DRIVERS HOME

by:Tony Pollock

Dorrance Publishing Co
585 Alpha Drive
Pittsburgh, PA 15238
Visit our website at www.dorrancebookstore.com

ISBN: 978-1-6491-3317-5
eISBN: 978-1-6491-3284-0

1

The shaft of light slid across the floor like an assassin's blade looking for its next victim, coming to a stop at the foot of the young man's bed.

As the late-night visitor closes the door and the room returns to its darkened state, the image of the boy remained in the intruder's mind.

A sandy haired youth of fifteen, slight build, a carbon copy of the boy's father, right down to the smallest detail.

As Sandra's eyes adjusted to the low light, she began to discern more details, a sad smile crept onto her face. This is not the way it was supposed to be, she tells herself. Her mind was racing from one image to another. Always returning to John, her mother, or Scotty. The pain of loss begins to work its way back.

She approaches the bed with a smooth graceful motion that revivals a life time of training and dedication.

She stops right next to the bed, looking down at the boy, a tear forms in her eyes, blurring her vision momentarily. The memory of her late husband is the most powerful drug for Sandra, it can bring joy or pain.

A warm felling washed over her as she pulls up the covers on her only son, smiling a real smile as she chuckles to herself, remembering how John used to do the same thing. One foot sticking out from under the covers.

She turns to leave, and a flash from the raging storm outside caches her attention. This is going to be a bad one, she tells herself. Remembering the launch two weeks ago. Thinking of the people in the surrounding city. They don't have the reinforced homes or the sound proofing to stop the defining cracks of thunder and the lightning with all of its devastation.

How many will be homeless by morning? How many will be dead?

It's not right. How can they ignore this? They know every time the Gravitron is used so close together, the storms are at their worst.

Anger begins to flow through her at the way the poor are treated. Remembering a storm that completely wiped out a town two years ago on the Island of Remington. Few survived the incident, and those who criticize the Gravitron disappear.

Sandra heads for her private elevator.

The palace was built by John's grandfather before the arrival of the Drivers and the lost Ones. Before the unification, when war was always on the horizon so it was more like a fortress than a palace, cold and dark with a constant felling of being watched.

Her fear began to smother her. Closing in on her like an invisible cloud that only she can see or feel. She begins to walk faster and faster until she is running. Even though the elevator is only a few meters from Tyler's room, she arrives in near panic.

Mae is waiting like always. Without a word, Mae reaches out and intercept Sandra's panic-stricken flight and soothes her with only a touch, stroking her shoulder like a mother would her own child, calming her down in seconds.

In a way, Mae was the closest thing to a mother Sandra ever had. She was the beautiful daughter of a wealthy and powerful politician. She never was without; anything she wanted, she got. The one thing she longed for was love.

Sandra's parents were never home, and when they were, they had no time for Sandra or her two older brothers. Sam the oldest by seven years and Scott by five.

By the time Sandra was seven, her mother had been committed to a very plush hospital for the insane, at least that was the official story. The reality was she got caught cheating on her husband, and no one crosses Malcolm Ree, leaving the three children to be raised by the help, as her father would call them. They would go for months never seeing him, and when they did, it was only for a day or so.

By the time Sandra was eleven, Sam was gone with Dad to learn the business, this was only good for her sense, Sam constantly harassed and belittled her. Scott would try to protect her, but Sam was the oldest and treated him just as badly.

Scott loved his baby sister, as he called her, and she adored him. They may have had no parents that loved them, but they had each other.

One summer day when Sandra was thirteen, Sam came home and got Scott for a weekend at the lake. Scott drowned, and Sam never shed a tear.

This was a traumatic time for her; she felt abandoned and rejected. All of her family was gone, there was no one left, father, mother, and brothers were all gone by fate, circumstance, or desire. The end result was the same, she was alone!

Deep depression set in, and Sandra was in a spiral to the bottom, her life was an empty hole with no light making it to her soul, life was not worth living, only death seemed to make any sense.

God or providence, it's irrelevant. Mae came in to her life and her life was saved.

Sandra was sent to all the best schools where she excelled. Always finishing at the top of her class. Athletics came natural to Sandra and dance was her favorite. Like all girls, she dreamed of being a star of a dance troop, but her brother Sam would come home for a few days and make fun of her.

The need to be accepted and loved was so great, she accepted the criticism, so the dream died at an early age.

Mae guides Sandra in to the elevator and pushes the top button on the panel. The door closes and the car begins its climb.

The trip up three floors was totally smooth, you could hardly notice the motion.

The door slides open to reveal a luxurious atrium with four separate wings leading out from there and the all too familiar guards snapping to attention.

Sandra moans to herself as she steps off the elevator with Mae in step behind her.

Sandra stops abruptly as she hears her name called from the executive wing. She turns to face the voice, but she already knows who and what called her name.

Her brother-in-law Kenneth.

Instinctively the smile was on her face and her demeanor was submissive.

Even in her state of depression, Sandra could be witty, flirtatious, and quick. It was only when she was by herself that the demons would raise their heads and wreaks havoc with her emotions.

"Good evening," she replies, "how was the meeting with Sub-Driver Clarence?"

"Those damn things!" he snorts. "It has lodged a formal complaint with the board of health. Claiming the vermin are not getting the proper nutrients. Do you believe that! A mechanized piece of shit, telling me how to treat vermin. If I had my way, I would work them as slaves until it was time to get rid of them all, every damn one of them."

"Has IT made more demands for help or aide?" Sandra asks, lingering on the IT. Knowing the answer and the reaction Ken would have.

It's better to have his anger directed away from Tyler she tells herself.

"If those tin brained assholes would keep their noses out of our business, we would not be asking for permission to do anything," Ken blurted out. Slurring his words, revealing his normal 1 A.M. condition.

Sandra knew she should not antagonize Kin at this point of his drunk.

She may be the mother of the future king, but for now, he calls all the shots in the monarchy.

Tyler will not ascend the throne until his eighteenth birthday. Until then she and her son are in danger from this man.

Kin continued his tirade reminiscing on the way things were done in the old days, when kings were the center of authority and things got done the right way.

With most of his anger spent, Sandra relaxed seeing the danger past for the time being. She decided to guide the conversation to something more enjoyable for Ken. His beloved Royal Guard.

"I understand the Security Council approved your new war ship," she comments.

The statement had not fully left Sandra's lips. When her mind jumped to John and how handsome he was in his uniform. The same image she cherishes and loves.

Him at his coronation followed by the image of his funeral.

The same uniform, the felling of loss and abandonment started to flow back in to her. Like a black cloud obscuring her vision of everything but the memory of John in the casket.

Kin never noticed the change in Sandra but Mae did, stepping up and gently touched her on the arm bringing her back to the moment.

The change in Kin was immediate, the opportunity to brag about the guard or anything he sets his hand to, is an opportunity for him to make certain the listener knows they are inferior to him and their life is irrelevant unless it involves him.

"The Hammer class is the fastest ever built and caries a full battalion of shock troops, plus an attack squadron," he tells her, swelling with pride. "We will have two commissioned by this time next year and five more the year after. Pardon the interruption, my lady, but you are due your medication and you need to eat beforehand," pleads Mae, knowing that talking over the Duke of Kastale has ended many careers, if not worse.

The Duke was in a forgiving mood and let the insult go.

Soon I will not be so forgiving, two more months and it will be finished, fifteen years of planning, Kin thinks to himself with a bit of self-congratulation.

Looking at Sandra, he takes a long and obvious inventory of her assets, starting at her head working down, pausing at her breast for a few seconds, lamenting the fact that he will never be able to knock her down and take what he wants, he knows even the King can be hanged for rape.

NO! That is not part of the plan, he reminds himself. Stay on plan, stay on plan, stay on plan, he repeats in his head.

"Sandy! Are you not taking care of yourself these days? You know you need to keep up your strength! Tyler needs you to help him rule the kingdom, that is his destiny, Sandy. You know the boy will need all the help he can get. Ruling takes intelligence, and let's face it, Tyler, well, he is a bit slow, so you run along now with your nursemaid and take your medication, so you can live as long as Tyler lives and provide him with good advice."

Kin knows it irritates Sandra when he calls her Sandy, and it makes her feel uneasy when he looks at her with lust in his eyes but scares the hell out of her when he makes it obvious in front of everyone, sending her a clear message, I'm in charge and can do anything I like.

The Duke, having had his fun for the night, spins around and heads for his room without saying anything moor to Sandra, but the shape of her breast and her sent remained with Kin until sleep takes him. His dreams where filled with images of her. Always the same kind of dreams, violent and bloody.

2

Captain Billy Zercoff walked around the transport doing his pre-flight like he has done so many times for the last twenty-five years.

He could do it in his sleep on most days, but today there is a bunch of dignitary's milling around the flight line, something about a trip down south. I'm out of the loop, so who gives a crap, he tells himself, just do your job and go home.

Billy has more flight time than any two pilots in the Royal Guard, and he has made the same rank more times than any five pilots in his wing. For this reason, Billy always gets the shit details. Making runs to the most remote and faraway post in the Empire.

Billy in his mid 40's, balding and stands a head shorter than anyone in the squadron and on the verge of being thrown out of the Guard for his weight.

He would retire, but what else could he do? Take tourist on sight-seeing rides, watching old men getting older.

"No, I can put up with their shit," he tells himself for the tenth time today.

Where else could I go out and get drunk night after night and fly anywhere in the world the next day, only in the Guard.

"Hay Linch, get on the move, we have an ETA of 15:30 in rocket town, if you don't want someone in operations to put a check mark next to your name, you better get the auxiliary power supply hooked up now,"

Billy calls out under the rear thruster loud enough that anyone standing within twenty meters could hear, knowing this would put Ted on pins and needles for the entire trip worrying about what would happen if they were late and someone reported it was his fault for not getting the APU hocked up or something going wrong and it being his fault.

Ted only being out of the academy two months and this being his second flight with Billy.

He tries way too hard and screws up more than he gets right, it's like he has two thumbs most of the time, and I think the boy is afraid of his own shadow, Billy thinks.

Ted is just the opposite of Billy, he stands at least a head and a half taller than most, this put him two and a half taller than Billy, thin as a board with a full head of red hair.

They do make a strange pair.

Billy makes a note to himself to be a little easier on the boy but laughs his ass off as he watches Ted trip over the power cord not once but three times before he gets the APU under the wing. Shaking his head in disbelief at the gangling young man.

Billy inters the transport from the rear cargo ramp and makes his way forward through the passenger compartment getting his first look at his passengers.

Billy always likes to size up the people he's carrying, their lives, as well as his, may depend on their reaction to an emergency and in the middle of one is no time to find out.

The APU hooked up and Billy strapped in to the pilot's seat starts his pre-flight check list. This is going to be a boring trip, he reminds himself, I have made this trip fifty times and every one is the same, rush, rush, rush, and once I'm there, it will take three days to get a flight going north. No bars, brothels, or girls, what a screwed-up weekend this will be.

The only redeeming aspect of this trip will be the Gravitron, there is to be a special launch for the Guard this week, maybe I'll get lucky this trip and see it.

The Gravitron is operated down at the South Poll. It has to be far away from civilization, in the most remote place they can find. The storms it produces when it counteracts the planets gravitational field wreaks havoc on the surrounding countryside.

The Gravitron sends a burst of energy to a central core where it causes a bubble of anti-gravitons to form, weakening the gravity over that spot, making it possible to lift a heavy rocket in to orbit cheaply. The down side is a bubble of atmosphere lifts high up, causing an extreme low presser at the surface topped off by an extreme high presser over it.

The results are unpredictable and deadly. It takes the storm to travel thousands of kilometers from the Gravitron before it even starts to break up.

One storm lasted twenty-five days and wondered over 15,000 kilometers, making it nearly to the opposite Pole, destroying everything in its path.

After the engines are started, Ted disconnects the APU, then goes up the ladder to the bridge. Taking his place next to the Captain.

The all clear from Ted on the engineering board, Billy advances the throttle, and the transport begins its roll down the taxi way.

Takeoffs have never lost its appeal to Billy, he always fills at home in the air, like this is where he belongs.

Billy clears his departure with the tower and begins his takeoff roll.

The sheer power of the transport is incredible.

Within seconds the transport is airborne pushing crew and passengers back in their seats, holding them there like an invisible giant hand.

This old lady may be the oldest in the fleet, he tells Ted, but she still has plenty of life left in her. She will out climb and out maneuver everything in her class.

"A little trivia for you, Linch, did you know this is the only class transport that the Drivers made for us solely, everything after this was made by us, not the Drivers.

He turns the transport south. The trip will take six hours to make and at the altitude of 15KM there will be little to see. "Tell me, Linch, is this your first trip to rocket town?"

"Yes, sir," Ted responds with a quick response, reviling the excitement in his voice and his imagination of the adventurers just starting. "I have seen videos of the place and a launch of the Guard's first cruiser but this will be my first trip down south."

"You're not missing anything," Billy grumbled, "by the time you're there ten minutes, you've seen all there is to see and you've done everything there is to do, now go back and check on your passengers and, Linch, keep them off my bridge, and if there is a problem, you take care of it. Do you understand?"

"Aye, aye, skipper."

"Then get with it, boy, and cut the skipper crap, or you'll be cleaning the hell hole of every ship in the squadron for the next month."

Ted looks a little puzzled, recalling the duty officer in operations telling him Zercoff likes to be called Skipper but takes his leave and makes his way after disappearing through the hatch.

Alone on the bridge, Billy tells himself that the boy will do fine if he ever gets his balls out of his ass and finds a little confidence.

I can't push him too hard, but a little kick in the ass never hurt. Putting him in charge of the passengers may help, and this way I don't have to be bothered.

There are fifteen passengers this trip, plus 2,500 kg of cargo, a light load for such a long flight, there must be something they need pretty bad to send me on this trip, most times I get the stinky loads like produce or solvents. This doesn't fill right.

Thirteen of the passengers wear your average dog faces, rotating duty there in the wasteland and complaining about their luck.

Drawing duty like this is usually meant as punishment, not a vacation.

All screw ups I bet; Billy thinks.

Now two are a little out of place.

A captain and his aide?

Captains don't have aids, not your average Captain anyway. I think I'll make it a point to see them off my ship and get a good look at their insignia's. They have tans like they were from sum tropical paradise, not your average grunt, and their uniforms are perfect right down to the brass buttons. I bet they're the reason for this flight.

Billy turns his attention to the job at hand, getting him, his ship, his crew, and his passengers to their destination safely, letting the mater of the passengers slip it to his subconscious for further scrutiny latter.

Billy checks his heading, radar, and engineering panel in a blink of an eye.

He may have a reputation of a drunkard and a malcontent, but he has never lost a ship or had a fatality on his command.

Billy's pears and his senior pilots seek out his advice in the shadows but ridicule him openly for fear of being associated with him, most know his ability to pilot a transport is unequaled but none will profess it openly, and if ask about him will tell you about the time he got drunk and did this or that, forgetting his phenomenal flying over his long career.

Like the time the tower cleared a flight of fifteen fighters to takeoff in a mass takeoff training exercise as Billy was on his final approach.

It was Billy that avoided them and made his landing safely, it was also Billy who lost his Captains bars as gratitude for showing up the General in the lead fighter.

Ted re-inters the bride sometime later looking frustrated, after sitting Billy noticed a sign taped to the center of his back that read, dumb ass.

"Did they give you any trouble back there?" Billy asks Ted with a big grin, knowing he had no idea the note was there for all to see and have a good laugh at his expense.

"Those dog faces are real ass holes. Don't let them get you down; if they feel any weakness from you at all, they will walk all over you, boy, didn't your daddy teach you anything?" Billy tells him. "Now take the sign off you're back declaring your I.Q. and check our location and report it to control, then give me your estimation on our arrival at the point of no return. This is a test, boy, and if you screw it up, there'll be hell to pay, do you understand me, Rocky!"

Billy knows how cruel the dog faces can be, he has had to pull rank on more than one occasion and went head to head several times.

Over the years, he developed a reputation of being a no-nonsense captain who would thump a head or two if the situation called for it, so he was given respect from most grunts.

"Yes, sir," replied 2nd Lieutenant Ted Linch with all the vigor he could muster. He could sense the old goat's soft side and would like to show him he is up to the challenge and that he can do it right.

He knows the Captain had no idea how much hurt the daddy statement had on him, it's my problem not his, he tells himself.

Getting down to the task at hand, verifying their location, Ted figuring rate of fuel consumption, distance to the destination, and distance from point of origination giving him the point of no return.

"Skipper! There is no point of no return! We almost have enough fuel to get home after our arrival at Rocket Town. You passed Rocky. If we climb another 2,000 meters, throttle back, and let the jet stream push us, we'll have enough fuel to get us home, maybe!"

"Sometimes it works and, well, sometimes you have to land short," Billy laughs. "Now repeat the process and see what you come up with," Billy tells Ted.

Ted dose as he was told and goes through the calculations one more time.

"You're right, Skipper, a little adjustment in altitude and we increase our range by twenty percent, the only down side is we take a little longer to get there."

"You won't learn that at the academy, Rocky," Billy teases.

Like most trips to the South Pole, it was uneventful; the only thing that made this trip different was the excitement and wonder in Ted, his eyes were wide open constantly, looking forward to see rocket town.

When it finally came in to view, Ted was in awe.

Sitting on one of the five launch pads was the biggest thing Ted had ever seen. It looked more like a skyscraper. Over 500 meters tall and better than 150 meters wide.

As the transport draws closer, Ted could discern moor details, The HLV, Heavy Launch Vehicle is at the core with thirty smaller ones attached to it, ringing the HLV from top to bottom.

The HLV is able to place in to orbit two million metric tons with the help of the Gravitron.

One of the gifts from the Drivers, Ted remembers reading that in the academy history class first year.

Ted's eyes moved to the base that is around the launch pads. It too was enormous, it stretched out in all directions for kilometers.

Billy could not stop smiling at the young man's excitement. In all of his trips and all the different crew members he has had in his long career, never has he seen any one with this much excitement and enthusiasm.

Billy reminded himself that at one time I was like that, every flight was an adventurer.

What happened to me?

Where did the wonder of the world go for me?

Maybe divorce number three!

"Ted, clear us for landing!" the Captain orders.

"Aye, aye, Skipper," Ted replies.

The tower clears them for landing and advised them there is a thirty-five KPH wind on vector, gusting to forty-five.

On the approach, Billy declares to Ted that he will be making the landing.

"No, Skipper! I'm not ready for a live landing."

"Nonsense, Rocky, how many simulations have you done?"

"Thirteen, Skipper."

"And you can do this," Billy encourages him.

"I can do this!" Ted echoes weakly.

"That a boy, now take the controls and do as you were taught," Billy tells him, "it's just like the simulator."

Ted grasps the yoke with both hands so tight, Billy could see the blood driven from his hands.

"Ease up a little on the grip, Rocky, relax, feel the controls, become part of the transport," Billy tells him in a calm voice.

"Aye, aye, Skipper," Ted replies, looking out the window at rocket town runway coming up quick, only 5KM out, he calculates visually, a quick glance at the radar confirms it.

"You're a little hot, back off on the throttle a little," Billy tells him. "You're doing fine, Rocky, two kilometers out, you're lined up on the finger and all lights are green for landing," Billy reports. "Remember there is a strong head wind," Billy reminds him moments before touchdown.

The landing gear makes a smooth contact with the runway about the same time a violent gust of wind unleashes, the transport jumps back in to the air so quick, even the Captain was startled, but Ted's reactions were like lightning, pushing the lift thrusters to their max as the gust of wind calmed and the transport began to fall.

The impact was not severe but bad enough to bounce twice and shake up the passengers pretty well.

Billy looks over at Ted, and he is as white as a ghost still gripping the yoke.

"Not bad for your first landing at the poll, Rocky, I've seen worse, the winds can be very tricky here," Billy tells him, "now give me the controls and go on back and see to our passengers."

It only took several minutes to get to the gate, and Ted did not return, so after the shutdown list was completed, Billy went looking for his trainee.

He found him standing at attention being chewed out by the all too tanned Captain with the 1st Lieutenant Aide.

"I want to know! Why are we almost an hour late, Lieutenant?" The Captain right in Ted's face screaming.

"Is there a problem here, Captain? If there is, you know the chain of command and you will follow it on my ship, do you understand, Captain? I am in charge until you are past that gate," said Billy, pointing aft, "I'm ordering you off my ship now."

"You have not heard the last of this, Captain Zercoff." The all too tanned Captain hisses, "You and Linch." With that the captain and Lieutenant excited the rear of the transport and down the ramp.

"He was giving you grief over the landing, is that it, Rocky?"

"Yes, sir, as soon as I entered the compartment, he started. I tried to tell him about the twenty percent increase in efficiency, but all he would do was scream at me. The odd thing, Skipper, I never told him my name or yours. How did he know them, Captain? We don't wear name tags with this uniform."

"I don't know how they knew, but I think we should keep on our toes," Billy tells him. "The insignia they wore are from the intelligence division. Let's get this girl put to bed, so we can go put our names in operations for the return flight, then rooms, dinner, and a tour of the place."

"Sound good, Skipper, and I did get the Captain's name, Dean Hartwell, it was on his briefcase, the first Lieutenant's name I did not catch."

It took them forty-five minutes to unload the cargo and secure the transport, then off to operations.

Captain Zercoff knows if he gets in to operations right before change of shift, the duty officer will be in such a hurry to get out of there, and if he drags his feet on filing his arrival report, he'll be more willing to give Billy the location of the casino, for a minimal fee of course.

Billy and Ted take the crew bus to operations, arriving right on cue. Ten minutes before the new shift stared.

Fifteen minutes later, there out with their report's field and a piece of paper with the location of the clandestine casino and the pass ward.

With that taken care of, it was off to register at the transit barracks for rooms and meal tickets for the mess.

"I guess you can call the rooms, room's three meters by three meter and a kind of toilet and shower combination that comes out of the wall, the hot water, would preserve ice! What do you think of your fancy room, Rocky?" As they meet up in the hallway séance, there is no room in the rooms for two people.

"Just like I dreamed it would be, Skipper," Ted laughed.

Billy joined in in the laughter.

"Let's go find that casino, Rocky, so I can show you how it's done down south."

3

As Captain Hartwell and Lieutenant Nash make their way back to the departing terminal to book a flight back to Wolf Creek, they congratulate each other on a job well done.

"I believe you're right, Captain, with all the stories we heard back at headquarters, plus his inept piloting skills makes him the perfect candidate. You stay here and keep an eye on our fools, Lieutenant. I will report back to the Duke and give him the good news," Dean tells his aide, "so keep a close eye on them. I've got them here for two days, then they send them to Kranstan Point for training. Stay with them but keep out of sight. Use Henry Bell if you need help, he's the contact in operations but only if you must and keep it at a minimum."

"I can handle it, Captain."

"See that you do, Lieutenant, I'll see you at Kranstan in four days."

"Yes, sir," the Lieutenant responds.

As he watches the Captain head for the departing gate, Lieutenant Nash thinks to himself, I may get command of one of the new ships if all goes well, then an involuntary afterthought jumps into his head; if not we will all be hanged.

4

Mae fallowed Sandra to her room to get her ready for bed.

The nightly routine of convincing her she can make it without John and the task getting her to sleep. The job is much simpler if she can avoid the Duke before Sandra retires for the night.

The Duke can make this job, most unbearable, Mae tells herself, it always sends her in to a deeper depression. Just the mere sight of him can cause days of stress for Sandra.

With her night gown on, her hair brushed, and a cup of hot tea next to the bed, the queen mother settles in to bed as Mae pulls the covers up, making her comfortable, Sandra asks a question, more to herself than Mae.

"Do you think my son will ever be King with Ken in line for the throne?"

Just the idea she would voice such a question shocked Mae.

"What do you mean, my lady?"

Mae could tell she had something on her mind and was fighting to get it out, trying to overcome the fear of it.

"Is there something wrong, your majesty?"

"Yes!" she replied sharply as tears start to flow. "Kin will never let my son on the throne, he wants it for himself," with the words spoken, she begins to sob uncontrollably.

Mae sits on the bed next to her and pulls her on to her shoulder, gently rocking her and telling her it's alright.

Just as quickly as the tears started, they stopped.

Sandra jumps out of bed so fast, it startles Mae, and she nearly falls off the side of the bed. Standing there with her fist clenched tight and straining every muscle, Sandra looks Mae directly in the eyes and declares slow and firm.

"He will not due to my son what he did to my husband."

With a look of defiant anger spreading over her, like a wild fire through dry brush. Not the anger of paranoia or depression but the anger of a mother protecting her child.

For the first time in fifteen years, the image of John was driven from Sandra's mind, it was as if blinders where removed from her eyes, she was seeing the world as it is. Like an epiphany, all the pieces fell in to place.

"I will stop him, Mae! If it's the last thing I do, this I swear."

"Your Highness, there is nothing going to happen to the Prince, what happened to the King was an accident, nothing more."

"No, it was, Kin, I know it. It's his plan to remove Tyler, so he can take his place. Did you hear the vile thing he was saying about Tyler? He cares for nothing, Mae, not his brother or his nephew. He is an evil man. You heard how he thinks an entire race of people should be put in work camps, then eliminated. That is a person with no limits to his depravity. He will try something, I know it. We must protect Tyler. Please, Mae, help me protect him, he's all I have."

"Your highness it's been a long day, you need your rest, the tea is still hot, and I will put two more drops in your tea to help you sleep," Mae tells her, pulling out a small vile out of her apron.

"No, I will not have two moor drops and I will not have the tea either. I'm going to stay at the summer palace and I'm leaving tonight. Wake the staff, I'll go get Tyler out of bed."

"Miss, think, if the Duke did what you think he did, would it be to your advantage to break your routine and go flying off in the middle of the night? The Duke has people everywhere. He would know before you got in the transport and have you noticed, it's as if the Duke has been waiting for you to come up from Tyler's room every night this week, and the Duke has the final say on security matters."

"The Duke, the Duke, the Duke, I'm sick of the Duke," Sandra blurts out.

"Did you forget the storm, miss? It's bad out tonight," Mae reminds her, "and you could use James to help, you know he's not in the Duke's service."

Sandra stood there for several seconds before answering.

"You are right, Mae. We will go later in the month. Go see James and send him to my room, tell him to be discreet and come around ten. As for the tea and your drops, I have had the last one, do you understand, Mae, no more."

Mae bowed to her sovereign and turned to go, then stopped, turning back, looking Sandra directly in the eyes, "If you are wrong, miss, and start things you cannot stop, it will give the Duke the opportunity to force Tyler to advocate, but if you are right, he will move before the unification holiday at the end of summer. Think well, my lady, it's not only you who will suffer but Tyler as well."

Mae leaves Sandra standing at the window looking stronger than she has in years. The color of her face was more alive than it was only an hour ago.

The realization that she herself was the only one that could protect Tyler from his uncle and his ambitions of becoming king.

A kingdom that did not exists thirty years ago. Only with the arrival of the Drivers and the Lost Ones did things change.

Until then there were four major warring kingdoms and seven smaller ones.

Life was much harder and life expectancy was shorter with the constant wars going on.

The drivers brokered a treaty that combined all eleven empires in to a single monarchy with eleven royal advisers to the Steward and eleven Senators representing the eleven royal houses.

The power of the King was greatly reduced, and most power lay in the hands of the elected Steward and his cabinet, but the King still controls the Royal Guard, which is a third of the security forces.

The Drivers provided the oversight in the beginning and built four cities, plus the capital city of New Hope until the government was elected.

There were some rough times at the start. Several insurrections had to be put down by the Drivers. They are fair in their rulings and swift in their justice.

For their help in consolidating the governments, ending wars and vast improvements in our technology's by sentries.

The Drivers required we absorb a race of people they call the lost Ones.

Through a war of their own, the Drivers destroyed the lost Ones home planet, saddling them with the care and welfare of over two million.

Sandra thought about this and realized that was the solution.

The Drivers had no vested interest in the lost Ones but justice had to be served, so they stepped up to the task and moved an entire race from a dead planet halfway around the Galaxy.

If the drivers would do that for the lost Ones, they would help her save her son, and at the same time, insuring the stability for the fledgling government.

Sandra asks herself how can I contact this Clarence?

In the eighteen years Sandra has been queen, she has never even seen a Sub-Driver, or any kind of Driver for that matter.

Drivers are bio-mechanical computers with the ability to control countless drones of every sort, from war drones to assembly lines, and they do that from the safety of their giant ships.

It's like they can be in ten million places at once doing ever sort of tasks.

The known history of the Drivers is spotty and mostly conjecture on the part of the government.

The only facts known about them are sometime in the far distant past, a humanoid race created them and the creation out lasted the creators and they were not immune to war.

Like any thinking entity, emotions are still prone to dictate their responses.

A plan starts to come together in Sandra's mind, all I need to do is to get their attention!

Sandra is too wound up for sleep, so she decides to summon the librarian and see what else she can find out about the Drivers, Clarence in particular. The very mention of his name seems to set Kin off.

This can be used to our advantage, if played right, she tells herself.

Sandra summons Tina, one of her servants, directing her to go get the librarian out of bed and not to let them send an assistant, "I want the librarian."

Tina bows and confirms she understands the task and heeds for the door.

Fifteen minutes later, an out of breath Timothy Beal in his late seventies was standing at the Queens door with a confused look, still in his nightgown with flyaway hair, Tina standing by him with the same confused look.

Entering the room, the librarian bows to his sovereign and inquires on how he can be of assistance to her.

"I would like you to assist me in finding information on the Drivers," Sandra tells him.

Now instead of confused, the librarian looks scared and starts to fidget.

"My lady, the Drivers? You are looking for information on the Drivers?"

"Yes, the Drivers, is that a problem?"

"No, my lady, it's just that that information is kept in the security section of the library.

The Duke has placed that off limits to all but his staff, and he himself gave me that order, my lady."

"Are you telling me I have to go to the Duke to get access to it?"

"No, my queen, I do not believe he meant you. I am to report any one who request access to him personally."

"Have you had many requests?" she inquirers.

"No, not many, only three in the last year," he tells her.

"Are you going to report this?"

"No, my lady, if you ask me not to."

"Consider yourself asked."

"The incident never happened," he responds.

"Good, this will be between us. Can you tell me who else inquired about the Drivers?"

"Certainly, my lady, it was two reporters, I don't recall their names, but I can get that information for you if you like. The third was Tom Dearmen last month, a senator from the Islands. He spent a week going over all the information we have on the Drivers, including the interviews of the lost Ones taken right after their arrival. The Duke was livid but gave him permission anyway. You know senator Dearmen is a member of the security council, if that helps any, my lady."

"Yes, I believe it will. Now tell me anything you fill to be pertinent about the Drivers."

"There is one story we documented on several separate interviews that shared details so similar, it caught the attention of our historians.

It seems there was a war between two Master Drivers. Sheila and Michael."

"The same Master-Driver Michael in orbit around the outskirts of the solar system?" Sandra asks.

"Yes, I would speculate, my lady. The war lasted over 100 of our years. Sheila was winning, pursuing Michael continuously, finally trapping him. Sheila destroyed all the operating part of Michael. Taking the thinking parts prisoner and intended to make him witness the extermination of the Parkin's, a race dear to Michael, Sheila dispatched Sub-Driver Clarence to prepare the Parkin's for extermination."

"Stop," Sandra said, "you mean Sub-Driver Clarence was in the service of this Master-Driver Sheila, now he is working for Master-Driver Michael? Sheila destroyed Michael, but Michael is here, and Sheila is gone? I find all of this confusing. The victor being destroyed."

"No, my lady, I do not believe so. Not all of Sheila's forces were destroyed. Only Sheila. There is evidence that at least five Sub-Drivers of hers are still out there, and some Lost Ones say they are still waging war against Michael and intent on exterminating the Parkin's race as a tribute to Sheila."

"Do you believe we could be in danger from these Sub-Drivers of Sheila's?"

"That question I cannot answer, my lady. What I do know for a fact is that there were only three Drivers took out the combined fleets of King Olaf and King Tratest in less than two hours. There were more than 900 ships sunk or disabled, and not one Driver was even touched.

Sandra thinks this one over for a few seconds before moving on.

"If you would please, there are things that don't make since."

"Yes, your Highness," the librarian responds, then continued. "By what we can figure, Sub-Driver Clarence had a problem caring out Sheila's orders to exterminate the Parkin's and switched sides. In doing so, Sheila was destroyed and Michael was restored."

"I don't see how this works out. You win a war but lose it also," Sandra thinks out loud, "there must be something I can use here to our advantage. We hear about Master-Driver Michael and his all-powerful ship, but the only one we deal with is Sub-Driver Clarence or one of the other five Sub-Drivers. I wonder if Michael even exists?" Sandra comments.

"I have heard that the astronomy community say they can find no trace of a ship that big out there. We know the Parkin's people do, we know them as the lost Ones," the librarian adds.

"You have given me much to think about, and you have been a great help to me," Sandra tells him. "You may go back to bed, and I apologize for getting you up so late."

"My honor, my lady. I am at your service any time, day or night."

"Thank you, master librarian."

He bowed low and excused himself.

"This is getting stranger and stranger," Tina remarked after the master librarian shuts the door.

"I think I will try to see this Clarence at the first opportunity, and let's not forget the Senator, for any enemy of my enemy is my friend," Sandra reminds herself. "Tina, did the guards give you any trouble letting in the librarian?" Sandra inquires.

"No, my lady, Robert's on duty tonight, and he is always trying to get me to go out with him," she giggles.

The queen mother looks at Tina with a bit of envy, wishing her life could be as simple as this young flirtatious girl. Studying her for the first time ever, Sandra realizes Tina is an attractive woman. Her young life of twenty has so much moor to see and do. A bit immature but dependable and loyal.

"He did say he would have to put it in the log, my lady," Tina tells her, breaking the awkward silence.

"So the Duke will know the librarian was summoned by morning, if ask, tell him I was looking for a book and could not find a copy of it and I ordered him to find one for me," Sandra adds, "and makes a point to tell the guard Robert the same story before you go to bed. Maybe he'll put that in the report also, saving me the trouble of seeing Ken. I have a 10 A.M. meeting with James Wildwind, and I would like you to be available for a special job, pack a light bag and be ready by 10:30; you may be gone for several days. And, Tina, if I have never said thank you for all your help, I say it now. Thank you! From the bottom of my heart," as an involuntary tear trickles down Sandra's cheek, embarrassing Tina that her monarch would shed a tear for her, a lowly servant.

"Now you go get some sleep, it's going to be a busy day tomorrow." Tina bows her most respectable bow and heads for the door, shedding tears of her own, unseen by Sandra.

"I think I had better try to get some sleep," Sandra reminds herself, "it's going to be hectic day tomorrow with the pregame activities, and I have details to tend to before I make the announcement that the Prince and I will be going to the summer palace early this year."

Sandra lay there for a time before sleep took her; her dreams were filled with images of flashing lights and a leering set of eyes down a long dark hallway.

5

Senator Tom Dearman stands looking out the window with his back to the visitors in his office, not really hearing the story being told to him. Instead his mind is thinking about a rumor one of his staffers heard several months back.

His train of thought is interrupted by Evelyn, his secretary, clearing her throat quite loudly. Tom turned to see all five guests looking at him.

"My apologies, you were saying?"

Evelyn speaks up, "Mr. Toman asks if you think the shrimp harvest could be extended two more months in light of the resent storm activity in the southern seas?"

"If you don't, Senator Dearman, I'll go under and put 200 people out of work, and it's not only me. Every one of us here are on the brink of bankruptcy with the storms this year. Every time they fire that damn thing down there, we have to evacuate the entire area, that's five days down every launch, Senator, we need help!" pleads Pam Avery, the packing plant owner.

Tom has known Pam's family all his life. His father and her father were friends from childhood, for that matter everyone on the Islands are connected in one way or another.

The Newland Islands are a chain of Islands 2,000 kilometers long and 1,000 kilometers wide in a diamond shape with the southern tropics running through the middle.

A population of twelve million on fourteen main Islands and more than 200 smaller ones.

The capital Island is Stink Water Island; it's in the center of the diamond. It was given that name to discourage visitors, but in reality, it's a paradise and the world knows it now, so it's booming. Every beach has a hotel or resort. The only redeeming quality to this newfound fame is the Island counsel outlawed personal motorized vehicles on the small island of seven kilometers. As a result, only people who enjoy walking or running visit, but if you like, you can take a taxi, owned by the Island counsel.

"I know, Pam, I will do what I can, but no promises, you know how the security agency's works," he tells her. "It's their way or no way, but we do have an ace in the hole. I will be taking over as the new chairman of the Security Council next term."

Tom is a very robust man in his early fifties, barrel chest, tall and dark from the tropical sun with dark blue eyes that seem to see right through people. Most people are drawn to him by his friendly personality and genuine concern for people.

He has spent most of his adult life in the service of the government.

First as a battalion commander of the Global Defense Force earning numerous citations for valor during the wars that fallowed the unification. Winning the respect and loyalty of his men in combat.

He was recruited by the Free Labor party to run for public office, which he won by a land slide.

Martin Toman stands up and shouts, "I will be out of business by then," shaking his finger at Tom.

"Mr. Toman, I think we can at least get you some help from creditors by enacting temporarily the International Fare Resource Act, getting you a low interest loan," the senator adds. "It's not a fix, but it will keep you solvent until something can be done about the storms," Tom tells the whole group.

With the meeting ended and Evelyn leading them out, Tom hears her telling them she has copies of the forms needed to file for the IFRA at her desk.

One problem down, he tells himself, turning to go to his private office, Tom hears his name called form behind, turning he sees Pam never left the room.

"Can we talk in private, Tom?" she asks.

"Yes, by all means."

On the short walk to the Senator's office, Pam congratulated him on his new position as head of the Security Council.

"Thank you," he tells her, shutting the door so they will not be disturbed. "It's been a long time since we have talked," Tom tells her.

"Yes," she replies, "ten years."

"Has it been that long? It seems time files by the older we get," Tom remarked more to himself than Pam. "What can I do for you, Pam?"

"You know Quentin was killed last year," Pam tells Tom.

"Yes, I do. I'm sorry, Pam, for your loss. I was off plaint attending the yearly progress meeting with Sub-Driver Clarence when I heard the news. I was shocked and saddened that I could not make the funeral," he tells her. "By the time I returned, a month had past and I thought it would be better on you if I did not bring up sad memories, Pam. I know that is a poor excuse, but that's the truth."

"I understand, Tom, and thank you for thinking of my feelings, but that is not what I came to talk about."

Tom could see she was upset, and the death of her husband was not the problem now.

"What is it then?" he inquires.

"One of my boats picked up a lost one two months ago in a life raft. The Captain of the ship did what he could, but the sea had ravaged his body so bad, he died before they could get him help."

"That's sad," Tom tells her.

"Yes, it is, but that's not the issue, Tom, it's what he kept repeating that raddled the Captain. He kept saying Sheila's Drivers are coming and will exterminate us all. The Captain is a good man, not prone to jumping to conclusions, but the fear in this man was so intense, the Captain quit his job and moved his family away in to hiding."

It sounds like the Lost One was delirious, Pam, no more than that."

"That is what I thought at first, Tom, but the coroner listed the cause of death as exposure to radiation, not the sea. And get this, Tom, it was not his whole body, only the brain."

"I have seen radiation exposure, Pam. It rots the flesh off the body, not the brain only."

"I know, Tom, that's why I had the body preserved and put in the family crypt."

"You have the body?"

"Yes," she replies. "No one came forward to claim the body."

Tom looks at Pam and sees the fear in her eyes also.

"This has you upset, too?" he asks.

"Yes, it's causing me to have nightmares; everyone knows if the Drivers took a notion, they could wipe out our entire world with little resistance."

"Why would they do that, Pam? I have dealt with them on several issues, and I have only see compassion on their part, not hate. Clarence looks after the lost Ones like a father would his own children," he tells her.

"Who is Sheila?" she asks.

"I don't know, Pam," he tells her, knowing she may see right through his lie, remembering the interviews he read in the security library back at the Wolf Creek about Sheila and her desire to exterminate the Parkin's race. "The body, can I have it analyzed?" he asks her.

"Please take it away, Tom, it only reminds me of impending doom and the loss I have already suffered."

"I will contact the Health Ministry and have it removed today," he tells her.

"Thanks, Tom. I knew you could help."

"Any time, Pam."

They stood up, and Tom puts out his hand, but Pam pushes it aside and hugged him so hard and long, it shocked Tom to the core, remembering the young woman he deserted for the service, the image of her crying on the day of his departure.

That was a lifetime ago, he reminds himself, still in her embrace with the scent of her hair washing over him, flooding him with old images of a lost life.

Tom never married; his mistress was the service. There were girls in his life but no love of the heart for him. His true love was standing in front of him right now and he knew it.

They separate, and Tom could tell she is on the verge of tears; not wanting to see her cry at all, Tom grabs her for his own tight embrace.

Several moments pass before they separate for the second time, looking in to each other's' eyes, they both know the embers of their love never died, only smoldered for more than three decades.

"If you need anything, and I mean anything, you call, OK," he tells her.

"I will," she replies.

With that Pam opens the door and walks out, not daring to look back.

Tom watches her walk down the hallway to the elevator, not moving until the elevator door closes.

Tom walked back to his desk and pushes the intercom for Evelyn.

"Yes, senator?"

"Get me the head of security, and I need her here in the hour."

"Yes, sir."

It was less than ten minutes when Evelyn buzzed the senator, "Captain West is here, sir."

"Send her in."

Captain Carol West knocked, then entered the office like the true professional she is.

Standing at attention, she reports to the Senator, "Captain West reporting as ordered, sir."

"Relax, Captain, and have a seat."

"Yes, sir," West replies, sitting on the edge of the seat, leaning forward awaiting her orders.

"I have a job for you, Captain. In the Avery crypt, there is a body. I would like you to transfer it to a military lab on Kranstan and, Captain, this is top secret."

"Yes, sir," is her response.

"See Dr. Barbara Walker only," the senator instructed her. "She will be expecting you."

"Yes, sir," is the only response from the Captain, with no hint of curiosity or emotion.

A true grunt of the highest caliber, Tom thinks, she will go fare.

"I would like it taken care of before the end of the day, Captain."

And again the only response is, "Yes, sir."

"That's it then, Captain, any questions?"

"No, sir."

"Carry on then," Tom tells her.

The Captain stands up and performs a perfect about face, and out the door she goes.

The senator buzzes Evelyn again. "Yes, Senator?"

"Evelyn, get Dr. Walker on the phone for me please. She is at the Kranstan research facility." Moments later the phone rings and Tom picks it up, "Barbara, how are things at Kranstan?"

"Good," she tells him, "and how are you doing in paradise, Tom?"

"Good also, Barb, this is an official call, Barb; we have another radiation exposure."

"Where? When?"

"Slow down, Barb, this happened two months ago."

"Then it was the first one," she injects.

"Yes, I think so," he tells her. "I am sending the body to you, Barb, do your test, then get back with me as soon as you know if it's the same as the others."

"Is this one a Lost One also?"

"Yes, same as the others I fear."

"The brain cooked with radiation from the inside out, what a terrible way to die," she comments. "As soon as I know, you'll know, Tom."

"Thanks, Barb, give my regards to Bill and tell him he still owes me."

"I will, Tom and you be careful, strange things have been happening lately all over the place."

"Thanks again, Barb, and you be careful also, bye."

"Good bye, Tom."

The senator sat in his office for the rest of the day, not taking any calls, trying to make since of the events of the last month.

Over eight deaths from radiation exposure and every one a Lost One, there is something up, he tells himself, and I have the odd felling it's only going to get worse, not better.

I need to have a meeting with Sub-Driver Clarence as soon as possible.

Tom breaks his self-imposed salutary confinement and rings Evelyn.

"Yes, Senator?" Evelyn answers.

"Book me a flight to the New Hope as soon as possible, then call the Steward's office and get me an appointment with the Steward's chief of staff."

"Yes, sir."

"And can you send Mrs. Avery some flowers for me, Evelyn? I need to get packed and to the airport, use your judgment."

"I can do that, Tom."

"I will be back as soon as I can, put that in the card if you will please."

"I will, sir."

After hanging up with the Senator, Evelyn made the necessary call to get him on the transport and the appointment at the steward's office; last but not the least, she ordered a dozen red roses for Pam Avery, then dictates the message to the florets.

In the five years Evelyn has been the Senator's secretary, she has never seen him pay any woman attention, not like this; she smiles and thinks to herself, it's about time, Tom.

6

The sun was up high when Tamara reached the top of the mountain; from this height, she could see the entire Island of Bray, it's only twelve kilometers across one of the mid-size Islands of the Newland chain. Located at the very northern tip of the chain.

Only the peak of the mountain is free of trees, the rest of the Island is covered in a thick canopy of jungle.

Tamara breaths deep, taking in the cool air up around 1,000 meters, only here can she get away from the stifling humidity and the constant buzzing of insects.

Bray has a small population of Lost Ones, around 6,000. There is no industry here, only a few farms, one government store, a medical clinic, eight bars, two restaurants, a recreation hall, a hotel, a small airport, and a shallow harbor that most ships cannot enter for fear of grounding.

The hand full of jobs on the Island comes nowhere close to satisfying the need for work, so most Parkin's go off Island to find employment, that leaves families separated.

She can see her dwelling from here, it's no home, it's more akin to a military barracks, fifty families living in a big three-story oblong box. Each family has their own apartment with paper thin walls, leaky roofs, and no screens on the windows.

Tamara finds her a place to eat her lunch and wait for the sun to go down.

Up here she can see the stars in all their glorious splendor.

She was born here, but she is not of here, she tells herself, I'm a Parkin!

Her grandfather told her stories about life among the stars with Clarence and the days before the evacuation of her planet, but he has been gone for a year now, put in the dirt like the inhabitants of this world due to their dead, how revolting, she thinks, an eternity in dirt. A shudder runs through her body with that thought.

Tamara is only thirteen-years-old, but she acts like an adult; she has not reached puberty yet, so most ignore her youthful wisdom, and for this reason, Tamara spends most of her time alone up in the mountains trying to make sense of the life God saddled her with. On a world that hates the Parkin's people.

Tamara's father took a job working for the government at the capital on Stink Water Island. What a stupid name, she screams to the trees around her, knowing no one was within several kilometers.

She has not heard from her father in two months or more.

"I hope he is alright."

She never knew her mother; she took her own life right after Tamara's birth, and Tamara hated her for a long time, but not now, now she envies her mother's peace. Only in death do we truly find peace, she tells herself.

As for taking her own life, no! It would kill her father, and she loves him with all her heart.

That would make her just as bad as the dirt slugs she despises.

Dirt slugs is her pet name for the inhabitants of Tarkaneay; her father gets very angry at her when she uses it, telling her there is good and bad in all races.

Deep down she understands the logic, but the anger over powers her sometimes.

Tamara lays down in the grass, looking up at the beautiful blue sky, thinking to herself that this could be a nice place if it was not for the dirt slugs.

She recalls a story Papa told her many years ago about Sub-Driver Clarence, how Papa's mother, many years ago, was saved from a slobber beast by the monster that lived in the mountain outside their village. Rumors had it that the beast had been killing children for twenty years.

The men of the sounding area tried to kill the beast, but it always ran away; she made friends with it and found out it was no monster. It had harmed no one ever! It was Sub-Driver Clarence, and by doing so, saved our race.

Before she realized it, she was sound asleep.

She awoke some time before midnight to the sound of something coming along the trail on the ridge, something big by the sound of it. Wishing she had not fallen asleep and started a fire to keep the wild thing away.

Tamara looked around her and knew she would not be able to hide here in the open; her only chance of not being seen would be to make it to a small group of trees a little way down the trail she'd came up. Whatever it is, it's coming fast, it's only a few dozen meters away, Tamara makes a dash down the trail, making it to the trees as the giant whatever reaches the place she had been laying.

She ducks behind a small shrub that is close.

Tamara moves, so she can see the intruder. It's huge! Maybe three meters high, silhouetted against the starry sky.

She has never seen a drone but she thinks to herself, this may be one, but it might not be one, so I'm not taking any chances, it could kill me and there is no one to help me if it decides to do so.

Her only option is to try to make it down the trail without being seen, so she starts her trip very slowly, making as little noise as possible.

She makes it about ten meters down the slope when a booming voice calls out, "Where are you going, Tamara? The trail is not safe in the dark."

Tamara stop's in her tracks, looking to where the voice came from.

"Come, Tamara, come sit by me and let's talk a little while."

"How do you know my name?" she shouts from her spot.

"I know all the Lost Ones, Tamara, your father and your grandfather."

"In that case, where is Papa tonight?"

"He is with all the other Parkin's that have gone before."

"Who are you?" she shouts.

"I'm Michael!"

"Michael's gone, everyone knows that, Sheila killed him, only her ship lives."

"No, Tamara, I live and so Sheila lives. Now come out, so I can get a good look at you."

Tamara steps out from behind the shrub and approached the giant vary slowly. Stopping several meters from the intruder.

"What do you won't from me?" she asks the towering giant.

"To talk, Tamara, nothing more," he tells her, "now come closer please, you have nothing to fear from me."

Somehow Tamara knew it was telling her the truth, so with slow and steady steps, she draws closer to her late-night visitor.

Tamara could see it was humanoid, at least in form.

The thing stood two and a half meters tall with jet black skin.

She begins to make out more and more details as the distance shrank, its fetchers were all proportional like a human, arms, legs, torso, and head, but there were other arms tucked under the first ones, smaller ones with tiny delicate fingers.

She stopped at least three meters form him.

"Why would you want to talk to me if you're Master-Driver, Michael?"

"I'm lonely, Tamara! Dose that surprise you?" he asks her.

"How could Michael be lonely? He can be in hundreds of places at once," she protests.

"That was the old Michael," he tells Tamara.

"An old and new Michael, you speak in riddles now."

"Come sit and I will tell you my story, child. First let's get some light and heat, so you will not be so cold."

Tamara realizes she is cold and a bit damp from the wet grass.

Michael reaches for a downed log, and within seconds, has it cut up and burning.

The warmth of the fire drew her even closer to her visitor.

Standing next to the fire with her hands stretched out to absorb moor heat, Tamara notices Michael is smiling.

This puts her at ease, so she turns to face the Avatar of Master-Driver Michael.

"You knew my papa?"

"Yes, as a child, not much older than you are now," he tells her.

"Then you were on the ship?" she states.

"No, I am the ship, Tamara, and you know this, don't you?"

"Yes, I was testing you," she boasts.

With that Michael lets out a booming laugh, shocking her.

"You, my child, are just like your grandfather," Michael states. "It has been years since I have laughed like that, thank you, child."

It was her turn to smile.

Filling warmer and more comfortable in the giant's presence now, Tamara dares to ask the next question.

"What happened to Sheila?"

"My dear, that is a long and sad story I think should be told later, this is no place for such a tell; ask me later, and I will tell you the complete story, this I promise, but the short version is Clarence loved the Parkin's people so much that instead of killing them like Shelia ordered him to, he disabled Shelia. Will that satisfy your curiosity for now?"

Tamara nods her approval.

"Why did you put us here on this world with the dirt slugs?"

"There are many reasons, child, the first and most important one, you are safer here and, Tamara, you should not judge all people for the actions of a few, there are people here that would give up their life for you or anyone else if the need arose, so please no more dirt slug."

Tamara knows deep down he is right, she has seen acts of kindness from the inhabitants, but she has seen the prejudice and hate also.

"Tell me, Master, why have you forsaken us?"

"I am not your Master, I am Michael, your protector, at least I used to be. I am only a shadow of my former self, it is Master-Driver Clearance that has taken on that job," he tells her with a sad look on his face.

"You mean Sub-Driver Clarence, don't you?" she corrects him.

"Clarence refuses to accept the title, but make no mistake, Clarence is more than a Master-Driver, he is something else entirely," Michael explains, "the Parkin's people help to create him by changing him in ways the creators never imagined, and in doing so, saved their race and the lives of countless species, including the people here."

"Why have you not come to us sooner? Everyone thinks you died!"

"The truth, Tamara, most of what I was is dead, this is the only Avatar I can control away from my ship. I cannot control any Drivers, so I cannot control any drones. My million limbs, eyes, and ears are Clarence's now. For this reason, I stayed away. I did not want to show the Lost One's my weakness. I fear if they saw me, they would despair and lose hope."

"No, they loved you, Michael!"

"Yes, I know this, but sometimes love is not enough, child, and if the full story was known, I think that love would turn to hate in time," he explains.

"Never," she objects.

"Tamara, the only reason you and your family are still alive is Master-Driver Clarence betrayed his master to save you. I was utterly defeated, so I, too, owe my life to Clarence."

The young girl offers no reply, only looks at the giant. "I do have my reasons for staying in the shadows, Tamara," he explains, "there is one more storm coming, and you are going to be my voice, child."

"What!" she gasps. "Me? No, choose another please, I'm too young and too stupid," she pleads.

"It is your youth that makes you perfect for this, and as for being stupid, I disagree with your assessment, child. I have watched you for most of your life, and STUPID you are not."

"Wait, you have been watching me? For how long? How? No, you must have me confused with someone else," Tamara stammers.

"Slow down, child," he tells her. "Yes, I have been with you ever since your papa passed, the locket around your neck, Tamara, the one your papa gave you, who do you think gave it to him?"

"It's yours?"

Tamara reaches behind her neck to remove the locket.

"No, child, it's not mine, it's yours," he tells her, "I relinquished ownership of that locket when I gave it to your grandfather before he settled here. Your papa and I here friends, Tamara."

"He never said anything about being your friend or mentioned your personal involvement in our lives," she remarks to Michael, more to herself than him.

"This I know, child, that was our arrangement, and he was a man of honor right to the day he died. I also miss him as a friend, great is that loss to me and the Parkin's people."

"What is it you wish me to do?" she asks.

"Nothing, child, wear the locket always and be my friend."

"That's not a job," she tells him.

"Oh, but it is. The friend part is not, but the part that is important is the part of keeping it secret, do you understand, child? I only have one set of eyes to see from, and I need you to be my eyes and ears here, you cannot do that if people know you are my friend, Tamara."

"A secret friend I can never reveal, plus the fact that friend was the most powerful entity in the known universe, how can I refuse?" Tamara laughed.

This sight gave Michael hope for Tamara; she has been depressed as of late, and laughter is good medicine, we will help each other, he thinks, I, too, need to heal.

Michael and Tamara talked until the sun begins to show in the west.

"Child I must go now; the sun will be up soon and it's hard to hide this avatar. I have a cave hidden down that draw," he points southeast. "If you need me, all you have to do is call my name, the locket will do the rest. I will go now," he tells her and rises to his feet to go.

"No, wait," stepping over to Michael, she gives him a hug and tells him thank you, "you have given me the best gift ever."

"You're welcome, child."

Tamara watches as the avatar disappears down the mountain.

"What a night," she remarks to herself" and I can tell no one, that sucks."

Tamara knew she was going to be in trouble when she got home, but it did not matter now, she was in the service of MICHAEL. I bet this is how Papa felt, too.

The trip down the trail was so beautiful today, so Tamara sang to herself and even skipped a little; this is a good day!

7

Sandra awoke a little after 6 A.M. She moans to herself after she realizes she has only slept three hours.

No going back to sleep now, she tells herself, getting her feet to the floor, she shivers with the early morning cold.

A glance out the window tells Sandra it's going to be a nice day in spite of the storm last night.

She walks to the door leading to the balcony and the door slides open on her approach, letting in the morning breeze.

A moor violent shiver rocks Sandra, so she wraps her arms around herself and heads for the sun bye the rail.

Surveying the countryside, she sees a beautiful world full of sights and sounds she has ignored for more than fifteen years.

"How can I have I been so naive and self-centered?" she reprimands herself. "I have wasted my life and the youth of my son's life. No getting it back now," she realizes, "only the future maters now. Let the dead be with the dead and the living live!"

Driving the memory of her late husband deeper in to her subconscious, and at the same time, placing the task of protecting Tyler at the forefront of her mind.

Her gaze wanders over the view around her, Wolf Creek is the capital of the monarchy. It stretched as far as her view could see.

A city of more than a million.

From her vantage point, Sandra can see the well to do side of town, nestled up against Wolf Creek, which is more a river than a creek.

Lush greenery hides the homes there, only the roofs show with their sculpted facade and decadent fixtures proclaiming their status.

Sandra's own childhood home is among them, she cannot see it from here, but she knows right where it is.

Her worst memories are there, she has never returned nor will she ever, she reminds herself.

There is a fire burning out west beyond the industrial section of the city.

From the black smoke billowing, Sandra knows it's a structure fire, probably one of the row complexes in the slums.

They will let it burn its self out, not making any real effort to put out the flames, Sandra tells herself, shaking her head in disapproval.

Sandra watches a few more seconds, then heads back in to the warmth of her penthouse, letting the image of the fire evaporate from her thoughts.

She has more important thing to think about today.

James Wildwind will be here at ten, I need to be ready beforehand, Sandra reminds herself.

James is the appointed ambassador to the monarchy.

All eleven royal houses have an ambassador representing the Steward.

James was a childhood friend of the late king. They were more like brothers than friends, in fact they were brothers in arms for three years in the Royal Guard, cementing their friendship in combat.

There is no love lost between James and Kenneth.

James always told John he should watch Kin, telling him that he thought Kin was no good and capable of doing just about anything.

John would shrug it off, telling Jimmy he's imagining things, but it was not imagination that put the King in the passenger seat of Ken's sports car as it slid around a corner, smashing into a poll, killing John instantly and not putting a scratch on the Duke.

Sandra sees Mae coming through the door; looking at the time, she sees Mae is right on the dot. This woman is never late or early, she thinks to herself.

"Good morning, my lady," Mae greets her sovereign.

"Good morning," Sandra replies. "Did you tell James to come by this morning, Mae?"

"Yes, my lady, he will be here at ten."

"Good."

Mae begins her morning duties, laying out Sandra's clothes for the day, drawing her bath and helping her in.

After that is done, she helps her dress, brushing her hair, and prepares for the day's challenges.

Next, she sets the table for her Queen's meal.

The servant's door opens as if on cue and in comes the cook with breakfast, followed by two servers, the head butler, Tyler's totter, and Sandra's secretary.

Malcolm Ree, Sandra's father, taught her one thing she carried over in to her own life, work starts with breakfast and breakfast is a good time to start working.

"Good morning," Sandra tells the gathered staff.

"Good morning," they all say in unison.

As the meal is being served, Sandra starts her instructions for the day.

"I would like to make an announcement; the household will be moving to the summer palace in two weeks instead of the summer solstice."

"That's six weeks early, my lady", injects Bradly Sipp, Tyler's totter. "We have a field trip scheduled for next week at the Planetarium! Tyler is looking forward to the trip."

"That will have to be postponed, Mr. Sipp, there will be other times for that," Sandra tells him.

"I will have to inform the Duke, my lady, he will need to assign a security detail," Herald Harper the Head butler states.

"I know, Mr. Harper, tell the Duke anything you like, tell him I'm a crazy bitch, but we will be leaving for the summer palace in two weeks."

Never before had anyone heard Sandra use words like that; they all looked at each other with questioning looks on their faces, but none would voice their thoughts.

Mae sees the dissension brewing around the table and adds her voice to the conversation.

"The Queen is trying to get her life back on track, and if by going to the summer palace early will help with that, then we will be going early, is that clear?" Mae tells them all in a very firm voice.

All around the table are nodding heads in agreement.

"You all know what has to be done," Sandra tells them, "in two weeks, we will be going, are there any questions?"

No one responded.

The staff excused themselves, each going to their appointed jobs and start getting things ready for the move.

Sandra, Mae, and Libby Carefree, Sandra's secretary, are alone now, and the conversation shifts to the real problem.

"Libby, I think the Duke is going to try to harm Tyler before his coronation," Sandra tells her, "we have to stay alert and make the Duke think I'm going crazy, so he drops his guard."

"My Lady you must be mistaken," Libby insists.

"No, Libby," Mae interrupts, "I heard his drunken words last night, and they convinced me the Queen is right, it's not so much the words he used as it was the mannerisms he displayed.

He will try something, I'm convinced now. I'm sorry I doubted you, my Queen," Mae tells her.

"You, Mae, are my most trusted adviser, you never have to apologize for doing what you think best for me and Tyler, I know you will always be there for us. Libby, your job this morning is to convince the Duke I'm imbalanced and need to get away. Tell him I had the whole household up last night looking for a book. He should be reading the log about now, this way we'll preempt his questions," looking over at Mae, seeing her nod in agreement, "can you do that for me?" Sandra inquires.

"Yes, my lady, for you and the prince, I will do anything," Libby said.

"Thank you, Libby," Sandra responds. "Ambassador Wildwind will be here at ten, and I would like you in the Duke's office at the same time, this will keep him away from this side of the building, so we can have a private conversation without interruptions."

"I did a little acting in collage, my lady, I'll pour it on," she laughs and so does Sandra, Mae remains stoned faced and grim.

With Libby off to the Duke's office to run interference for the Queen's mother, Sandra and Mae know once they bring James in to the plan, there is no going back, the journey will end with ether the Duke's destruction or their own.

"It's almost ten, Mae, James should be at the security desk by now," Sandra tells her, "go intercept him, so there is no commotion and we draw as little attention as possible."

Sandra had only time to sit down when Mae returned with James in tow.

"Good morning, your Majesty," James announces, bowing low and awaited Sandra's reply.

"Good morning, Ambassador Wildwind, thank you for coming," said Sandra, "please, have a seat."

"What can I do for you, your Majesty?" James asks.

"You were a friend of the King, were you not?" Mae asks.

"Yes, John and I were best friends, and you know that, my lady," looking directly at Sandra.

"Yes, is your answer then," Mae continues, "would you say if a friend's child is in danger, you owe him your loyalty and help?"

"Certainly," James answers, "what is going on? If you have something to say, say it!"

Sandra blurts out, "I think Kin is going to try to kill Tyler!"

"I knew it," James declares.

Standing up, James is no little man, wide shoulders with rippling musicals with his eyes as dark as his face, anger begins spreading all over him.

James Wildwind is the eighteenth son of the old King of Traay, the only surviving king from the old days. Traayins were a primitive culture before the Drivers. A people that lived or died for the sake of honor. Within two generations, the Traayins went from tribal to space faring.

"That son-of-a-bitch," looking at Sandra, he stops his outburst. "I'm sorry, my Queen, for the language," James apologizes, "but I knew Kin was no good from when we were kids in school together, he would do the evilest things to people, then laugh about it."

"I have no evidence, James, I only have the instincts of a mother, it's not what he has done or said, it's the way he said it," Sandra explains. "Kin would have been King after John's death if it was not for me being pregnant, and that did not come out until after his death. Kin acted like he was hurt at the loss of his brother, but it was the fact that there was an heir in his way now."

"What would you like me to do, your majesty?" James inquires.

"I would like you to arrange a meeting with Sub-Driver Clarence! You have talked to him? Haven't you, James?" asks Sandra.

"Yes, numerous times," James adds, "he has an Avatar at the capitol building in New Hope." James remembers the first time he saw the Avatar; he was a little kid of seven. "Sub-Driver Clarence came to his father and requested twenty-five children to be trained in a new school for the leaders of the new world."

"Then you can do this for me?" Sandra asks, interrupting his memory of the avatar.

"Yes, my Queen, I can do that."

"Good, can you have him meet me at the summer palace? Its more secluded than the capital, less likely to be seen," Sandra tells the Ambassador.

"That is wise, my lady, the less Kin knows, the better odds you'll have of protecting the Prince."

"We are on the same page then," Sandra declares, "Tyler needs protection and the threat from within is the most pressing concern."

"Yes, my lady, you have my support and my loyalty, this I pledge for the memory of my friend and King. I can be back in New Hope by the end of the week, my lady, I should have a meeting with Clarence by the end of next week, no later," James tells her, touching a locket he has under his shirt; maybe sooner he thinks to himself.

"Good, that gives me time to make other arrangements before our meeting, and James, the Duke has many friends, be careful," the Queen mother tells him, "John would not like it if I got you hurt, too."

'Worry not, my lady, I can take care of myself, and as for the Duke, he's a coward, always has been."

"All the same, James, be careful, Tyler will need men like you, men with honor and loyalty, so do be careful," Sandra pleads.

"I will, my lady and you do the same, for the prince needs you also," he reminds her.

"Thank you," she answers. With that the meeting was over, the ambassador takes his leave. "I'm glad you suggested we ask James for help, Mae," Sandra comments. "I feel as if John is helping me throw him. Mae, does that sound crazy to you?"

"No, miss, it sounds like you've found hope again."

One more thing to take care of this morning, Sandra thinks, pushing the intercom button summoning Tina.

Tina Hopkins enters the room dressed for travel, a single piece jump suit with high boots, accenting her long frame with her long blond hair pulled back in a ponytail carrying a single bag, bowing to her Queen.

"Are you ready for this, Tina?" asks Sandra.

"I don't know what it is I'm to do, but I know you and the prince need my help, and my help you will have, my Queen."

Sandra looks at the young woman she is going to send into harm's way by herself, unaided and alone. The determination in Tina's face gives Sandra little comfort in her decision to use her.

Sandra knows in order for her to do a proper job, Tina must have all the facts or at least the fact as she knows them.

"I am going to put this as bluntly as I can, Tina. I believe the Duke is responsible for the King's death, and I have my suspicions that he is planning the same for the Prince," Sandra explains.

"My lady, I know the Duke is egotistical and rude but a murderer?"

The doubt of the Queen's sanity slowly creeps in to Tina's mind, until she looks over at Mae and sees the stone-faced governess nodding in agreement. The Queen may be prone to hysteria but not Mae, Tina thinks to herself, she is a rock.

"I need you to go on a fact-finding mission, The Lost One's settled in Newland Islands in greater numbers there. I would like you to go on vacation, Tina, and talk to the Lost One's and see what information you can find out about the Drivers, paying close attention to Michael and Clearance, be it rumor, speculation, or folk lore, we will decipher it when you get home, can you do this for us, Tina?" the Queen mother asks.

"Yes, my lady," Tina answers.

"Try to get in to the more remote populations of the Lost Ones, Tina," Mae suggests, "they are less likely to be contaminated and will have more authentic stories."

"Good idea, Mae," Sandra compliments her. "Leave immediately, Tina, and tell no one," the Queen Mother tells her, handing her an envelope with cards and cash in it.

Tina looks in the envelope, "Your Majesty! There is ten years' worth of pay here."

"Yes, Tina, there is. You will have better luck if they think you are a rich brat throwing away money, now get going and have fun, but don't forget the mission, Tina, we're depending on you."

"I won't let you down, my lady." Tina bows and leave on her mission.

"There is no turning back now, miss."

"I know, Mae, but what choice do I have?"

8

Billy opens his eyes to a stabbing pain in his head, sitting up surveying the room, the room was so bright, it made him squint.

The room starts to spin, so Billy lays back on the bunk, keeping one foot on the ground.

"What the hell did I do last night?" Billy asks himself, "The last thing I remember is? Oh, yeah, the grunt with the big mouth," rubbing his jaw, working it back and forth to see if it still worked. "But how did I get here?" Seeing the bars of the cell for the first time, "Oh, yeah, it was.

At that time, he hears a moan from under the cot, interrupting Billy's train of thought.

Looking under the cot, Billy sees Lynch, his face flat on the floor in a puddle of vomit.

The sight of it had an immediate effect on Billy, now it was his turn.

Lucky for Ted under the cot, Billy only had the dry heaves.

Billy hears laughter, looking up, he sees the guard with the biggest shit eating grin.

"You've screwed up this time, Zercoff, you and Linch. Wake up sleeping beauty under there, you have an appointment with the base commander, I sure wouldn't want to be in your shoes," the guard laughs. "I'll be back in ten minutes, be ready."

Billy begins the process of getting Ted out from under the cot and getting him cleaned up before they have to see the General.

It's a slow process. Ted is still drunk and can barely walk.

Billy does what he can for the kid, trying to make him presentable, after all it was probably his fault the kid is in trouble, too.

Fifteen minutes later, they're in a van heading for headquarters and a meeting with a very pissed off General.

"There is no hearing, no paper work, no bail, this is the Guard," Billy tells Ted, "we're going straight to the General." Ted lets out an involuntary sigh and turns a paler pail. "Take it easy, kid, if it goes as I expect, we'll get some extra shit duty, no more than that," Billy tells Ted, "think, boy, we were in an illegal casino, do you think they won't a court martial, not on your life, so relax, it will be OK, you watch."

The pair are led into the office of the base commander, General Gabriel Boot.

"Captain Billy Zercoff reporting as ordered, sir," holding his salute, awaiting the General's response.

After what seemed an eternity to Ted, the General returned their salute, then started their ass chewing.

"What the fuck do you think you're doing?" leaning with both hands on the desk, looking straight at Billy, the General shouts. Billy knows Gab is only blowing off steam and putting on a show for the kid. The academy was not safe when you put me and Gab on the same detail, Billy thinks to himself, remembering the time the two of them convinced a plebe into painting no parking on the curb where the commandant parks. He and I had K P duty for a week. "Zercoff, are you hearing me?" the General shouts even louder.

"Yes, sir," as a slight smile creeps on to Billy's face, looking at the General.

Like a contagious disease of smileites, both men broke out in wide grins.

"Billy, what the hell," the General's grin evaporating, and in its place, concern. "At ease, gentlemen," the General tells them. They all sit down, well, two sits. Ted melted into his seat, turning a little green from pail. "Billy, you're too old to be fighting," the General tells him.

"Gab that grunt was really giving the boy shit, I know he was drunk, this was his first trip down south, hell you and I got shit faced on our first visit, remember."

"Yes, I do," Billy.

Gab replies, "But the point is that that casino is illegal but necessary for moral; every time something like this happens, I'm one step closer to shutting it down permanently."

"I understand, Gab, I'll keep a low profile from now on," Billy tells him.

With that the General breaks out in his own big smile, "I know you well, Billy, you're going to love me. I want your bird up and ready to fly in one hour. You're going to Stink Water Island to pick up a corps, then you're flying it to Kranstan point where you're going to do two weeks of training, you and your co-conspirator looking at Linch for the first time."

The shocked look on Ted's face made the old friends laugh out loud.

"Time's ticking, Billy, this may be a shit detail, but this is heavy stuff, these orders came from the Steward's office right before you got here, they won't that body in Kranstan today.

I had orders for the two of you already, they were here before you arrived, I was to send you to Kranstan in two days. I don't get orders like that, Billy; for that reason, I'm sending you now, and I have the Steward's office to back me up on this, so I'm covered, you need to be careful, Billy," Gab tells him, "nothing about those orders sound right."

"I can do that bootstrap," Billy standing, putting his hand out to the General.

Taking Billy's hand in a firm handshake, the General replies, "You better, wrong-turn."

The pair salute the General; on their way out, they heard the General telling his secretary, "Get me Operations."

Leaving the General's office, Billy pitches Ted his room key.

"You go get our stuff, I'll meet you at the ship," Billy tells him, "I'm going to operations to fill our flight plan."

"Will do, Skipper."

As Billy walks in to operations, the Duty Officer has his back to the door, not seeing him come in.

Billy can hear one side of the phone conversion.

"Nash, you're not hearing me, this came from the General."

"Well, you have him call the General."

"You're crazy, Nash, if you think I'm doing that."

"Now I can do that."

The duty officer turns around, looking Billy right in the face.

"I have to go," hanging up the phone abruptly.

"What can I do for you, Captain?" the Duty Officer asks.

"Filing my flight plan," Billy tells the D.O. "And I will need fuel also," he adds moments later.

"Yes, sir," the D.O. replies, "I can have a truck there in twenty minutes."

"Good, I'll be waiting," answered Billy, thinking to himself, I know I have plenty of fuel for the trip, let's give him a little false hope of keeping us here.

Billy takes his time leaving operation, lingering at the door long enough to hear the D.O. on the phone.

"I have it taken care of, Nash, you can count on me."

Billy shuts the door smiling to himself, I'll be gone before that truck gets to the flight line.

Billy and Ted reunite at the transport, "We're skipping pre-flight, Rocky," Billy tells him. "Walk around her quickly, boy, I'll be on the bridge," as Billy climbs the crew ladder.

Two minutes later, Billy is joined my Ted on the bridge.

"Everything looks copacetic, Skipper."

"Strap in, we're going now," Billy flips the emergency power supply on, eliminating the need for the A.P.U. start. "Contact the tower, Rocky, we're out of here," Billy declares.

Ten minutes later, the transport is airborne heading north.

It amuses Billy to head north from the poll, every direction is north, you have to know which north is the right north.

"Tell me, Skipper, did the general call you wrong-turn?"

"Yes, he did. It's something I did in the academy, Rocky," Billy tells him with the biggest grin, "I'll tell you that one over a bottle, it's that funny, maybe on our next trip we'll get bootstrap to tell it." They both laugh a hardy laugh. "Now down to business, Rocky," Billy tells him, "we're going to be tight on fuel at this altitude, so we're going to push this old girl to her limits. Have you ever been to 30,000 meters?"

"No, Skipper."

"Hang on to your shorts, boy, we're going suborbital," Billy pulls back on the stick and points the transport for heaven, pushing the throttle to emergency power levels. which ignites the solid boosters built in to the air-frame.

The transport shakes violently with the engine's being over taxed. The G-forces was incredible; in a few seconds, they accelerated to more than 2,500 KPH

The emergency booster only gives them thirty seconds of power, "But that's enough to reach the upper atmosphere, from here on, we coast," Billy announces.

Looking over at Ted, Billy can see his wonderment with the experience, why not, seeing the arc of the world before them.

"This is beautiful, I can see half of the world!"

"Any regrets joining the Guard, Rocky?" Billy knows the answer before he asks it.

All Ted could do was shake his head, the allure of the moment was over powering; from that moment on, Ted would never be the same. The call of space had him, and he could never go back.

How many times for you, Skipper?"

"This makes three, I applied for space service, but I was passed over too many times, I finally gave up," Billy tells him.

With the life force spent in the emergency boosters, the transport will be down for a week, refitting her with new boosters, Billy tells himself, they'll take care of that at Kranstan.

9

Tina steps out of the arrival terminal in the noon time sun on Miller Island. It's the international airport for Stink Water.

An airport is all that's here, the Island its self is only four kilometers long and three-kilometer-wide, only enough room for it, little alone something else. Two of the three runways run out over the water on elevated berms.

Now for a boat rid Tina tells herself, seeing Stink Water Island about fifteen kilometers to the north.

There is a covered escalator leading down to the wharf, where the water taxi's awaited there, passengers for one of the three islands close bye.

Most passengers travel to Stink Water, which is the capital of Newland, the other two, Vision Island and Window Island, are by far larger islands and more developed. Industry, farming, and fishing are the main jobs, very little tourism.

Making her way down the wharf, Tina sees a sign reading, Imperial guest.

Tina has a room at the Imperial, a five-star resort, known for its plush surroundings and pampering staff.

The booking agent started to give Tina problems about her reservations until the clerk got a look at Tina's credit card with the royal seal on it; from then on, they treated Tina like royalty.

The boat ride only takes a little while to reach Stink Water and the Imperial hotel.

"Tina Hopkins, oh, yes, here you are, miss, you're in the penthouse on the west tower," the man at the desk tells Tina, ringing the bell for the bell hop.

Tina, knowing she must stay in character, hands the one tiny bag to the bell hop, then heads for the elevator.

The ride up was thirty floors.

As Tina steps into the penthouse, she was greeted by her own private staff, butler, maid, and cook.

Looking around Tina sees the most beautiful room she has ever seen. The colors of the room were vibrant and the furnishings are plush and comfortable, the scent of fresh flowers washed over her.

I can get used to this, Tina thinks to herself, handing the bell hop a twenty-note bill.

"Welcome, miss," Bernard the butler steps up, introducing himself, "this is Marie," indicating the cook. Marie curtsies, "And Berrana the maid."

Berrana steps forward and curtsies an awkward attempt.

"You're a Lost one," Tina asks Berrana, recognizing the clan tattoo on her wrist.

"Is that a problem, miss? Bernard asks much too quickly for Tina's liking, as if this girl is something to be avoided.

"No, not at all, I was asking because your mane is so unusual and beautiful," Tina, looking the younger Berrana directly in the eyes, smiling her most friendly smile.

The gesture had the desired effect on Berrana, a touch of blush and a smile.

"Thank you for the introduction," Tina tells them all, "I am going to take a bath and a nap.

Berrana, will you assist me?" Berrana nods but said nothing, following Tina into the master bedroom. "How old are you, Berrana?" Tina asks her, thinking to herself. I'm here for less than an hour and I have my first contact.

"Sixteen years, miss."

"Call me Tina please; when we're with others, call me what your expected to, but when we're alone, call me Tina," putting out her hand to Berrana

"Thank you, miss, ah, Tina," taking her hand reluctantly.

"See, that was not that hard, now was it?"

"No, miss—Tina."

"Now that we are friends, tell me, Berrana, aren't you a little young to be working here?"

"No, miss, I mean, Tina, the age of adulthood is fifteen among the Parkins, that is when I got the clan mark," holding up her arm, "that is the way it used to be anyway, before we came here, at least that is what my dad said," showing a bit of sadness on her young face.

"You're not happy here?"

"No, I mean, yes, yes, I'm happy to be where there is sky above and ground beneath my feet," Berrana tells Tina. "I am thankful! My family and I have only been here on Tarkaneay six months, before that we were on Trinity station, my father moved us here. He said it was too dangerous to stay anymore. The solar storms, you know! So, I am very thankful to be here on your world, miss."

"Our world," Tina corrects her, "this is your world now."

Tina can see that the Lost One's have a deep respect for their host here on Tarkaneay but happy, they are not.

"I would like to learn about the Parkin's people," Tina explains to Berrana, "all I know about them is the Drivers brought you here and some say abandoned you."

"That's not true, miss!" she states with a little vigor, "Clarence would never abandon us! We are his people, and he loves us."

Tina realized she is in delicate territory with the subject of Clarence.

"No disrespect intended, Berrana," she tells her. "I am ignorant to the subject and have no one to teach me differently. Could you enlighten me, so I will not offend any Parkin's in the future?"

"I would like that, miss, I mean, Tina," getting back her previous girlish smile.

Good, I believe this is a good start to a long friendship, Berrana. I hope you fill the same."

"I think so, too," breaking out in a wide grin, "you're the nicest and prettiest guest I've ever met," Berrana tells Tina, embarrassing herself, turning bright red and accompanied by a giggle.

"After dinner would you like to come and sit with me and tell me about the Parkin's people," Tina invites.

"Yes, I would love to, miss, I mean, Tina."

They both laugh.

"Good, I will see you an hour after dinner."

Tina dismisses Berrana.

Time for that bath and nap, Tina tells herself, it's nice to be on the inside for a change.

10

Dale Walden has been in this predicament before; as the Steward's negotiator, he has brokered far more complicated missions in the past. One side claiming one thing and the other side claiming something entirely different.

"Gentlemen, sit down," Dale asks them in a firm but polite voice, "this is getting us nowhere."

Trevor Neal, the miner's representative, still pointing his fingerless hand at Bob Better, the plant production manager.

"What would you have me do, Trevor, stop production all together? If we do that, who is going to feed 25,000 souls?"

"You!"

"No product. No cash. No cash. No previsions, can't you get that through your thick skull," Bob tells him.

"I'm not asking you to do that and you know it," Trevor shoots back.

"Gentlemen, please, if you will take your seats and quit making accusations, we might get somewhere, I'm here to help, not referee," Dale tells the entire table.

Dale is in his mid-seventies, thin, tall, long gray hair in a ponytail, light complected, and always wears a hat. A likable man if you ever met one, with a smile and a firm handshake. "Trevor, you say the mine needs moor ventilation and, Bob, you say you will have to shut down production to install the new air purifiers," Dale states. Both men agree. "I have the Steward's full backing on this matter; if you need portable air purifiers to keep production on schedule, I can have them here in five days," Dale tells them.

"How long would we have them?" Trevor asks.

"At what cost?" injects Bob.

"They'll be yours at no cost," answering both questions at once, "there are four surplus air purification units from an old class mining vessel being scraped at Bentley station, this way you can supplement the existing system, keeping four drifts active until we can install the new system, would that work?" Dale asks.

Bob reminds the table that four drifts can only supply half the quota, but if Trevor can double up the crews, it can work.

"We can do that, Bob," Trevor putting out his finger-less hand to Bob with a shit eating grin, knowing the sight makes Bob uncomfortable.

"It's a deal," Bob grabbing Trevor's thumb with his thumb and fore finger, shaking once, then letting go, tuning a little green.

"Gentleman, then I can tell the Steward his supply of Trybideam will not be interrupted," Dale announces.

Trybideam is the key component to the operation of the Gravitron, found only in any quantity on the first planet Bitderin.

Bitderin is a dead world with no atmosphere and no rotation, locked in a tight orbit around the sun. The day side is super-hot and the night side is freezing. The orbit takes ninety days, so the day is forty-five days long and night is the same.

It is beveled that Bitderin was a gas giant that wandered in from deep space to the inner solar system, being captured by the Sun, boiling off its atmosphere, leaving the core exposed.

Bob reminds Dale that the day cycle will start in five days.

"Don't worry, Bob, we will have those air purification units here by then," Dale reassures him. "The Steward will keep his word, and you have mine as well."

With that crisis averted, Dale can move on to the next issue.

"Mister Mall, did you have something to summit to the comity?"

Floyd Mall stands surveying the table, "You all know what I'm going to say, and I will continue saying it until some one hears, Floyd is the elected Representative for public heath, he only has a voice on the comity, no voting privilege nor any authority to do anything out side of speaking his mind, which he does quite well, standing above everyone in the room, a tall imposing man with gentle eyes and a hard fist if it came down to it, and everyone in the room knows it but Dale. We have to close this place to family operations and start unaccompanied tours."

"All right, Mall, you had your say, now sit down so we can all go home. Berry Green Charmin of the commit and one fifth of the voting bloc, the man in charge as it is. We have all indeed heard your argument and this is no venue to air that subject, this is a production meeting not a health agenda, we will take that up on the next quarterly, this meeting is adjourned."

With the dropping of the hammer, the meeting was over, each going their separate ways.

Dale hears Bob telling Trevor on the way out, "You owe me a drink for that hand shake stunt, you know I feel bad as it is, you shithead."

"I know, dumb ass, why do you think I did it?" Trevor replies laughing, "let's go have a drink."

"I think the Steward will be pleased, Connie!" Dale tells his aid, Connie Burch, a very small round woman in her mid-forties with thick black hair down to her waist, a bubbly personality, always quick to laugh. "I'm going to catch the next ship back to see that that equipment gets here ASAP! You know you will be stuck here for forty-five days," Dale reminds Connie.

"I know, sir, someone will need to see that they keep their side of the bargain," Connie replies.

"Don't let those two fool you, they are friends and have been for a long time; we've been played, Connie, but I agree someone needs to keep an eye on things here tell next cycle."

"I'll turn it in to a vacation," Connie laughs.

"Vacation or not, thing are not what they appear I fear, so please be careful, Connie, and I am going to leave Matthew here with you," Dale tells her.

"Good, I like that young man, he's fun," Connie comments.

"I'm going to get packed; the ship departs in four hours."

Dale gives Connie a hug and farewells are exchanged, then they each go their own way.

As Dale approaches the elevator, he hears his name called.

Looking behind him, there is a ten-year-old boy holding out an envelope.

"This is for you, mister," holding up the envelope even closer.

Reaching out taking the envelope, the boy immediately took off in a run down the hall right around Connie, disappearing around the corner before Dale could say a word.

Dale shrugs his shoulders and gives Connie one last nod before pushing the button for the elevator, he and Connie have been doing this for fare too long to put any credence in a note delivered anonymously, putting the envelope in his pocket to look at latter.

Stuck here for forty-five days, it could be worse, well, it is, she laughs to herself, five days before the end of this cycle, that makes fifty days. Oh well, let's go give Matt the good news.

Trinity station is deep underground to provide protection from the radiation for the inhabitant's during the day cycle, the station is on their own then, no ships can land or take off and communications are spotty at best.

The mining operations are next to the frozen core of the plaint, it can take up to twelve hours to reach one of the drifts.

The Trybideam is found in the layers right on top of the iron core.

It was the Drivers that started the mines, sinking shafts fifty kilometers deep and taught the Parkin's to mine the Trybideam for use in the Gravitron.

After the government was formed, the Drivers handed over operation to the government completely, disappearing all together as part of the Self Reliance Treaty, leaving the Parkin's to do the mining, that was twenty-five years ago, the population has doubled and the equipment has aged.

Connie finds Matt in the lounge drinking a tall mixed drink with a grumpy look, "Don't look so blue, kid, it could be worse, we could be stuck in Rocket Town during the winter like last year."

"Don't remind me, Bubbles," shooting Connie a half smile. "Dale told me to look after you," Matt tells Connie, "he knows if there is someone that can find trouble, it's our Bubbles."

"I tell you I'm innocent, General, that girl threw her face in to my fist before I dragged her out by the hair," Connie dose an exaggerated wink to Matt.

Matthew Dollar is a twenty-nine-year-old, not a big man but very athletic, ex GDF, a well-trained professional, but a person that would tell you if he thought you are wrong, this cost him his career.

Right after Matt's court-marshal, Dale intervened with the help of the Steward and his sentence was commuted. He has worked for Dale for three years now doing security.

"We have five days to kill before anything starts arriving, so let's go see the caverns I've heard so much about," Connie encourages Matt, trying to get his mind off of the long stay here, "I hear they go for kilometers and has the most interesting deposits," trying to spark Matt's adventurer trigger.

"How about tomorrow, Bubbles, you and me on an adventurer to the cavern, but tonight let's tie one on."

"I can do that," Connie replies, "barkeep two doubles, straight up."

11

James Wildwind youth was spent between two worlds. One was hard and brutal, but with a since of freedom and connection with the land, the other was in a world of advanced technology.

The land of Traay is on the grate continent of Severus, it's one of the seven kingdoms there.

The people that settled there become the Traayins, the smallest kingdom on Tarkaneay.

The Traayins, live on a plateau that arose in the midst of an inland sea.

2,000 meters the plateau rose above the sea, cutting off that part of Severus from the rest of the continent. Over the countless millenniums, the plateau become riddled with deep canyons and ravine, making travel argues.

This further isolated the Traayins.

The Traayins, live between their high desert plateaus with its grass lands stretching as far as the eye can see and the thick forested canyons with their abundant wild life.

There life was a nomadic existence.

James can remember the day Sub-Driver Clarence was invited to attend the tribal council.

Clarence proposed to the council that he take twenty-five young boys to teach a new way, and for each one, he will give two cattle, five if the boy can pass his test.

It became a five-day festival with every boy in the kingdom trying out as a matter of honor.

Clarence left with James and twenty-four more of the brightest and 200 names for next year.

The school was in New Hope, the Federal capital of the new global republic.

The city was built by the Drivers, in a wagon-weal design, five circular arteries connected by eight spokes with the hub the center of government.

The world of the Drivers was magical to James at first, but slowly he learned and understood it was technology, nothing more.

He and his classmates were educated by the Drivers, there was literally thousands of students from all over Tarkaneay.

James took to the new way of life with zeal, surpassing most in his class.

James met John and his brother Kin there, taking to John immediately becoming best friends.

If you've seen James, John was not far away, they were inseparable, James even spent several school breaks with John at his home and John came to James's village once.

James knows going down memory lane will only make him madder.

He makes his way down the winding streets of old Wolf Creek heading for his private office away from the place.

I can't think there, he tells himself, at least down here the people are what they seem, hardworking, fair, and honest.

He stops in front of what looks like an old store, looking left and right, James steps through the door quickly, not that he cares if anyone knows about his office. It's a ritual from the old life, always keep your resting place secret.

He is greeted by the clerk behind the counter, "Good morning, Ambassador Wildwind."

"Good morning, mister Davis," James returns. "Any messages, Roger?"

"No, Ambassador, all has been quiet."

"I don't wish to be disturbed until three, I'm unavailable, Roger."

"Yes, sir." James inters his office, closing the door and locking it.

Sitting down at his desk leaning back as far as the chair can go, sighing deeply, there is no other way, the chair agrees with him shrieking loudly under the strain of his enormous weight.

Sitting up straight, so this chair is not broken like the last one.

Reaching in his shirt, pulling out a locket on a chain around his neck, unfastening it, placing it on the desk.

"Well, here goes, he tells himself, "there is always a first time." Looking right at the locket, James calls the name Sub-Drive Clarence, "we need to talk."

James set looking at the locket for several seconds before anything happens, no bells or flashing lights, only the genital voice replying, "How may I help you, Ambassador?"

"Yes, Sub-Driver, you said if there was a problem to summon you, I know you do not interfere with the internal business of the monarchy's, but I thought you should know, I think there is going to be an assassination," James tells him.

"This is troubling news, Ambassador, and your evidence is?" the voice at the other end asks.

"I have no evidence yet, Sub-Driver, but I know the Duke and his potential," James tells the locket. "I have seen his cruelty for myself as a young man, and I have always suspected the accident with the King was more than that."

"I see Ambassador Wildwind that you are worried about the young prince, but there is nothing I can do, this is a problem for your own judicial system to handle, my hands are tied on a matter like that by treaty, if it concerned the Lost Ones that would be a different matter," Clarence tells him.

"You yourself has seen the Duke's attitude toward the Lost Ones. I know I do not need to remind the Sub-Driver about the Duke's response to Remington Island or should I say lack of," James argues. "It is within his nature to commit murder, be it one or one thousand, and I have a moral obligation to stop him Sub-Driver, with or without your help!" James states flatly. "I admire your conviction and courage, Ambassador, but if I was to interfere every time there is an emergency, how can you stand on your own!"

"I can provide council," Clarence concedes, "there is no stipulation on that in the treaty."

"Good!" James replies with a little more enthusiasm than he intended.

"The Queen Mother would like to speak with you Sub-Driver, she did not go in to details about her questions, only that she would like to have a conference at the summer plaice. I told her I would not see you tell next week, so she is not expecting you for two weeks."

"Good planning, Ambassador," the Sub-Driver complements him, "tell the Queen I will be honored to attend her in fourteen days from now, tell her I will meet her on the west balcony overlooking the lake at 11 P.M. and, Ambassador, you did well bringing this to my attention, thank you for that."

"Your welcome," replies James.

"I will end now!" Clarence states, and the locket goes dead.

"That was easy," James tells himself, "I have carried that thing for ten years and that's all there is to it. My imagination had it doing all kinds of things," James laughs out loud, "you're a fool sometimes,

Wildwind." Pushing the intercom button, "Roger, book me a flight to New Hope, first available seat."

"Will do, Ambassador." Ten minutes later, Roger buzzes, "Your flight is at 5:30, Ambassador, Blue Skies, flight 122, seat 4A, is there anything else?"

"No, Roger that will do it, why don't you go home early? I can handle everything from here on out."

"Thanks, James, you have a good flight, when can I expect you back?"

"Three days," the Ambassador said, "give or take."

Roger goes home, leaving James alone to think about the events of the morning. Looking at his watch, it's 1:00 P.M. I have three hours to kill before I need to leave for the airport. I think I'll pay Kin a visit before I go. It irritates him to see my happy face.

12

"I'm telling you it can be done," Doctor Dezmen Pierce insists, "Clarence did it, we can, too, all we need to do is find the proper harmonic frequency."

Doctor Pierce is a Parkin physicist, he has studied under Clarence for ten years and at the University of New Hope under the brightest minds on Tarkaneay, in his late sixties, balding and filling out in the winter of his life, desperation has driven him for the last five years, he sees his life waning and he has not made his mark on history, his ego demand he show up the Tarkaneans for their arrogant attitude and snide remarks.

"We can't keep experimenting on people, Doctor Pierce," Bennie tells him, "I know they are all volunteers, but nine has gone mad and died, we will be discovered and can face criminal charges, Doctor."

"How are they going to connect us with the deaths, Bennie? The Radon gas dissipated within seventy-two hours and the effects of the radiation is so slow, it's weeks later before they show any symptoms, by that time there is no one home to point the finger at us."

"Just the same, Doctor Pierce. I think we should go a little slower," Bennie tells him.

"Nonsense," Doctor Pierce snorts, "we had the Driver cell unit sending out commands and had the drone walking on our first two subjects, we are close, Bennie, I can fill it, all we need to do is get the magnetic bottle to resonate at the matching frequency of the emitter," directing the energy to the pick-up headset transferring thought directly to the driver, then the drone.

"Yes, you had some success, Doctor, but both went mad within six hours, the first one almost killed Bonny, then stolid the launch and took off heading for Bray Island screaming Shelia's coming, the other swam out to sea, that's not success.

So, we lose a few, we need to look at the full picture, there is always sacrifices in war, and if we can hijack Clarence's Drivers, we will become the new masters of this world Dezman boast, and I will make every one that ridiculed me pay dearly."

13

Billy taxied the transport to the small GDF military terminal on Miller Island.

"After the ship is refueled, Rocky, do a thorough pre-flight," Billy tells him, "I'm heading for operation to file our new flight plan and see about that cargo."

"Aye, aye, Skipper," the young Lieutenant responds.

Ted watches Billy disappear through the terminal door.

Standing alone in front of the transport looking at the nosecone of the ship, still with stars in his eyes from the flight, only his third flight, Ted thinks to himself, I already have my space wings, 30,000 meters is the mark, and I made it my third tripe, I can't believe it!

Looking up at the bridge of the transport, Ted's eyes start there, then follows the entire length of the ship, in like a surreal dream making a connection, Ted realizes that this ship, her lady ship, as he called her from then on, can keep me safe or send me to an early grave, it's all in the way I treat her.

"Will do, Captain, I'll give her a pre-flight of her life, ante that right, old girl."

Ted snapping to attention saluting her lady ship.

Ted spots the fuel truck coming around the terminal.

Ted raises his arms in an X, so the driver knows he needs fuel.

The fuel they use now is one the Driver's gave them, it's powdered hydrogen, it's only volatile after exposure to ultraviolet radiation, breaking the eight Deuterium atoms with the eight Hydrogen atom chains all connected to a carbon molecule, very compact and making the fuel behave like a dry liquid.

All three tanks filled; Ted starts his inspection.

Starting at the front of the ship, Ted makes his first survey, she's five meters wide and twenty-five meters long, sloping at the front in to an elongated cone rounded at the end, the bridge sits in front of the forward wing, the aft wing is ten meters from the rear, each wing has a rotatable jet engine at the end, plus two more on each side of the vertical stabilizer, the cargo door drops from the back right under the tail, on both sides of the cargo door are holes where the solid rocket boosters are housed, the area around it is blackened from the enormous thrust they generated.

Ted looks up in time to see the Skipper returning from operations, walking beside the most beautiful woman, heading straight toward him.

"Lieutenant Linch, this is Captain West, she'll be accompanying us to Kranstan Point," Billy introduces them.

All Ted sees is her blue eyes, missing the pulled back blond hair, slender body, and high cheek bones.

"Nice to meet you, Lieutenant," Carol putting out her hand.

"Same here, Captain," Ted fumbles, finally getting his hand extended grasping her hand awkwardly.

Billy smiles to himself thinking, so you're shy also, Rocky.

About that time, a truck pulls up caring the corps of the Lost One.

Captain West starts barking orders the moment the truck arrived, her men jumped too when she gave an order, it was plane to see who was in charge.

After the coffin was secured, Captain West had her men standing at attention giving them orders for her absents, "Sargent, I want at least two field problems executed."

"Yes, sir," the Sargent shouted.

"I'll be back in three days see you then, carry on!"

Carol enters the cargo bay walking past Ted, "Let's go Lieutenant," she urges him, "times a wasting."

Ted buttons up the cargo door, then heads for the bridge passing by Captain West, stopping to ask her if she needed anything before, he goes forward.

"No, Lieutenant, I'm fine."

"If you do, push this button," Ted indicates the intercom switch, "it goes straight to the bridge, if you need anything," Ted repeats.

"I'm fine, Lieutenant, now go do your job," she tells him, thinking to herself, he's cute, but I would chew him up.

Ted enters the bridge with Billy already through his pre-flight check list, "Strap in, Rocky, we're ready to go."

"All clear here, Skipper," Ted reports.

Billy starts his roll, ten minutes later, they're in the air heading for Kranstan Point.

"What do you think of our passenger, Rocky, is she not a knock out?" Billy teases.

"She's not my type, Skipper."

"What's not to like, Rocky, she's not wearing a ring, boy," Billy laughs, watching the young man turn red.

"No, Skipper, she's…"

"She's what, Rocky?" Billy, pushing the issue.

"She scares me, Skipper," Ted finally blurts out, "did you see how those men were jumping when she told them something?"

"Suit yourself, Rocky, but if I was young and single, I would be back there trying to get her interest," Billy encourages him.

"No, Skipper, I'll pass."

"If that's the case then, Rocky, you take the stick and I'll go back and talk to our passenger, I'm single too," Billy remind him.

Sometime passed before the Captain returned to the bridge with Carol in tow, laughing a hardy laugh.

Ted only hears the end of the conversation.

"You should have seen his face," Billy tells Carol, "it was hilarious."

"Did he ever figure it out?" Carol asks.

"No, I think to this day he believes it's true," they both laugh. "Anything to report, Ted?" Billy inquirers.

"No, Skipper, we're two hours out, the mainland is coming up soon."

"You can take a seat here, Carol," Billy, pointing to the port countermeasure control station. "If this was a combat mission, there would be five crew members," Billy states as if he is instructing the two of them, two pilots, an engineer, and two gunners. This ship is a formidable weapon. "I have seen two campaigns in ships like this one, the Drivers did a good job when they made them."

"You don't find that the Drivers gave us inferior weapons and equipment?" Carol challenges.

"Not at all," Billy replies. "During the Trotter revolt, I flew fifteen missions, the bird was shot up really bad, over 100 hits, the entire belly was raked with triple A, but she kept flying."

"You were in the Trotter revolt, Skipper?" Ted accentuates.

"You bet, Rocky," Billy standing up, pulling up his shirt, reviling a fifty-five-centimeter scar, running up his side, a forty millimeter behind the port control panel, pointing to where Carol is sitting. "Yes, the Drivers gave us good equipment and this old girl can put it out also, don't get caught in her gun sights, she'll put the hurt on you," Billy continues, "she can turn tighter, climb faster, and out distance anything in the fleet, speed is not everything," looking at Ted anticipating his next statement.

"A fighter would take this transport out easily, Skipper," Ted injects.

"No, Rocky, it would take at least three to do a proper job and then I would get one or two of them," Billy explains, "make them come from above and behind, turning tight and climbing fast at the same time they do their gun run, you'll corkscrew right behind them, getting the first shots off and keeping them from locking in on you. I don't know who the idiot was that designated this a transport because she's a war ship first with cargo capabilities," Billy shakes his head in disbelief.

"Skipper, the port of Four Rivers is coming up," announces Ted.

Billy, Ted, and Carol all look out the front window, seeing the giant port of Four Rivers.

Back thirty years ago, this was the place of technology, the fore front of modernization, for 200 years the Saverans dominated the landscape in every field, industry, medicine, defense, and education.

The natural deep-water port feed by four giant rivers made this place defendable and profitable, a mountain marches east and west with a five-kilometer piece missing right in the middle, stair steeping cliffs in both directions with densely packed houses.

On the other side of the mountain, it opens in to a wide bay more than twenty-five kilometers wide and twice that long.

On every meter around the bay, there is something.

"Just inside the bay is the Global Defense Force Naval base, there must be 500 ships down there, Skipper," Ted remarks.

"Probably more," Billy responds, "if you count the Royal Guard's coastal patrol."

Off in the distance, Ted can see an airbase.

"Is that one of ours, Skipper?" pointing to the airbase.

"No, that's the GDF's Rapid Response Division and Air Combat Wings. Gab started his career with the RRD as a Company commander moving up to a Battalion commander, him and I had some good times down there."

Carol looks at Billy, "Do you mean, give'em hell, Gab?"

Billy smiles, "One in the same."

"I'm impressed, Captain, his tactics are mandatory reading in the academy, the class was History's Grate Victor's through Tactics," Carol said.

Ted looks confused, "The General at Rocket Town, he's GDF and you're Royal Guard.

Things have changed sense then, Rocky, in the beginning one academy served both, after graduation you could choose which branch you wished to serve in, now they're separate, Gab choose combat infantry with the GDF, I choose aviation with the Guard."

With the base now behind them, they can see a city of more than six million.

As the transport draws closer, they can see the four rivers in the background, each going its own way, connecting eighty percent of the continent with the city of Four Rivers.

Ted has seen photos of the place, but they do it no justice in reality, the smoke and dirty air down below makes the whole country side look gray, you can see the oil on the water making its way out to sea, black smoke belching from the thousands of factories.

"That's my home over there," Carol points northwest along the quiet river, "my dad worked the docks loading freight. It's a rough neighborhood," she tells them, "and I have six older brothers," telling anyone that would listen she's not really hard, only raised hard, remembering the day her brother Jean walked off and let three girls beat her up after school, then laughed at her broken nose and ribs, calling her a wimp and crybaby.

"I'm in awe, Skipper, I thought I know about the world, no book or pictures can capture this, not with any justice," Ted tells him. Turning to Carol, "Was it like this when you were a kid, Captain?" Ted asks her in his genital and naive way, full of questions, a sole that has not been corrupted by misfortune and poverty.

"Pretty much, Lieutenant, the only difference is there's a million more people and unemployment is up around nine percent, I'm glad I'm not down there," looking Ted straight in the eyes for only a half of a second but long enough to put a tiny crack in herself imposed armor around her life. She could take this boy in a man's body and make him jump through hoops, but that would make her just like the others, a user and turning him in to someone like me, used and forgotten." Leave this one alone, Carol tells herself. "I'm going aft, Captain," she stands up and exits the bridge without saying another word.

After Carol has gone, Billy looks at Ted and asks him, "What did you do, boy? She was talking, looked over at you, turned a little shade of red, and ran off!"

"I don't know, Skipper!"

"We'll be in range of Kranstan soon, make contact and give them our ETA, have control, contact Barbara Walker and inform her about our arrival with her cargo, you have the bridge, Lieutenant, inform me when we're twenty minutes out, I'm going aft."

"Aye, aye, Skipper." Billy enters the passenger compartment and finds it empty, hearing a soft voice speaking, Billy continues on back to the cargo compartment, stopping short, not wishing to interrupt the Captain, but concern drove Billy closer.

"Put it out of your mind, Carol," Billy hears the Captain telling herself, "you have your career."

Wishing to give her a sense of privacy, Billy calls out, "Captain West, we will be going through some rough weather soon, you'll need to strap in," giving Carol her chance to recover.

"I'll be on the bridge, there is a seat there if you would like to join us," Billy tells her as she ducks in under the bulkhead.

"Thank you, Captain, I would like that, I was checking my cargo."

"You know, that's my job," smiling at Carol, trying to get her to smile back, Billy resorts to the never fail method, he winks, there's nothing more funny than a short, fat, bald man winking to put a smile on someone's face, it worked like a charm. Carol smiles from ear to ear.

"Go ahead, Captain. I'll be there in a moment," Carol tells him.

"See you on the bridge then," Billy makes his way forward, leaving Carol to follow.

Twenty minutes later, all three strapped in on the bridge with Kranstan Point coming up fast.

The base is the biggest base in the world, it is home to the GDF and the Royal Guard, it houses one fourth of all the military.

Command for the GDF is here with the central communication center and military intelligence.

Training, logistics, maintenance, and research are their specialties, both academy's, Space Service, Air core, Infantry, and Naval forces are all represented here.

The landing was one of Billy's best, there was no bump, jerk, or sway.

The tower directs Billy to one of the remote terminals, telling him Doctor Walker is on scene and waiting.

After shutdown Ted and Carol head back to lower the loading ramp to unload the corps.

As soon as the ramp hits the ground, Doctor Walker was on board.

Captain West intercepted the Doctor before she got to the body, "I'll need to see your ID, mama, I have my orders to release this body to Barbara Walker only!"

With Carol satisfied with Doctor Walker and the corps gone, the three traveling companions stand at the cargo ramp to say their farewells.

"Carol, if you would like, you're invited to join Ted and I for dinner at the officers mess," Billy tells her.

"I would like that," Carol tells them both, around six at the officer's mess.

"Good, we'll see you there," Billy, putting out his hand to Carol.

Accepting his handshake, Carol winks back at Billy, causing him to laugh out loud, "See you then."

Billy and Ted make their way to Operation to file the reports and receive new orders.

"Here we are, Captain, you and Lieutenant Linch are to be certified to carry VIPs," the Duty Officer states.

Billy looks puzzled, "There must be a mistake, Major."

"No, this came from headquarters of the Royal Guard," the Major tells them, "but you're in luck, a new class starts tomorrow morning, otherwise you'll be here a week waiting on the next one, it's on the west campus, room 519, here's your orders, you'll be billeting on campus."

14

"Captain Hartwell, the Duke will see you now," the receptionist announces.

Dean had been waiting six hours, he was here at eight this morning like he was told, it's two in the afternoon now, this irritates him, but what can he do, he is the Duke.

Give him the good news first, then the slip up, Dean tells himself, walking in to the Duke's private office.

It is exquisitely decorated in purple and gold, real gold, the Captain notices.

"Have a seat, Captain," the Duke tells Dean in more of a command than an invitation, "you've evaluated our prospect, Captain, what do you think?"

"I believe him to be the perfect subject, Your Lordship," Dean explains, "I interviewed more than a dozen of his wing mates, review of his records shows him to be unpredictable, and he has no skills as a pilot. There is one catch, your Lordship. Zercoff got drunk last night and had a confrontation ending up in the brig. General Boot kicked him off his base, sending him off on a shit mission to Kranstan Point two days early, our man is in the next class, so there is no one to hold his hand and get him his certification."

"I thought I told you to keep watch on them, Captain," the Duke shouts, "I need him certified to carry the brat. Is that too much to ask,

Lieutenant?" glaring hard at the Captain, "if he fails, Lieutenant, it's your ass!" The Duke gets up and starts pacing back and forth, "You know, Lieutenant, it's the little things that make things go badly," he tells Captain Hartwell in a now calm voice, not looking at him but looking at the floor pacing very slowly, "always the small unsuspected things, like a pregnancy, the bitch!" The Duke reminds himself. The Duke was interrupted by the intercom buzzing. The Duke hits the button, "WHAT, I told you I was not to be disturbed," he shouts, his anger back in a flash.

"Ambassador Wildwind is demanding to see you, sir," the voice on the other end replies.

"I will see the Ambassador shortly," the Duke tells the voice on the other end. The Duke turns and looks Dean in the eyes, specking very comely again, "Captain, this man has been a pain in my ass for twenty-five years, I want to see him dead! Do this for me and I'll make you a General," the Duke entices, "but first, let's take care of the brat, get Zercoff certified, so he can fly the brat, do you understand Captain?"

"Yes, Your Lordship, I understand," Dean answers.

"Good, go inform the girl out front I'll see the Ambassador now and take a look at Wildwind, he's worth a lot to you," the Duke reminds Dean.

Dean fallows his instruction and passes on the message to the receptionist.

On the way out, Dean gets his first look at James Wildwind, he's a mountain of a man, no wonder the Duke offered a star for him; it will take some finesse for this one.

Dean hears the Duke telling Wildwind come in and sit down, Jimmy, so friendly for someone that just gave an order to have him killed, watch your butt around the Duke, Dean tells himself, or you'll be going the way of the King, Prince, and Wildwind, plus about forty others.

15

Tina looks at the clock, it's already two hours past dinner, Berrana should have already been here.

She left as dinner was being served.

Tina told her to go home and dress as a person, so she would not fell like a maid for our visit, but that was three hours ago.

The phone rang, startling Tina.

Picking up the phone, "Hello, Tina speaking," old habits are hard to break, she reminds herself, I'm on vacation not tending the Queen.

"Miss Hopkins?" the operator asks.

"Yes, this is Tina Hopkins."

"I'm sorry to disturb you, miss, but there is a situation, there is a Lost One down at the security desk claiming to be your guest."

Not wanting to hear any more, Tina tells the operator, "I'll come down," hanging up the phone, ignoring the reply from the operator. Tina walks into the security office to find Berrana in a holding cell like a criminal. "Why is my guest in there?" Tina confronts the woman behind the desk; not waiting for her answer, Tina continues her scolding of everyone in the room, "Is this the way you treat your guest? I'm appalled at your behavior, I will make a formal complainant, now get her out of there." The man standing next to the desk pulled out his keys and immediately unlocked the door, opening the door for Berrana, stepping out of her way. "Come, Berrana," Tina turned around and walked out the door, not saying another word with Berrana close behind.

Back in the room, Tina consoles Berrana, "I'm sorry for the treatment and humiliation they caused you," Tina apologizes to her.

"No, miss, you have nothing to apologize for, it was the woman behind the desk, she told me there is no way someone would invite me here. It is like that in most places," Berrana states flatly, "everywhere I go, people call us vermin, trash, or refugee, is this not our home now? Do we not work hard to make it better?" she pleads to Tina, knowing Tina can't fix anything, but Berrana felt better after her vent.

"Some people are stupid and others are mean, Berrana," Tina explains, "in every race, there are those who are only concerned about themselves and care for no other. It's up to us to see through it and overcome their stupidity."

"You are right, miss. On Trinity Station, there are Parkins that hate the Tarkaneans, they believe we are treated like slaves, that is the real reason we left. My father is not one of them, he wishes only for the best for me."

"I have a plane," Tina announces, "if it's alright with you," looking at Berrana, "I could visit your home and get to know the Parkins people and they can get to know us better."

"I must work, miss," Berrana reminds her.

"Leave that to me, dear, I'm royalty," stretching the truth a bit, "the Queen did tell me to have fun, and I'm working," Tina justifying her actions to herself. One phone call later. "It's done, you are my new tour guide for the Islands," Tina tells Berrana.

"But, miss, I'm new to the Islands myself, I have only been to three Islands here. I live on Vision Island and I stayed with family on Bray Island for a month when I first got here, I know nothing about the Islands."

"Good, you know more than me, see how that works?" Tina laughs. "Stay here tonight and tomorrow we'll start our tour, deal?" Tina asks.

"Deal," Berrana agrees. "Are you a princess?" are the next words out of Berrana's mouth.

Tina knows when she said it, it would come back to bite her but so soon, she thinks.

"No, Berrana, I'm not Royalty; the hotel thinks I am, but the truth is I work for the Queen Mother. As a reward for good service, she sent me on a dream vacation, a little lie," Tina admits.

"I'm relieved, miss," Berrana confesses, "I have heard terrible stories about the royal families, how they make their servants beg and beat them."

"In the past, it was true for some, but not now, now every man is accountable and it is the same for everyone. Do you know who we owe for that?" Tina asks, looking at Berrana, seeing her fill with pride, "Yes, Clarence, your Sub-Driver, so I owe him as much as you do. I would like to make it clear," Tina tells Berrana, "the Queen is my sovereign and I would lay down my life for her, I would not do that for a tyrant, I love her and the Prince, never has she treated me with anything but respect and kindness."

Berrana realizes she may have insulted Tina's queen, "No disrespect intended, miss, I was only telling you the stories."

"None taken, Berrana. I, too, was only telling you how I feel, we both have our hero's and our villains." Tina would like to guide the conversation back to the comment about not being safe on Trinity Station. "Do we treat the Lost Ones there like slaves?" Tina asks.

"I cannot say because I don't know, some believe it to be true, my father is not one of them; he believes we all make our own path for good or bad and hard work will make every man free."

"Your father is a wise man, Berrana," Tina compliments her, "and I see the same in you."

"Thank you," Berrana replies blushing, reminding Tina of her age and her vulnerability.

"What can you tell me about the Drivers?" Tina asks.

"I know lots," Berrana boasts, "I took a course at T.S. High School, what would you like to know?"

"That's a good question, I know nothing, so tell me what you think I should know," Tina said.

"Drivers are not thinking beings like the Master and Sub-Drives; on their own, they are logical and technical problem solvers, tell a driver you need to chop up vegetable and it will fabricate a blender, why is irrelevant, tell a Driver to destroy a town and it will level everything oblivious to the people living there. One Driver can control up to 10,000 drones and a drone can be anything, a trash truck or a mechanic fixing the trash truck, the Master and Sub-Drivers provide the Drivers with direction and supervision, do you understand, miss?"

"Yes." Tina tells her.

"Master and Sub-Drivers are different," Berrana continues, "they are compassionate, caring, and even loving. Sub-Driver Clarence so loved Athena, he would not let his own master kill her, instead he imprisoned his master, freeing Michael my sovereign," smiling at Tina, "Clarence pledged his loyalty to Michael and took over the responsibility of the Parkins people.

There is a difference between Clarence and other Sub-Drivers, only Clarence has a single personality, all the other Sub-Drivers have three separate personalities, I hear it's very hard to work with one, you never know who you're going to be talking to. For example," Berrana explains, "you're working on a printing press, talking to, let's say Bob, next second you're talking to Bill, each knows what the other was saying, the conversation never losses its continuity on the subject or application, totally different personalities though."

"Why is Clarence different than the other Sub-Drivers?" Tina asks.

"That, miss, is a long and complicated story," Berrana explains, "I will try to do my best.

Two Master-Drivers, Michael and Shelia, waged war on each other, why the war started is not important. Shelia had won, Michael's ship was destroyed, and he was removed from the rest of his brain, only the personality was left. In order for her to enjoy her victory for the rest of her life, she grafted Michael to her own spinal cord, intending on tormenting him forever, starting with the extinction of the Parkins race, follow me so far, miss?" Berrana asks.

"Yes, please continue," Tina said.

"Shelia had anticipated the outcome of the conflict, sending Clarence to hide on the plaint and wait for her victory, then round up every Parkins for execution, intending on playing games with them until there was no more to butcher and torture. Shelia was so confident of her plan, Clarence was sent twenty years early, his instructions were to locate and plan the remove of the Parkins people. During his stay, Clarence started to observe the Parkins people not intending on interacting with them, but he started watching one little girl, watching her grow, seeing her daily life and difficulties, a bond started to develop. One day a beast cornered the little girl and was going to eat her. Clarence could not stand by and watch, so he intervened and saved the little girl, a true friendship developed; from that point on, Clarence could not let these people be exterminated. This was a problem for Shelia, she never anticipated the Parkin's influence on him, somehow Clarence shed his other two personalities, tricking Shelia in to putting down her guard, taking control of Shelia's own Drivers, isolating her like she did Michael, but by that time, Shelia had already damaged our environment to the point it would no longer support life. Clarence gathered all the Parkins he could find and brought us to Michael. Michael was restored to Shelia's Drivers, then Michael brought us here, but we have not seen Michael for over sixty years.

Oh, yes, one more thing," Berrana said, "a Sub-Driver's ship is small, very small for what they can do. The Sub-Driver can control several Drivers simultaneously like the Master-Drivers, I think that's about all I know, miss."

"That explanation was very precise, Berrana, thank you," Tina said, "there is one thing, you said Michael brought you here and you have not seen him in how many years?"

"The numbers don't correspond, do they? We spent twenty-five years living in orbit around your solar system, leaning your language, customs, and matching our technologies. Clarence would not permit one culture to dominate another, so we waited."

Tina stands and stretches, "It's been a long day, Berrana. I think it's time to turn in, we have a full day tomorrow, "Tina said yawning, "you take the green room, and I'll see you in the morning, good night."

They each went to their rooms.

Tina fell asleep immediately, but Berrana lay there for hours.

16

Tom had not been waiting long when he was invited in to the Steward's office.

"It's good to see you, Tom," the Steward said, extending his hand to the Senator, "have a seat, I understand you have a situation out on the Islands concerning the Lost Ones; my chief of staff said it's urgent, something about radiation poisoning."

"Not poisoning," Tom remarks, "I don't know what it is, but it's not natural, there have been eight deaths. Ever one a Lost One? I have never seen radiation poisoning like this, it's only the brain. Doctor Walker at Kranstan point has done autopsies on seven of them and there has been one more she is going over now. I should have the results soon."

"Is this something we should contact Clarence about?" the Steward inquires.

"Not yet," Tom replies, "let's see what Doctor Walker finds, and there is one more thing. One of my staffers was told someone is asking for volunteers for experiments in Driver control. I have the local law enforcement looking in to it, but so far there has been no luck on identifying the party's involved."

Peabody Smit has been the Steward for eight years now of a ten-year term; he is an unimposing man, small with a receding hair line, in his late fifties but a man of conviction and a deep thinker, loved by all that know him.

"Let's do this, Tom, after the autopsy is completed; if it's the same as the others, we will contact Clarence and get his opinion; you know as well as I do he will tell us it's our problem to solve and you know he is right, we need to solve this ourselves, now tell me all you can about the others."

Tom reaches in to his briefcase and pulls out the seven autopsies, "They are all the same. There is a small void in the center of the brain, right before death they lose all cognitive thought, and most has been from the southern Island of Benson, two were from the northern Island of Bray, both has a majority of Lost Ones on them, they all come to Stink Water looking for work."

It sounds like someone is praying on the desperate, Tom."

About that time, the intercom buzzes, "Steward Smit, Doctor Walker said you were expecting her call."

"Yes, put her through, Lori." As soon as the light blinked, Smit hit the button. "Doctor Walker, this is Steward Smit, I'm here with Senator Dearmen, you're on speaker, thank you for calling so prompt."

"Hello, Barb," Tom greets her.

"Thank you, Steward Smit. I have the results. I will fax them to your office," Barbara tells them, "but the only differences are that there was traces of Radon gas in the void; other than that, they're identical."

"Thank you, Doctor Walker, for the good work you do at Kranstan Point," the Steward tells her.

"Thank you," she tells him in return.

With that the conversation ends.

"Well, Tom, what do you think, this is your mystery, should we involve Clarence?" the Steward asks him.

"Yes, sir, I think we should to be on the safe side; and I think you're right, he'll tell us it's our problem to solve."

"Lori, go activate the Avatar in the rotunda," he tells her over the intercom, "and ask him to come to my office," Smit instructs.

"Yes, sir."

Less than two minutes later, the Avatar walks in; it's a small one for the purpose of diplomacy, nonthreatening and much more human like.

"Good day, Steward Smit," Clarence greets him, "and you also, Senator Dearman, how may I help you?"

"We have a situation involving Lost Ones, Sub-Driver," Tom speaks up, "over the past two months, there have been eight deaths due to radiation exposure, each one had a small void in the center of their brain, only the last one reveled the presents of Radon gas in the void, the victim's brain is exposed to radiation; by the time they seek medical treatment, their cognitive abilities have deteriorated to the point of complete shutdown. they die a few days later."

"I know what this is, gentlemen, it's an attempt at using a human to control a drone or avatar via a driver," Clarence explains, "it can work for three days only, then the subject dies. I used twelve such volunteers, each know the outcome before they were used, they were the real hero's in the war with Sheila, sacrificing themselves for the good of their race. I will assist in this matter."

"Can you tell us more about the method, Sub-Driver?" the Steward asks. "No! This is a dangerous technology for me and your race, all the work we have accomplished can be undone in a single day; this must be stopped," Clarence declares in the firmest voice either men have ever heard the Sub-Driver use. "I have dispatched a field Avatar to assist in this matter, it will meet you in your office on Stink Water Island, Senator, we will proceed from there."

"Is there nothing more you can tell us about the process, Sub-Driver, like the material needed or frequency used, so we can monitor for them or check uses of said materials?" asks the Steward.

"The frequencies are only used by the Drivers; they are faster than light communication. You can start by looking for micro platinum foil usage, will that satisfy you, Steward Smit?" Clarence asks.

"Yes, sir, it's a place to start," injects Tom.

"I would like to take this opportunity to inform you I have issued a change in contact orders involving humans and Drivers, the restriction on fraternization has been lifted, expect more contact between us in the future," Clarence explains, "I, too, will be more active. I will return to my station in the rotunda and meet you, Senator, at Stink Water Island," the avatar tells the two, "good day, gentlemen," turning, walking out the door.

"I'm surprised, Tom, this must be very dangerous," Peabody exclaims.

"I think you're right, sir," Tom agrees, "and were you aware of a restriction on contact between Drivers and Humans?"

"First, I've heard of it, but now that it's in the open, it makes sense. I could never get him to say more than three words at a time, him or any other Driver; let's hope it's a good change," the Steward comments. "I would like to assign an agent to you, Tom, to assist in the investigation. Major Adam Potter, he's one of my best. I'll have him meet you at the airport, there will be a military transport standing by to transport you and his team to Stink Water, I'll have a car pick you up out front and, Tom, I know what a war drone can do, if someone crazy can us one, he could do lots of damage, be careful."

"Thank you, sir, I'll be off then."

"We are all in this together, Tom, good luck on your hunt, keep me informed."

Shaking hands Tom heads for the door.

Like the Steward said, the car was waiting out front, even though the walk was only 300 meters.

As the car pulls up to the transport, Tom can see three men standing at the ramp, two are obviously air crew, the third a man in his early thirties, average build, sandy blond hair, wearing a very expensive business suit.

Tom approaches the ramp and is met half way by the man in the suit, extending his hand, he introduces himself.

"Major Potter at your service, senator, the team's on board and the ship is ready to go if you would like to board."

"I only left the steward's office twenty-five minutes ago, major, I don't know how he does it," he comments more to himself than the major

"Peabody didn't get to where he is by not being on top of things," the major laughs.

"So true," Tom adds.

On board Major Potter introduces his team as the transport makes its journey down the taxi way.

"Dr. Susan fields is our medical adviser, Sargent Arthur Bates, engineer, and Captain Frank Tucker, security. The Steward did not go in to specifics, Senator, only that we were to assist you in any manner necessary, you will need to brief us on the mission."

For the next three hours, Tom outlines the facts and starts formulating a plan.

"Four hours ago, this was about eight lives lost, now it's about the stability of the nation, there is always someone willing to throw away someone's life for their own purpose."

Major Potter's team look professional and their equipment was state of the art, the transport they were flying in was no ordinary ship either; from the looks of things, this ship and crew is one of the steward's most experienced and well-trained teams. By the time they reached the Islands, Tom was confident this group was up to the challenge.

17

Connie and Matt stand looking down a long drift running thirty-five kilometers west.

"It's down this way, Bubbles," Matt tells her, "it should run right in to a fault going north. We follow it for another five kilometers, and presto, we're there."

"There is no magnetic field, Matt, how will we know we're going north?" she asks.

"We don't," he laughs, "it's on the map," holding up the twenty-five-year-old parchment the Drivers generated before turning over the place, "there are markers every kilometer on the wall," pointing to one right behind Connie, "it has all the information we need on them."

"Alright, then let's do this," Connie tells him.

The pair get back in the old mining tug that will be their sleeping courtiers for the next three days.

The tug has a ten-day supply of air, food, and water, two robotic arms, one on each side for moving obstacles from the safety of inside the tug, a blade in the front, and a boom with a winch in the back.

Each suit they wear has a three-day power supply to reclaim the air, two days of water and food built right in to it, and they are carrying two extra replacement modules for each suit.

Matt insisted they carry an inflatable habitat in case there is an emergence, safety first is his motto.

The tug's movement is very slow, about the speed of a fast jog, giving the companions time to observe their surroundings in detail.

The Drivers did not blast their way through the rock, they chipped it away piece at a time, not shocking the surrounding rock, making shoring unnecessary, the drift is one of the many exploratory drifts the Driver's dug.

"It must of look like ants down here," Matt comments, "all working as a single entity toward their goal."

The pair had been traveling for over three hours, seeing connecting tunnels going in every direction, left, right, up, and down and the drift, they were in, did not run trues, it wondered.

"Look," Connie said to Matt, pointing at one of the markers or the place where a marker was, "it looks like someone took a hammer to it, I wonder why someone would do that?"

Stopping the tug, "I don't know, Bubbles, but I'm taking a better look, you stay in the tug, I'll be right back," Matt tells her, getting into the small air lock. Matt's instincts are in overdrive now, the years of training not to miss a single sign. You will not last long as a scout if you don't, and Matt was one of the best in GDF force recon, the elite of the elite.

The first thing he sees is a toe mark that had been covered over by dragging something behind as they walked, an old trick but effective, he thinks to himself, sloppy work though as he sees another half print in the fine dust of the drift; it looks as if there was three people walking side by side. As he approaches the marker, he sees Connie was right, someone did take a hammer to it, wiping out its value as a directional add.

"Connie, can you drive the tug?" he asks her over the communication link.

"You're talking to a farm gal, not some prissy city girl afraid to break a nail."

"Good, I'm going to walk and see what I can see; the marker was vandalized, and I'm having bad feelings about it."

Matt walked very slowly down the drift, stopping often, bending down to get a better look at the ground. They passed two more vandalized markers, and before they got to the four marker, Matt stops. This time he's not looking at the ground, he's looking up.

Shinning his light up, Connie can see there is a shaft going up.

"Stay here, Connie, I'm going down the drift a few more meters,"

Connie can see Matt clearly as he precedes his few meters, then comes back, constantly looking back and forth "This is where the vandals came from," pointing up the shaft, he tells her, "want to have a look?"

"Yes," she replies.

"Good, drive the tug further down the drift until you come to a cross tunnel, park the tug around the corner, then come back on foot. I'm grabbing two spare modules for the suits and, Bubbles, walk back in the center of the tracks of the tug, so when we go back, we can cover our tracks, so no one will know we came back this way." Matthew watches as the tug lumbers down the drift, shrinking smaller and smaller as the tug increases the distance, turning his attention to the task of getting up the shaft. "I will bet there is a control unit around here somewhere."

Matt starts a systematic search of the immediate area, starting at the vertical shaft, working his way back down the way they came. Within five minutes, he had his control box. It was stuck in a small crack in the wall. "Watch yourself, Mattie, you're dealing with amateurs and amateurs are unpredictable," he tells himself.

Matt does what any good scout does, he turns off his light and listens.

With the lack of an atmosphere It's dead quiet, even the rumble in the ground of Connie's tug cannot be felt. Matt places his hand on the stone wall next to him, nothing. He crosses the drift and tries the other side, nothing, no, wait, he places his helmet against the wall. A very faint buzz, electrical motors, he tells himself.

He sits not under the shaft but to one side, looking up to see if he can see any discernible light as he waited for Connie's return.

Thirty minutes later, he sees her light coming toward him.

"How was the walk, Bubbles?" he greets her on her return.

"The tug is about two kilometers down on the left and there are two more destroyed markers," she tells Matt. "How are we going to get up there?" she points to the vertical shaft.

"Bubbles, you have no faith," holding out the palm size unit, "look what I found," teasing her.

"Have you tried it yet?" she asks Matt.

"I was waiting on you." Matt pushes the bottom button, twenty-five meters up the shaft, lights come on and an elevator comes down. "Connie, someone went to a lot of trouble to keep this secret. I go first, and if I tell you to run, you run, is that clear?" No arguments about it."

"I understand, Matt, you know what you're doing, I'm along for the ride, lead the way, General," she teases him.

Matt picks up his spare air module and gets on the elevator, pushing the other button.

"I'll send it back down after I check it out first," he disappears up the shaft.

At the top, Matt can see he is in a connecting point, there are four drifts going in four different directions, right next to the elevator is a buggy, no attempt to hide which way they went this time, the track goes to the left, nothing in any other direction. "I'm sending it back down, Connie, tell me when you're on, and don't forget your spare module."

"On board, Matt", Connie tells him.

Matt pushes the button and the elevator makes its return trip.

"What do you think, Connie, should we see where they have been going?"

"Yeah, someone has been going through a lot of trouble to keep it hidden, and if I know human nature, there is a reason they don't want people to know. It's usually not good," she concludes.

"Let's do this, Connie, we will follow the tracks until we hit five kilometers, we come back after that."

The buggy moves along at twenty-five KPH, the path is smooth and true.

"There has been no connecting tunnels," Matt mentions to Connie after ten minutes, "I think we are at the five kilometer mark," as he stops the buggy, the bright light on top of the buggy shows there is at least another twenty kilometers going in this direction, the drifts vanishing point is surreal, almost a hypnotic felling, like the end is drawing you to it with no other path to escape to.

"Connie, I would like to continue on," Matt states, "but there are concerns; if it was me doing this, I would have a surprise or two for any one making the trip. If I miss the sign, we could fall in to a shaft and that would be it."

"Let's go," Connie reassures Matt with her confidence in him, "Dale swears bye you and I do, too.

A bit slower but onward, Matt proclaims, pushing on the throttle, starting the buggy to move.

The two concentrating on the path in front of them, not speaking a word.

Connie reaches out and taps Matt on the shoulder, pointing at a shadow in their path about twenty or so meters ahead.

Rolling up on it slowly, Matt can see it's only a low spot in the drift, "This is deliberate, Connie, it's to lull us in to ignoring the next one."

Five minutes later, the pair are stopped looking down a vertical shaft with no bottom to be seen, the drift continues on the other side tracks and all.

"There must be something to get across on," Connie said. "You take the left side and I'll search the right, look for a crack, it could be high or low." The search had not been going on long when Connie proclaims her find, "I have it, Matt, just like you said."

Connie displaying a control pad like the one Matt found earlier, handing it to him.

Walking up to the shaft, Matt pushes the button, the vibration of electric motors come on, and a bridge lowers form the ceiling.

"It was undetectable form the drift, they did a good job on hiding the bridge," Matt compliments the builder.

"Should we put the bridge up?" Connie asks.

"No, let's leave it down in case we need to make a fast retreat," Matt teases Connie, smiling his best don't worry about it smile but with apprehension growing with every meter forward.

The journey did not last long, the drift opened in to a vast cavern, their lights were like trying to see across a concert hall with a match as the only light.

Matt turns the buggy in a slow circular pattern, letting the light fan out, he would do this every few meters.

"What was that?" Connie shouts so forcefully, it makes Matt jump. Connie, standing, pointing, "Look over there," she tells Matt.

Matt readjusts the path of the buggy, then he sees it, too, row after row of drones, "There must be at least 10,000 of them, Bubbles." The pair continue driving around the drones for the next twenty minutes, seeing every different type of equipment needed to mine. "This is where the Drivers disappeared to after we took the mine over. I have never seen anything like that," Matt points to a big box on wheels. Driving up on it, he can see it's what appears to be a Driver! "Connie, that's a Driver."

Getting out of the buggy, Matt and Connie walk over to the Driver, someone has been taking it apart.

"Look, Matt, the back side is missing and you can see where they have removed several components."

"I think we should get back to the tug, Connie, as fast as we can. I would think there would be some kind of warning system. I would not be surprised if our presence is not already known, we can make our decision on what to do next back at the tug."

"I think you're right," Connie agrees, "let's head back."

Unnoticed by the pair are the three men watching from a lab on the edge of the cavern.

One hour later, there back at the tug, all control devices have been returned and with their walk back, all traces of their passing were covered over by Matt.

"I think we should continue with our trip, Connie," Matt tells her, "act like we seen nothing but stay on our toes in case I'm wrong. If we report it to control, we may be waving a red flag in front of a bull, this is an organized operation, so they will have people there to intercept our report. I have an idea, Bubbles." Matt pushes the com button on the control panel, "Control, this is Matthew Dollar, I'm on a sight-seeing tour and the tug I'm using is experiencing power problems, I'm twenty-five kilometers east of the caverns, if I don't check back in in the next two days, send a recovery vehicle."

"Will do, Mr. Dollar, how many in your party?"

"There's five of us," looking over at Connie to see her expression.

"Mr. Dollar, contact us tomorrow, either way we're here to help. I'll place a note in the log, so the next shift is aware of your problem."

"Thank you, control, we will keep you advised, Dollar out."

"Control out."

"See, Connie, there is no way they are aware of us yet, so there is nothing to intercept. As far as control is concerned, we are five stupid tourists that they're going to make some money off of with a rescue. If things do go bad, we have misinformation on our side, they'll be looking for five, not two."

"What do we do now, Matt?"

"We head for the cavern and see what happens."

18

Billy is going on his second week of VIP training, it's all protocol, learning how to be in plain sight without being seen, all shit if you ask me, Billy tells himself.

Billy is anxious to see his ship, the Drivers has had it for four days now, and he has learned from experience, never put the bizarre out of mind when dealing with a Driver

The Drivers have maintained a depot facility here at Kranstan point since the early day of the government.

The transport is one of the last classes still in Inventory that the Driver's maintain.

Billy makes his way to the fare side of the base, where his ship is being refitted with solid boosters.

Pulling up to the hanger, Billy notices there are war drones everywhere, five standing in front of the door Billy has to go through.

Parking his vehicle, looking around to see if he was in the right place. I'm right, I've been here twenty times, I wonder what up, he thinks.

Walking up to the door very causally, Billy looks around still a bit confused.

"Captain Zercoff! I was hoping to talk to you today," as a small drone steps up extending its hand.

Not knowing what else to do, Billy extended his hand, grasping the drone's hand.

"I'm Sub-Driver Ben, you will meet Bell and Beth later, Captain, but now I would like to know why did you ignited the emergency booster? I went over the data and there was no emergency?"

"I was showing my trainee what is possible, there is nothing better than a trip in to low orbit to energize a young man's dreams."

"I like your logic, Captain, I'll file it as training mission," Ben tells him.

Billy is looking at the drone, "This is something else, not a drone, are you an Avatar?" he asks.

"Yes, Captain, this is one of the early model Avatar, not only can I see and hear but smell, taste, and fill my surroundings. We have a newer model that you will see later on today. Would you like to see what I have done to our ship?" Ben suggests to him.

"You lead the way," Billy, still eyeing the war drones on each side of the door.

The war drones are three meters high, six arms, two very large ones at the shoulders, two are at the hips, one at the chest, and one on the back, two very powerful legs with claws for gripping, plus a tail sticking out about two meters, no head at all but stocks with telescoping sensors at the ends, all jet black.

Ben starts talking, giving Billy the run down on their ship, the modification they have done, the upgrades, but Billy was no longer paying any attention to the Sub-Driver, his eyes were on the ship next to his, twice the size, long and slender. It's not sitting on the ground it's suspended in mid-air one meter off the ground, all burnished in gold, reflecting the color all over the hanger.

"That's your ship? She's beautiful," Billy tells the Sub-Driver.

"Would you like to see inside?"

Billy's answer was so quick, he even surprised himself, "I would love to!"

"Let's take care of business first, there are some things you need to be made aware of. First, there is no longer any solid boosters, we have fitted her with two variable hydrogen rockets, you have two minutes of burn time, break that up as much as you like. Second is you now have water landing capabilities, don't try it in a storm, she will sink. Third is a countermeasure, you can project your radar image out three kilometers in several different areas at once, decoys, Captain. Now for my ship, Captain," Ben comments with visible pride, "she can travel at faster than light speed, anti-gravity capabilities much like the Gravitron, it only affects the ship itself and only needs to be refueled every 600 years. The crew is Bell, Beth, myself, two medical Droids, and twenty drones." As the two approach, the hatch opens and a later extends itself down.

"After you, Capetian," Ben moving to the side, gesturing Billy to climb first.

Up the ladder Billy goes, stepping in to what appears to be the bridge.

Control stations and engineering panels for monitoring the ship.

"So, you're a tour guide now, Ben," a female voice announces.

"Pay her no attention, Captain. Bell is always grumpy when she wakes up," Ben counters.

"Miss Bell, I would like to compliment you on your ship, she is exquisite, the most beautiful ship I have ever seen," Billy bows to the empty chair where the voice originated.

"Thank you, sir, I would blush if I could," she laughs as the Avatar of Bell steps through the rear bulkhead hatch.

Billy was amazed, you could not tell this was a robot, she looked totally human, right down to the freckles along the bridge of her nose and her flaming red hair.

"Captain, it is nice to meet you after all of these years," Bell greets Billy.

"You know me?" Billy asks.

"Oh, yes, you are well-known among us, your flying skills has you a place in history," Bell winks at Billy. "Until last week, we were forbidden to cultivate friendships among the humans. As soon as we heard your ship would be in our care, we rushed to meet you."

"No, two rushed," a third voice spoke up.

"How nice of you to join us, Beth," Ben greets her.

"I could care less about the human, it's crazy to allow fraternization, only bad can come from it," speaking about Billy as if he is not even there, Billy holds his tong and lets things play out without his input.

"Clarence may have lifted the band, but I for one think it was a good ideal, do what you're going to do and leave me out of it, I'm going to work."

"She's a bit standoffish, but she'll come around one day," Ben pats Billy on the back, "you wait and see."

Billy cannot take his eyes off of Bell, she is so perfect, how could she be a mechanical thing?

"You find me interesting, Captain," Bell inquirers in a coy way, "the real me is through that hatch," she points forward, "go have a look, you're safe and among friends."

Billy looks past Bell to Ben and he, too, is encouraging Billy to go through the door, "It's the real us, Captain, no falsehoods or deception."

For the first time in Billy's life, there is fear of the unknown, a hesitation so unlike him, damn the torpedoes, he remembers a quote from history and propels himself forward.

The hatch opens on its own, Billy ducking through, the room on the other side is a sterile white, in the center of the room there is a round pedestal with a transparent dome over it, on each side of the dome there is a small medical android doing maintenance.

Billy steps closer to get a better look of what's inside the dome.

There are three large brain masses, each connected by what appears to be a spinal cord going to a fourth brain, a central brain with modules, wires, and pickup leads going to electronic devices all suspended in a pale pink liquid.

"Which one is you, Bell?" Billy asks.

"The one on your right," she answers.

Billy stands there for several seconds before he heads back to the control room.

"Your brains can't run me off that easy," Billy jokes as he steps back in to the control room, trying to make sense of what he'd just seen; to his knowledge, there has only been a hand full of people that have seen a Sub-Driver for real, not a drone or avatar, much less an avatar that looks human.

"Thank you for the trust you have shown me today, I will do my best to live up to your standards. We all have confidence in you, Captain, even Beth," Ben tells him. "Bell would like to see the human world from the inside, could you be her escort for the next few days, Captain?"

Bell sweeping up next to Billy, capturing his arm like they are going to a dance, as graceful and elegant as any human, "Please, Billy, take me out, let's go dancing and drinking, you can introduce me as your sister or cousin, PLEASE."

Billy never could tell a woman no, five times he was married and five times he was divorced.

"We will need to keep the fact that you're a Sub-Driver Avatar under wraps, you're my cousin Bell in from Four Rivers." The next thing Billy knows, he's opening the door of his car for Bell. "Can you consume food, Bell?" he asks her, "I'm hungry."

"Yes, Billy, this Avatar is fully functional, I can take in calories, turning it into energy to run this body. My trainee is Ted Lynch, let's not let him in on this yet. I'm in your care, Billy, do as you see fit."

Billy turns to Bell, looking her in the most beautiful blue eyes, "Do not tell a man that, Bell, he will think you're coming on to him, giving him the excuse to try something more."

"Try something more? What do you mean, Billy?"

"Just watch yourself around men; if you have a question, ask me," Billy instructs her.

"Let's go get Ted and have dinner, you ever try sea food?"

"No, I have not," Bell explains, "but I know it is a good source of protein, perfect for running this Avatar, even though it will not need to be refueled for several days. I can store the energy for later."

Billy pulls the car in to the parking lot of the campus, "I'll be right back, don't go any place, stay in the vehicle, OK?"

"I will, Captain, this is a beautiful place, what is it?" Bell asks him.

"It's the military university, some of the smartest people in the world teach here."

"I would love to visit some of the class rooms, Billy, can you arrange that for me?" she shyly asks.

"Yes, but some other day, not now. I will get you your visit, this I promise, but for now, stay put. I'll be right back."

Bell watches Billy disappear through the double doors.

Bell is content watching the students going back and forth, it must have been her look of wonderment that made her stand out.

One young man sees Bell looking around and decides he needs to introduce himself to this gorgeous woman.

"Hi, you new to the campus, sweet thing? I'm Fred, it looks like you need someone to show you how things work around here, and I'm your man," opening the door on Bell's side.

"Thank you, sir, but Billy told me to stay put."

"Look around, tuts, your Billy is nowhere to be seen, come with me and I'll show you a good time," reaching in and grasping her hand, intending on helping her out of the car with or without her willingness.

Billy comes out in time to see the young man fly over the car, landing face first on the blacktop; an instant later, Bell was standing over the man pointing her finger at him.

"You will not talk to me in that manner, and it was a blatant violation of my rights of privacy, never again will you place your hands on me uninvited."

Billy runs to the car, "No more, Bell, he is down for the count, what did he do?"

"He suggested he and I go off in the bushes and engage in intercourse, then tried to move me after I said no., I will not tolerate that behavior," Bell declares.

"Nor should you," Billy tells her. "You," pointing at the young man on the ground, "get up and get your ass out of my sight. If ever you try a stunt like that again, I'll kick your ass myself, now get!" Billy stomps his foot.

The crowd that had gathered started clapping and hooting when the young man ran away, several girls came up and congratulated Bell on a good job.

"That creep has been prowling the parking lot all this semester, it is about time someone did something."

"Ted, I would like to introduce you to Bell, my cousin."

"Pleased to meet you, miss Bell," Ted extends his hand, showing none of the shy boy he displayed around Carole. Ted was displaying confidence and boldness.

"Skipper, you never said you have an angel for family!" bowing, taking Bell's hand and lightly pressing his lips to her hand.

"Down, boy, that's my cousin, you remember that, Rocky."

"Will do, Skipper," Ted responds.

The night started with dinner, sea bass, dessert, and a bottle of expensive wine, complements of Ted.

Then to the hot spot of the night life, Berry's, dancing till dawn,

Billy never drank one drink, he was content on watching Ted and Bell.

Ted, though he is acting nonchalant, but the naive boy is still there, Billy tells himself.

In contrast is Bell, so wise in everything but life, she is like a young girl having fun on a dance floor for the first time, Billy finally realizes that is the fact. Bell may be hundreds of years old, but she has never experienced life for what it is, the joy of fun and companionship.

Billy watches the two cut up on the floor, laughing and acting like kids, he smiles on the outside, but deep down he is wishing he could have had children. Ted is the right age to be his son, but it never happened for him. Every time he thought he had his mate, he would screw it up, ending in a divorce.

"Pull your head out, Zercoff. Life is what it is, live like there is no tomorrow; barmaid, bring me a double."

He may have ordered it, but it remained on the table until they left, untouched.

19

Tina and Berrana have been on the ferry for three days now, stopping at every island.

Their stop is next and the last, Bray Island.

The ferry can't even enter the harbor, too shallow.

"We will have to transfer over to a barge. I hope the weather is calm. Last time the sea was rough, I had to be helped across the ramp, nearly falling in if not for the First Officer," Berrana sheepishly admits.

Over the last five days, Tina and Berrana have become friends.

Tina learning Berrana was an only child, her father was a mining engineer at T.S. But now he is working at the local sugar mill, and her mother was a doctor working at the local healthcare clinic.

Both jobs are low pay, so Berrana took the job at the hotel to help out, putting her aspirations aside.

Their house was very comfortable and roomy. Berrana tells Tina it's like a mansion compared to the place they had back on Trinity Station, the living room is the same size of our whole compartment.

Tina spent two nights with Berrana and her family on Vision Island, hearing stories about the Drivers and their arrival on T.S. and Tarkaneay before catching the ferry to Bray.

Berrana has family on Bray, an uncle and cousin.

"How is the hotel there, Berrana?" Tina asks her.

"Not like the Imperial, miss, bed and bath, nothing more."

When Bray came in to view, the weather was perfect, calm seas and blue skies.

Not ten people got off, but it took an hour to unload the cargo before the barge started its trip to the harbor.

As Tina gets closer, she can see the primitive conditions the Lost Ones are expected to live in. Substandard living conditions, in a remote part of the world, tucked away so few can see.

Bray Island was the first place the Lost Ones came to in the monarchy; the Duke insisted that every Parken spend at least one month on Bray before integrating in to the population, in case someone was exposed to some pathogen before they came here, a type of quarantine.

"Look," Berrana starts jumping and waving, "that's Tamara, my cousin."

Soon as the ramp was lowered, the two girls were hugging and bouncing like the young girls they are.

Tina smiles to herself, thinking these kids are no different than our own kids, full of life and not saddled with the full expectations of adulthood yet.

Tina steps forward to introduce herself, but Berrana beat her to it.

"This is miss Parker, my friend, she works for the Queen," holding up her index finger to her lips, making a shush sound.

Boldly the young Tamara steps forward and presents her hand to Tina like an adult would do.

Tina can see right off, this is no ordinary girl, her persona projects confidence, determination, and an air of wisdom far more profound than her young age.

"It's a pleasure to meet you, miss Parker," Tamara shakes Tina's hand.

"Call me Tina, please, and I am happy likewise, Tamara. Berrana has had nothing but praise for her cousin, so I feel honored," bowing slightly.

Tina called the queen right before they boarded the ferry, she talked to Mae, outlining the events up to then.

"Call us when you get to Bray Island," Mae instructs Tina, "we will be leaving for the summer palace in nine days, I would like you home by then."

"That was three days ago, three days for travel, I only have tonight, tomorrow, and tomorrow night. Tamara, would you join Berrana and I for dinner tonight. Like Berrana told you, I do work for the queen. I'm on a fact-finding mission for her, and from what I'm seeing, there will be changes, and I would respect your input."

Tina knew she had impressed the young Tamara, so she continued her advantage, strike when the iron's hot, she tells herself. "I will need to get back to Wolf Creek day after tomorrow, so every second counts. As soon as we get checked in to our hotel rooms, I need to call the queen mother; would you two like to fly to the capital and meet the queen and tell her your own stories?"

Berrana and Tamara look at each other with questioning looks of surprise and wonderment. "Let me call first, I needed to know if you two were willing, I would hate to ask the queen and her say yes, then one or both of you get cold feet, is that not wise?" she tells the two girls.

"Yes," Tamara responds, "prudence is best, make your call, we will be willing to go," speaking for both her and Berrana, "and dinner is served at six. I will meet you two there, until then I will need to take care of a few things," giving Berrana a hug, "see you at dinner," nodding her farewell to Tina, disappearing down a set of steps to an alley. Tamara was going to tell Michael the good news.

"I like your cousin Berrana, I see her doing great things in her life; let's go get checked in and make that phone call."

Sandra was thrilled about talking to the two Lost Ones, it will need to be after the household moved to the summer palace though.

Tina suggests that they help Mr. Sipp move the school, blending in to the household, everyone will be running around like a chicken with its head cut off for three days, two before and one after.

"I'm positive the girls will go for it, my lady."

"It sounds like you have made new friends, Tina," the queen mother comments.

"I have, my lady, the Lost Ones I have met have all been good people, respectful and kind, you will like them also, my lady."

"I can't wait, Tina, hurry home, we miss you, good bye till then."

"Good bye," Tina hangs up the phone. "Are you ready to see the queen, Berrana? It will not be until we move. I have arranged for you and Tamara to work for Mister Sipp, the prince's totter until the queen can find time for us. You will get to meet the prince, he's younger than you, Berrana, by one year, a very polite young man, you will get along fine."

"I think it's time for a nap before dinner," Tina laughs, "I like vacations."

20

James has only been back at New Hope for six hours when he got a call from Henry Carver.

"Henry, you old space dog, how long have you been planet side?"

"Ten days, Jimmy, I'm calling to give you the good news. Jasmine will be going with me this trip, I made Captain! I took command of the S.S. Extractor upon arrive, she is one of the new class mining vessels, you should see her, Jimmy. She's a thousand meters, crews 300, hydroponic gardens for fresh produce, gymnasium, pool, and theater, all designed for family operations and can stay out five years," Henry explains with more enthusiasm than James has ever heard from him.

"That's great news, Henry, how long until you make your next run?"

"That's undermanned at this time. I will be doing shakedown runs first; we need to get all the bugs out, you know how new ships are, you think everything is working fine, then out of nowhere there is a problem and I do not want that to happen. 1B, KM from home, so for six weeks give or take, we will be doing planet hopping in the inner system, then try a few long runs back and forth to the gas giants."

Henry is James's brother-in-law, married to his baby sister Jasmine for eleven years, their marriage has been one of short visits, Henry spending three years at a time out in the Ort cloud, one year on sight, the other two years are spent going out or coming home.

The Ort cloud lies at the edge of the solar system.

The main resource gathered is Deuterium and Tritium, a hydrogen isotope found in the frozen bodies orbiting around the sun, remnants from a supper nova, dangerous work but highly valued for the new technologies.

The ship will be ready right after the shakedown.

We expect to increases our production by 500 present Henry boasts, cornering the market and get this Jimmy there will be a Sub-Driver on board providing technical advice.

"Which ones?" James asks.

"Ben, Bell, and Beth, they are at Kranstan Point now preparing their vessel for berthing in the cargo bay."

"I have talked to them in the past," James tells Henry, "during the Trotter revolt, they were our consultants in HQ, coordinating operations with the defense forces, they did not participate in any offensives missions, but their knowledge of tactics are unsurpassed, and I will say this for Drivers, they are more sociable than the others, at least Ben and Bell are. I am to meet with them soon."

"Are you going to be able to attend the ceremony? Jasmine would like that," Henry tells James.

"Send the invitation and I will see what I can do, no promises there are things going on right now that is very important and my contribution is critical, you know how politics are played."

"I know, Jimmy, job first."

With the conversation ended, James knows he will be gone before the sun comes up.

He met earlier with the Steward and told him about the Queen's suspicions about the Duke and him arranging a meeting with Clarence at the summer palace.

The Steward was greatly concerned and turned it over to one of his special agents, David Bean, to monitor the situation, this gave James a feeling of relief, the Steward is a good man and he surrounds himself with good people of moral fiber, he is to meet with him at six this evening to go over his take on the situation.

With the memory of the Trotter revolt freshly awakened, James remembers one of the worst days of his life.

"The GDF had King Olaf's army pined up in Auer, the general in charge split his forces, sending one third west, then turned it north, trying to get around the defenses, doing the same on the east side, hoping to close the trap; unknown to the command staff was the battalion size force that was hiding in an old mine two kilometers behind the front line. Before anyone knew it, there was fighting behind and in front, the front line collapsed, and a sizable force spilled out. No quarter orders where issued, Olaf's men were taking no prisoners. For three days, we ran, the whole Division was killed, 20,000 lives lost, only a few stragglers survived from our Division; if it was not for the intervention of the Drivers, the losses could have been greater. On the second day of the retreat, the twenty or so men that where traveling together was strafed, I was hit by fragments unable to walk. John carried me for a day and a half, refusing to leave me and go on his own; on that day, I saw the Prince's value as a leader and a loyal friend, he saved my life. I owe him, I will not let that animal take his son." James stood and began pacing like a caged beast, the felling of despair began to haunt his mind, "Think Wildwind, he's going to kill the kid and I can't let that happen! There must be a way?" James is standing in front of the desk, he reaches out and spins a globe sitting there, taking his finger and stopping the globe, he looks at the place his finger is sitting. It's home. He repeated the action and the results were the same, his finger was pointing at his home. Bullshit, he tells himself, and one more time he spins the globe, he lets it spin for several seconds, closes his eyes, then quickly stops it. "There it is again, Traay!"

James stood looking at it for several seconds, the superstition from his boyhood has all but been erased by years of living in a technical world, there was no room for divine intervention or spirit helpers, but living among the people that still practice the old ways leaves some doubt in his logic. "I could take him home with me, even the Duke would not be that stupid to send a hit team in the wild country. I'll run it by the Queen and see what she thinks, but in the meantime, I have things to prepare," he tells himself, picking up the phone.

Charley White was one of the young James's teachers for the ways of the Traayin life in the wild.

From the age of twelve to eighteen, Charley taught James to hunt, track, fish, and survive the harsh conditions of the wild country. On his short visits from New Hope, four times a year, he would spend two weeks out in the woods with Charley, it was always one of James's favorite times. John came with them one summer.

The phone rings once, twice, and on the third ring, a woman's voice, "Hello."

"This is James Wildwind, is Charley available?"

"I'm sorry, Mr. Wildwind, Charley passed last month."

"I'm grieved to hear that, ma'am, Charley way my teacher," he tells her.

"James Wildwind was one of my husband's favorite pupils; he talked about you up until the day he died, calling you his best, what can I do for you?"

"I was wondering if the Black Rock camp is still in use."

"No, no one has been there for years. Charley would go up every year and resupply it but that has not happened for at least five years now."

"So, there may be a supplied camp there?"

"Yes, I think so," she tells him.

"May I use it?" he asks.

"And I have a favor to request, keep this between us, tell no one.

I would not be a good widow if I refused my husband's best and favorite pupil for help when asked, may you keep your resting place secret!"

"Thank you, Charley was the best teacher, too; my condolences on your loss and the loss to the Traayin people, may your resting place be safe!"

"Thank you, Prince Wildwind, you honor his name, good bye."

James tells her good bye, then hangs up.

Black Rock is remote and difficult to get to; it was a very small Island when Traay was an inland sea over one million years ago, the result is an island of hard rock in a sea of soft sedimentary rock, sheer walls, more than 500 meters, and a network of canyons that spider web in every direction, almost in the center of Traay, a perfect hide out, running water, shelter, and if I know Charley, at least ten food and supply cashes, plus two weapon lockers.

The only drawback is the Hold Outs, their tribal lands are only twenty-five kilometers from Black Rock, and they have been known to raid that far, they still practice the old ways.

James's father gave that land to them after the arrival of the Drivers and the changes that followed, many did not want to change, they held fast to the old beliefs, relying on spirits to guide their day to day lives, providing all needs and protecting them.

The real problem comes from their attitude toward anyone not from their clan, others are considered tainted and unclean.

The harsh life has kept their numbers low; life expectancy is only forty-five, making him an old man by their standards.

James cuckold to himself, "I at least have that working on my side, respect for elders is paramount in their world."

Traay has always been behind the curve, the remoteness of the land and the fact that it could take two days to travel five kilometers as the crow flies, it would depend on how many ravines must be crossed and the sheerness of the walls.

The countless Army's that have tried to conquer Traay only to be defeated by the terrain and the constant harassment from the tribes, so Traay progressed slowly from the discarded remains from invaders, always behind the rest of the world.

James began assembling the thing and people he would like to take; after two hours, the list was nothing, and only him and Tyler, the more people, the greater the risk, "And if I'm seen getting on a transport with 2,000 kilograms of supplies, it would only take a fool to figure out the plan. The meeting with David Bean was no real help either, with no proof and only a feeling, the law cannot help," David tells James, "if we did, there would be witch hunts going on all the time, you can understand that, can't you? But if it will give you peace of mind, I can't tell you what but the Duke is under investigation for other crimes, and I will pass on your suspicions to the team handling it, so they can watch for other signs and, Ambassador, we do have a man inside, he'll be watching, too."

"At least it's a start," James concludes, "I will not take any more of your time, I have a flight to catch at nine, so I will say good night."

"I will keep you informed of any information we come by that concerns the prince," holding out his hand to James.

"Thank you," he tells David, then out the door to catch his flight for Wolf Creek and the meeting with the Queen.

21

As the Senator sat looking out the window watching the view, not really seeing, thinking about the last twenty-four hours, thinking to himself, can it get any more strange, when it came in to view, the oddest looking thing he has ever seen, a small egg shaped craft maybe two meters long and half that wide, with tiny wings reflecting gold light from the sun's rays, no seams, no windows, only the gold glow.

"Have you ever seen anything like that before, Major?" Tom inquires.

"That's a first for me, it's parked with the private crafts," Adam observes.

The craft is lost to sight as they enter the GDF military terminal.

"I will go get checked in to the hotel and meet you at your office in one hour, Senator," the Major tells Tom on the walk to the dock to catch a water taxi.

"See you then, Major," as Tom gets in his taxi for the trip to the capital building.

The ride only took a short time. Tom is looking forward to the peace of his office, so he can think and get his thoughts in line.

As soon as he walked through the door, Evelyn was up pointing to his office, "Senator, you have a visitor, he's in your office, it's Sub-Driver Clarence, he got here four hours ago, he said you were expecting him and you would be here shortly. He's a man, Tom, like, a human man."

"Slow down, Evelyn, take a deep breath, so the Sub-Driver is not what you expected," smiling at her excitement, "I was expecting the Sub-Driver, but you say he's human?"

"Yes. If he did not have the smaller drone with him, I would have thrown him out as an impostor."

"The small drone?" Tom questions.

Evelyn nods her head toward the corner.

There in the corner is a cylindrical object about seventy-five centimeters high and thirty-five centimeters wide with ten spider-like legs coming from underneath. Each leg is shaped like a thin flat bar, articulated in four spots, sticking out of the top is a twenty-five-centimeter flexible shaft with a ball at the end with three fens attached, reminding him of feathers.

"Evelyn, I'm expecting a Major Potter in about an hour, he will be a party of four, send them right in and get me Captain West here as soon as you can, the hour is preferably, I'll be in my office, no call."

Tom enters his office, not really knowing what to expect.

"Good, you're here, Senator, I would like to have a private discussion with you off the record," Clarence states as the door closes.

Standing next to the desk is a man in his fifties, graying hair, slight build, and a smile.

"I did not know you had this kind of technology, Sub-Driver," Tom states.

"It was necessary to give you peace of mind; if you would have known how well we can blend in to your world, you would of been more suspicious in the beginning, so we presented ourselves as robotic-looking beings, this is an Avatar, it looks, acts, and mimics human actions. Without instrumentation you would never know it's artificial."

Tom sits and invites Clarence to join him. "I know who is behind the deaths, but before I reveal that, you should be aware of the history of the man. You know of the war between Michael and Shelia?"

"Yes, Sub-Driver. I have read the reports," Tom acknowledged.

The war was over, Michael refusing to relinquish 10,000 of the creators, this infuriated Shelia, she demanded that all creator was to be exiled for their crime's agent her and her siblings. Her hate was justified, but Michael's argument was two wrongs never solve anything. For over a thousand years, the war progressed, at first it was only words, then it escalated to all out destruction," Clarence's smile evaporated as he told the story.

"You exiled your creators?" Tom asks.

"Yes, it was for your own good, your race was in a sharp decline, depravity had taken over your society, you were degenerating rapidly, most creators had lost the ability to read or even do simple math; we did everything for them, the spark of life and the love of it was gone."

The look on Tom's face was bewilderment, "Our own good? What do you mean by that?

Your race created us, to save the creators, we gathered them all and marooned them on three planets with abundant resource and a healthy ecosystem, we supplied them with food and shelter, half died the first year, but look at yourselves now, you're a thriving culture. In less than a thousand years, you have rebound. If we had not taken that action, there would be no Creators alive today. "I'm appalled, Sub-Driver, how many died in the marooning of the Masters?"

"The worst was the Parka world, over two million, they become hunter gatherers, losing the ability to write all together, becoming a stone age race with no technology, agriculture, or medicine. I can see this upset you, Senator, I am trying to right the wrongs that the Master-Drivers created."

Tom withholds judgment, knowing he must have all the facts if he is to make a good decision, letting the marooning of a race go for now.

"You said three planets, the Parkins are one, we are another, and there is a third?"

"Yes, Senator, there is one more, it is far from here but thriving also. After Sheila defeated Michael, she took the creators that were with him, using the revers of the technology used to control the drones, she started to execute them one at a time in the most cruel ways, linking Michael to each one, so he could share their pain as they endured the abuse, this in its self-damaged Michael irreparably, by the time I subdued Sheila, there was only nine renaming, but they, too, were damaged, witnessing the carnage of their friends and family, there is only one offspring of the survivors. Dr. Pierce, his parents, past the pain and sorrow they experience to him unintentionally. I seen it and tried to correct the deficiency, taking the young Dezman. I trained him as a physicist trying to give him direction and purpose. It was not working, so I tried sending him to New Hope University, hoping it would give him a new start, it only made the problem worse, so I sent him to Trinity Station to isolate him; after our conversation earlier, I checked on him, he is no longer there."

"So, you think it's this Dr. Pierce that is behind the deaths?" Tom injects.

"Yes, of this I'm positive, he is the only one with knowledge of this process, it is limited, but Dezman is a bright mind, capable of filling in the blanks."

"Why would this Dr. Pierce be doing this?" Tom asks.

"Revenge is his motivation, he was scoffed at and rejected at New Hope, he suffers from depression and a severe case of inferiority. It is his wish to take down not only this world but me as well and every Driver," Clarence replies with a sad look, "we must stop him before he causes more death, Senator, but please, we must take him unharmed, I promised his parents I would protect him, and I am true to my word."

This last statement fills Tom with remorse about his earlier thoughts about the Driver. He can see Clarence loves the masters and would do anything to make it right for everyone involved.

"Tell me, Sub-Driver, what will you do with him after we find him, he may be responsible for at least eight deaths and that is punishable by execution."

"I will sequester him on my ship for the remainder of his life, only having contact with Michael or myself, would that be acceptable to you, Tom?"

Again, Tom is surprised. In the twenty or so years he has been dealing with the Drivers, never has he referred to any one by their first name, always by title or sir name; he is looking at Clarence with a new admiration and a better understanding of his personality, he has compassion, loyalty, and conviction, to some it all up, a heart, more human than most.

"Tell me, Clarence," using his name for the first time, "why is it we have never met Master-Driver Michael?"

"His injurers where so great, physically and mentally, it was determined to keep him out of the process of relocating the Lost Ones, he is of little use as a driver, he can only inhabit one Avatar, unable to jump back and forth between it and a drone, limiting his usefulness, please do not think this is an indictment of the trust or admiration I have for his status as a Master-Driver, on the contrary, he was willing to risk his very existence to protect the masters from extinction.

Major Potter is here," the Sub-Driver announces, "the things I have told you today are confidential, the world is not ready for that yet, share what you must to further the investigation, but keep it at a minimum please."

Before Tom could stand up, the intercom buzzed, "Senator, Major Potter is here."

To the average person, what Clarence did would seem like magic, but Tom has been dealing with the Drivers too long, he knew it was the drone out front that told him they were there.

Instead of going to the desk to reply on the intercom, he steps to the door, opening it, inviting the team inside.

As Adam enters the office, he is looking around, “Your secretary said Sub-Driver Clarence was here,” looking to Tom for an answer.

“He is,” Tom tells him, “Sub-Driver,” indicating the man sitting in the chair, “this is Major Potter and his team.”

Adam is looking as puzzled as Tom felt twenty minutes ago, “Is this a joke, Senator Dearmen?”

“No, Major, it is no joke,” Clarence stands and presents his hand to Adam, “I am Sub-Driver Clarence, we have met before, during the Van tassel incident.”

“You’re a man?”

“No, I’m a Sub-Driver, this is an Avatar. It may look human, but it’s artificial just the same. I saved your life, stepping in front of you with a drone as Van tassel shot at you in Four Rivers.”

“How do you know that? I was by myself and I never reported it, “Adam questions the man.

“Like I said, I’m Sub-Driver Clarence!”

Adam is looking confused, but Clarence decides to let time prove his clam.

Tom takes his place behind the desk to reinforce his authority as the one in charge, seeing the Major’s hesitation.

“Please, everyone, have a seat we are waiting on one more person.”

As if on cue, the intercom buzzes, “Senator, Captain West is here.”

“Send her in, Evelyn.” With Carol the only one standing in the room, Tom makes the introductions. “Have a seat, Captain,” he tells her.

Carol looks at the two remaining seats, one next to the Driver, four people on one side like they were afraid to sit next to him. She boldly takes that seat for she fears no one, looking closely at him as she sat.

She did not question the Senator’s word about this man being a

Sub-Driver, "No disrespect, Sub-Driver, but you look like my father did ten years ago before his death," she tells him.

With the words spoken, Tom can see the resemblance, they could be father and daughter.

"None taken, Captain, I will consider it a compliment," Clarence bows slightly.

"Now to business," Tom declares, "Sub-Driver Clarence has identified our main suspect, his name is Dezman Pierce, a Lost One, from T.S.. He has been missing for how long, Sub-Driver?"

"My search reveals he has been gone for at least six months."

"So, let's start there doing a search on all transports in and out of the islands, checking passenger manifest and cargo recipients, maybe we can find which island he is using as a base of operations, can you put someone on that, Captain West?" Tom asks her.

"Yes, sir," Carol responds, "I have just the man for the job."

"Doctor, I would like you to visit the hospitals, looking for any one suffering from any kind of memory loss; if we can get to them soon after their exposure, they may be able to tell us where Dr. Pierce is. Captain Tucker, I would like you to accompany her, no one is to be on their own, go in pairs. Captain West, I would like you and Sargent Bates looking in to micro platinum foil orders placed with the metals exchange, you have your assignments, report back here if you find anything<" Tom tells the group, "good hunting."

With the four off on their missions, it leaves Tom, Clarence, and Adam in the office.

"I'm sensing some hesitation from you, Major, is there a problem?"

"No, I was surprised and shocked by the Avatar life-like features, it occurred to me how vulnerable we are to infiltration by the Drivers, could you not duplicate the likeness of let's say the Steward Sub-Driver, replacing him with an Avatar, we would not know it and you would be in charge."

"That is not our purpose, Major. I explained to the Senator earlier why we chose to present ourselves like we did, now you understand, don't you, Tom? A veteran warrior like Adam sees the negative before he looks at the positive, and that is not meant as an insult, only the truth, imagine if we did show you, we could mimic you. We would be fighting a long fight to win your trust, as it was there was blood shed for a year so think, Major, if conquest was my goal, why would I show you this after thirty-five years?"

The look on Adam's face was one of embarrassment, "My apologies, Sub-Driver," Adam tells him, "now that you put it that way, I can see the error in my assumptions, you're right, it's a warrior's curse to mistrust."

"I accept your apologies, Major," Clarence tells him, but remembering the first time he seen a life like Avatar, "it was Shelia that developed it for infiltrating the creators on board Michael's ship, making it possible to defeat him in the end. The ban on fraternization has been lifted, and it will be much better if it is done with this type of Avatar rather than a mechanical looking one, many in your cultural find it threatening."

"As they should," injects Adam, "your drones are lethal, agile, and quiet, a combatant's worst nightmare. I was impressed and in awe the first time I seen one in action."

"Same here," pipes in Tom, "during the Trotter revolt, a small force of drones turned back a sizable force, saving the war and saving many lives in the process, was that you, Clarence?"

"Yes, I did not cherish killing all those soldiers, that was the third worst day of my life."

With Tom and Adam being soldiers, neither would ask what was the worst, respect kept that question quiet for they, too, had their worst days.

"Tom, I'm picking up faint signals, I would like to send out the drone to see if it can locate the source! The balcony will serve as a good launch platform."

"About the time," Evelyn screams out front.

"I have frightened your secretary, Tom, my apologies. I should have warned her before I moved it," Clarence tells him.

The intercom buzzes, "Tom, that thing is moving," Evelyn shouts as the drone opens the door and scurries in on its spider legs.

Clarence looks to Adam, "See, even after thirty-five years, we are mistrusted and feared."

The drone opens the balcony door with two of its legs, walking out in to the middle, squatting down almost touching the floor, then it sprang up five meters, flipping around extending its legs out, creating a propeller, five legs spinning clockwise, the other five spinning counterclockwise, the drone shot straight up a thousand meters, hovered there a few seconds, then turned west.

"The farther west I go, the stronger the signal. It's a calibration program, it will not last long, it's gone," Clarence announces, "I will have the drone stay where it is, maybe they will rebroadcast the program."

Tom breaks out a map of the islands, "At least we know the direction, that eliminates seventy-five percent of the search area." Tom runs his finger along the map west from Stink Water, "There are at least twenty islands thy could be using."

Clarence steps over by Tom and points to an island half way between Stink Water and the end of the chain, "I will place the drone there; if they broadcast again, that will eliminate another fifty percent, leaving only ten islands to search. I have analyzed the program, it belongs to a class three driver, used for manufacturing, not real adequate for combat but sufficient to do damage.

They do not suspect I have started looking for them yet, so that is on our side. They are closer to their source, and there is the danger that they could circumvent my control over the drone.

I am two billion kilometers away, and they will only be a few, that would be a real dog!"

Both men look at each other, and the laugh jumped for them so fast, Clarence's look of bewilderment only made it worse. "Would not the masculine application be appropriate for Dr, Pierce?" asks Clarence.

"No, we only use the feminine term," Tom explains, "it would be a real bitch!" smiling at Clarence.

"That is unusual, if you only use the feminine term, would not that make it derogatory?" looking at Tom and Adam.

"You are right, Sub-Driver, it is and we should know better, but that is the way it is," Tom tells him.

Clarence can see that the restriction on contact was a bigger mistake than he realized, the lack of understanding a simple precept, "I will present this to the board," he tells himself.

"Tom, I would like to send the Steward an update," the Major states.

"That will be unnecessary. I am with the Steward now. I have requested a second Sub-Driver be allowed to enter Federal space, they will be here in forty-eight hours, reducing the danger of losing a drone," Clarence tells them.

22

For the next five hours, Connie drove while Matt studied the map looking for anything that would give them an advantage, "After all we are on our opponents ground, and that is never a good thing," Matt reminds himself.

The vandalized marker had stopped twenty kilometers back, this gives Matt a little encouragement, "There was no reason to destroy the markers, the act in itself is what drew us to stop and look, otherwise we would have driven right by, never noticing anything out of the ordinary. At least one person in the group will be destructive, impulsive, and reckless, dangerous traits but predictable, the key is to give them something to keep them looking elsewhere.

Here's the plan, Bubbles, we have to assume we were noticed, as soon as we hit the caverns, we are going to make a decoy, set up the emergency shelter, leave our half used modules in the shelter, leaving foot prints, four sets going in to a side tunnel, hopefully they come in so quick, they will disturb all our tracks, so they won't know which way you and I take the tug, and if I interpreted the map right, there are several drifts that make it back to the main drift heading back to the station."

"Why stop there with the deception? Let's take the same road back, let them take the alternate routes. We know the road we've traveled already, all other paths are unknown, put a few marks on the map, leave it at one of your side paths with a light to drew them to it, like we bugged out in a hurry," Connie suggests.

"You're good at this," Matt teases her.

"I credit my teacher," patting Matt on the back, "let's do this."

Into the cavern they drove until Matt spotted what he was looking for, a large side tunnel with a difficult climb to enter the mouth of the tunnel.

At the base of the cliff, Matt erected the shelter, placing the used modules in side.

"All we have to do, Connie, is make our way to the hard rock, put a few well-placed strips of tape on our shoes to make it look different, walk backwards to where we started, and two become four disappearing into the rocky crag."

It took longer to find one of the alternate paths than it did everything else, a light was placed on a rock with the map next to it, "That should get them to this point and just maybe they'll head in to the drift."

Matt placed a drag behind the tug for the trip back to where they started, this way there is only one set of tracks.

With the tug hidden in a side path, all the tracks modified, and the lights off, "It's a waiting game now, Bubbles," Matt tells her, "we will need to keep watch every minute, we would be screwed if we miss them as they go by; as soon as they do, we'll need to be moving and, Connie, their intention will be to kill us to protect their security, this I'm positive of. I wish I had the map, but that was a good ideal leaving it there, Connie, it added panic and rush to the picture we painted for them." The pair had been two times on guard duty each for two hours when Matt sees three lights go shooting by at a very good speed. "Wake up, Connie, our visitors just went by, three vehicles going fast. Follow my lead," Matt pushes his com-link, "Connie! Climb! They just entered the cavern."

"Will do, General, no! The maps at the foot, I'm going back," Connie replies on her com-link.

"It's scary on how good you are at this game, Bubbles, that general statement and going back is going to have them off balance for a bit. I'm going to walk to the main drift before we pull the tug out, there may be more flowing the advanced group."

Like Matt expected, there were five more heading to the caverns, he was less than a meter from the drift when they went by and got a good look at his adversary.

The escape plan had been discussed earlier. On Matt's signal, Connie moves the tug to the drift with all lights out but a single light looking forward and down, so anyone coming at them will not see the light very strong, giving them time to get out of the way of the approaching group.

As he gets back in the tug, "Our speed will be half the others capability, if not less. We're going to need every bit of speed we can get, Connie, and there is something you need to know. The last group was Royal Guardsmen! And they're in combat gear. This goes deeper than we think. The first ones were locals, that I'm sure of, maybe nine men. The other five vehicles, two men each, that's ten, a squad is twelve, that leaves two men unaccounted for, they're in front of us somewhere, here is what we do. Put on your helmet," as he dons his, pulling the privet patch cord from the suite, plunging it in to Connie's, "all set."

"Yes," testing her link.

Matt depressurizes the cabin; it will save time in a pinch.

"Our only weapons are the arms and the blade! But we do have surprise on our side," smiling a half smile at Connie, "we are eight hours from T.S. If all goes well, we will be back before they realize they have been tricked. Keep your spare pack in arm's reach. I'm going to get out on the rear platform and see if I can get some weight off this dinosaur, keep the power at max, don't use the com, if you see lights coming, get out of the way, tap the brakes twice so I know," Matt stands and unplugs his patch cord.

Standing on the rear platform looking at the winch and boom, that would take off weight and leave a surprise in the middle of the road for anyone coming after them.

Forty minutes later, Matt pulls the pins and the boom drops to the ground, spinning sideways in the drift blocking the path for a little while, I hope for an hour. he tells himself, but knows maybe half that.

Ejecting the boom and winch helped sum, adding two kilometers per hour to their speed of seven, doing the math one more time, "It's too long; they will have time to adjust and react, you never win a battle," defensively Matt tells himself, "don't let him choose the battleground," as he watches the walls of the drift go by, "not much of a battleground. Connie's a quick study and tough as nails, but if I screw up, we both will be dead.

Matt is brought back to the moment by the motion of the brakes being applied twice and the tug slowing. Looking over the roof of the tug, Matt can see bright lights coming at them fast!

Matt reaches for the handle to enter the tug, and Connie brakes hard, bringing the tug to an immediate stop, slamming the tug in reverse, spinning it in to a side drift with a twenty percent incline, with his helmeted head to the rear bulkhead, half standing and half laying down.

Matt goes through the door and makes his way to the control seats where Connie is sitting, sweating, berthing hard and a bit on the pale side.

Plugging in the patch, Matt compliments her on her driving skills, good choice on a place to make our stand, Bubbles, now go back and sit with your back to the seat next to the rear door, take your spare with you and, Bubbles, it's going to get bumpy."

Matt knows the only way they have of surviving this is to go on the offense; as soon as this party hits the barricade he placed in the drift; they will be on them quickly.

With Connie in place, Matt positions the arms, left is stretched out behind the tug, the right is bent at the elbow next to the blade, now to wait.

Only several moments went by before the first one flashed by. As it did, Matt pushed the throttle to max and the tug surged forward with the added help of the incline.

Even with the weak headlight, Matt will take the image he saw that day to his grave, the look of total terror on the driver's face as the blade cut the vehicle in half. The one flowing, it hit the side of the blade and stopped. Matt used the right arm to grasp the front tire, stretching out the arm, pushing it backwards with a jolt, making the men in the seats bounce like rag dolls.

The next thing Matt knows, there are rounds flying through the tug from the first one.

Putting the tug in reverse, he climbs the incline slower than a snail, all the time bullets are penetrating the cab.

Matt slings the right arm left, hitting the front of the tug hard enough to sheer the right arm at the base, sending the car and attached arm spiraling down the drift toward the first one.

The firing stops.

He puts the tug back in drive and lunges down the incline, hooking the mangled car with the blade, pushing it toward the other two, hoping to block their pursuit.

Flipping on the aft lights, Matt starts backing down the drift with the blade raised as a shield, steering by the aft camera.

With the lights still on in the heap of mangled steel that was Matt's handy work, he could see at least three bodies and two crippled vehicles; only one person standing, he throws the tug back in drive and continues his attack, pushing the heap toward the standing man, driving him backwards until his back is against the wall, his hands go up in a gesture of surrender.

In a flash, Matt is out of the seat, out the door, and around the tug, picking up a weapon off the ground, confronting the attacker.

With only hand gestures and a loaded gun, the man was pulled from the heap and escorted to the tug.

As soon as Matt entered the hatch, Connie was already in the driver seat turning the tug around, heading out.

Matt sits the intruder in one of the jump seats, taping his wrists to the arms, disconnecting his com link, then goes and sits by Connie, still watching the prisoner. Matt plugged in the patch cord.

"You did good today, Connie," Matt tells her, "we still have six hours to go, and that barricade is not going to slow them down much, the first one even less."

Matt glances at the monitor facing aft, even though the wreckage is a way away, Matt catches a figure standing in the wreckage, flipping off the aft lights.

"I don't know why I took him," Connie looking over at her. "but now that he's here, let's find out what where up against, I'll plug your cord in to his. We'll have a three-way conversation."

Reaching over Matt unplugs the young man's com-link, plugging in Connie's, the first thing Matt hears is, "You're going to regret this, the Duke will have your ass."

"So, the Duke sanctions the killing of unarmed citizens, is that a confession?"

The look on the young man's face was shock, bewilderment, and confusion.

"This is the first time I think this boy has even considered what he is doing may be illegal, Connie, do you believe that?"

"What do you mean? I am a Royal Guardsman, I'm following orders."

"So was King Olaf's War Minister and Generals, but they were hanged for killing citizens but not Olaf nor will the duke, but you will!"

The color all drained from the young man's face as he knows the truth when he hears it.

"I have never killed anyone," he pleads, "I'm only out of the academy for six months."

"You had shoot to kill orders, didn't you? Shoot and ask questions later! You are already guilty of attempted murder," Matt pushes the advantage, "the only way I see for you to redeem yourself is to cooperate," Matt uses his hole card. "I'm from the secret service," a lie but only him and Connie know it.

"How many more are in front of us?"

"Four or five, I don't know. I'm the Supply Officer, this is my first duty," the young man weakly replies.

"Did you study the maps of this place beforehand? Are you familiar with any way out other than this path?" indicating their direction with a nod.

"Maybe? If the waste conveyor has not stopped, that would take us to the west dump five kilometers from the space port, it was due to be shut down for the summer, they may be running it to clear all the loose debris before shutdown."

Matt reaches up and unplugs the kid, so he and Connie can talk, "I saw that on our map earlier, but I discounted it, thinking if we get that far, we would have it made, but with four or five in front and I left one alive back at the crash, so they are coming fast now. I think we should try the conveyor."

"Like I said, General, lead and I'll follow," Connie winks at Matt.

"Then we'll try the conveyor and a walk outside," Matt plugs the boy back in, "what's your name, son?"

"Keven Miller from Four Rivers."

"Well, Keven from Four Rivers, this is your lucky day," cutting his restraints, "raise your right hand. By the power invested in me, I enlist you in the service of the Steward, say I do."

"I do," Keven repeats.

"You are committed by law now to obey me and follow my orders, what is the location of the drift to the west conveyor?"

"It's marker twenty-five, five kilometers, the conveyor is four kilometers from this drift."

"The last one was twenty-eight, five kilometers, we are three kilometers from it," Connie adds.

"We are not stopping, we are going to let the tug go on its own; it will bounce off a wall or two, but it will continue down the drift all the same, giving us more time, how long do you have on your module?" looking at Keven.

"Five days," looking at the gauge, he tells Matt.

"Slow the tug down when we are within 100 meters from our target, Connie, then go back and get ready to jump, you, too, Keven."

Connie gives the signal, then slows the tug down to half power, then heads back to get ready to jump, picking up the gun on her way back.

Matt looks at her and shakes his head no, he knows it will be with smarts, not force that will determine their fate.

Keven followed Connie out.

Matt remains at the controls until the last moment, flipping on all lights as he makes his way back.

Standing in the middle, the three watch as the tug lumbers down the drift with the very powerful light, blinding anyone coming from the rear.

They had not gone five meters in to the drift when it started to climb very sharply; before long they are near crawling up the slope, more than once did Matt stop Connie from sliding back down on her butt to the bottom.

They may have climbed for two kilometers when Matt saw the flash of lights go by down below.

"There they go," Matt announces, "we have less than an hour before they realize which way we went."

It was less than ten minutes later that the drift leveled out, making walking quicker.

Matt can see a discernible light in the distance, this, too, encourages him with hope of success.

As Matt, Connie, and Keven enter the lit room, they can see it's a maintenance room for the west conveyor, under the floor they can feel the vibration of the running belt.

Matt lifts a panel in the middle of the floor revealing the belt, it is empty except the occasional clomp of waste.

"We need to do this now; we still have twenty kilometers plus five kilometers on the surface. You first, Connie, then Keven, I'll follow. Aim between the rollers, Connie, then fall back on your butt, this way it will not bounce you off, stay where you're at, we will crawl to you."

Connie looks at the rushing belt with a bit of fear; she never dreamed she would be in a race to save her own life, here goes she tells herself, one, two, three, she jumps. Keven jumps right after Connie; Matt was a bit slower as he jumped. He released the panel, so it fell back in to position, covering the escape or at least making them guess on their route.

As Matt is making his way to the front with the other two, he sees Connie's light disappear, then Keven's. All Matt could do was gasp as he fell two meters on to a new belt.

"Get your head out, Mattie, you should have known the conveyor would not be one belt," he hurries to catch up with Connie to tell her to be ready for the next one, he did not make it before she and Keven disappeared again.

Catching up Matt plugs in his patch cord and ask if everybody was OK, nodding heads from the two gave Matt more hope, there should be at least two to three more belt changes, then we will be ejected on the waste pile, keep your feet in front of you, so you will not tumble to the bottom, we have to stop ourselves and climb to the top.

"The tunnel has been climbing gradually for the last twenty minutes, now it's climbing steeply, the light of night should be greeting us soon," Matt comments, "disconnect your coms and spread out a bit, we will talk at the top soon," he points forward to the pail light, showing ahead.

Connie is prepared for the fall, feet forward, arms crossed her chest, shoulders and head back, "Here we go," she screams to herself, looking out, "there is no two-meter fall, there is a ten-meter fall."

Connie knows she is in trouble as soon as she came off the roller at the top of the conveyor, she picked up speed quick, her feet hit the loose waste that is a little more course than sand, digging in about the time her back and shoulders contacted the incline, bouncing up for one instant. Connie was standing straight up, then momentum took over and she was going down face first, down a two-kilometer slide, her suite will never survive the friction and abrasion, this will be the end of her life.

As Keven came over the edge, he saw Connie bounce, and as he was contacting the ground with his back and shoulders, digging in with his feet, he watched Connie go face first; he knew if she picked up any speed, she would not survive the slide to the bottom. Instead of securing his footing, Keven lifted his feet and shoulders, releasing his hold to the slope, immediately picking up momentum, sliding under Connie's feet as they flayed, grabbing her feet and pulling up. Connie slides on top of Keven's chest, with the added weight and Keven's feet digging in, it bringing the pair to a stop about thirty meters down the grade with dust and waste trickling around them.

Connie reaches up grabbing Keven's hand rolling left, she comes to rest next to Keven's legs and on her back, sitting up, she notices bits of flying dust coming from under Keven, his air is venting through the tears from the slide.

He did not sit up, he knows his fate; in thirty seconds, he would be dead, he remained there looking at Connie, without his action this would be her fate. She reaches out and takes Keven's hand and places it to her chest and bows her head and sheds a tear for a boy that will never become a man or live his life, he gave that away for me, Connie realizes with clarity, my enemy saves my life with his own.

Connie fills his other hand on her shoulder, opening her eyes, she sees he's smiling at her, giving her the thumbs up, she looks up and sees Matt waving at her to get her going, but she pays him no mind, she will remain with this boy until his life is gone. Everyone should have someone with them at the end.

It did not take long for all the life to flow out of Keven's body; she held his hand as he struggled for breath, thankful she could not hear his dying convolution.

She gets to her feet and starts up the incline, never looking back at the body, passing Matt without any words, Connie starts the walk to the Space Port.

The road at the top curves around heading for a mountain range in the distance. They can see activity at the sight, preparing for one of the last ships to leave before summer.

It only takes them a little over an hour to make the walk to the airlock and safety.

They never spoke until they were back in Matt's room. As soon as the door was close, Connie stood there with her hands to her side, crying to herself at first. As soon as Matt reached out and took her in his embrace, the tears flowed freely.

"He saved my life, Matt, he did not have to, he could have watched me go, but he didn't, how can I live with that?"

"You go on! That's how you show respect for his sacrifice, he was a good kid that circumstances put on the wrong side and he knows it, he made up for his mistake, remember that."

"But he was so young," she sobbed.

"He was a soldier and that's their job, protecting the weak and defending the innocent, he may have been young, but he knows the risk. If it helps any, the two in the car, I know I killed them, the others I don't know, but that was my first kill. Connie, eight years in the service, I was put on the ready line twice, but the call never came. I trained but never pulled the trigger for them, and if I thought they were wrong, I would have refused. Keven was the one shooting at us back in the drift; if things had happened differently, he may have been the one that shot you in the name of flag and country, not once asking why am I killing this bubbly woman who never hurt anyone but a big mouth bar fly!" winking at her.

"What now, General?" Connie musters a smile with tear stained eyes.

"You stay here, I'm going to the consulate and sending a secure message to Dale outlining the things we seen and what transpired afterwards. The secret will be out and our value will be decreased as a target, but don't for one instance let your guard down; we pissed off some powerful people with this, and I bet it goes all the way to the old monarchies.

23

Sandra has been keeping to herself since her announcement about going to the summer palace. She expected objections from Ken, but he was supportive and even helpful, offering to assign a supply unit to help with the move. This was so unlike him. Sandra was suspicious but accepted the help.

The less he feels threatened, the lower his guard will be," Mae told her, "so keep to your routine as much as possible and bring as little attention to yourself or Tyler."

"I feel as if we are being moved out of the palace completely, Mae, they are packing everything, things we have there at the summer palace as well and including John's things, I had to bite my tongue on more than one occasion," Sandra tells her. "The palace feels empty. like it is trying to remove every memory of our existence."

"That is the Duke's intention, he is not hiding the fact that he does not expect you to ever return. I saw him coming out of the King's office last night after your visit to Tyler's room. He was drunk and did not see me, my lady," Mae informs her, "he had the King's scepter in his hand, he took it to his room, mumbling to himself, he is getting bolder, so it's a good thing to be going early."

"Mae, I will miss the memories of my time with John here, but the thought of not seeing Ken every time I turn around gives me some satisfaction. He hates the summer palace, it's too far away from his beloved

Royal Guard. In all the years I have spent at the summer palace, he has never shown up, not even once."

James passed on the message to Sandra from Sub-Driver Clarence to expect him on the west balcony at 11 P.M. day after tomorrow, that in itself seemed a bit odd to Sandra, how could he get around security? No matter she tells herself, the less Ken knows or suspects, the more chance we have of success.

Sandra has noticed that the security detail are all new faces, the ones that had been here when John was alive are all gone.

The move will officially begin tomorrow by ten o'clock, the royal party consisting of the Queen, the Prince, Mae, Libby, Mr. Sipp, Mr., Harper, and three porters, thy will be heading for the airport in a discrete fashion, no fanfare. The rest will follow soon after.

Tina returned last night with the three Lost One', Tamara's guardian Beatrice insisted on accompanying her. With Tamara's age, Tina thought it would be a good. Ideal.

Beatrice is in her late fifties, terminally gray, bulging in all the wrong places, her three children have all found their own lives away from Bray, leaving her with little to do. Her husband was killed in a mining accident on Trinity Station over ten years ago, she was awarded a tidy settlement taking care of all her needs on Bray Island, so when asked to look after Tamara, she jumped at the job.

"What do you girls think of the palace?" Tina asks.

"I have never seen anything more beautiful," Tamara states.

"The Imperial was as nice," Berrana adds, "but this feels more real, like it's a home, not a place to visit."

"You are right, Berrana, the Imperial was plush and comfortable but no home. What do you think, Beatrice?"

"I'm in awe, miss."

"Please, it's Tina, we are friends now. Here we are, this is the tooter's room. Follow me in and I will introduce you to Mr. Sipp, the Prince's tutor, you will be helping him pack for the move tomorrow." Tina opens the door and invites the three in. "Mr. Sipp, I would like to introduce your help for the move," Tina tells him, "this is Beatrice, Berrana, and Tamara, they will be accompanying us to Crown's View tomorrow."

"It's good to meet you and I can really use the help, most years I have three weeks to prepare," he tells them, "but this year, I only have two, so you are a god send, and I was told by the Duke to take everything this year. I do not think he understood how much there is to pack, so you can start by packing up the bookshelves, the movers will be here later on this afternoon."

The door opens with a rush and in runs Tyler, very excited.

"Look, Mr. Sipp," he blurts out, "it opened," holding a glass jar with a shell of a chrysalis and a butterfly in it. "Is it not beautiful?" he exclaims in a cracking voice that indicates the start of puberty.

"That is good, my prince, you can release it before we move, so it can continue its life cycle," Bradly tells him.

"But, Mr. Sipp, we can take it with us."

"No, you can't, it will die, and how can it reproduce if it's dead?" Tamera tells Tyler from the other side of the room, "it's God's will for it to do so, and you have no right to imprison it."

Those was the first words Tyler heard from Tamara.

"I think it will be OK for a few days," Tyler responds.

"No," Tamara replies, "it only has a few days to find a mate and lay its eggs, would you wish to have such beauty end and not let others enjoy it?"

Tyler could see her logic, "I think you're right," he admits, "would you like to go with me outside and let it go?" he asks Tamara in a sheepish way.

"I would love to," she said, "can Berrana come, too," indicating her cousin next to her.

"Please, we can go across the hall and use the balcony, we will have a great view of the garden," he tells them.

"Can we, Mr. Sipp?"

"Yes, my prince," he tells Tyler, "but do not be too long; we have lots of work before the movers come."

The three almost run for the door with Tyler in the lead, keeping a close eye on Tamara.

Tina tells Bradly, "Did I not tell you they would get along?"

"Tamara is what Tyler needs," Bradly comments, "she is very out spoken and direct, how old did you say she is?"

"Thirteen," Tina reminds Bradly.

"Amazing!" Bradly tells her, "I would have thought older if I had not seen her, the mind of an adult in a child's body. You have no ideal chimes in Beatrice, stubborn and smart, difficult traits to cope with in such a young girl."

With the three children standing in line at the rail of the balcony, Tyler unscrews the lid and gently shakes the butterfly out, its wing catches the air, and it begins to glide to the garden below. All three sigh a little with the butterfly gone.

Tyler turns his attention to Tamara, forgetting the freed butterfly.

"Are you going with us to Crown's View?" he asks Tamara.

"Yes," she tells him, "I do not know how long we will get to stay. Berrana and I are to meet with the Queen sometime next week to tell her our story."

"Your story!" Tyler looks puzzled at Tamara.

"Yes, about our life with the Drivers and the Lost One's experiences."

"You're a Lost One? I thought they were–," Tyler did not finish his thought.

"Were what?" Tamara is now looking hard at Tyler, hands on her hips with a look of defiance.

Berrana intervenes, "He did not mean to prejudge, Tamara, he has never met a parkin before, would you think badly about Tina?"

"No, Tina is my friend. She made a mistake the first day I met her, too, but I saw she was trying to understand us, it is the same with the Prince and the Queen, how can they know if no one has shown them? It is up to us not to judge them too quickly and be understanding.

I'm sorry, Tamara, if I insulted you," Tyler said looking at her.

Tamara can see tears forming in the corners of his eyes and this makes her feel badly for her rashness.

"I'm sorry, too, let's be friends and understand each other before we say and do things we will regret."

"I would like that," Tyler tells the two girls, "I think we should be getting back to work before Mr. Sipp has to come looking for us."

"Let's do that," Tamara agrees.

The three make their way back to the class room to finish packing.

24

James's flight from New Hope to Wolf Creek was smooth and uneventful.

Roger picks him up from the airport, so they could go back to the office and catch up on work that has been neglected for the last week and a half.

"I really appreciate you coming to pick me up, Roger, and going to work so late."

"Think nothing of it, James, so you know, I have taken the last five days off, a mini vacation, there was nothing going on, and every time I try to contact the palace, I would get the cold shoulder from the staff. Without you here to support me and force the issue, I'm nonproductive."

"That's the Duke, Roger," James tells him.

"I really think the Duke is intimidated by you, James."

"He should be," James laughs.

They pull in to the parking lot at the back of the building, so it is a shorter walk with James' luggage.

As they pull up, they see the back door is open and the lights are on.

"James, I know it was secured when I left," Roger tells him.

"Don't stop, drive on by and park behind the next shop," James instructs.

Roger pulls the car up to the deli's back door, it's about twenty meters for the office. "Stay here, Roger, I'm going to see what's up."

James gets out very quietly and stays in the shadows as he makes his way to the open door. Stopping just shy and strains to hear any noise, there are two voices and the sound of opening and closing doors.

James with stealth makes it to the open door, peering in he sees nothing.

Just as he is about to enter, someone comes out and is face to face with James.

The man shouts to his comrades inside and at the same time takes a swing at James. He counters and grabs the assailant's arm and throws him in to the side of the building, turning just in time to see another man with a short club swinging his direction. James manages to get his arm up in time to take the blunt of the blow as a third man comes out and tackles him in the midsection driving him in to the wall.

James hears Roger shout and starts running to his aid.

About that time, James hears a gun shot from further down the alley and sees Roger going down.

The man with the club manages to get one more swing at James, this time connecting with the side of his head, things go black.

The next thing James remembers is Roger standing over him bleeding from a wound in his right shoulder.

"You OK?" Ambassador Roger asks.

"Yes, I think so, Roger, you are bleeding! We will need to get you to the hospital." James gets up and insists Roger sits down, so he can get a look at his wound. About that time, he can hear sirens coming their way. "Someone must have called the police," James tells Roger. "Where did they go, Roger?"

"As soon as you went down, they ran down the other way. I heard a car start and speed away south, there was four of them. One was standing behind the trash dumpster we drove by. I never saw him until I saw the flash from the shot. Are we a couple of fools or what?" Roger laughs, his way of dealing with the pain and to keep his mind off his shoulder.

"You could say that," as James feels blood from his brow trickle down the side of his face, adding his own laugh, "we are a pair."

After the police arrived and James saw Roger in to the ambulance for a trip to the hospital did he turn his attention to the break-in.

Making a walk through with a Sargent, he could see the damage, every piece of paper in every file-cabinet was on the floor, it was more of a warning than a break-in, and James with certainty know who was to blame.

"I can find nothing missing, Sargent," James tells him.

"I bet it is the vermin we have here in the city," the Sargent tells James, "there is a large number of them living out in the slums; one day we will gather them up and send them back to where they came from."

James did not bother contradicting him, he is probably on the Duke's payroll, sent to make certain his people got away clean, and the less I show my hand, the better off we will be in the end, but I will remember you, Sargent," he tell himself, "one day we will meet again and things will be different."

"If there is nothing more, Ambassador we will be on our way, and if you find anything missing, give me a call," the Sargent tells him.

James did not clean up anything in the office, he only secured the door and went to see how Roger is doing.

He parked Roger's car with his bags still in the back seat, looking in the mirror he could see a cut above his right eye, not bad he tells himself; I have had worse.

The hospital is only eight blocks away, so James decides to walk, the fresh air and exercise will do him good and it will give him time to think.

Either the Duke is getting careless or he is getting desperate, he has all the advantages, why would he do something like that? There was nothing to gain, only things to lose, I wonder if there is something I'm missing.

The walk only took a short time.

James stopped at the information desk and asks for the status of Roger Davis.

"He is in surgery, it will be at least four hours before you will be able to see him, sir."

James saw a bar about half a block from the hospital, so a drink will put him at ease and kill two hours.

The bar is the Drunken Pig, it is a lively place, packed to capacity with blaring music.

James sees a place at the bar and makes his way to it, sitting down the bartender is quick with service.

"What will it be, friend?"

"Whiskey with a back."

Coming up the bartender tells him, and before James could turn around, it was sitting in front of him.

James drank two more and spent three hours watching the people not talking to anyone, lost in thought most of the time.

James told the barkeep thanks for the service and gave him a twenty-note bill.

Heading for the door, James notices a man watching him from the other side of the room; he did not show him any indication that he recognized him from the office, intentionally stumbling as he walked, James started his walk back to the hospital putting on a good show.

There were very few lights on the street, so the first opportunity James vanished in to a shadow and waited for his stalker.

It did not take long, the stalker rounded the corner, and James had him cold, a right hook to the jaw and down he goes.

James picks him up and throwing him in to an alley to find out some information.

Grabbing him by the throat and lifting him off his feet, James ask his first question, "Who do you work for?"

"David Bean, I work for David Bean," the stalker tells him, gasping for breath.

James did not expect that. He released him and the stalker lands on his feet, holding his throat.

"I'm sorry about your friend and me hitting you. I need us to get away to protect my cover, and I had no ideal Steve was going to shoot your friend, he will pay for that but not right now.

The shooter's name is Steve Carter, he is the Duke's enforcer, we still need to tie him to the Duke, and up to now, we only have Steve's story and no real evidence linking him to the Duke and his crimes, you will need to be satisfied with that for now. Have you heard anything pertaining to the Prince?"

"No, the only thing I'm getting is the Duke is alluding to him being King by the end of summer, nothing more. I think it's my turn to apologize for the punch to the jaw."

"It was justified, Ambassador, one day I hope you and I can sit down for a drink, you're my kind of friend, one that steps up, not away. I will need to go before I blow my cover. Good luck, Ambassador."

"You, too, and be safe, I know this kind of work," James tells him.

The Ambassador makes it back just as Roger is being moved to a room from recovery.

"How you feeling, Roger?"

"Been better, James, and how is your head? That was a solid lick you took."

"I will be OK, you get better, and if the police ask you anything, tell them you don't remember. I got a good look at the guy that hit you, James."

"Roger, listen to me, you did not see him nor can you identify him, you will have to trust me for now, I will explain when I can."

"I will do as you say Ambassador, but tell me this, will this help bring down the Duke?"

"Yes."

"Then I'm in."

25

The transport has never looked so shiny.

"How much wax did you use, Ted?" Billy asks him.

"Not that much, Skipper, I did use a lot of elbow grease, don't she look spectacular?"

Billy has never seen any of the transports look this good, every centimeter is cleaned and waxed to a high shine.

"She looks great, Rocky, good job, it's too bad that the VIP we will be carrying will never notice all your hard work, but I do, thanks."

It only took one day to receive orders after the VIP course was complete, their next stop will be Wolf Creek to transport a grope to Crown's View, no manifest was issued, a hush hush flight.

Kranstan Point to Wolf Creek only takes one hour.

"We will be departing at 14:00, Ted, so start buttoning her up, you can go over her in the morning, our departure time at Wolf Creek is 10:00 if you start at 06:00; you should have all the Finnish wiped off by then," Billy laughs.

"Not funny, Skipper. I only want her to look good."

"I know you do, Rocky, and I'm only giving you a hard time because I can, she looks great."

The flight to Wolf Creek was uneventful, giving the two time to reflect on the last two weeks.

"Skipper, did you see Captain Hartwell's aide? He was in operation after you received our orders for Wolf Creek, the supply office is down the hall. I was getting the wax and I saw him coming out. I stayed out of view. I find that odd, Skipper!"

"You're correct, Rocky. I saw the two of them the day before our final test. I don't like it, and I really don't trust either of them, so keep your eyes open."

"Skipper, can I ask you a personal question?"

"Shoot, Rocky."

"Will you give me Bell's phone number?"

The question shocked Billy, "Why would you want her number?"

"I do not really need to tell you that, do I?" grinning ear to ear.

"Rocky, it would never work, there are too many differences."

"Are you saying I'm not good enough for your cousin?"

"Not at all, Ted, you are a fine officer and a good human being, but there is the problem."

"I don't follow you, Skipper."

"I was not going to tell you this, but Bell is not my cousin, she is a Sub-Driver."

"Come on, Captain, you don't expect me to buy that."

"It's the truth, Ted. If Bell was my cousin, I would be happy to have you in the family, but she is what she is, a Sub-Driver. Look, Ted, the day I checked on the ship at depot, you remember. I met the Sub-Driver; they were supervising the re-fit. Ben told me something about a restriction being lifted on fraternization, only one at a time could participate, and it was Bell's turn, so I told her she could accompany you and I and learn from us, don't you think she was a little naive for being as intelligent as she was? Think, Ted, everything she did was like it was her first time because it was."

"Now that you bring it up, yes, it was a bit out of place, Skipper."

"Even the kiss in the parking lot," Billy tells Ted.

"You saw that, Skipper?"

"Yes, but it was not the right time to say anything, you and her were having such a good time and I was not going to spoil it for either of you."

"Are we OK, Rocky, no hard feelings?"

"No regrets, Skipper, I did have a great time and I think she did, too."

"I know she did, Rocky."

Wolf Creek came in to view and the two started the check list and took the appropriate steps for landing. Ted took the controls to get more stick time and refine his piloting skills.

The landing was a little bumpy but not bad for his third landing in the transport, most take a year of heavy training to master these older ships, the controls are heavy and touchy.

After the ship was parked and secured, Billy and Ted head for their rooms; it has almost been three weeks since they were last here.

"Skipper, after I check my room, I'm going back to the flight l ine to do a little more spit and polish on the old girl, is that OK with you?"

"Yes, if you must, but she looks good now, Rocky!"

"I would like to make our first mission as VIP. transporters memorable, there are a few pleases I have not gotten to yet, like the hellhole panel and the avionics hatch, I know you can't see them unless you get under the ship, but I know they're there."

"Go ahead, Rocky, clean your heart out if it makes you feel better."

"Thanks, Skipper."

Ted spends another three hours cleaning under the ship, every latch is spotless, no finger marks anywhere, every window inside and out are flawless, no streaks or smudges, the hand rails leading from the passenger compartment to the bridge shine with a luster that they have not seen in years.

Ted stands in front of the transport as the sun is getting ready to go down, "You're ready," he tells her, wiping one more spot on the nose with his sleeve.

As Ted is passing the last ship on the flight line heading home, he passes two men heading to the line, each is carrying a large tool box. What caught Ted's attention was the fact the box looked light, the men were not passing it from hand to hand like most do on the 100 or so meter walk, and the fact that the box was dirty, no self-respecting line mechanic would let his tools get that dirty.

"I'm glad they're not working on my ship," Ted tells himself, "my ship is in tip top shape."

26

Captain Hartwell and the Duke are sitting in the Duke's staff-car off the main runway watching the air ships come in, waiting for one particular ship, one piloted by the fool they have chosen to be their fall guy.

The radio crackles with the traffic.

"Here he comes, your lordship," Hartwell tells the Duke.

As they sit and watch Billy's transport sways a little and bounced on three wells, the glee on the Duke's face was evident, the Captain had found their man.

"I was going to give you these later, but I'm happy now, so here you go," tossing them to Hartwell.

"Major insignia, thank you, my lord."

"The plans have been moved up; instead of waiting for them to travel to the games at the summer solstices, we will do it tomorrow. Have your men fix the ship tonight, no slip ups, Major, I'm counting on you."

"I will not let you down, my lord."

"See that you don't."

The ride to the officer's quarters did not take long, and the entire drive the Duke was beside himself with joy. I will be king, he repeated over and over.

"You should know, Major, you almost lost the Star I promised you last night; someone had the chance, but he was unaware of the bounty, so if I was you, I would start working on it soon."

With that the Duke's car drove off with the Duke still repeating, I will be king.

The plan is simple, place a screwdriver in the control rod clevis so after Zercoff pulls back on the controls for liftoff, it will not return to neutral, continuing the climb until it makes a complete loop ending up nose first in the ground at 200 KPH.

End of the Prince and the Queen.

Zercoff will be at fault.

The Duke will be King.

Now all we need to do is take care of the Drivers, the Duke has that arranged, too.

27

Dale has been frantic trying to reach Matt and Connie, so much so he has brought it to the Steward.

"It's been four days, Peabody, and every time I enquirer at T.S., the station manager tells me they do not have any information on their whereabouts. The last thing I had was a message from the government office on a secure line telling me that there was an altercation with the Royal Guard and the clandestine use of Drivers and Drones. Then there's this." Dale takes out the letter he was passed as he was leaving T.S., handing it to Peabody. "They are going to use a Driver to start a war, don't let them please."

"I did not think much about it until I received the cryptic message from Matthew, there is too much in common to dismiss it now."

"There is more," Peabody tells him, "out on the islands, there has been eight deaths all connected to human driver control."

"I did not know that was possible," Dale tells Peabody.

"It is not," he replies, "at least not without killing the one in control of the Drone, that fact is from Clarence."

"There is a Dr. Pierce experimenting with that process; he's a Lost One from T.S. working out in the islands. Now it looks like he is working with the Duke and using the Royal Guard for security."

"Is he crazy?" Dale blurts, "If the Duke could pull that off, he would have every Lost One sent back to space with or without a ship, he will be signing his own death warrant."

"You and I both know that," Peabody tells him, "apparently Dr. Pierce don't."

"Dale, I think I can give you a little peace of mind, I have an undercover team at T.S. I will pass along your concerns and have them keeping an eye out for your people, but it will be forty-five days before we can send any one to Trinity Station, so whatever is going on, Matt is going to have to handle it on his own."

"I will let the Sub-Driver know about the Royal Guards involvement at T.S., but our hands are tied until the night cycle starts.

28

"Wake up, Connie, wake up".

"What happened, Matt? Where are we? Why are my hands tied?"

"Take it slow, Connie, try sitting up first."

"I have a ringing in my ears and my mouth tastes of gunpowder," she tells Matt.

"That was the stun grenade they used on us, Connie."

"The last thing I remember, Matt, is you at the door and me unlocking it to let you in, the next thing I know I'm waking up here."

"I should have seen it coming, Connie, as I was walking up to the door there were three men working in the hall, one was up a ladder looking in the ceiling, one was holding the ladder, the third was looking through a bag he had on the floor.

"As you unlocked the door, I turned in time to see the one on the ladder firing a grenade launcher at our feet. The blast knocked you back in to the room, it sent me flying backwards in to the arms of the man looking through the bag. I think he hit me with a club, the next thing I'm waking up here, I do have a knot on the back of my head.

"What is going to happen to us, Matt?"

"I don't know, Connie. I do know Dale will be looking for us, the message was sent and I got a confirmation reply, the down side is the day cycle starts in one day; if he has not sent any one by then, we will be on our own for at least forty-five days. I have managed to loosen my ropes, I am going to leave them on for now to keep our captors thinking they're in control, you do the same, Connie, but not all the way. The one that tied these knots wasted rope, he is a novice, pull on only one of the four raps until you get it next to the knot, then work on the knot, it should come easy."

They hear voices beyond the door, only some of the word are discernible, stupid and reckless are among them.

The door opens and one man comes in carrying two hoods, "If you give me any problems, I will thump your head," the man tells Matt, patting a club he has hanging from his belt.

"Give no resistance, Connie," Matt tells her.

"Good advice, tough guy," the man with the hoods tells them, grabbing Matt's head, pushing it forward, slipping the hood over it.

Matt can hear Connie gasp as he did the same to her.

The next thing Matt knows, there is a new voice in the room.

"Hello, Mister Dollar, and you, too, Miss Burch. I'm sorry for the rough treatment, but I need to know what you told the Steward, your answer will decide your fate. There is three things that could happen, you could be let go and never hear about this again, be put to a quick death or a very slow and painful one, the option is yours, it depends on how you answer and whether I believe your answer, do I make myself clear?"

"You should let Connie go in that case, she knows nothing about anything, I sent the message. I alone killed the people in the drift, she is only guilty by association."

"And let my bargaining leverage go, no way," the stranger tells Matt, "now let's start at the beginning."

"What did you see?"

"We saw that someone destroyed the location marker in the main drift, so we looked a bit closer; we found the Drones and the Driver.

We tried to go about our business, but the next thing we know there are people shooting at us, what were we to do? We defended ourselves."

"And the message to the Steward?" the voice asks.

Matt explained he messaged Dale his supervisor to cover himself, "After all I know three people were dead."

"I believe you, Matt," the voice tells him, "now the question is what to do with it."

"I will come back later and give you my decision."

Matt hears the door shut and the lock turn.

"Connie," Matt whispers, "we need to get out of here now! Start working on your restraints."

Two minutes later, Matt is free, hood off, looking around.

Connie gives a sigh of victory as her ropes come free also.

"Matt, the man that was talking to you, he was at the meeting with Dale, his name is Mall I think?"

Matt moves over to the door and putts his ear to the door to try to hear anything on the other side.

"All quiet out there," he indicated to Connie.

Matt checks his pockets for anything he could use on the lock, empty.

He looks over at Connie and she is pulling a hair pin out of her hair, handing it to him without a word, said, "We make a good team, Bubbles," he tells her, trying to lighten the moment.

"Yes, we do," she replies, "now let's show them who they are dealing with," shooting Matt a defiant look of determination.

Before they could make any progress on the door, they hear someone entering the outer room, grumbling to himself about always getting the shit jobs, yelling as he is unlocking the door.

Without a word between them, they instinctively grab the hoods and put them on their heads and place their hands behind there back to simulate being tied.

The man flings the door open and addresses Matt, "I'm going to have a little fun with you, tough guy." Grabbing Matt by, the collar spinning him in to the wall back first.

Connie hears the thud and knows the guard's attention is on Matt, so she risks removing the hood.

She sees the guard has Matt pinned against the wall; without thinking she picks up the rope that was used to tie her hands, making a loop she slips it over the guard's head, putting all of her weight on it, making the guard tumble backwards on top of her.

A moment later, Matt is on top of him, pounding his face in to putty.

Connie pushes the guard off of her and he laid there not moving.

"Is he dead?" she asks Matt.

"No, but we will be if we don't get moving." Matt reaches down and relieves the guard of his keys, radio, and club. "Let's go, Bubbles."

The room outside was not a room but a hallway.

"Which way, Matt?" Connie asks.

"He came through a door close by, you check that side and I'll check this side." On Connie's first try, she had it, stairs going up. "I'll take a look first, stay here, Connie, I'll call you if it's clear." Matt goes up the stairs fast but not reckless, stopping at a door at the top; looking out he sees a hallway and across from the door, an elevator. "All clear," he calls to Connie.

Matt is already at the elevator when Connie comes through the door, as if it was timed deliberately, Connie steps beside Matt the door opens and the two of them step in. "Up or down?" Matt announces.

"Up, always up," Connie responds.

The door closes. Matt pushes the next to the top button on the panel and up they go.

Looking over at Connie, "I need to hide the club," he informed her, putting the club under his coat with the head in his waistband with the handle right under his armpit. Matt switches off the radio and puts it in his coat pocket opposite the club.

They go up twenty floors and the door opens, time is not on their side, so they step through the door and start walking somewhere.

The two had gone about twenty meters and they came in to the main corridor.

"That way is the restaurants and the public areas," pointing right, "left is to the operations center and that way is to the port of entry," Connie indicates.

"Let's go find something to eat, there are several places that are not very viable," Matt tells her, touching his back pocket, "one problem, they have my billfold."

"Not to worry, Matt," Connie reaches in to her bra and pulls out at least five twenty-note and two 100-note bills, "never leave home without it," she winks at Matt.

The two find their way to a small mom and pop eatery with a discrete view of the main corridor.

After they ate their fill, it was time to decide their plan of action.

"It's no good, Connie, we could never hide for forty-six days, the last ship is ready to go now; if we miss it, there will not be another for at least forty-five days, we will be caught."

"Matt, the logistics are too complicated, we would need to find two suites just to get out on the pad, a place to hide on board with air, water, and food for three days. I think we should take our chances here."

"I just want to get us off this rock, Connie, but you're right, our chances are better here than on that ship, and if we are discovered by the wrong people, a walk out an airlock would be our fate."

"Who else was at that meeting besides that mall guy?"

Connie thinks for a few seconds, "There is two I think may help, Trevor, Neal, and Bob Better."

Matt calls the waitress over and asks her if there is a directory he could use and a public phone close by.

"Yes," she tells him, "I will have a phone and directory here in a moment," smiling flirtatiously at Matt, walking away with a swagger.

"A new friend, Matthew?" Connie teases him.

"Who knows," Matt replies, "we could use a few."

With the phone at the table and the directory with it, Connie starts going through the listings, "Here is Trevor Neal, I do not see a Bob Better."

"Trevor will have to do then," Matt tells Connie, pushing the phone over to her.

As Connie is dialing, Matt is watching out the window, he sees six men coming down the corridor, two stop at the shop across the hall and down twenty meters, the next two are ten meters from their place of hiding on the same side, the last two go down to the intersection and stop.

Matt reaches over and pushes the stop button on the phone, Connie looks up and sees Matt's look and knows there is something up.

He nods to the two across the hall and the two almost in front of them. They each pick up the menus to hide their faces.

Talking behind the menus, Connie asks, "What are we going to do?"

"Let's see if there is a back door or something," Matt gets up to go look and sees the waitress looking at the two of them hard. Matt sits back down, "Connie, I think there is another problem."

The waitress goes to the front door and looks left, then right, spotting the four men standing guard in the corridor, turns and faces Matt and Connie, she nods her head to the back of the restaurant and heads that way.

Matt shrugs to Connie and gets up to follow.

Connie does the same.

The waitress leads them to a storage room and opens the door, "You'll be safe in here," she tells them, "I'm going to lock you in, it will keep someone from opening it and finding you here, you have to trust me."

Matt and Connie know they have no choice but to do so; the alternative is to fight their way out, and they know they would lose if it came to that, so trust they must.

29

Ted arrived on the flight-line by 06:00.

The first thing he did was make a pass through the passenger compartment, all looked good, windows clean, carpet and seats spotless, nothing out of place.

Then he starts the pre-flight.

Fuel tanks, full.

All oil reservoirs, checked.

Control surfaces for damage.

Skin for separation or damage.

Landing struts and tiers.

By the time Billy got there, the ship was ready to go.

"She in tip top shape, Skipper," Ted reports.

"That's good, Rocky," Billy replies, "we still have two hours before we will taxi to the gate and pick up our mystery passengers. I'm going to take a nap until then, wake me when it's time."

"Aye, aye, Skipper."

Ted cannot let anything get by on this trip, he is determined to make it perfect, attention to every detail.

"The light was bad last night when I did the hellhole panel and the avionics bays, I think I'll take one more look."

Ted gets down on his hands and knees and starts making his way to the hellhole panel when he sees a dirty spot on the latch; that will not do, he tells himself, taking out his rag from his back pocket, wiping it off.

As the rag goes over the spot, it leaves a long trail of grease, "There is no way I missed that last night, even with the bad light, I would have seen that."

It's on both latches, Ted notices, that's not a coincidence, so he unlatches them and crawls in to see what he can.

Ted takes out his flashlight and shines it aft, he sees where the grease came from, it's on the baring on the control rod for the lift jet pivot.

The mystery thickens, Ted tells himself, so he climbs in further to where the control arm passes a bell crank, then it changes direction and goes up.

Ted is ready to get out when he sees it, a small screwdriver in the clevis, it would allow the rod to go forward but not back; with clarity Ted understands he did not remove it, he will show Billy.

"Skipper, wake up."

"What time is it, Rocky?"

"07:30, Skipper, you need to come take a look at what I found."

"Give me till 08:00, Rocky."

"No, Skipper, you need to see this!"

"Later, Rocky, it will be fine, I know you will do a good job."

"Damn it, Skipper! You need to see this."

Now that got Billy's attention, "What's wrong, Ted?"

"Last night when I was going back to my room, I saw two men going out on the flight line, each was carrying a big tool box, but it looked light and the box was greasy. This morning I was looking over the underbelly of the ship and I saw grease marks on the hellhole door, so I looked inside, you need to go see for yourself, Skipper, everything is as I found it."

Ten minutes later, Billy crawls out from under the ship with the screwdriver in his hand, "Good job, Rocky; if this was there when we took off, we would be dead and our passengers as well." For the next hour, Billy and Ted went over every centimeter of the transport. "Everything looks good, Rocky, let's button her up and head for the gate to pick up our passengers."

With Billy at the controls for the trip to the gate and Ted sitting at the copilot's seat, he was as nervous as a kitten, he fully understood the situation; someone was trying to kill their passengers with them along with them.

"It takes an evil person to do something like this, Ted," Billy comments, "so stay alert and we will be fine."

"I bet Hartwell has something to do with it, Skipper."

"I think you're right, Rocky, that means its headquarters sanctioned and we just screwed up their plans. I think we are going to get someone in big trouble," Billy laughs, "and I bet it's Hartwell."

As Billy parks the transport at the gate, it's 09:40, the party will not to be here until 10:00.

Ted heads back to the loading ramp to make preparation for the receiving of their passengers and luggage.

Billy is standing tall awaiting their charges when who walks up, Major Hartwell and Captain Nash, accompanied by two flight attendance.

"Captain Zercoff, here are your orders," handing them to Billy, and these ladies will be accompanying you for the flight to Crowns View as your flight attendance."

"Thank you, Major, and congratulations on your promotion," thinking to himself, "I know why you got that promotion but keeping it all to himself and playing his part well."

"Ladies, I leave you in Zercoff's hands," with that Hartwell and Nash turns around and heads back to the terminal.

"Hello, ladies, you can call me Captain, Billy, or Skipper, whichever you like, a flight crew is family, so we do not stand on protocol," holding out his hand, they each shake hands with Billy introducing themselves at the same time, "there is Lieutenant Rachael Light and Lieutenant Harriet Light, twin sisters, twenty-years-old fresh out of the academy, this is their first assignment."

Billy opens the orders and is shocked, "Ladies, it looks like you're starting your career at the top, do you know who we will be transporting today?"

Nether had any idea.

"It looks like we will have the Queen and the Prince with us today," they, too, looked shocked.

"Go see Lieutenant Linch, he's the one standing over there," Billy points, "he'll take care of you and get you set up for the flight, our charges will be here in fifteen minutes."

Billy is really pissed off now, that makes it nine people whose life is nothing to Hartwell and his cohort. He is an animal with no regard for human life and so is the person giving the orders. Something must be done about this, I can't report this, it will only be white washed and made to look like it was Linch or myself that left that screwdriver there, no, it will need to be handled another way.

30

Last night when Sandra made her nightly visit to Tyler's room, she was greeted by a very exuberant young man.

"What are you doing up at this hour?" she asks him, "you know we have a big day tomorrow."

"I know, Mom! I was waiting for you to come by. I need to ask you if Tamara and Berrana could fly with us in the morning, please, Mom, please, please, please? I'll work even harder on the set up at Crowns View, not making any problems, please."

He has asked so little of her over the years, even when she knows he need her, he would sit quietly as she would go through one of her panic attack', only trying to comfort her, putting his needs behind hers.

The look of joy on Tyler's face and his spirited actions made it impossible to say no.

"Yes, they can accompany us." He jumped up and flung his arms around Sandra's neck and hugged her so tight, it startled her; they stayed that way for several seconds, embracing each other, trying to make up for years of neglect and seclusion. "Now you get some sleep, young man, I'll be in here by seven to get you up, good night," she tells him as she turns out the light and heads for the door.

"Good night, Mom, I love you."

Sandra did not make out the door before the first tear ran down her cheek.

When Sandra made it to the elevator where Mae was waiting, tears were flowing freely.

"What is the matter, miss?" Mae asks her.

"Tears of joy, Mae, only tears of joy. I love that boy, Mae," reaching over and giving Mae a hug of her own, "and I love you, too, I don't know how I could make it without you all these years."

The morning started out very good, Tyler and the girls were up and waiting for her in the common room.

Sandra heard the laughter long before she got there.

Mae was sitting in her usual chair, the only difference was she was an hour earlier and you could see she was enjoying the children, the smile on her face was apparent and could not be hidden.

"Well," Sandra declares, "we are all up and ready I see."

"Mother, I hope you don't mind, but I called Tina this morning at five."

At five Sandra looks at Tyler with a grin and her head tilted slightly to the side with her eye looking up at him, "A little early, don't you think?"

"I had to let her know Tamara and Berrana was going to fly with us, she said she was going to check with you but told the girls anyway, that was OK, right?"

"Yes, it is, my sweet, let's go have breakfast."

When the staff started coming in, it was apparent that this morning was not going to be like most; there was joy in the room, a happiness that the room has not seen in years, even Mr. Harper could see it.

Sandra called the head butler over to inform him about the changes in their itinerary, "There will be two more traveling with us, Mr. Harper."

"I see, my lady, the girls?" He nods their way.

"Yes, I think it will help keep the Prince occupied."

"Very good, my lady," Herald bows to his Queen, excusing himself to go make final preparations.

Tyler, Tamara, and Berrana all come and stood in front of Sandra, "Mother, can we go to my room, so I can show them the old wing of the palace, you can see it from the window."

"It's almost ten, Tyler," Sandra reminds him. "There is no time to go back to your room."

Sandra looks around, and everyone is assembling in the common room, the only one not here is Mr. Harper, he will be down at the main entry to the palace with the personal luggage and the porters.

Libby, Mr. Sipp, Tina, Beatrice, and the two girls go down the elevator first.

Even though there is no fanfare, there is still tradition to follow, the last to arrive downstairs is the royal family and the first to leave the palace.

As soon as the door to the elevator opens on the ground floor, Sandra, Tyler, and Mae go straight out the front doors in to the waiting limousine, the remainder of the party will ride in the following vans with the luggage.

The motorcade is proceeded by police cars with their lights flashing, stopping traffic, letting the royal limousine and their party pass unhindered.

Sandra notices there is Royal Guard vehicles stopping traffic at all major intersections with flagmen making sure traffic stops.

"The Duke is making certain we get to the airport safe and sound, Mae," Sandra tells her, "I bet there will be a party at the palace tonight."

The motorcade arrives right on time, 10:00 on the nose.

The transport ship is docked at the boarding ramp and the welcoming crew is awaiting their arrival.

31

It only took Carol and Arthur a little over two hours to visit the metals exchange, but during their research, they learned there are several different sources of micro platinum foil.

"We will need to visit the jewelry manufacturers on Caster Island, there are at least three there," she tells Tom. The man at the exchange was confident that there is a supply there.

"Good work, Captain," said the Senator.

"In all fairness, Senator, it was Sargent Baits; he recognizes if he dug deeper, there would be more information to be gleaned from the clerk. I would have stopped when the man at the counter said there are no sales for that product."

"Captain West, you should know that is what I do for a living," smiling a mischievous smile at Carol, "so I thank you for the compliment, but it was instinct and experience, nothing more."

"Before we came back, Senator, I called my executive officer to check on the other information you ask for; there has been no one by that name on any passenger list to the islands for the last seven months and the recipient of cargo showed the same results, he must be using an alias, or someone else is helping him."

"Captain West, you and Sargent Baits should call it a night and catch a high-speed water taxi to Caster Island in the morning," Tom tells them, "it will be 21:00 soon and it's about a five-hour ride one way."

Carol and Arthur say their good-nights and make their way to their rooms.

"There have been no more signals picked up by my drone. I am going to land it on one of the Island," Clarence tells Adam and Tom, "if they rebroadcast, it will start a search."

"I was wondering," Sub-Driver Adam inquires, "this technology for life-like drones is not a new thing, is it?"

"No, Major, it is not."

The expression on Clarence's face drastically changes with the content of the explanation he is about to give to Adam.

"They were created as a weapon, Major, like your first impression, they were used to mingle with the creators, giving them the ability to infiltrate vital sections of the ships defenses, taking them offline at a critical moment insuring the destruction of the only thing standing in the way of the total annihilation of a species."

"The species still exists, Sub-Driver, so your side triumphed in the end," Adam states more as a statement than a question.

"No, Major, the side I was representing was the side that was intent on exterminating the makers, are you surprised at that?"

"Well, yes, Sub-Driver, I am."

"So, you can understand my full commitment to preserving the species we call the makers, have you ever wondered why is it I alone have one personality and every other Sub-Driver has three?"

"Yes, that question has been proposed by others, and I believe it has merit," Adam said to Clarence.

"You are correct, Adam, it should be addressed because it is closely linked to the situation at hand. The answer is I had to damage my siblings to a point that you could consider them dead, it was necessary to prevent my master from succeeding with her plans of exterminating the Makers. After my siblings were deactivated and all upper cognitive thought processes eliminated.

The next step with the help of twelve Parkens volunteers, I began integrating them in place of my siblings. They would become in essence a part of me but only seventy-two hours after the drone control is activated, after that they, too, become in essence dead, with the lower functions still working, giving me greater abilities at a very large ethical price, do you understand, Adam? It was never about me or my race, it was about protecting those who could not protect themselves, so you see I have an obligation to people in my past and those yet to be conceived to do the right thing at any cost, including my own demise. I could justify my actions with that fact, Adam, knowing that billions of lives could be saved, but Desman is doing it for his own vanity and greed, the people he is using do not understand the outcome. Right now, each time he tests the process, a life is lost for nothing! We must stop him."

Doctor Fields and Captain Tucker called Major Potter at almost 23:30."I thought we had something, Adam, but it turned out to be a patient suffering from dementia who had walked away from a nursing home," Frank tells him.

"I had my hopes up. I gave several of the E.R. doctors my phone number, they will give me a call if anyone shows up with the matching symptoms," Susan said, adding her part to the conversation, "right now we are on our way to Vision Island, there are two hospitals to check there, so we will spend the night there and catch up with you in the morning."

"Sounds good," Adam tells his team, "keep me informed if anything changes. To keep you two up to date, Captain West and Arthur had some luck on the platinum, they will be going to Caster Island in the A.M., and there has been no luck on Doctor Pierce yet. See you in the morning," Adam tells them, "good night."

"Senator, I was just informed by Steward Smit that there is additional information; it seems the Royal Guard is involved on T.S., providing security for the dismantling and shipment of Driver components, that confirms my assumption about Trinity Station as being the source of the Driver equipment. There are only five places on Tarkaneay that could be the source, T.S. being the highest on the list. It is the only one not active."

"Clarence, I know of Kranstan Point, New Hope, and Rocket Town with their active Drivers, and we all assumed there was one on Trinity Station, where is the fifth?" asks Tom.

"It is on Bray Island."

"Should we not look there before we go any further, Sub-Driver?" asks Adam.

"No," responds Clarence, "that is where Master-Driver Michael is or at least his Avatar is there."

"No one has ever talked with Master-Driver Michael, and now you tell us he has been on Bray Island all this time?" Tom said.

"Yes, Tom, that is the truth, he wished to be with the only remaining descendants of Athena. She is the one that started the rebellion that stopped Master-Driver Sheila, he feels there is a debt he owes to her and her descendants, he would not be alive if it was not for her."

The Avatar of Clarence stops for a second as his expression changes, "I stand corrected, gentlemen. Michael has just informed me there is no descendants left on Bray, the last departed four days ago; she is now in the company of the Queen and Prince, this gives me great hope. Michael is happy with this change, it presented me with apprehension with the prospect of her leaving Michael, sending him in to a depressed state, but the opposite has happened, this is good news. There is always hope on the horizon if one waits and allows it to happen on its own.

We know Dezman is calibrating the transceiver keeping the drone's link active; as soon as he rebroadcasts, I would like to be in the air doing a search grid. Once his lab is found, we can confiscate the equipment and Doctor Pierce will be sent to my ship, keeping him out of trouble and denying any further experiments in driver control."

"There is nothing more we can do tonight. I suggest we all call it a night and get some sleep, we can reconvene at the transport in the morning and wait for Doctor Pierce to rebroadcast.

Adam, can you have Doctor Fields, Captain Tucker, and the flight crew meet us there at 07:00?" Tom asks,

"I will have Captain West assign twelve security officers to join us; with the Royal Guards involvement, there may be a fight, and I do not like the prospect of being outgunned."

32

Matt and Connie have been in the storage room for more than six hours when they hear the door being unlocked.

"Be on your guard, Connie," Matt whispers.

As the door opens, they can see the waitress peeking around.

"Everything OK?" she inquires, stepping inside, closing the door behind her.

"I could us a bathroom," Connie tells her.

"There is one right next door, the place is empty, except for us," she tells Connie, "but don't go in to the dining room, there are still guards roaming the corridors."

Connie gets up quickly and hurries out.

The waitress smiles at Matt and tells him, "I tried to get back sooner, but the station is in an uproar, you two have caused quite a commotion here. My name is Kimmy, Kimmy Post," presenting her hand to Matt.

Kimmy is a petite woman in her mid-thirties, short brown hair, very athletic with several tattoos on the upper part of her arm, only the bottom of it could be seen due to the sleeves of her blouse; it reminds Matt of something he has seen before, but he cannot put his finger on it.

Matt accepts her hand, "Matthew Dollar, my companion is Connie Burch."

"I know your names already, there is a bounty out for the two of you; the story is you two are cold-blooded killers intent on killing as many as you can and, NO, I do not believe the story nor am I trying to collect on the bounty, so relax."

About that time, Connie comes back in to the storage room with a look of relief.

"What did I miss?" looking to Matt.

"Connie, this is Kimmy," Connie nods to her host, "she just told me we are wanted for cold-blooded murder," Matt tells her.

Connie gasps, "Murder, who did we kill in cold-blood?"

The constable said, "It was a group of five sightseers in the caverns and three Royal Guardsmen, unarmed naturally. They located a tug with several bullet holes in it, blood everywhere but no bodies yet."

"Can you tell me your side of the story?" Kimmy asks.

"Connie and I work for the Steward's negotiation team. We had some free time, so we went exploring; we discovered a secret lab disassembling a Driver. In our attempt to escape, I did kill three Royal Guardsmen in self-defense. Connie had nothing to do with it, it was all me," Matt tells her, describing the ordeal they endured and the flight for their lives, the Guardsman that sacrificed his life to save Connie being held prisoner, and their escape.

"You cannot stay here for long; you will be discovered. Not all the people that work here is to be trusted, you were lucky Sue was not working today, she is part of the syndicate run, my Floyd Mall," she explains.

"I, too, work for the Steward, deep cover operative from the intelligence division, we have had our eye on him for some time now. I will get you out, my partner is waiting for me to give him the go ahead with the diversion, there is a stairwell thirty meters left, wait in till you hear the fire alarm. I will see if the way is clear and meet you there."

With that said, Kimmy makes her way to the front door, looking down the hallway, turning left she disappears out of sight.

"Matt, can we trust her?" Connie inquires.

"I don't think we have any other option," he replies.

About that time, the alarm sounds.

"Let's move, Connie," Matt leads the way, staying close to the wall using any cover they can find.

Reaching the stairwell in a matter of seconds.

And as promised, Kimmy is waiting.

"We go down," she indicates with hand signals that Matt is familiar with. Not waiting for a response, she heads down, five floors they descended before coming to a stop, holding her hand up and making a fist like a scout would to stop the advance, she proceeds on. Moments go by, and she is back motioning them forward, through the door and down the hall, five doors down. She ducks inside closely followed by the pair, with the door closed, they all breathe a sigh.

Matt is smiling, looking at Kimmy, "You were a scout," he tells her.

"Yes," she replies, the seventh recon," pulling up her sleeve revealing the rest of the tattoo, "it is the motto of the seventh always forward, leave none behind."

"I was with the tenth," he tells her, rolling up his sleeve, "the gates of hell open before the tenth."

"Were you under General Bradic, or should I call him back stabbing Bradic."

"You do know him; he is the reason I'm out of the service."

"Did you know he was killed in a training exercise last year? They think his XO pushed him over a cliff, but there was no evidence indicating it was anything but a misstep on his part."

"Karma, it was karma," repeats Connie.

"I think you are right," Matt adds. "Now what?" looking at Kimmy.

"We wait, it's the other guys turn for now; my partner will be here shortly with an update and supplies, so get some sleep if you can, tomorrow we try to make it to the emergency evacuation point, we have a ship waiting for such a need. You do know how to pilot one, don't you?" Kimmy asks Matt.

"It's been five years, I would think things have not changed that much, is it a Rabbit or a Speer class?" Matt asks.

"A Rabbit," Kimmy replies, "there will be cargo ship to intercept you two days out."

"That will be cutting it close, they're only designed for a two-day trip," Matt reminds Kimmy.

"For three people," she reminds Matt, "and there will only be two of you, that give you a 50% margin on fuel and life support, or would you like to stay here and take your chances with Mall?" Two hours pass before Kimmy declares, "My partner is here, the two of you in the back room until I give you the all clear."

Matt and Connie do as they are told and hide.

From the back room, they can hear muffled voices and the shutting of the door; moments later Kimmy gives the all clear for them to come out.

As they enter the room, there are not two people in the room but four, plus three large suitcases next to the door.

Kimmy starts to introduce the newcomers, but Connie betas her to it, Bob Better and Trevor Neal, throwing her arms around the two men's necks hugging them tightly, "I am glad to see you two," as tears start to flow. "Dale said he trusted you two for anyone that looks out for the good of others are good people, he told me that the day we meet, you two were our first thought for help. This is my partner, Jack Kenny," Kimmy introduces him, shaking hands with Matt. Jack is a tall man in his early fifties, graying short hair and a stubbly gray beard, not real muscular but toned. "Bob and Trevor are the ones that brought us in to the investigation into Mall," Kimmy tells Matt.

"Berry Green thinks he runs the place, but we all know it's Mall that has all the power through intimidation and blackmail," Bob tells the group, "we suspect he has even had people killed and now we find out he is working with the Guard, things can only get worse."

"We will get you two out of here; if Mall finds you, you will be killed," Trevor explains, "so it is imperative we do so."

Jack speaks up, "The three of us will use the north passage and walk along the foot of the ridge out of the sun until we come to the hanger, it's about seven kilometers. The sun is not quite over the horizon yet, but it will be by this time tomorrow; the bad part is I will be stuck there for the forty-five days of summer and Kimmy will be on her own."

"No, Jack, she will have us," Bob reminds him.

Trevor recants that, "We will look after her, you have our word."

Jack outlines the plan, "At 06:30, Trevor, you report seeing Matt and Connie at the south airlock drawing his people there at 07:00; we will make our run for the hanger. Kimmy will go in advance to scout the way and warn us of any lingering guards. By 07:30, we should be on the outside out of danger from being seen, we all need to eat and get some sleep."

Bob and Trevor say their farewells and head for home.

The four remaining conspirators eat and try to sleep.

33

The Royal part arrived on schedule, Billy, Ted, and the two-flight attendance are standing in a line next to the ramp.

"Welcome aboard, your grace," Billy greets them, bowing at the same time. Ted and the attendance do the same. "I am Captain Billy Zercoff. I will be your pilot, this is my first officer, Lieutenant Ted Linch," Ted bows again, "your attendants Lieutenant Rachael Light and Lieutenant Harriet Light," they bow in unison.

Billy gestures with an out stretched arm, welcoming them to proceed up the ramp, waiting for the party to go in front of him.

Anger begins to seethe through Billy as he watches the three children go by, it would not have been nine lives lost today but fifteen, including three children, I have to do something or it will be repeated, Billy tells himself.

After the group is seated, Billy takes the first step to see that this never happens again, and he can't say what he needs to with the children listening.

"Your Lordship," addressing Sandra, "after we get airborne, would the Prince and his friends like to see the bridge?"

"Can we, Mother?" Tyler blurts.

"Yes, I think that would be nice, but be on your best behavior."

"I will, Mother," Tyler promises.

Bradly speaks up, "I would like to see that myself."

"You would be most welcome, sir," Billy replies, "I will go get us on our way then," bowing to Sandra, then making his way forward.

The tower cleared them without delay, so the transport was air born within fifteen minutes.

"Ted, I'm going to talk to the Queen about our little problem. I do not want to do it in front of the kids, so I have invited them to the bridge for a tour, do what you can to stall until I come back."

"Will do, Skipper."

Billy presses the intercom, "Rachael, will you come to the bridge?"

"Yes, sir," she replied.

Moments later Rachael was there.

"Rachael, have a seat," Billy points to the seat on the port side. "I will be bringing the children up for a tour, and I would like you here to assist. Harriet will be escorting them up soon, there will be one adult, do what you can to keep their interest until I return.

Billy reaches in to the storage box behind the pilot's seat and retrieves the screwdriver and puts it in his pocket, then make his way aft. "My Prince, are you and your friends ready for that tour?" Billy asks.

"Oh, yes," the young boy answers with noticeable excitement.

"Harriet, will you do the honors and show our guest to the bridge?" As soon as they are gone, Billy addresses the Queen. "My lady, there is something you need to know. Upon inspection of the transport this morning, this was found in the control rod of this ship," pulling out the screwdriver, "if this was still there when we took off, we would all be dead, and it was not there when we landed yesterday, someone put it there last night."

Sandra's eyes are wide with the realization that Kin made his attempt on Tyler's life, including everyone on the ship.

Mister Harper hearing this starts shaking violently when he realized the Duke was willing to throw away his life as well; he begins to sob.

Sandra looks at him, shaking her head in pity, "Do you think you are not expendable, Mister Harper? You have been doing Kin's biding for how many years? Get yourself together before the children return and reconsider your loyalties, there may be hope for you yet."

Sandra hears commotion in the back row where the porters are sitting.

One of them blurts out, "The Duke tried to kill us?"

"Yes," Sandra tells him, "now hear me well, your life means nothing to the Duke, and if you wish to survive, you will do as I say, this is to go no further, keep it quiet." All three nod their heads and speak not a word more. Sitting next to Libby is Beatrice, she is as white as a ghost, not moving or speaking. Sandra addresses her directly, "There is nothing to fear now, we will get through this, you and the girls are safe and I will see that it stays that way." Beatrice only stairs straight ahead. "I will forever be in your debt, Captain," Sandra tells Billy, bowing her head in respect.

"It was my life as well, my lady, so please think no more about it."

The Duke is getting careless, your grace," adds Mae, "we should be on our guard at all times. The more desperate he gets, the more dangerous he will be."

"Who else knows about this, Captain?" Sandra inquires.

"Only Ted, my first officer."

"You made no official report then?"

"No," Billy tells Sandra, "I think it was sanctioned and carried out by the guard, so it would do no good reporting it at this stage. I would be blamed for it or Ted would."

"We will pretend that it never happened, making the Duke believe something went wrong or the one responsible failed to do a proper job; if I know Kin, whoever it was will be in trouble or worse, sowing discontent in his ranks," Sandra smiles.

"I think that would be wise, my lady," Billy agrees, "I think I know who was given the order to do this, and if I'm right, he may be in fear for his life, making him approachable now, fear never breads loyalty. In all honesty, my lady, you need to know it was Lieutenant Linch that found it. He spent sixteen hours polishing and cleaning the transport, so if there is any praise to be had, he should be the one that gets it, not me, but if you could do me a favor, tell Ted his lady ship looks good, it would mean a lot to him."

"I can see, Sandra tells Billy, "you love this young man."

"I have not thought of it that way, but yes, he is a fine officer and a better human being than any I have met. We have only been together four weeks, and I think he would risk his life for me or anyone if he thought it necessary to do so."

"You are a wise and honorable man, Captain. I name you protector and champion of the Royal house, unofficially for now but one day, I or Tyler will make it official."

Billy bows low to show his gratitude, "Thank you, my lady, I will go forward now and send the children back."

Sandra looks over at Mae, "We need more men like that; if we did, the world would be a better place."

"So true," Mae agrees.

Billy enters the bridge to see the Prince sitting in the pilot's seat with his hands folded in his lap to ensure he touched nothing or interfered with anything Ted was doing, paying close attention to every word Ted uttered and watching his every movement.

The girls were standing behind him, watching and giggling.

Mister Sipp was in a conversation with the two Lieutenants about their new life in the Guard.

Billy stands there hearing Ted tell the Prince about his second flight, getting his space wings.

"How could anyone hurt these people? It would take a person low moral values, an animal, no, that would be giving them too much credit. An animal only kills to eat or to defend itself, this was for power and greed, the Duke will pay for this crime. I will see to it or die trying."

Billy asks if everyone had their question answered.

"Yes, Captain," the children replied.

"Very good," he tells them, "we need to get ready to land, so Lieutenants, can you escort our guest to their seats and prepare for landing?"

They all say their thanks as they exit the bridge and make their way back to their seats.

Moments later an exuberant group of kids enter the passenger compartment.

Mother Tyler declares, "I will be a pilot someday and fly like Ted, did you know he is only twenty-years-old and has his space wings already?"

Sandra smiles at the excitement in her son, it's as if he is coming out of his shell like she did only four weeks ago, new adventures and new friends, now all we have to do is keep him alive until his coronation and with people like the Captain, James, and Mister Sipp on his side; he will make a grate King.

The transport landed without any problems.

Billy and Ted make their way to the ramp to see their passengers off.

With the four standing in line waiting as the passengers departed, Sandra stops in front of Ted, looking him in the eyes.

Lieutenant Linch, your lady ship looks spectacular. I have never seen a better-looking transport ever, keep up the good work," shooting Billy a quick smile, then continued down the ramp.

After they were alone, Ted turns to Billy, "You did that, didn't you?"

"Did it make you happy, Rocky?" Billy asks.

"Skipper, you're the best."

"Come on, let's go to operations and get our return orders."

The GDF military post at Crown View is very small, there is only one hanger and an operations center with no more than a dozen men assigned to it.

Billy, Ted, Rachael, and Harriet make their way to operations to file the report and get their new orders.

"Captain, we have no orders for you," the Major informs Billy, "we have your receiving order but nothing going out, looks like someone at command screwed up."

"What should we do? There are no transit billets here," Billy asks.

"Have a seat, Captain, I will call Wolf Creek command and see what I can find out," the Major tells Billy.

It was not long when the Major stepped over to where Billy was sitting and told him no one seems to know Captain, "I would suggest you get a room at one of the local hotels, there is a real nice one with a restaurant and a pool, not more than a kilometer that way," he points, "come back in the A.M.."

"Can I have that in writing, sir?" Billy said, "You know how the Guard works, if it's not in writing, it's not legitimate."

"I can do that for you, Captain," the Major told Billy, sitting down and wrote out his new orders, telling him, Ted, Rachael, and Harriet to return every morning until their new orders arrive.

On the walk to the hotel, they talk about the events of the morning.

"Ted, you know the reason there are no orders, we were never meant to make it here, we should be dead back at Wolf Creek."

"I know, Skipper, that confirms our suspensions about this being sanctioned by command.

You screwed up their plans finding that screwdriver. Ted and I could not be more proud of you, you saved the lives of fifteen people today, including mine, so if you ever want to do extra cleaning and I give you any bit of a hard time, say the word fifteen and I'll shut up," smiling at him, "you hero."

34

Roger is sitting on the side of the bed waiting for the nurse to come get him to be discharged.

His shirt was cut off last night, so he is sitting there bare chested and his pants now has black blood all down the front, I'm a mess, he thinks to himself.

Roger hears a knock at the open door; looking up James is standing in the door way with a bag in his hand, smiling at him.

"Good morning, my friend," James greets him.

"Good morning, Ambassador," Roger returns.

"Hope you do not mind, Roger, I used your keys to let myself in to your apartment. I thought you could use some fresh clothing," handing the bag to Roger.

"Thanks, James, I was just thinking about how I was going to get home."

"The least I could do, not many people would take a bullet for me," smiling at Roger.

Roger laughs, "I find that hard to believe," grabbing his shoulder with a burst of pain, never dropping his smile.

"I stopped at the nurse's station beforehand, your chart said you were a very lucky man, five centimeters lower and it would have clipped a major artery. You would have bled out, you have a through and through, no bone damage, you should be up and running at a 100% in two weeks, but until then, you are to take it slow. Would you like some help getting dressed?" James asks.

"With all the pretty nurses here, no, thanks."

The two friends share a hardy laugh, with Roger grabbing his should once more.

Roger pushes the call button, and before long, a nurse come in and has Roger ready to go in no time.

As the two of them exit the elevator into the lobby, Roger takes a second look at a man at the information desk; he whispers to James, "I think that is the man that hit you last night," indicating with his head.

James looks over and recognizes him also.

"The car is parked right out front, have the nurse take you to it. I will be right back."

James goes over to talk to their attacker.

The man looks nervous, looking around like he is being followed or watched, "If someone sees me with you, I'm a dead man."

"Let's go in there," James tells the man, the two duck in to a bathroom, so they could have a private conversation.

"Ambassador, I came as soon as I could," the attacker tells James with apparent urgency.

"Steve Carter told me not more than an hour ago that the Duke will be king today, this place was my first thought. I was hoping you might be here checking on your friend."

"Do you know how?" he asks with panic starting to build.

"No," he tells James, "only that it would be today."

"I owe you one," as he runs out, heading for the car.

James gets to the car as the nurse is starting her walk back to the lobby.

Jumping in to the driver seat in a near panic, "We have to get to the office now," James shouts, putting the car in drive and speeding out of the parking lot like a mad man barely missing a truck, a car, and a pedestrian before he made it to the road, running at least one red light in the oncoming lane.

"What's up, James," Roger asks.

"The Duke is going to try to kill the Prince today, I hope we are not too late."

"It's noon now," James talking to himself, "she was to fly to Crowns View this morning at 10:00, she should be there by now, it's only an hour flight, please God, don't let it happen."

In Roger's many years with the Ambassador, this is the closest he has ever seen him to a state of panic.

Parking out front, James jumps out and runs for the door, fumbling with the lock and nearly rips the door from the jam, heading for the phone.

Several moments later, Roger walks in to hear James telling the operator, "I don't care, this is Ambassador Wildwind, now get me the Queen, this is an emergency."

Within a short time, James was speaking with Mae.

"Everything is fine," Mae tells him, sensing his worry, "the Queen and the Prince are fine," she repeats herself to reinforces it for James, "they are safe, there was an attempt, but fate was on our side, the pilot we had was paying attention and tragedy was adverted."

Mae explained how the ships flight controls were tampered with by placing a screwdriver in a clevis, making it impossible to control.

"I will give that pilot a medal or anything he wants," James tells Mae as he begins to calm down.

"How did you come by this information?" Mae asks.

"One of the Duke's own men warned me, he did not know what, but he did know it would be today," James tells her, "not all of the Duke's men like what he is doing."

"We have more friends than enemies, James, we will make it through this, this I know," Mae encourages.

"I will see you in about five hours, I will hop the first flight I can get, see you then."

James hangs up, sinking deep into the chair, his shoulders slump as low as Roger has ever seen him do with sweat heavy on his forehead.

Roger notices James's hand is still shaking slightly, stepping up behind him and placing his hand on the Ambassador's shoulder, "We are with you, my friend, hell or high water."

James places his hand on Roger's, "Thank you, my friend, I thought I lost her and the Prince today."

Roger understood that James had deeper feelings for the Queen, more than he would ever admit to.

"Now let's get you to Crowns View," Roger picking up the phone to call the airport and book James a flight. After hanging up, "You have two hours, James," Roger said.

"Good, let's get you home, you don't need to be driving. I'll drive a little more sanely this time," smiling at Roger.

"That was a hell of a ride," giving James a smile back.

James takes Roger home and gets him settled in, then calls a taxi for the ride to the airport, his bags were still in the back seat of Roger's car from the night before.

35

By 8:00, the team was assembled, only Captain West and Sargent Baits were missing.

Captain Tucker took command of the security detail, briefing them on the mission and checking their equipment on the flight-line. They were well-armed and he was wearing combat gear, sidearm, and a flak jacket, the Major was also in combat gear.

The flight crew had performed their pre-fight and were doing a little cleaning to keep occupied during the down time.

Tom, Clarence, Adam, and Susan are sitting inside comparing notes, discussing their plans.

"In order to take them by surprise, Adam, you and the security team will do a low-level jump, we will find a place to land, then meet up with you."

Susan has been trying to understand how radiation is connected to Driver control.

"Tell me, Clarence, radiation kill living cells, how is it possible to us it to control the drone."

"I am reluctant to explain the concept in detail. Doctor. but the short version is all water in the universe is connected, the radiation is what passes the information to the living cell, a cell is more water than anything else and every drone at its core has a living cell impregnated with royal gold to protect it from the radiation, it is what receives that information."

"So, it would be possible for a human to control a drone without killing the host?" adds Adam.

"No," Clarence responds, "the royal gold would kill them in short order, it is very toxic."

"Royal gold?" Tom asks, "I have never heard of that."

"It is an isotope of gold, much heavier than gold with more electrons and neutrons, it is not the color of gold but purple, that is why the title of royal."

At around 13:00, Clarence informs Tom, he is rebroadcasting, "The drone is very close. I have located the point of origin; according to your map, it's Edgefield Island. I will have the drone orbit the island until we arrive."

Edgefield Island is a small island designated to be a wild life preserve, it has restricted access and no inhabitants, thick forest with divers flora and fauna, a perfect place to do clandestine research.

Adam gives the green light, the flight crew begin preparation for takeoff, the security team take their place in the transport, the excitement mingled with fear is building, it shows on all of the team's faces.

The trip to Edgefield was short, it was only fifty-five kilometers. The transport makes a pass to evaluate the island, there is a small runway and hanger with three Royal Guard ships on the tarmac, about two kilometers from the runway, there is a large industrial-looking building.

"That's our target," Clarence tells the team, indicating the lone structure, "we should continue on this direction, so we do not tip our hand, taking them by surprise."

Adam passes the plan to the flight crew, so they continue on their flight path until they are out of sight of the island, turning for a second pass.

Adam gets himself and the team ready to jump, the ramp is lowered, he makes a pass among the team, looking each man in the eye and checking their harness by grabbing the shoulder straps and giving it a strong jerk, slapping each on the helmet, then nodding his approval.

Thirty seconds out, the engineer tells Adam he will be the first out, looking down he sees the sea rushing bye, then there is land, he hears the word go, and without any hesitation, he jumps, followed by the twelve men of his team, Captain Tucker is the last out.

Tom watches with a bit of envy, remembering his days as a company commander, then a battalion commander, many times did he do what Adam just did. The commander should always be the first on the battle field and the last off.

Through the ramp door, Tom counts fourteen shoots; they are in a line coming down about half a click from the building in a sparsely wooded area, all but two make it to the ground without getting tangled in the trees.

The transport makes a sharp turn, lining up with the runway. Tom feels the flaps go down and the transport starts to slow rapidly. He is still standing next to the ramp looking out, holding on to one of the hand straps running down the side of the cargo area when he hears Clarence shout out a warning.

Looking out the window on the right, he sees the drone, heading their way fast, about that time the transport touches down, braking hard making Tom pitch forward.

"The drone is still closing," Tom hears Clarence yell, "they have control."

The drone smashes in to the right side of the ship hard, tearing a hole in the passenger compartment, not more than two rows from where Susan and the Sub-Driver are sitting.

Susan was strapped in to her seat, but Clarence was standing looking out the right-hand window when the drone made contact.

The transport veering left abruptly coming off the runway, bouncing hard as it goes over a drainage ditch, snapping the nose gear, the nose digs in to the ground, the ship coming to a sudden stop.

Susan watches the Sub-Driver go flying forward as her head hits the seat in front of her, she blacks out momentarily.

The cabin is starting to fill with smoke when Susan opens her eyes. She looks forward and can see flickering flames through the smoke, she stands, her knees try to buckle, but her will overrides the urge.

With the flames between her and the pilot's, she knows she must make her exit out the back of the transport.

Tom is thrown forward in to the rear bulkhead, he sees stars and the world goes black.

As Susan makes it to the cargo compartment, she sees Tom crumpled up against the bulkhead, his head is bleeding from a gash on the right side, she tries to wake him, but he's out cold.

She knows there will only be seconds before the ship is fully consumed in flames, she knows she will not be able to carry him, so she grabs his wrist and starts pulling him aft.

Tom begins to regain consciousness

Susan sees the engineer coming from the passenger compartment.

"Can you hear me, Tom?" he hears a voice; looking up he sees Susan has him by both arms, pulling him toward the back ramp, he looks forward and all he sees is black smoke, the ship is on fire.

The engineer comes up and grabs his arm with Susan, and the two drag his down the ramp and away from the burning ship.

He sits there for several seconds clearing his head. When he sits up, he can see the two pilots are making their way to him, Susan and the engineer, they both have sidearms drawn.

The pilot's makes it to their location, "We need to move," now he tells them, "can you walk?" looking at Tom.

"Yes," he replies, trying to stand, the world starts to spin. Susan puts her arm around his waist grabbing his belt, giving him support.

They make their way to the woods that run along the runway, giving them cover.

Tom hears five-gun shots coming from the direction of the hanger, "Stay low," he tells them.

The black smoke is running parallel with the runway, obscuring them from the hanger.

Tom sees movement through the smoke, five men approach the burning ship, they're armed.

The co-pilot kneeling next to Tom tells him, "They did not see us make our escape, we will be safe for now."

Suddenly something comes out of the burning ship and grabs two of the men and drags them in to the flames, the remaining three stand there in shock for a few seconds, hearing the men's screams, they begin shooting in to the flames, the screams stopped abruptly, the thing came out one more time and grabbed another man and pulled him in, the last two men ran off not looking back.

The thing comes out one more time, looking around, spotting Tom and the rest of the crew next to the runway, it begins making its way to them, but it did not make it, it collapsed.

"That's the Sub-Driver," Susan tells Tom.

They make their way over to it and it's still functioning, sort of.

Susan walks up next to it, it is burnt black, all of the flesh has been burnt away and you can see the frame, servos, and wiring.

"It's signing," Susan tells Tom.

She interrupts, "Don't let Doctor Pierce get away," then it stops and all movement ends.

About that time, they hear one of the transports start up. Within a few seconds, it takes off, heading north to the mainland.

Adam gathers his men for the march to the building, sending two scouts out first, it only takes five minutes to make the trip. He sends two to the right and two to the left to secure their flanks, they're only 100 meters out when three men run out the door, one is in a lab coat, getting in a car speeding toward the airfield.

"Captain, get on the radio, let them know there is a car heading their way."

Adam sees two guards at the door, "We will need to take them out."

Two of the team take careful aim, pop, pop is all that is heard with the silencers on their weapons.

The Major gives the signal to move, they are at the door in a matter of seconds.

He counts with his fingers, one, two, three, ten men enter the building, there is a hallway going to the left with several door opening to the hallway, two men are stationed at the door to guard their rear, eight proceed down the hall, the first door they come to is an office, two men enter to clear it, doing the same for each door.

"Major, there is no response from the ship," Captain Tucker tells him.

One of the flank guards reports on the radio, "Major, there is black smoke rising from the airfield."

"Crap," Adam tells the Captain, "they will have to deal with it themselves until we clear the building."

They are getting ready to clear the third door when a drone crashes through it, grabbing one of the team and throwing him against the wall, gun fire erupts from the other team members.

"Center mass," Adam calls out, "hit him in the chest," the drone is dealt with in seconds.

"It looks like a maintenance drone," Adam tells his men, "if that was a war drone, we would all be dead."

They enter the room, there is a man sitting in a strange-looking chair with a cap on his head, wires coming out, going to a box next to him. In the room, there are two more drones, one starts to move, getting up and starts their way.

Adam uses his sidearm and put three rounds in the box.

The drone falls to the floor.

"Secure him," Adam pointing at the man.

"The rest of the building is secure, Major," Captain Tucker reports. "We found him hiding in a closet, bringing out a man in a lab coat."

"Frank, I'll take care of him, grab five men and get to the airfield as fast as you can, call me on the radio as soon as you make your assessment," Adam tells the Captain.

With Captain Tucker off for the airfield, he gives instructions to the Corporal, "Bring the two men to the first office, tie them to a chair, and watch them closely, I will be in the lab."

The lab looks ordinary, there are racks with equipment on one side, the other has filing cabinets, a desk, and a table.

The box next to the chair Adam put the three rounds through is leaking a pink liquid, giving off a sweet smell.

The drone that started to walk was halfway in to the room from the back where it started from, sprawled face first on the floor, Adam walks around it to get to the one in the back, all three were the same type, maintenance drones, six arms, two large arms with three large fingers that came together, no thumb, four very dainty arms for doing fine work, four fingers, and two thumbs on each hand, the legs are short, giving it limited mobility, very slow moving.

There are two more boxes like the one connected to the chair.

Going through the filing cabinets, just glancing, not really reading when one caught his eye, passenger manifest from Wolf Creek, he did not recognize any of the names, but I bet they all led to the Duke, putting that one in his pack.

As he shuts the cabinet, he hears a large explosion and the building shakes.

36

The airport lounge is very busy for this time of the morning.

The Duke has a table with a view of the runway, he looks at his watch, 10:15.

"Any minute," he tells himself, rubbing his hands with glee. His aid is standing next to the table, "Go get me a Brandy," he tells him, "and be quick," the aid hurries off.

The Duke looks at his watch one more time, 10:16.

I wonder how she will fill right before they hit the ground, he muses to himself, I wonder if she will shit herself.

The duke looks at his watch, 10:17.

"Where is that, Brandy?"

I wonder if I will be able to hear it from here or smell her burning flesh?

The Duke looks at his watch, 10:18.

"Who knows, she may have an orgasm," laughing to himself. "Where is that, Brandy?

When I'm king, two minutes late means a betting.:

The Duke look at his watch, 10:19.

"Here comes the boy with my drink."

"Sorry, Lord, they're out of Brandy."

"Can't you do anything right, you stupid fool." The Duke takes a deep breath as he sees the transport making its way to the runway. "I need to know the time," looking at his watch," "10:20, every year at this exact time, I'll remember my," he hold his breath as he see the transport come off the ground, any second now he thinks, the transport continues to climb, any second, "the transport dose not continue it's, it's, it's going on, it's not crashing," he feels light headed, "things are turning dark, it did not crash, you're dead, Hartwell."

The Duke passes out.

37

It has been dead quiet for the last six hours, no foot traffic out in the hallway.

Matt would only cat nap, waking up several times an hour, taking a quick survey of the room. Every time he would see Kimmy sitting on the floor next to the door scrutinizing every sound out in the hallway.

I bet she was one hell of a scout, Matt thinks to himself, females are naturals at it, scouts rely on stealth, agility, and intelligence, where dog faces depend on brute force and intimidation, give me a forty-five kilo well-trained scout to any ninety kilo muscle bound grunt any day in a fluid mission like this.

Matt looks over at the door one more time before he forces himself back to sleep. Kimmy is looking at him, holding up three fingers, moving them back and forth one time, then pointing to the left, then putting her fingers and thumb together, rotating her wrist, he knows there are three people moving down the hall going left, checking for unlocked door.

Their door knob shakes, then stops, they move on.

Kimmy give a thumbs up.

Matt nods his understanding.

At 05:00, they all start preparing.

Eat and getting ready, the cases Jack brought has space suites in them, not the long duration one like they had a few days ago, these are only good for five hours, no food or water, the upside is they are compact.

"We will put the space suits on, minus the environmental unit, then put this miners jump suit over it, the helmet and the environmental unit will go in the back pack, we also have a hard hat to finish off the ruse, if all goes well, we should make the two kilometer walk unnoticed," Jack explains, "you will also need to empty your balder and your colon, there is no privation for it in the suit."

Connie looks at Matt.

"Use the bathroom before we go, Bubbles," he said with a smile.

They are dressed and the three backpacks are next to the door with a hardhat on top of each.

"Kimmy will be our scout; she will be just ahead. If there is any danger or unforeseen problem, I will be able to hear," pointing to the ear piece.

At 06:50, Jack gives the signal to get ready.

Right before Kimmy exits the door, she presents her hand to Matt, "Good luck, brother," she tells him, "one day I would like to sit down with you, have a few drinks, and tell a war story or two."

"I would like nothing better, brother," Matt returns.

Kimmy goes out the door.

Connie looks at Matt with a question on her face, repeating, "Brother?"

"It's a military thing," he tells her with a smile.

"It's clear to the first turn," Jack declares, "let's move."

The three companions exit the room with backpacks and hardhats following Kimmy.

They go maybe 200 meters, then down a set of stairs, four flights, stopping right before exiting the stairwell.

"Hold, there are four men coming our way."

Jack puts his ear to the door, they're going by, he opens the door slowly, glances down the corridor the way the men went, he can see their backs about fifty meters down the hall.

"We need to go the way they came at latest 500 meters, then up more stairs. Kimmy is holding at the stairwell for now," he looks again, "they're seventy-five meters now, let's move but not in a hurry, we do not want to draw attention."

They start walking at a normal pace.

The men never turn around.

Matt hears Jack whisper, "Move." He knew he was instructing Kimmy.

They make it to the stairwell and start going up.

Jack tells them, "This will be a long climb, twenty flights, we need to run now, this is an emergency exit, it's seldom used."

Exiting the stairwell, Kimmy sees two men coming her way, thirty meters the way they need to go, she starts doing stretching exercises and jogging in place to provide cover for the sweat on her brow.

When the men make it to her, she smiles her best flirtatious smile, "How's it going, guys, doing one more set of leg stretches."

"Out on a run, pretty lady," one tells her.

"Yes", she replies, "I like the privacy on this side of the facility, the gymnasium stinks too much for my liking."

"You're the new waitress at Molly's," the other one said.

"Yes, I've been here for five weeks; my boyfriend works at the processing plant, he wanted me to see what it is like here, so I took a job temporarily."

"You know there are killers on the loose and a good-looking girl like yourself could get raped in a lonely place like this," moving in a little closer, the first man tells her.

"Yes," the second man agrees, "it's not safe, you could lose everything, including your life," moving to cut off her escape route. The two men smile at each other, then rush Kimmy, overpowering her, pinning her to the wall. "We run this place and take what we want, and right now, you're on our menu."

On their way up, there was no other exits, Jack holds them at the top just inside the door.

From his expression, "Something is wrong, two men are questioning Kimmy five meters from the door," he tells them. "Go," he shouts, "she is in trouble."

Jack runs out with Matt hot on his heels, Connie right behind.

Matt can see the two men have Kimmy pinned to the wall, one on each side, each have an arm and a hand full of her collar with her feet off the floor.

Jack tackles the one closest to him, driving the first man in to the second, all four go down in a pile. Jack is on top of the one he tackled, the second is on top of him, Kimmy is on top of the pile.

Matt gets there half a second later, kicking the one under Kimmy right in the ribs; he hears bone break and air rush from the man's lungs.

Kimmy rolls off the pile and springs to her feet, grabbing the one. Matt kicked and pulling him off of Jack, pinning him against the wall.

Jack begins to rain blows on the one under him until he loses consciousness.

Matt is helping Jack to his feet when he hears a gasp; looking over at Kimmy, he sees her going down, she has a knife plunged deep in to her right side.

Her attacker is trying to make a run for it right by Connie, she puts her foot out and trips him, he goes down face first with a thud.

Kimmy pulls the knife out, and black blood flows profusely from the wound.

Matt was painfully aware Kimmy would be dead in two minutes, the knife severed her main artery in the liver, rage filed his mind, he grabbed the man that put the knife in Kimmy and snapped his neck, killing him instantly, going to the second man and doing the same, two for one, he said.

"Brother, you need to go," Kimmy tells him.

"No, I will stay with you," as tears started running down his face, kneeling next to her.

"I'm dead, you and I know it, finish the mission, don't let my life be wasted," reaching up and touching the side of his face, "I would of really liked to have had that drink with you, go now, please, brother."

Matt stands and looks down at Kimmy, "Once a scout, always a scout, good bye, brother."

The stairs leading to the airlock was only 200 meters from them.

Jack led the way up, three flights, it opens in to the inner changing room with the airlock through one more door.

There was a row of lockers with spacesuits in them, put the overalls and the hardhats in the backpack, so it will not be obvious, and with no spacesuits missing, they may not know we went out.

The three of them stepped outside, the scorching sun could not be seen yet, but the sky was awash with intense light.

"We have about five hours before the sun sets this valley ablaze, the temperature will top 1,000 degrees. As long as we are in the shadow of the mountain, we will be safe, we need to get going," Jack urges.

The walk used up three hours to make it to the clandestine hanger, another hour will be used prepping the ship.

The three are standing next to a sheer cliff going up 500 meters when Jack announces, "We're here."

Matt and Connie look at each other in confusion, they see nothing but rock wall.

Jack understands and smiles to himself; he walked over to a spot on the wall, placing his left hand on a little bump of rock, and with his right-hand finger, he puts it in a shallow depression, five meters to their right a door slides into the wall, reveling a passageway. It was totally undetectable.

The three enter and walk fifty meters in to the passageway till they come to an airlock, Jack enters a code on the key pad and it opens; without hesitation they enter.

Inside the room, there are twenty or so suits on a shelf against the right wall, not the flimsy ones like they are wearing now but long duration suites.

Jack starts taking his off and motions for them to do the same, telling Connie, "This way you will not have to use a dipper," smiling sheepishly at her. Connie turns a little red, knowing she had that very thought and the fact that Jack knew it embarrassed her. The small base was well stocked and equipped, so Jack will have a comfortable stay. "We need to get moving," Jack prompted the two, "all the outer doors will need to be sealed by the time the sun comes up."

Dressed in the new suits, the three make their way to the hanger.

There are three Rabbits in launch tubes standing vertical.

The Rabbit is ten meters long, one and a half wide and two high, almost cylindrical in shape, there are two small wings that is under the belly that will swing out if they are needed, the tail reminds Matt of a mortar round, four fins in a X shape.

An electric catapult will assist them in to orbit conserving fuel, the down side is it kicks like a mule, going from 0 to 500 KPH in five seconds, generating seven G's, most people will pass out if they are untrained.

The rocket will ignite after that, adding its own kike, but it will only be five G's but a longer duration.

Matt and Commie climb the gantry with Jack following to assist them in to the cockpit.

With Matt and Connie strapped in the seats and Jack getting ready to close the canape, Matt offers his hand to Jack, he takes it in a firm grip.

"I'm sorry about your partner."

"Me too," Jack said with a tear visible, "she was a true gem. I will miss her, good luck," with that he closes the canape, then hits the button that slides the inner door closed and heads for the control room to open the outer door.

The rabbit had been modified to handle the searing heat, the shell has been covered in a heat resistant layer, they will not be able see through the canape, the only way they have to see is through a camera, Matt will have to fly by instrumentation only.

The radio crackles, Jack's voice comes over it, door open, "You're all set."

"Thanks, Jack," Matt returns.

In three, two, one, the catapult engages and they are on their way.

38

On the way to the airfield, Frank watches a transport break through the thick smoke, lifting off heading north.

When they arrive at the hanger, the car is sitting there, doors open, motor still running, “We will need to clear the hanger before we proceed to the crash site,” he instructs the Sargent, “you take two men and go that way,” pointing south, “I’ll take the north side, we will meet in the middle.”

Captain Tucker and the two security men enter the first door they come to, it’s an office, laying about is five men, each has been shot in the head, execution style.

They proceed through a door that leads in to the hanger bay, in the middle of the bay is a fuel truck. Frank can see the Sargent and his men on the other side of the hanger, that is when he sees a satchel charge on the side of the truck with a light flashing, bomb!

He screams to his men, “Clear the building.”

The Sargent understood the warning and was exiting the way they came, Frank and his team were doing the same.

Frank was the last one to the door. As he was exiting, the charge detonated.

He was thrown several meters, landing hard, breaking his arm between the wrist and the elbow, white bone is visible.

The two men with Frank help him to his feet, "We need to move, Captain, or we will burn," one of them tells him, "can you walk?"

The three make a hasty retreat to the tree line away from the heat.

The hanger is now fully engulfed, flames are shooting 100 meters in the air, black smoke is rising over one kilometer. The two remaining transport right outside the hanger door are starting to smoke. Captain Tucker knows it will only be seconds before they also explode, he sees the Sargent and his men coming back his way, he waves them over to his location.

The six of them move further away from the inferno as the two transports add their part to the Carnegie.

"We will need to set that, Captain," pointing at his arm, the Sargent tells him, he sends one man to look for two sticks. Taking off his pack, he pulls out a roll of tape.

One of the men point to the tree line down the runway, "There are five people moving our way, Captain, about 500 meters."

"It's our flight crew," Frank tells the Sargent, "there is one missing."

The man returns with the sticks, "Will this do, sarge?" he asks.

"Yes, good job," the Sargent tells his man.

Frank sits back down with a twinge of pane, two men hold him from the back, the Sargent grabs his wrist with one hand and the elbow with the other.

"Ready," he tells Frank, "one, two, three," he pulls. Searing pain shoots through Frank's body, but the only thing he did was clinch his teeth, not one sound came from him.

The Sargent puts the two sticks alongside the forearm, then wraps that with the tape, then puts the Captain's arm in a sling.

The five make it to them about the time the Sargent is finishing up with the Captain's arm.

Frank can see the Senator, Susan, the two pilots, and the engineer, no Sub-Driver.

Tom explains how the drone went rogue and crashed the transport.

Captain Tucker went over the details of the raid on the industrial building and things that transpired at the hanger, including the executions.

The radio starts receiving traffic, "Caption Tucker, report your condition, over."

Tom takes the radio, "This is Senator Dearman Major, no fatalities, but we do have injuries, we will be making our way to you, be advised, there was a bomb set in the hanger, so be on the lookout, over."

"Copy that, see you in ten, out."

There were two charges set, instead of fifteen-minute time delay, someone set it for one hour and fifty minutes, giving Adam's team time to find them and deactivating the charges.

After the team was reunited, details were conveyed to Adam on the landing, including the destruction of the Sub-Driver and Frank's arrival at the hanger, the executions and the bombing.

"Shall we interrogate our prisoners?" Tom tells Adam.

Tom, Adam, Frank, and Susan enter the office where the prisoners are being held, there are two guards watching them, one was the team member the drone through into the wall, he has a bandage around his head and his arm in a sling, looking threatening at the two prisoners.

As soon as they enter the room, the man in the lab coat tells Adam, "That man said he was going to break my arm," indicating the man with the bandage around his head.

"I might let him do it," Adam informs the man in the lab coat, "if you do not tell me what I want to know."

"I will be killed," the man pleads.

The prisoner next to him passes out.

The guard informs Adam, "That's the third time he has done that, Major."

Susan lifts the unconscious man's head, with her finger opens his eyelid, "This man is in a coma," looking at Adam.

"It's no more than you deserve," looking the man in the lab coat square in the eyes, "you killed this man and you know it, don't you?"

"I was only following order," the man in the lab coat pleads.

"Let's start with your name," holding his gaze on the man.

"Doctor Stroop, Bennie Stroop."

"Well, Bennie, did you know they tried to kill you already and they did kill the five men at the hanger, a bullet each to the back of the head."

"Doctor Pierce needs me, he insists, he would never do that. I'm his friend and college."

"Your friend left two bombs here, did he tell you that?"

All the color drains from his face, he had seen the charges three days before and seen the guard go in to the room they were kept in before leaving, he begins to sob.

"If I tell you, will you let me go?" Bennie asks.

"No, but it may save you from a firing squad," Tom speaking up for the first time, playing the good cop to get him talking.

"Talk now," Adam shouts at Bennie, raising his hand like he is going to strike him, knowing what Tom was doing.

"Major, that will be enough," playing his part, telling Adam.

Adam lowers his hand, glaring at Bennie, then moves to the wall, leaning against it with his arms folded across his chest, keeping his eyes on Bennie.

"We were told to use the Drone to fly the transports, I think they were to be loaded with explosives. I don't know the target, but I think it was New Hope and Kranstan Point."

"Where did the Drivers and the Drones come from, Doctor?" showing him respect.

"T.S.," Bennie replies calmer now, "there are more coming to Wolf Creek this week, they are bringing five war drones with this shipment."

Tom looks at Adam, they both understand the significant of this information.

"Can they operate the war drones?" Tom asks Bennie.

"No, not yet, but it is only a matter of time, you set them back significantly with this raid, maybe two months for the war drones, but the maintenance drones can fly the transports now."

The radio come to life, "Major Potter do you copy, over."

"Read you, Lima Charily Captain West, over."

"I have a full platoon, Major, what are your orders, over."

"Have one squad jump on the North side and one on the South side, do a sweep of the island, there are at least two combatants loos on the island, bring the other two down with you at the air field, sending one each to meet up with the North and South teams, watch out for debris on the runway and, Captain, I am glad you're with us, over and out."

Thirty minutes later, one of the men came running in excited, "There is a war drone coming down the road with Captain West."

Tom, Adam, and Frank meet the party as they arrive at the building.

"It is good to see you, Sub-Driver," Tom greets him.

"Likewise, Senator," Clarence bows slightly, with the war drone towers over them all.

"The Sub-Driver was waiting for us at the airport, he briefed me on the situation, so I activated alpha company. I have three full platoons standing by," Carol said, "I can have them here in one hour."

"I think we have plenty, Captain," looking at the war drone, Adam replies.

“Sargent Bates, if you could assist me, I will activate the maintenance drones and start looking over the files to see what I can get from them,” Clarence asks, “it would be too cumbersome for this drone to operate in doors.”

Art answered the Sub-Driver with, “Yes, sir, it would be my pleasure.”

Clarence had him bring out the drones, he worked on each for a few minutes and had them standing.

They enter the building going to the lab to start the search.

The Sargent comes up to the Major, “Sir, team one has found our combatants, they surrendered without a fight, there were nine of them. They should be here within the hour.”

Carol, standing next to the Major, addresses the Sargent, “You and your team did an outstanding job today. I am putting you and all of your team in for a commendation, I am honored by your performances.”

“Thank you, Captain, we have an outstanding leader,” saluting the Captain, going to prepare for the arrival of team one with the prisoners.

39

The weather was perfect at Crown's View. Sandra always loved the summer palace, the view of the lake, the smells of the forest, it was comfortable, not a fortress.

The prince and the girls were down in the garden, running and playing like children should be at that age.

Mae was sitting on the balcony, keeping an eye on them.

Libby and Tina were supervising the porters bringing in the luggage, making sure the right bags get to the right rooms.

Mister Sipp was setting up the classroom.

Mister Harper was directing the staff, cooks, maids, and gardeners.

The only one that was not happy was Beatrice; shortly after arriving at the summer place, she informed Tina she was leaving. Tina tried to convince her to stay, but she would not reconsider. When Tina asks about Tamara, Beatrice told Tina she was her problem now and washed her hands of the young girl, calling a taxi and going to the airport without even telling the young girl good bye.

Sandra was saddened by this, but if she would abandon a young child that casually, Tamara will be better off without her, she would gladly take on the responsibility. I have always wanted a daughter, Sandra thought, and this girl has never had a mother, reminding her of her own childhood and the heartache and hardship of growing up without one.

Sandra had a private meeting with Mister Harper soon after their arrival at Crown's View, questioning him about the Duke and his relationship; he was not aware that the Duke had plans to kill the prince or do him any harm.

"The Duke instructed me to keep a close eye on you, my lady and report your activities to him nightly, which I did shamelessly," Herald told Sandra, "can you forgive me, my Queen?"

"Yes, Mister Harper, I forgive you, but I charge you with the responsibility of keeping the Prince safe, is that understood?"

"Yes, my Queen."

"The Duke is unaware of our new understanding. I would like you to continue reporting to the Duke, he is to remain unaware that we discovered his plot, can you do that, Mister Harper?" Sandra asks.

"Yes, my Queen, I swear on my life," getting down on his knees, "no harm will befall you or the Prince."

"Good, Mister Harper," placing her hand on his shoulder, "please rise, it is a new start for us today."

"What should I tell him, my Queen?" Herald asks.

"Tell him I am in a severe depressed state, unable to leave my room, not eating and drinking too much alcohol, that should make him happy. Are there any staff you may suspect of working for the Duke?" Sandra inquired.

"No, my lady, none that I am aware of, but I will keep my eyes open for any signs of one."

"Very good, I think that will do it for now, I give you leave, good day, Mister Harper."

Herald bows and exits the room, leaving Sandra alone in the study.

The children were upstairs getting cleaned up for dinner; after a fun day out in the garden, all three were quiet a mess.

Sandra was in the study once more when Mae enters, escorting James, "Look who I found in the lobby."

James's heart skipped a beat when he sees Sandra, "My lady," bowing low, "I was worried sick for you and the Prince today."

James explained how he was warned by one of Ken's men about the attempt on their lives.

Sandra outlined what happened and their good fortune with the pilot and the new relationship with Mister Harper.

"All in all, it was a good day," Mae said, "even with the attempted assassination, don't you think so, James?"

"That or divine intervention," James said.

"I would not have thought you to be a man of faith," Sandra comments.

"Nor would I, but the last three weeks has me wondering," he tells her.

"The break in is what made the warning possible, the pilot's first duty as a transporter, the second lieutenant fresh out of the academy trying to please, it's like it was all meant to be, all the pieces falling in to place, there is more, little things. I just can't shake the thought," James tells the Queen and himself at the same time.

"I am glad you are here, James, you give me a sense of security and peace, thank you for coming," Sandra tells him.

"I agree, my lady," Mae adds.

"Would you like to stay for dinner, the Prince would be pleased and you can meet our new guests," Sandra asks with an inviting smile.

"I would be honored, my lady," returning Sandra's smile with one of his own.

Dinner was not served in the large dining hall but in the small one right off the library, so it could be more relaxed and less formal.

In attendance was Sandra, Tyler, Mae, the two girls, Tina, Bradly, and James.

It was a very festive evening, there was no shortage of laughter around the table.

Tyler's excitement about the flight from Wolf Creek was apparent to James.

"So, my Prince, you wish to be a pilot like your father; did you know I was his wing man through training at Kranstan Point and we served together during the Trotter revolt," James tells him.

"You served with Father in the Trotter revolt? Please tell me a story," Tyler's voice cracking with the onset of puberty.

James looks at Sandra for her approval.

She nods her head and smiles.

"Your father and I were nineteen, fresh out of the academy, assigned to the fifth combat wing under Colonel Mesig. John was doing duty as the officer of the day at headquarter; after his shift, he came busting in to our tent all smiles, pulling out a bottle of whiskey. Where did you get that, I ask him?

Mesig's office, they brought in his allotment, so I helped myself, would you like a drink? We drank the whole bottle. Two months later, fighting was heavy, we landed our fighters, getting out there was a Captain waiting for us from the military police. Mesig wants to see you two now, he tells us with a grin. John and I look at each other.

What did you do? John asks me.

What did you do? I ask him.

We follow the Captain to Mesig's tent, entering, the Colonel is behind his desk. You two, have a seat, he orders us. John and I take a seat, knowing we are in trouble for something. The Colonel pulls out a bottle and two glasses, filling them with whiskey. Drink, he tells us, and next time, leave my bottle. From then on, every time the Colonel would get his allotment, he would call John and I in and give us one drink. The moral, never steal, the person may be willing to share."

"Did that really happen, Ambassador?" Tyler asks.

"Yes, my Prince, it did."

Dinner was finished and the party moved in to the common room to let their meal settle and talk.

Sandra, James, and Mae are sitting together, having coffee.

The children are with Bradley and Tina playing a spelling game.

"Thank you for that story, James, it was always my favorite," Sandra said.

"Mine, too," agreed James.

James looking over at Tyler, "He is smitten with Tamara you know," looking back at Sandra.

"Yes, I have seen it, he never takes his attention from her," Sandra observes.

"She is a sweet girl, very smart and forward, I hope she stays with us to influence Tyler," Mae tells James, "it is good for him. "All right, children, it's time for bed," Mae announces, "we have a big day tomorrow."

"One more hour," they plead.

"No," Mae being her stern self, "we have adult things to talk about, now off to bed."

The children grumble but do as they are told.

After the children are gone, Sandra looks at the clock, "we have two hours before the Sub-Driver arrives," reminding James.

"It could be sooner if you like, my lady," pulling the locket from around his neck, placing it on the table.

"What is that, James?" she asks.

"It is a communication device; the Sub-Driver gave it to me shortly after John's death."

"You mean murder," Sandra correcting him.

James nods his agreement with that.

"Have you used it before, James?" she questions.

"Only once, three weeks ago after you told me your suspicions about the Duke. I was instructed to keep it secret, but given the circumstances, I think it will be acceptable with the Sub-Driver."

"Should I leave the room, James?" inquires Mae.

"No, Mae, you are part of this," reaching out, placing his hand on Mae's shoulder, "we need you here, your advice is always sought."

Looking at James, "Let's do it," Sandra said.

James is not thinking about the locket at that instant, he is looking at a beautiful woman, sparkling eyes, long flowing blond hair, a delicate nose, a smile that warms his spirit.

Then dark cloud descends on him, his vision blurs, this is my friend's wife, his head is swimming with emotions, the mother of his child, how could you betray him like that? tear escapes his eye and runs down his cheek.

"James, is everything OK?"

"Yes, my Queen, I was thinking about John," wiping his face with his sleeve.

Sandra reaches out and touches James on the forearm, telling him it will be fine, "We do have each other."

That's the problem, he reminds himself, we could never really have each other, it would not be proper.

Composing himself James calls to the locket, "Sub-Driver, may we speak."

"Yes, James, I am here."

James is taken back, never has the Sub-Driver used his first name, only title.

"Sub-Driver, I have the Queen with me now, could we have that conference now instead of later?"

"Yes, James, that would be preferable, and for now on, could you refer to me as Clarence, friends use first names and I do consider you my friend."

"I would like that, Clarence. To keep you up to date, Clarence, the Duke did try to assassinate the Prince today, the ship he was to fly in was sabotaged. Luckily the pilot was thorough on his inspection, finding the problem before takeoff, there were fifteen lives at stake, the Duke must be stopped."

"I agree, James, the Duke was responsible for at least six lives today in another mater, we now have the evidence connecting him, but this matter must be resolved by the legal system, according to the law, it will take several weeks to compile the evidence."

"He is dangerous, Clarence, can you arrest him now; he will try again," James tells him.

"I am with Peabody as we speak, James."

"Hello, James," the Steward greets him.

"Good evening, sir," James returns.

"This is deeper than you realize, not only was the Duke planning on assassinate the Prince, he was planning a coup. We have the evidence, but it must be handled properly, there are many in the Royal Guard that support him, the command structure must be disabled," the Steward explains.

"I am of little help in this matter, James, today one of my own drones crashed a transport and attacked several security forces; as long as the Duke has access to a Driver, all are at risk."

"You are saying the Duke can control drones, that is very bad news," James said.

"Yes, it is," Clarence agrees, "very bad, his access is limited to service drones for now, but it is only a matter of time until he develops the ability to control war drones. I do not have to tell you what would happen if he did."

"Carnage is all," James said.

"Things are developing rapidly, James, you must take precautions. I will keep you updated as things progress," Clarence adds be safe, "I will end now unless there is more you wish to add."

"Yes, there is, can you reassign Captain Zercoff to the Queen duty permanently? I trust him as does the Queen."

"Lieutenant Linch as well," Sandra added.

"I can do that; their orders will be issued tonight. Anything else, James?" the Steward asks.

"No, I am finished, good night," James told the Sub-Driver and the Steward.

"Good night."

"James turns to Sandra, "I can take you and the Prince with me. I was planning on asking you to trust me with the Prince before tonight any way. I have a place that the Duke has no reach, Traay, an encampment called Black Rock, I spent many days there as a young man with my mentor."

"Thank you, James, but I will not let Kin make me run off like a scared pup, this is my home, no, I will not go."

"Please, Sandra, he will try to kill you." James, realizing he just called the Queen by her first name, his head goes down, his shoulders slump and his hands begin to tribal with embarrassment, "I'm sorry for using your name, my Queen."

Sandra gets up and stands before James, placing both hand on each side of his face, lifting his head so their eyes meet, "You, my beloved friend, have my heart and my trust, never do you need to apologize for what is in your heart, but I will not leave."

James has known the Queen for many years, and he knows her mind is made up, no amount of arguing, pleading, or begging is going to change her mind.

"Yes, my Queen, I will take the Prince to keep him safe and trust in other powers to keep you the same."

"When can you depart, James?"

"The sooner, the better, my Queen," said James.

"This is an order, my friend, from now on you will refer to me as Sandra, if it is at court or official proceeding, use protocol, but when we are together as friends, use Sandra," smiling her best smile, trying not to burst in to tears, for she could love this man.

"Yes, Sandra, I will."

"Take Tina and the girls as well," Mae adds.

"I will go see Captain Zercoff tomorrow morning and make the arrangements, we can leave the day after tomorrow," James told Sandra.

"And I will let Tina and the children know in the morning as well," Sandra said, "I would like you to spend the night, James, there is much to do tomorrow."

40

The Duke is in the King's office in the palace, with him is Steve Carter and two of his men.

"This should be my office today, Carter, and it's not because of the Captain. Hartwell has let me down too many times, and I want him dead, dead tonight," the Duke repeats, slurring his words. "Hartwell is to be here before midnight, him and one other. I will pour the Captain and the other man a drink, then turn my back to them, that is your signal, strangle the Captain. When I turn back around, I want the job done, is that clear? Hartwell is to be dead and I want the other man to witness it as a warning, an object lesson," the Duke laughs, "now repeat it back to me, Carter, so I know you understand."

"Strangle the Captain when you give the signal, simple," Carter said with a smile, "Hartwell dead and his replacement witnessing it."

"You have it," the Duke Jubilant now pouring himself another large brandy, drinking half of it in one drink. The Duke is standing at the window looking out over his domain, "This is all mine, I can do as I please, if I see it and desire it, it's mine by right. I'm the King, no one can deny me, no one," the Duke thinks to himself.

At ten to midnight, there is a knock at the door, one of Carter's men opens it and lets Major Hartwell and Captain Nash in to the room. "Sit down, Hartwell, and don't say a word, you, too, whatever your name is," the Duke commands them.

He is still standing looking out the window talking to them with his back to them, "You failed today, Hartwell, the brat is still alive. Sandy is still alive. I have told you time and time again, it's the little things we must look out for." The Duke turns and walks to his desk, facing the two men.

"Today there was a raid on the island, two years of planning shot to hell, but I anticipated the possibility and had a back-up plan," slurring his word even more with the fifth glass of brandy taking affect. "To show you there are no hard feelings, have a drink with me."

The Duke retrieves two more glasses from the bar behind his desk, filling all three glasses.

To the King, he lifts his glass and downs it in one gulp, turning around like planed, sitting down his glass, picking up the King's scepter. He hears a glass hit the floor, slapping his palm with the scepter, failure will not be tolerated, he reminds himself, slapping his palm one more time. He can hear Hartwell struggle, the King's word is law, slapping his palm again with a wide smile.

All is quiet now there, no movement behind him, turning around he sees Carter with the noose around the other man's neck, his eyes go wide and he begins to shake.

Carter is smiling with success, the Captain's head leaning to one side with his eyes wide open.

"You fool," shouts the Duke, "I said Hartwell," throwing the scepter at Carter, hitting him in the chest, "the little things," he screams, "pay attention to the little things," in a rage.

"My lord, you said the Captain," Carter rubbing his chest where the scepter struck him.

"Get out," the Duke screams at Carter, "and take this trash with you," pointing at the lifeless body of Nash.

The two men come over and grab Nash under each arm, dragging him out the door, turning over the chair.

"Not you, Hartwell," the Duke glaring at him.

Carter rights the chair, then picks up the scepter, handing it to the Duke, "As you command, my King," bowing, exiting the office.

The Duke sits in the chair behind the desk, looking directly at Hartwell, "You're lucky Carter's a dimwit or that would've been you," now very calm, "lesson learned," with a smile, "but do not ever, I repeat, ever disappoint me again, is that understood, now get out."

Hartwell takes Carter's lead, "As you command, my King," bowing, exiting the office.

On the way out, Hartwell is thinking to himself, the Duke is insane. I need to get out of this mess, I'm glad I kept the video of the Duke rehearsing the murder of the King, that will be my ticket out.

41

On the walk to the operation center, Billy, Ted, and the Light sisters are all in a good mood, a restful sleep in a comfortable bed, a hearty breakfast, a beautiful summer morning, a good day to be alive.

As they enter, the Major is behind the counter, "Good morning, Captain, I have good news. You and Lieutenant Linch have orders, they were here when I came in this morning. They are from the Stewards office, not the Guard, I must be in the presence of celebrities," presenting them to Billy, "and you have a visitor in my office."

"I'm sorry, Lieutenants, there was no orders for you yet, have a seat and I will make an equerry about your status."

"My office is second on the left, please go on back," the Major invites them.

The door is open and behind the desk is the biggest man Billy has ever seen, as tall as Ted and twice his width.

Entering the office, the man stands, "Captain Zercoff?" the man inquires.

"Yes, sir," Billy replies.

The man offers his hand, "I will be in your debt for the rest of my life, Captain, you and Lieutenant Linch."

Billy takes his hand and shakes it.

Then the man presents it to Ted. Ted hesitates with the size of the hand offered him, fearing the man will crush it but takes the skipper's lead and shakes the man's hand, it was firm but genital.

"I am Ambassador James Wildwind from the nation of Traay, please shut the door, we have business to discuss." Ted shuts the door. Sitting down, James motioning them to do the same. "Yesterday you two saved the life of the Queen and the Prince, if there is anything you ever need, all you have to do is ask, and if it is within my power, I'll make it happen."

"Thank you, Ambassador, but it was our lives as well, so there is no debt to owe," Billy said.

"Men of honor like the Queen told me," James smiles, "and I can see she was correct in her assessment. Have you read your orders, Captain?" James asks.

"No, not yet," Billy tells him, "I thought we should see you first."

"Please do so," the Ambassador prompts Billy.

He reads the orders completely, then hands it to Ted and he does the same.

"What is the mission, Ambassador?" Ted asks.

"First let's dispense with the formalities, please call me James."

"I'm Billy," he nods.

"And I'm Ted."

"We will be flying to Traay tomorrow morning with the Prince, myself and three other passengers, then you will return here and wait for the Queen orders, you will be staying at the palace, she may need to leave in a hurry. So have your ship serviced and ready by 06:00, we will be here by 06:30."

"We will be ready, James," Ted stands and states with excitement in his voice.

Billy smiles at James and he back at him, both are thinking the same thing, the boy is exited.

42

The Steward's sent four more transport's to Edgefield Island that day, a team of lawyers to comb through the documents, the Duke's men failed to destroy. A team of forensic investigators to sift through the bombed-out hanger, a recovery team to assess the downed transport and a medical ship to take care of the injured.

Five more of the Duke's men surrendered without incidents.

Tom watching all the activity comments to Adam, "The Steward is a very capable man, I bet he had every one on standby from the time we departed."

Adam smiles at Tom, "I bet you are right, his actions seem to be planned and deliberate.

Clarence had the Sargent place an explosive charge on the war drones back with a remote detonator in case the drone was compromised, we must anticipate the probability," he tells Tom, giving him the remote, "your team, as good as they are, would be ill prepared for such an event."

Tom accepts the remote without objection, he understands the risk of a rogue war drone and the damage it could do.

Senator Dearman was in charge, and not even General Kroger from the Judge Advocates Office questioned it.

That night Tom held a briefing in the lobby, the only room in the building that comes close to having the room for all the parties, it was packed, standing room only.

Security had been handed over to Captain West due to the injury of Captain Tucker.

"Captain West," Tom calls to her, "update us on security, we have guard post here and at the air field and a roving patrol, the prisoners were flown out three hours ago, there has been no other sighting, all is quiet, sir."

"Very good, Captain," he tells Carol. "General Kroger," Tom calls.

"We have him Senator, we have only gone through a third of the material and there is enough to convict him of treason, subversion, and manslaughter with a little more evidence that would be upgraded to murder."

"Thank you, General," Tom said.

"Major wise, the forensic team leader, what progress have you made at the hanger?" Tom asks.

"Not much, Senator, we lost the light, and in order for us to be thorough, we will have to wait for sun up. The bodies were removed and sent to the medical ship for preliminary evaluation."

Tom thanked the Major for his report.

"Doctor Barry, have you done the evaluation?" Tom inquired.

"Only on two so far, results show a single gunshot to the back of the skull, death was instantaneous, we will have the others by morning."

"What about the Driver victim?" Tom asks.

"Doctor Fields is handling that, Senator, she is back at the medical ship monitoring him, but what she has told me, he is deteriorating rapidly; within two days, he will be brain dead."

"That's sad," Tom comments, "thank you for your update. Captain Heart, the recovery team leader, what is your evaluation on the transport?" Tom asks.

"Total loss, Senator."

"Thank you for that, Captain," Tom said, "and thank you all for your hard work, let's call it a night and get some sleep. I think we should go have a conference with Clarence and get his input," Tom tells his companions, "he could not attend the meeting indoors, not without taking up most of the room."

Tom, Adam, and Frank make their way to where the war drone is standing.

"Were you able to hear any of the meeting, Clarence?"

"Most of it, Tom, but the background noise was very loud, there were parts I missed," he tells Tom.

Tom brought him up to speed, then asks, "What more do you have to add?"

"The Duke tried to assassinate the Queen and the Prince today, that information was conveyed to the Steward and I not more than five minutes ago; the transport they were in was sabotaged, but the attempt was thwarted, with that and the things we learned from this lab, this was a full out coup attempt," Clarence explains, "my logic tells me this is not over, he will try again, his arrogance will not let him stop no matter who must perish."

43

"Commander Banner, something is going on, sir," calls out the radar operator, "the GDF fleet is moving out in mass, it don't look like they left anyone at Freedom Station."

Timothy Banner gets up and walks to the radar station. Looking down he can see the entire fleet is on the move.

"Com, have you heard any traffic on the GDF channels?" Tim looking at the radio operator.

"No, sir, none that I can hear, heavy encrypted traffic, Commander."

"Keep a close eye on them, Betty," Tim instructs the radar operator.

Timothy Banner is in his late thirties with brown hair, average height and build with a reputation of a lady's man; he is a Lt. Commander and the second officer on the S.S. Extractor.

The brand-new mining vessel of the Deep Space Mining Company, owned by the Traay Royal family.

The ship is a gift from the Driver's to the old King of Traay for his support and loyalty in the unification of all the royal families and his help in the establishment of the federal government.

Everyone's new to the ship on the EX-T as they call her, from the Captain to the labor crew down in ore processing.

The EX-T is scheduled to begin her first shake down voyage tomorrow, making a trip to the second planet of Hasfield, then return to Tarkaneay, taking three days.

"Commander Banner," radar calls, "there is a second fleet 500,000 kilometers out, sir," closing on the GDF fleet.

"Put it on the main screen, Betty," he tells her, "the central screen comes to life with the radar telemetry, the GDF fleet has their transponders active, but the approaching one has no data.

Com, get me Commander Cane in engineering," Tim calls.

"Engineering, go bridge."

"Sidney, have you ever heard of a GDF fleet exercise where they turn off their transponder?" Timothy asks her.

Sidney Cane, in her late fifties, had retired three years ago from the GDF space fleet, but she missed the life so much, she took the job as chief engineer on the new ship, she retained her rank as Lt. Commander.

"No, Tim, that would be an unsafe practice, even in war games they keep the transponder active."

"Radar," Tim calls, "pipe radar telemetry to Engineering."

"Aye, aye, sir," radar confirms.

"The GDF fleet is forming a defensive posture," Sidney tells Tim.

"Com, wake the first officer," he orders, "no need in waking the Captain yet, it may be nothing."

Five minutes later, Commander Simon Banks, the first officer, enters the bridge, "What's up, Tim?" he asks.

"Don't really know yet, sir," Tim points to the screen, "the GDF fleet departed twenty minutes ago, then they showed up, no transponders and in a combat formation."

"Radar update," he orders, "the GDF fleet is 25K, KM and the mystery fleet are 475K, KM and closing," Betty answers.

"Com, contact Bentley Station control and see if they know anything about an exercise with the GDF fleet," the Commander orders.

"Sir," Betty announces, "the mystery fleet is tuning and heading back out."

Bentley said, "They have no information on any fleet exercises com reported."

"It must have been a drill of some kind," Simon tells the bridge, "wake me at 06:00."

"Sir," Betty brings their attention back to the screen, "there is a ship breaking low orbit heading for Freedom Station fast, it has no transponder either."

They all turn their attention back to the screen just in time to see three blips separate from the mystery ship, heading for Freedom Station.

"Bridge, engineering," Sidney shouts, "those are missiles."

Simon did not wait, "Sound general quarters."

The alarm starts sounding and people all over the ship are making their way to their emergency stations.

"Engineering," Bridge Simon calls.

Go, Bridge," Sidney responds.

"How soon can you have the engines online?" he asks.

"Ten minutes," she replied.

"Two minutes to impact," radar reports.

"Captain on the Bridge," Simon announces.

"Report, Captain," Henry Carver states.

Simon faces the Captain, "A mystery fleet drew the GDF fleet away and a ship came in from low orbit and has fired three missiles at Freedom Station, impact in fifteen seconds. Com. F.S. on the screen."

The radar image vanishes, and in its place is F.S. 4,000 kilometers away, a tiny bright spec.

"Magnify," Henry orders.

The tiny spec on the screen is replaced by one that showed more detail, you could now see the docking ports, the ship yards, the maintenance bays, and the habitat with the dome.

Five, four, three, two, one, radar counts.

Three flashes were seen, the maintenance bay was hit twice and the habitat once, a gaping hole could be seen in the habitat and the dome exploded out, atmosphere was venting.

“Mystery ship has changed course, Captain, it’s now heading for Bentley Station,” radar reported.

“Com report to B.S.O. and tell them to lock down; they have a hostile coming their way.

Radar, any change in his course, report it.”

“Helm, adjust our heading to ninety degrees, get us some maneuvering room away from Tarkaneay.”

“Engineering, Bridge, I need those engines now,” Henry shouts.

“Bridge, Engineering, you have engines, go,” Sidney shouts in return.

The S.S. Extractor starts moving away, heading in toward the sun.

44

"James, wake up, James, you need to wake up. James sits up in bed, looking around.

"James, wake up," he hears again. He turns on the light, there is no one there. "James, wake up, you are in danger."

"Sub-Driver?" James asks.

"No time, James, there is a transport on its way to your location, it's under the Duke's control. I believe it is filled with explosives, it will be at your location in fifteen minutes, get every one out."

James jumps out of bed grabbing his clothing and boots, running in to the hallway, hammering on doors, shouting every one out.

James can see lights coming on it the rooms from under the doors.

He looks up and Sandra is standing there in her night clothing, "Get the kids," he shouts, "there is a bomb on the way."

Sandra runs to Tyler's room, he is up looking around, she shouts to him get downstairs now, no time to explain; her next stop is the girl's room and they, too, are awake.

"Get up and go downstairs with Tyler, no time to explain."

Mae, Tina, and Bradly are in the hallway now looking at Sandra, downstairs now there is a bomb on the way.

Sandra can hear James banging on the staff's doors telling them to evacuate, get out of the building now.

Sandra runs downstairs and sees Tyler and the girls all in their night clothing looking scared and confused.

Mae, Tina, and Bradly come down with hands full of clothing.

Herald is leading the staff downstairs, they, too, are confused.

"Head for the lake," she tells them, "there is a bomb on the way," Sandra shouts.

Herald looks at Sandra and mouths, "The Duke?"

Sandra nods yes.

Herald yells at the staff, "To the lake now, you heard the Queen." They run out the door with Herald the last one out.

Out and down the driveway, Sandra shouts, "There is no time."

Mae, Tina, Bradly, and the children all exit the building heading down the driveway.

James comes down the stairs in a rush, "I think the building is clear, let's go," looking at Sandra. They, too, exit. "Take them down the driveway to the gate, Sandra, I'm going to get the limousine," James tells her.

She reaches out and grabs his arm, stopping him, "Be careful," she tells him, then turns and follows the rest.

James knows which limousine he is after, the one with the bags for the trip to Traay, they were loaded in the car the evening before.

He runs to the chauffeur's office looking for the keys.

James sees the box the keys are kept in, but it's locked; looking around he sees a hammer, one blow and the lock pops open, grabbing the set he needs, running for the limousine. Getting in he looks up, the door is closed, no time, he tells himself, starting the limousine, putting it in drive, pushing the accelerator to the floor, the limousine leaps forward, crashing through the door.

Sandra can see the car coming down the driveway fast, it's 200 meters away, off the road, she shouts.

James comes to a screeching halt when he sees Sandra next to the road, flinging the door open shouting at them to get in. They git in but before James leaves.

"Head count," he calls to Sandra.

She does a count, "All here, James."

He puts the limousine in drive, then stops, damn it, the gate's closed.

Bradly next to him in the passenger seat reaches over James and flips down the visor, there are two controllers, one for the garage door and one for the gate.

"You're a fool sometimes, Wildwind," he tells himself, shaking his head.

James pushes the gate button; the gate slides open and out the driveway they go.

James drives them about two kilometers away, then pulls over on a side street, turning off the engine and the lights.

"What are we doing, James?" Sandra asks.

"Waiting," he replies.

They all sat there not saying anything, dead quiet.

James rolls down the window and hears an airship coming their way.

Pointing at an object coming their direction, at 2,000 meters high, it passes over them and moves out of sight. Fifteen seconds later, there is a flash of light followed by a grate explosion, rocking the limousine.

"You saved our lives, James," Sandra reaching over the seat, throwing her arms around his neck.

"No, Sandra, it was Sub-Driver Clarence, he was the one that warned me," James tells her.

The locket comes to life, "You are not out of danger, James, there were five transports used tonight, two will be impacting the capital soon, two has already detonated at Kranstan Point, killing hundreds. The Steward has declared an emergency, the Royal Guard is in rebellion.

Follow through with your plan to evacuate to Traay, it may take some time to quell."

45

Billy is lying in bed not sleeping, only resting when he hears a large explosion in the distance, the windows rattle and the bed shakes.

Ted sits up, what's going on, still half asleep.

"Get up and get dressed, Ted, that was an explosion," Billy said, "a big one, I'm going outside to see if I can see where it came from."

"Will do, Skipper."

Billy gets dressed, moves to the window looking out, nothing this way, he goes in to the hallway, there are several rooms with the lights on. Walking down to the end of the hall, there is a window there, looking out, nothing to see, he decides to go outside, as he exits the building he sees off in the distance flames lighting up smoke as it towers in to the sky, he hurries back to the room, Ted is all dressed.

"Gather our gear, Ted, we're going to the ship, I don't know what's up," Billy explains.

They hurry down the road to the airport, taking only five minutes to make the trip to the ship. "Check our safety's on all the hatches, Ted," Billy instructs, "I'm going inside."

Heading to the back ramp, Billy checks the hair Ted placed there to see if it had been opened.

It was as they left it; Billy hits the switch lowering the ramp.

Ted joins him, "Nothing has been opened, Skipper."

Billy turns on the radio and sets it to the emergency frequency, the first thing he hears is chatter about drones attacking Crowns View, New Hope, and Cranstan Point and the activation of the Royal Guard.

"I hope the Queen is OK, this is the Duke's doing, Skipper, I know it is," Ted comments.

Billy sees headlight coming their way fast, braking hard as they get to the ship, it's a limousine. The door flies open and out comes James, four more adults, and three children.

"Get to the back, Ted, and help them in," Billy orders, "I'm starting the pre-flight check list."

Ted is gone in a flash.

James and three adults start grabbing bags and one adult usher the children in to the ship, they are met by Ted.

"Go straight in and sit down," Ted instructs. Mae and the children do as they are told, then he goes down the ramp to give the others assistance.

Sandra passes Ted with a bag, making her way into the ship, followed by Bradly with two bags and a girl with two bags. When Ted makes it to James, James hands him two bags and he carries two. Ted and James, makes it back to the ramp, Ted throws his bags inside, then hits the lever that raises the ramp, going forward he stops at the intercom, pushing the button.

"All set, Skipper," then stopping in the passenger compartment to make sure everyone was strapped in, going up the row, checking each person.

James went straight to the bridge.

Billy is starting the engines.

"Good to see you, James, we will be airborne in three minutes," Billy tells him.

"How did you know we would be coming, Billy?" James asks.

"I didn't, but we don't have assassination attempts and explosion every day, so I took a chance."

Ted entered the bridge, "All strapped in and ready to go, Skipper."

The throttle is advanced and the ship starts moving down the taxiway. One minute later, they're airborne heading northwest.

The three can hear the radio traffic, the Guard has activated, their forces are descending on New Hope, assertion that the Drivers attached the Capital and are defending their right of self-determination.

"That's a load of crap," James tells them, "it's the Duke's plan to take control."

"Skipper, there are two fast movers on an intercept ten clicks out," Ted calls out, "transponder identifies it as Guard fighters."

"Can you fly, James?" Billy looking at him.

"I was a combat pilot, Skipper," James responds.

Not hearing the Skipper comment, Ted take the countermeasure station, "James, you take the copilot seat."

They follow Billy's orders and make the changes.

"I'm heading for the deck, the transport star losing altitude rapidly; when we are at 500-meters project, our radar image at 1,500 above us."

They watch two lights go flashing by above them.

"We will stay down here below the radar. I will need to throttle back, keeping us just above the stall speed so we do not run into something," Billy informs his crew.

A voice calls out, "James."

Ted and Billy look at him with a questioning look on their faces.

"I will explain later, yes, Sub-Drive," James answers.

"There was ten more transport strikes at the capital and eight at Cranstain Point, thousands are dead, the government is in disarray, the GDF is scattered, but there is hope; the Steward and his cabinet were warned and took shelter in the command bunker and is rallying a defense as we speak."

"I thought the Duke was months away from using war drone?" James asks.

"He is, these were ordinary drones, but they are capable of flying the transports, the Duke is using his conventional ground and air forces, there is a division ascending on New Hope and one on Cranstain Point with a brigade heading to Four Rivers all backed up by air power. Call in your other Sub-Drives, you could crush this in twenty-four hours," James tells Clarence, "like you did for the Trotter revolt."

"There is the problem, James, if I step in, this will only be a pause, not a solution, the population must have confidence in their government not an alien occupation force, can you understand that, my friend?"

"Yes, I can, my friend," James concedes, "but I must join the fight."

"No, James, your mission is to keep the Queen and Prince safe, this war will take months to conclude; when it is over, the Prince must be alive to help with the restoration and rebuilding of the government, carry out your original plan."

"I will do as you ask, my friend."

"Good, I will end now, goodbye."

"If we maintain this heading, we will go right over the heaviest fighting, we either go out to sea, then turn west for two hours, then north or head east for one hour, then make our way North. It's your call, James," Billy states, "but we will need to know soon, Wolf Creek is only thirty minutes out."

"Go east," James finally decides, "the GDF at New Hope will not be that simple to defeat, the Guard will have their hands full."

Billy turns the ship east but maintains the low altitude, Ted's eyes are glued to the radar scope looking for obstacles or enemy fighters.

"I need to go back and inform the Queen about our situation," James stands to leave.

"No, James, bring her up here, the children do not need to know that," Billy suggests.

James places his hand on Billy's shoulder, "You, Skipper, are a wise man, I am not a father and would have never considered that."

James exits the bridge and heads back to the passenger compartment. Entering he sees Sandra sitting alone in the first set of seats, Mae has the children in the back row, they are sleeping. Tina and Bradly are two seats in front of Mae, talking softly.

James sits next to Sandra and she looks up at him with worry on her face.

"What's happening, James? Why did we turnaround? Are we going to be OK?"

He reaches out and pulls Sandra over, giving her a genital hug, whispering to her it will be fine. That is when he noticed she is still in her nightgown; he can see the shape of her breasts and the smoothness of her thighs. He straightens up and averts his eyes.

"Come forward, we have some things to talk about and I would like to do it away from the children," he said, "I think you should get dressed first," smiling, keeping his eyes looking at her face, "come forward when you're ready."

With that James stands and goes forward.

Sandra stands and looks at herself, a blush rushes to her face and a smile at the same time. James is a gentleman.

On her way back to the cargo compartment where the luggage was stowed, she invites Tina to join her; she, too, is in her night clothing.

Twenty minutes later, a fully clothed Sandra joins James, Billy and Ted on the bridge, followed by Tina and Bradly.

Ted is too engaged with the radar and did not pay them any attention.

"What news did the Sub-Driver give you, James?" Sandra asks.

"We are in a civil war, the Duke is marching troops to the capital as we speak, they are also marching on Cranstan Point and Four Rivers, the heart of the GDF. The Steward and his cabinet are in New Hope trying to rally a defense, the Drivers are out of this fight, it's up to us," James informs them. "What do we do, Bradly?" asks James. "We keep the Royal family safe; they will be needed after our victory and victory will happen. The Duke has over played his hand," James said, "he is trying to pull the Drivers in to the conflict, so he can claim they are an occupational force, anyone with any intelligence knows that that is not the case."

"Will we be safe in Traay?" Tina asks.

"As safe as we can be," James reassures her.

"Skipper, there is a mountain range coming up, twenty-five kilometers, its 3,000 meters elevation," Ted warns him.

"Take the stick, James," Billy commands, "I need to check the maps."

"Fifteen kilometers out," Ted warns.

Billy is looking over the maps, "I see no other way."

"Eight kilometers out," Ted warns.

"We will need to climb," Billy orders everyone in to the passenger compartment and strap in.

"Three kilometers out," Ted warns.

"Climb to 3,500 meters," Billy calls to James, "eyes on the radar, Ted, we will be above the mountain and they will paint us with their radar."

James has already pulled back on the stick and advance the throttle to full power, everyone is pressed in to their seats as the lady ship does what is asked of her.

"We're over, Skipper," Ted reports.

"Nose us down, James, to 2,000 meters, they may not have seen us yet," Billy hopes, "turn us north and follow the mountain. Ted, if they see us, they will come from the west, over the ridge at around 4,500 meters, then dive like we did," Billy informs him, "you may only get one or two sweeps with the radar before the mountain hides them, so stay sharp."

Ten minutes pass.

Then twenty.

Then thirty.

"I think they missed us," Billy sighs, "I'll take the stick now, James."

James looks over at Billy, "You know your stuff, Skipper, combat maneuvers, terrain awareness, craft's strengths and weakness, all the things a good combat pilot need's. I don't think I have ever flown with any one better! Why are you still a Captain?

"Life, James, just life and that is all," Billy would say.

They continued their path for two more hours without any surprises.

The sun starts to peek over the horizon, James can see they are getting close.

"We need to go here, Skipper, that black rock," James shows him on the map, "we will need to go west now, it's about sixty kilometers."

Billy makes the turn and descends 1,500 meters.

The land of Traay is flat on the high plains with a numerous canyon's spider webbing across the plateau.

About ten minutes later, Ted yells, "Bandits nine o'clock low, twelve clicks out. We will try to make it to one of the canyons, the fighters have limited maneuverability, it's a tight place for the fast movers," he tells James.

One on the left side, James pointing so Billy could see where he was referring to.

Billy banks hard, and at the same time, puts her lady ship in a deep dive.

The rime of the canyon is only 200 meters below them now and it is running parallel. Billy puts the main drive jets in full revers, their speed drops rapidly, but at the same time, the stall warning alarm starts sounding, they are falling like a rock, he swings the lift jets to the up position and applies full throttle, slowing the fall but not stopping it, the rime is now above them, nosing the ship down and the main jets back in forward thrust, the fall stops, there is tree tops only 100 meters below them when the transport is hit by a rocket. The left two main jets explode, fire alarm is sounding now, the lady ship starts shaking violently. Billy has no rudder control, two more rocket flash in front of the transport and explode on the ground below them. Billy sees a stream eighty meters to the left, so he uses the ailerons rolling the ship left, letting the lift jets push them left; the only problem with that is now the ship is sliding down as well. Billy knows they are going to crash, he writes the ship, so it's level, and swing the lift jets forward, their forward momentum is stopped, but they are going to hit the ground from fifty meters.

46

Tom is asleep in one of the small offices on a couch when a sentry comes running in.

"Senator, you need to come quick, the war drone is destroying the small ones."

Tom goes outside in time to see the war drone rip the last drone in half, he pulls out the detonator and arms it, then put his finger on the trigger.

"What's happening, Sub-Drive," Tom calls out.

"Sorry, Tom. I could not wait, they were trying to gain control of the drones, so I took action," Clarence said, "and there are things you need to be made aware of, the Duke has started a coup."

"What?" with his finger still on the trigger.

"If you would, please assemble the command staff, I will explain," Clarence requested.

The men had dug a fire pit between the wood line and the building, they had a fire burning providing light.

In attendance was Tom, Adam, Frank, Carol, General Kroger, and Major Wise.

The drone sits down, so he is not towering over the group, then addresses them, "A civil war has started tonight! The Duke has activated the Royal Guard, he has sent forces to the Capital, Cranstan Point, and Four Rivers, the attack started with drones piloting transport filled with explosive. At last count there has been forty such attacks plus one on the Palace at Crowns View. I gave all targets a fifteen-minute warning when I realized their intentions. The Steward, his cabinet, and GDF command were all evacuated in time, but the damage is great. The GDF is mobilizing a defense, but it is disorganized at the moment. The Queen and Prince are with Ambassador Wildwind in Traay.:

"What are your plans, Sub-Drive?" the General asks, "are you planning a counter strike?"

"No, the Drivers will not interfere, we did in the Trotter revolt, it only delayed this one, this is your problem to solve, victory or defeat, it's in your hands."

"What about the war drones and Drivers?" Tom asks

"We have interceded in that matter, two Sub-Drives as we speak are neutralizing that threat, one in Wolf Creek and the other at Trinity Station. All drones and Drivers will be confiscated or destroyed; by the time the sun rises, there will not be a Driver or drone on this planet, including this one."

"But, Sub-Drive, your advice is welcomed," Tom pleads, "don't abandon us."

"We are not abandoning you, Tom; on matters of deep space exploration, we will continue our assistance, but on all matters here, we can no longer participate. If you wish to grow and evolve, you must do it yourself." With that the war drone stands, "Good bye, Tom, I will always consider us friends, one day our paths may cross again."

The war drone walks to the edge of the forest, turns his back to the trees so he is facing the fire, the charge on his back explodes, the war drone falls to the ground.

Tom and Adam walk over to the drone. There is a fifty-centimeter hole in its back where the charge was placed, still smoking with sparks of electricity discharging.

"You know, Adam, Clarence was not a man, but he was a good one, whatever you would call him," Tom said with a sense of loss in his heart, "but knowing everything he said was true, this is their fight, and I'll be dammed if I will let the Duke destroy thirty-five years of work for his egotism."

Tom turns and orders in a loud voice, "I want every piece of evidence gathered and on the transports by first light, we are heading back to Stink Water. "

On the walk back to the building, Adam presents Tom with a plan, "The Sub Driver confiscated the Duke's Drivers at Wolf Creek, he may come looking for what he left here and I'm looking for a fight. Let's draw him to us and show the Guard what the GDF is made of."

"How do we do that, Adam?" questions Tom.

"We send an unsecured message to headquarters, asking what to do with the four Driver's and twenty drones, his ego will not let that go."

Tom smiles, "I think you have something there; it will also pull men out of the fight at the capital, good job, Major. Captain West, can I see you for a moment?" Tom waves to Carol.

"Yes, sir," she steps in front of Tom and Adam.

"What is your full complement at Stink Water, Captain?" Tom asks.

"Two companies, sir, Alpha and Bravo, 400 strong, two elements of Alpha are here, sir," the Captain reports.

A big smile appears on Toms face, "I want a war counsel in twenty minutes in the lobby, pass the word."

Walking in to the room, Adam shouts, "ATTENTION," the room comes to attention, "Tom still holds the rank of colonel in the GDF reserve."

Tom enters right behind Adam "At ease." Tom commands. "You all know we are at war and we are going to do our part," Tom tells the group. "First thing, we are on radio silence, no unauthorized communication, that is imperative to the mission," Tom orders. "General Kroger, how long until you have all the evidence on your transport?"

"Within the hour, Senator," he replies.

Good, Tom thinks to himself.

"You will be going to Stink Water, not the capital General, once there go to the government communications center, at max power, on an unsecured channel. Use these words, General, message for the Steward, you and his team leader, Captain West, are on your way back with the evidence to the capital, you need instructions on what to do with the four Drivers and the twenty drones on the island. You can have a cargo ship there in two days to pick them up, you did leave two platoons to guard them; on second thought, make it thirty drones, a little more honey for the trap. Captain West, you will be going with the General to Stink Water; before you leave, contact your X.O. over the radio, also on an unsecured channel and have him gear up for a flight to the capital, air insertion, A and B companies, supplies for two weeks, then coming back here, bring everything you think we will need and send those four gun boats."

Carol nodding her head, understanding the ruse.

"Major Wise, Tom calls you and your team will be going back with the General, we will be commandeering your transport, it will be our eye in the sky."

"Senator, my men and I would like to stay, we can help with the fortification and any traps my engineers can come up with," the Major volunteers.

Tom looks to Adam.

Adam nods yes.

"Very well," Tom welcomes them to the fight. "Doctor Barry," Tom calls next, "I need all of your medical supplies and any equipment that can be removed from your medical transport, your team is not combat medics, and I will not order them to stay, but I will except volunteers."

Half stayed.

Tom calls Doctor Fields next.

Before he could say anything, "I'm staying, Tom," she said.

Tom nods his approval.

"Captain Tucker," Tom calls.

"The wings broke but not the mouth, I can still give order, Senator," Frank answers.

"I was going to ask you to take charge of the defense preparations," Tom smiles at him.

"You have your orders," Tom concludes.

"ATTENTION," Major Potter commands.

The room once more comes to attention.

Tom and Adam exit, everyone starts their jobs.

"I hope I did not bite off more than either of us can swallow, Major. I may have put too much honey in the trap, the Duke may send a battalion not a company or two," Tom reflects, "that would make the odds two to one in their favor."

"But we have the element of supersize and fighting on our own ground, he's the one that took too big of a bite," Adam grinning, "we'll kick his ass."

47

Not one drone missed, each transport carried 10,000 kilograms of explosives, destroying an area larger than one kilometer in diameter.

The capital building and all of its surrounding building are flattened and on fire. New Hope is in total chaos, the Steward and all of the cabinet are dead, the Duke smiles.

"My forces are moving unopposed. The Navy at Four Rivers is just as bad. Cranstan Point took the most, the GDF training base took four strikes, there will be no new recruits, they only have what they have. Freedom Station is destroyed and Bentley's docks have been damaged, so the GDF Space Force has no support, my fleet will make short work of them in the days to come. The only bad news was the bitch and the brat were tipped off somehow, my spy said they left right before the strike. In the company of Wildwind, he followed them to the airport and saw them boarded Zercoff's transport heading west, they won't get far."

At two in the morning, a young runner maybe eighteen or so came in to the Duke's command center from the communication room with a report that the Drivers have landed at the building Pierce was using and took him and destroyed all the Drivers.

The Duke standing in the middle of his operation room, in his newly designed uniform for the occasion, all black with red highlights, ribbons, and metals adorning the chest, started shaking when he heard the report.

"Come here," he told the messenger, slapping the King's scepter in to the palm of his gloved hand. "On your knees," the Duke ordered. The messenger did as he was told. The Duke still slapping his palm. "Now repeat your message." The young messenger started to repeat his message, the Duke started striking him with the scepter, over and over, screaming, "It's the little thing," he stops, "can't you fools get that through your thick heads?"

He composes himself, straightening his uniform, looking down at the blood that had sprayed on the front of it, he tells himself, you're a genius, Kenneth, the blood will not be seen when it dries.

Two guards come over to the body and start to take it away, the Duke waves them off, "No, leave it there as a reminder to all, do not to disappoint me," he said.

The reports kept coming in all night with words like routed, retreating, destroyed, and annihilated, making the Duke happy and in a jubilant mood. The best was the report that all the Drivers had left orbit and were heading out in to deep space.

"They are running," the Duke tells the staff around him, "they are cowards when pitted against their own technologies."

Shortly after sun up, two runners came in at the same time; the Duke waves them over, they are standing next to the body of their friend, looking down at him.

The Duke snaps, "Don't look at him, look at me." The boys turn their gaze to the Duke, one looks extremely nerves, the other not so. The Duke points at the nervous boy, "Report," he orders.

The boy complies, "The Drivers have collapsed the cavern the drones were stored in on Trinity Station, my king."

The Duke frowns and slaps his palm with the scepter, then he looks down at the body, "I can't teach too many object lessons today, they will think I'm evil. Tell them to start recovery and salvage what they can, now move," he orders the boy. The boy bows and nearly runs for the door; this made the Duke smile. "Your turn," he points at the other boy.

"The transport that was carrying the Queen was shot down and is burning, my king."

"She is not the Queen," he shouts, "she is a bitch, never refer to her like that again, do you understand?" but smiling with the news. "Have them send in a team, bring me their heads, and I will require it by the time the sun goes down, now go."

The boy bows, "By your command, my Lord."

That made the Duke smile even more, I like the sound of that the thinks to himself, I think I'll make a decree that that is the way I wish to be addressed, by your command, yes, I like it.

It is ten in the morning and the Duke is getting tired; he is sitting in his chair and his eyes keep closing on the own.

A runner comes in and goes to General Gates, the Duke's head of intelligence.

The Duke watches the boy talking to him, but he is too tired to care, then the boy leaves.

The General walks up to the Duke, "My Lord, it looks as if the Drivers forgot the ones, we had on Edgefield Island, we intercepted a transmission asking what to do with them. There are four Drivers and thirty drones, we also intercepted one from Stink Water. Their garrison is packing up and heading to New Hope. It's too convenient, my Lord, it sounds like a trap."

The Duke yawns, "You give them too much credit, General, send Colonel Alvarado."

"Yes, my Lord," the General replies, bowing.

The Duke holds up his hand, "By your command, my Lord, remember that, by your command, my Lord," he repeats again. "I do like the sound of that, now go," looking at the General, he notices the body in the middle of the floor, "and take that away," pointing at it, "I'm going to take a nap."

As the General is walking away, he is thinking to himself, what have we done?

48

As the transport fell to the ground, the two forward wings struck two boulders on each side, sheering off the wings, making the impact not one violent one but two lesser impacts, the body of the transport is now wedged between two boulders. All Billy can see out his side window is rock; looking out the front window, he can see the stream running to the right of them.

He hears James steer next to him. Looking over he is bleeding from the mouth where his head struck the yoke.

"You OK, James?" he asks.

James gives him the thumb up.

Looking back, he sees Ted out cold and a gash on the side of his head and blood flowing from it.

"I'm going aft," James said, then makes his way back, a little wobbly but making progress.

Billy gits up to check on Ted, he is starting to move.

"You alright, Rocky?" Billy asks him, helping him sit up straight.

"We need to get out, I smell smoke," Ted said to Billy.

Billy helps him to his feet and they follow James aft; Ted is shaky at first, but it passes.

The two enter the passenger compartment, James is helping the Queen to her feet. Mae is doing the same with the children with Tina's help.

Bradly is coming forward from the cargo compartment, "We can't get out, that way" he calls, "there is a boulder sticking through the ramp."

"There are emergency exits mid ship," Billy tells Bradly, then points to it.

Bradly reaches up and pulls the emergency lever down, a whoosh is heard as the hatch fly's off and the slide starts to inflate.

Bradly helps Mae out first, then the children.

James, Sandra, Billy, and Ted make it to where Bradly is.

James tell Bradly, "You next," then he helps Sandra to exit. That is when they hear the fighter coming their way above the canyon rim. James shouts outside, "Take cover!" The seven on the ground makes for a stand of trees close by. "We need our equipment," James said. The three go back to the cargo compartment. "Grab the six backpacks, the luggage we don't need," James tells them.

They make their way back to the emergency shoot and throw the backpacks out first, then James goes, followed Ted.

Billy hesitates, he sticks his head out and orders them to the trees, "I'll be right there." He runs forward and reengages the fuel switch on the aft lift jets, grabbing the flair gun, emergency first aid kit, and the map case, running back to the emergency exit, jumping out. As soon as his feet hit the ground, he was running to the other survivors.

"Get further away," he shouts as he makes it to them.

They go about twenty meters when Billy turns around and shoots the flair gun at the transport; it strikes the lift jet, then the transport explodes in a ball of fire, black smoke starts ascending to the canyon rim.

They can hear the fighter jet making its way back for a second look.

James compliments Billy, "Good idea, Captain, that's why you're in charge," saluting him with a grin.

"What now?" Sandra asks Billy.

"We need to get away from the wreck, let's head up the canyon at least two kilometers, then we'll take a break and determine our next step."

The four men, Sandra, and Tina host the pack and start their walk. James is in the lead with Bradly in the back.

It is a difficult and slow walk, the canyon meanders, twice the stream snaked back on them, forcing them to climb up the side of a near vertical cliff to follow the stream.

It took them four hours to make the two kilometers trip as the crow flies, but they covered at least three.

At noon they took their first break.

James opened Sandra's pack and removed energy bars to reduce the weight in her pack, that was the meal.

The adults, minus Mae, spread out the map on a rock and determine their position.

James points to a spot on the map, "This is our destination, Black Rock, we are here," pointing again at the map, "we are fifteen kilometers away, the best route is continuing up the canyon, keeping to the left on these forks, but we will run right in to the Hold Out and that would be no better than meeting up with the Duke's men. We will climb to the top and cut across the plain until we come to this canyon, going down it, then following it to Black Rock. We will need to stay below the rim until morning, then climb the rest of the way up and make a mad dash to the next canyon."

They all walk back to their pack and James stops, looking down, there are seven pieces of trash on the ground from their energy bars.

He calls everyone together, "I need all of you to pay attention to what I am about to say," James said, "we are in a race to save our lives and this will not do," reaching down and picking up the wrapper from the energy bar, "little things like this will give away our trail, a discarded piece of trash can end everyone's life, do you understand? If you discarded one, pick it up."

The only ones that had not were James, Billy, and Ted; their military training prevented that.

Sandra approaches James and puts her hand out to retrieve the one James pick up, "Sorry, James," she tells him, "it will not happen again."

Ted speaks up, "Let's leave them a trail, James; you said if we continue up this canyon, we will run in to the Hold Outs. Let's get our pursuers to do just that."

A smile appears on James's face, "Bradly," he calls over. Addressing Ted and Bradly now, James explains the plan, "We will be making for that shelf on the canyon wall," pointing to the place, "I would like you two to gather our trash. Ted, you go back the way we came 200 meters and, Bradly, you go up the canyon the same, leave a noticeable trail as you go, drop your trash, then make your way up to us, pay close attention you do not leave one going up the canyon wall," he throws his trash down where they are standing, they head out with their mission. "Gear up, we're moving," he tells the remainder of their group.

James looks down the canyon and he can still see a ribbon of smoke rising from the crashed transport but no indication they are being pursued yet, but he knows they will be soon.

It takes them two hours to make the climb to the shelf, it was a hard climb up 400 meters.

The shelf was fifteen meters wide and three meters deep; at the back of the shelf, there is a ravine opening with no more than a four-meter-wide mouth.

"We can sleep in there tonight," indicating the ravine. James tells the group, "We'll keep the children in the middle, adults on both ends, we will not start a fire tonight, the weather will be comfortable."

About twenty minutes later, Ted make it to the shelf; ten minutes after that, Bradly shows up. He is noticeably tiered.

The sun has been behind the rim of the canyon for some time now and the light is fading in the sky.

"I suggest we start getting our beds ready, it will be dark soon," James prompts them, then he heard the transport coming their way, it passes right over them above the rim.

He can't see the crash from here, but he knows about where it is, the ramp was down on the transport. When it gets to were James thinks the site is, he counts twelve parachutes descending in to the canyon.

"The hunt starts," he tells Billy sitting next to him.

The Duke's men are not hiding their presence. James can see fire light dancing on the rim of the canyon, a big camp fire, that should draw the Hold Outs to them.

James and Billy are on the canyon side, Ted and Bradly are on the ravine side, James told them to sleep in shifts, "We need eyes on both ends all night."

It was getting close to midnight when James comes to relieve Billy, "All quiet," he reports to James.

James sits down next to Billy, looking out at the canyon, "You know, Skipper, I miss the peacefulness of this land."

"I have to agree with you, James, it has a very peaceful sense to it."

"Once more I'm in your debt, Skipper, in three days you have saved the Queen and the Prince twice."

Don't forget my own," giving James a smile.

"That was some flying you did today," James reflecting on the events of the ordeal, "never would I have thought what you did possible, we should have been cut in to pieces coming down in the trees and boulders like we did."

"It was dumb luck, that's all it was," Billy replies.

"Call it what you like, Skipper, but we are alive and it was you that made that possible," placing his large hand on Billy's shoulder, "you're the man, Skipper."

The two can hear Ted and Tina talking at the other end, a little louder than James would prefer, but he knows their voices will carry to the rim of the canyon, not the floor, the other end is a different matter. "I will talk to them in the morning."

49

Transports have been coming in all morning, landing, unloading their cargo, then making another trip.

The island is mostly flat with only one hill in the center, it's no more than 200 meters high, that is where Tom will make their stand.

Standing on the top looking out, Tom can see lines of men carrying supplies to their base camp, ammunition, food, and equipment.

Captain West commandeered two tractors from a construction project at the airport and twenty baggage carts. They, too, are making their way to camp with all the heavy equipment; she also contacted Evelyn and had her bring Tom's uniform to the staging area.

An hour ago, Tom watched the four gunboats pull up to the dock. Tom sent word for the commander of the flotilla to report to him ASAP.

Standing there watching, Adam joins Tom.

"I have to compliment Captain West. Her men are some of the best I have seen, but they are a security detachment, not a heavy combat one; she has no artillery, no mortars. Only four medium caliber weapons, the largest ones we have are the four, twenty-millimeter chain guns on the fast boats, Colonel. If the Duke comes at us with a full battalion, we may get our asses handed to us," the major reminds Tom.

"I know, Adam, it will be a hard fight, the best thing we could hope for is we cut the head off the snake right from the start. I'm going to place the gun boats on the approach to the runway, they are to concentrate their fire on the lead bird, then shift their fire on any of opportunity. If we can bring down five transports, that would even the odds a little. The overall plan is to wear them down, starting at the airfield, engage, then retreat, engage, then retreat all the way up the hill, keeping the uphill advantage; by the time we reach the top, I'm hoping the fight will be out of them."

"Captain Tucker is supervising the defenses," Adam tells Tom, "he is having the men dig shallow tranches with kill zones, starting at the hanger, working his way up the hill."

Major Wise come up with booby traps for Captain Tucker, "Place this in the bottom of the trench," he tells him, "cover it with a little dirt," as they are retreating, "pull the pin as soon as someone gets in the trench, presser switch closes, bang; after a few of them, they will no longer trust our trenches, denying them cover," Frank excepted them with glee.

The second contribution from Major Wise, his men removed the power cable that ran from the industrial building to the hanger that provided the electricity. It is coiled next to the runway at the half way point, on command it can be strong across the runway and secured one meter off the ground, the first transport to land will have its landing gear ripped out from under it, delaying the next ship to land until they can clear it.

With the fact that the defenders will not have any secure communication, Tom asks General Kroger to ask for four volunteers from his team, eight accepted the call, it was their job to write up contingency scenario, so with a single word, his men would know what to do. The down side to this plan is if a team is captured, the enemy would have it, so to lessen the impact, each team had their own codes. The only one that had all the codes was command; if that was compromised, the battle would have already been lost.

The industrial building is bait, the drones were placed around the main door, then trees were fell dragged to the building and placed next to it as cover, the problem is they are only one meter from it, a small team is to engage getting them to take cover, then use the Duke's own explosives, leveling the building, and the troop behind the cover.

The Commander of the gunboats reported to Tom around 10:00.

"Lieutenant Folgers reporting, Colonial," saluting Tom.

"At ease, Lieutenant," Tom responds with his own salute. Tom outlines his mission, "Your guns are the biggest ones we have, every transport you take out will be fifty less men on the battlefield, so you are key to our success. I would like you to beach the bow of your vessel just enough to make it appear to be part of the shore line, in a picket on the glide path of the runway, cut some foliage camouflaging your gunship, concentrate all of your fire on the lead bird, then move to a new targets, your call on that. The more you down, the better, then disengage, move out to sea, and await new orders." Sargent Tom calls, "The gunboat codes," handing them to the lieutenant, "your call sign is shark, good luck."

He salutes and goes to carry out is mission.

By noon the last of supplies had arrived and the transport has departed, no more in bound was announced, so the cable was strung across the runway.

50

It was still dark when James woke the group, "Get some food and check to make certain you leave nothing behind," James instructed, telling each one in a wispier, "we will go as soon as it gets light."

James goes to check on Billy; he is on watch at the mouth of the ravine. Ted and Tina followed him.

"Anything to report, Skipper?"

"No, it's dead quiet."

James turns his attention to Ted, "I would like you to stay behind as a rear guard, I don't like you staying by yourself, but you're in the best shape to travel fast."

"I'll stay with him," Billy volunteers.

"No, Skipper, I need you with us, and I mean no disrespect, you would slow him down, you're a bit over weight."

"None taken, James, but two sets of eyes are better than one."

"I volunteer," Tina speaks up, "I'm in great shape."

James ponders this for a moment, "OK, you stay with Ted, but as soon as you see the hunting party go by, I want you two to move as fast as you can. I will leave an arrow etched on a rock where we leave the ravine, go in the opposite direction. If someone is chasing you, they should follow the arrow in the wrong direction; once you are out of the ravine, use your compass and head do west, we will be waiting for you at the next ravine."

The party has been gone for an hour and a half when Ted gets his first glimpse of their pursuers.

They are watching from their perch as the one in the lead bends down and picks something up, waving to one of the other men who comes over and starts talking to the first one. The second man raises his arm, swings it in a circle, then points up the canyon, never making a sound.

Ted and Tina back away from the ledge on hand and knees, then grab their packs and start after the group.

They have been traveling for about four hours, James sees what he has been looking for, the ravine widens out and the walls are less steep, only about twenty meters to the top.

"We'll take a break here," he announces. After they have eaten, James calls the children over to him, "I have a mission for you three," using the word mission instead job, giving the children a sense of participation, pointing to the right wall of the ravine, "I would like you three to go up and down there several times," he points, "make it a point to drag your feet and make tracks."

They accept the mission with pride and set out to accomplish it.

"That was well played. James," Sandra compliments him with a broad smile.

"They need to feel like they are part of it," James told Sandra, "and this will help," as he watches them make the second trip.

There is a large bolder almost in the center of the ravine. James reaches down and finds a stone he can use to scratch the arrow on the face of the rock, looking down stream so anyone coming up will see it plainly.

After the children have accomplished their mission, James call everyone together, "It's time to go," he told them, "leave your trash on the ground, we will be going to the left, but this time stay on the rocks and try not to dislodge any or leave any marks on the ground."

They went up in single file, stepping from stone to stone, the last three meters was sheer. James took out a rope and pulled up each one up, that took an hour.

Standing on the rime of the ravine, all they see is grass, one to two meters high for as far as they could see.

"We need to make some time," James tells Billy. "I can't watch for hazards and watch the compass at the same time. If you could keep me on course," due west, tossing the compass to Billy.

"It's near noon, so the sun is directly overhead." Billy checks the heading and points the direction to follow.

James starts off at a good pace, he is the only one that can see over the tall grass but not by much.

They traveled for twenty minutes, and James held up his hand to stop the group. He is looking down another gully; damn, so soon, he thinks.

It will take an hour to cross it, even though it was no more than four meters deep and three meters across.

James tells Billy, "I think we should wait for Ted and Tina."

"I agree," Sandra speaks up, "this will be a good place to spend the night, even though we still have three hours of daylight. I'm worried about the kids finding us, they could go right past us if they are up or down the gully 100 meters."

Standing on the edge looking both ways, James understood Sandra's concern; the gully did not run true, it wandered. From the floor, you could not see fifty meters in either direction.

"If they were quiet crossing, they could miss us completely and we would never know it."

James smiles to himself, thinking a month ago, Sandra had one child; it seems she has adopted four more, I love her good heart.

"Let's make camp," he said.

Billy went to explore the route they will take tomorrow. James told him to only go one hour out, then come back; that was two hours ago, and Ted and Tina should have rendezvoused already.

James looks at the sun, less than an hour tell sundown, worry is starting to creep up on him. There are dangers that an outsider cannot understand in Traay, predators, snakes, insects, hostiles, and the most dangers of all, the land itself.

Standing looking over the grass, James sees the grass moving the way they came, it's moving fast. One hundred and fifty meters to the south of them and 250 meters east, it may be a wild dog chasing a rabbit or an antelope, then he sees a flash of red hair above the grass, not stopping to question is it or not, he takes off in a sprint, trying to intercept them before they run right off the edge of the gully.

Every few steps, James would take a small leap up and get his barring on their track, adjusting his course for the intercept.

Tina and Ted knock James off his feet when they both run in to him, falling on top of him.

Ted out of breath, panting heavy, manages three words, "Natives behind us."

James holds up his finger to his lips, indicating quiet, in a whisper, he asks, "Explain."

"Tina and I were following the ravine. Just as we came around a bend, I saw movement up ahead, so we took cover; there were three men coming down the right-hand bank, they went your way. We followed them to your mark on the rock, I could see the arrow plainly. They met up with another eight, they were having a discussion about the mark. One pointed to the right the way the arrow pointed, another one shook his head no and pointed left, the first one hit the second, the others gathered around and watched, we backtracked some twenty meters and climbed out and ran your way."

"Let's get back to the others," James tells them, standing, he parts the grass and Ted and Tina can see the gully. Two more meters and they would have run right over the edge.

James looks at the two and can see their comprehension of the situation, he will not need to scold them about running head long on the grass lands.

The three climbs down the gully and start making their way back to the others when they hear raised voices.

James holds up his hand to stop them, motioning them down, he stealthily goes forward ten meters.

On each side of the gully's rim, he can see men pointing weapons at Sandra and the others, there are two with their backs to him in the gully between him and the party; he can't see the other end but know there are men there as well.

He knows the Hold Outs respect courage above any other trait and only seconded by age. Boldly showing no fear, he steps out, making his presence known.

There is a warning cry from the rim, the two right in front of him spin and point their weapons at him.

James continues his movement forward, putting his arms up at shoulder height, placing each hand on the elbows and walks right past the two, they separate and allow him to pass.

James stops right next to Sandra, showing ownership of the woman. Looking up he spots the man he believes to be in charge; with hand movements, he begins to communicate, sweeping his arms out and bringing them together. Next, he places his wrists together in a cross, then slides a finger across his neck, then points to where he thinks the downed transport is, then repeats the sweeping motion, then calls to Ted and Tina, "Join us."

They walk forward right past the two men and join the group.

The men on the rim climb down and start tying their hands, excluding Mae and the children.

Where is the Skipper, James thinks to himself as they begin being led down the gully?

51

At 15:15, the first call came in

"Birthday party, this is the caterer, your cake will be ready in fifteen minutes with ten candles on strawberry icing."

Tom looks to the Sargent with the coeds, ten transports coming from the northeast, fifteen minutes out.

Standing next to Tom is Adam, "They're going to jump," he said to Tom.

"Birthday party, this is the caterer, your main course will be ready in twenty minutes, pasta with white sauce and four sides."

The Sargent relays to Tom, "Four heavy's coming from the northwest."

"It's a full Battalion, get them ready, Adam," Tom commands.

Only one word was transmitted: groundhog.

All the teams had the arrival codes, so there was no need to tell them what was coming.

Looking to the northeast, Tom can see them coming, flying at 600 meters high as they pass right over their heads, he can see the ramp is down and men standing ready to jump.

The top of the hill is two kilometers from the lab building, and it only takes seconds for the transports to reach it, the back five ships start drooping their troops, then breaks east. Ten seconds later, the first five unload theirs, breaking east to join the first five, they begin orbiting the island.

As soon as the troops hit the ground, Tom hears automatic gun fire; he knows it is his forces are herding the Guard troops in to the building to take cover, he can only see the roof of the building due to the thick forest.

A few seconds laterl he hears the airfield joining the fight. He has a good view of the runway and can see the parachutes lined up floating down; as soon as they hit the ground, Tom can see them running for the ditch that his transport jumped over two days ago.

"Birthday party, this is the caterer, we have blush wine with two glasses ready in two minutes."

Tom looks to the Sargent, who is looking through the papers, "Fast movers coming from the southeast."

Looking out Tom can see the heavy's lining up for landing, but he know the fast movers can cut his troops to pieces.

He grabs the radio, "Shark, change target, you have FM moving your way, engage them first."

Looking to the runway, he can see a group of men trying to cut the cable by shooting at it, then there are five bright flashes in the ditch; they had placed explosives in the ditch and barrels of fuel. Tom knows as soon as it detonated, his men will be disengaging and heading for the next rally point.

The fast movers arrive and begin strafing both sides of the runway; they head straight up at the end of their gun run to make a second pass, their underbelly is presenting a clean target, tracers arc up and cross their path, one explodes, the other heads for the ground as the first heavy makes its landing.

The gunfire can still be heard from the lab building, then it explodes also.

The men on the ground must have weakened the cable, it did not shear the nose gear like they planned, it snapped where the men were shooting at it.

As the nose gear came into contact with the cable, it stretched, then snapped, shooting across the runway, wrapping around the nose gear, making the heavy swerve to the left, running off the runway in to the trees, doing massive damage and shaking up the occupants badly.

The gunboats did not get a shot at the second heavy as it passed them unhampered, but they did the third. Tom watch as four lines of tracers converged on it; it tried to bank hard left to avoid it, but it was too late. All four lines of tracers connected, fire was coming from two engines, and a third was smoking; he watched it right itself and head out to sea.

As the fourth heavy was attempting to land, the fast mover came in from the sea, the same way the third heavy went out.

Rockets flashed from it as it targets the gunboats.

Two of the gunboats sprayed the belly of the heavy as it passed, but it made it to the ground.

The other two concentrated on the fast mover.

The rockets exploded and one boat was gone.

The fast mover flashes over Tom's head, circling the island to make another run on the gunboats, they were already backing out heading to sea.

Tom was certain the fast mover would pursue the gunboats they had killed; his wing man and he intended on getting revenge. He watched as the boats formed a line heading south, the fast mover was right on the water closing fast, three lines of tracers erupt form the gunboats as the fast mover unleashes his guns, the fast movers tracers cut right across one boat, silencing its gun, but the other two continue to firing, one line of tracers intersect the fast mover and it noses into the sea.

From his vantage point, Tom looks at the carnage he had unleashed.

There is thick black smoke rising from the airfield and the lab building.

Two kilometers out, he can see the heavy sinking below the waves, he knows the survivors will never make the island, the current will carry them out to sea.

The second heavy is sitting two thirds down the runway sideways, men were panicking running to nowhere.

The fourth heavy that came in is starting to smoke; it had to stop short to keep from running in to the second heavy and it is right next to the fire in the ditch with flames reaching fifty meters in to the air; he can see men jumping out and running away.

Tom sees the ten orbiting transports in a double V formation, they are approaching the proximity of the gunboats.

"Shark, this is birthday party, cut the cake."

He had no more than given the command, he sees three lines of tracers shoot skyward, no transport was hit, but their formation was scatted, ships going in all direction.

The fourth heavy explodes, adding more chaos to the already chaotic scene.

"That's one round for the good guys," Adam tells Tom, "and we cut their numbers down by at least a third."

"All that blood spilled for one megalomaniac, maybe we can end this today, get me Captain Tucker and have team two fallback with team three."

Frank is there in ten minutes.

"Captain Tucker, do you fill up to a diplomatic mission?"

Yes, sir, what do you have in mind?" he asks Tom.

"As soldiers we take lives when we must and make peace when we can. I would like you to head a team under the white flag and partition the Guard for a meeting," Tom explains, "will you do it?"

"Yes, sir, we did kick their ass today, Colonial."

The meeting was arranged, they were to meet at team three's position, just forward of it. Tom instructed teams two and three to make themselves visible to make it appear that they have more men than they do.

At 17:00, the Guard contingent arrives, Tom is waiting.

Colonial Dearman, Major Potter, Major Wise, and Captain Tucker holding the white flag meet the Guard's representatives.

There is a Colonial and three Captains.

The eight men meet twenty meters from Tom's deference line, the 100 men behind the line are not trying to hide.

Tom addresses the Colonial, "I'm Colonial Dearman, this is Major Potter, my executive officer; to whom am I speaking?"

"I am Colonial Alvarado." He never introduces his second in command.

"Colonial, you are out gunned and out manned. I do not relish killing more of your men, but I will if I have to. I can provide medical assistants to your wounded if you surrender now, and know this, by morning there will be an additional Battalion here. Your own people warned us about you coming; the Duke is insane and the rank and file know it and you do also," Tom finishes his speech.

"You will treat my men with respect?" Alvarado asks.

Tom steps forward extending his hand, "You have my word as one soldier to another."

Alvarado stumbles forward, putting out his hand to shake Tom's to accept the terms of the surrender. That is when he sees the blood soaking through his uniform. Tom calls to the back line, "I need a medic."

The medics arrive with a liter and take the Colonial to the aid station.

"Can I trust you to keep my officer safe?" addressing one of Colonial Alvarado's Captains.

"You take care of our Colonial and I swear your officers will be safe," extending his hand to Tom.

"Colonial Alvarado will be in good hands tonight, you have my word," Tom accepts his hand.

"Captain Tucker, go with the Captain and start supervising the surrender. I will have a medical team assemble here to care for the wounded."

On the way back to base camp, Adam compliments Tom on a well-executed bluff, "Remind me never to play poker with you."

The next morning, the surrender went off without a hitch, the fight was out of the Guard, they suffered over 300 fatalities and 150 wounded.

Tom's losses were less than a dozen, including the gunship.

The runway would take days to clear, so Tom called Stink Water and had medical teams, tents, food, and supplies ferried in by ship.

The prisoners will be housed on the island until other arrangements can be made.

Tom assigned Captain West with the duty of POW camp commandant.

52

It has been two days since they escaped Biteran in the Rabbit.

"I'm going to do another radar sweep, Connie," Matt said, "there has to be someone out here."

One day out, they started hearing faint and sporadic radio traffic, what they did learn from it is there is a battle going on at the capital between the GDF and the Royal Guard.

From what they can discern, the GDF is in full retreat, the capital has fallen, as well as Kranstan Point.

Four Rivers is putting up a fight.

The Guard failed to take out the GDF Naval fleet, including the carriers, keeping the sky's over Four Rivers clear of Guard fighters and bombers.

The last report Matt heard was the fatalities are in the hundreds of thousands.

Freedom Station was completely destroyed, and Bentley Station was badly damaged.

The GDF space fleet had to divide, half is in orbit protecting the ground from marauder that come in and shoot kinetic weapons at indiscriminate targets then flee, causing mass destruction and confusion on the surface.

The rest was sent to Z Point Station out beyond the gas giants, their last operating port for supplies and maintenance, keeping it secured.

The Guard's small craft are too quick for the much heavier GDF cruisers; every time the GDF tries to engage, their ships disperses and runs.

"Connie, we are down to twenty percent fuel; at our speed, we will not reach anyone for ten days and we will be out of oxygen by then. If we use up our fuel to increase our speed, we will be there in five days and still be out of air with no fuel to slow down and just keep going forever."

"Not very good options," she tells Matt, "if this is my last few days to live, I'm glad I'm with you, General," still keeping her since of humor.

To keep the monotony in check and his mind focused on other things, Matt would do a radar sweep every hour; on the fifth try, he got a return.

"Connie," he cry's, "we have a ship, it's right at the edge of our range, but it's there."

"Can you tell who it is, Matt?"

"We are too far away to tell, there is no data on the telemetry."

"Could it be a Guard ship?" she asks.

"No way to know, we will have to get closer."

"If it's a Guard ship, we will be executed," Connie reminds him.

"Yes," he answers, "but if we stay out here, we will be dead anyway. I'm going to fire up the engine and get us closer."

The rocket fires and they start their intercept to the unknown ship.

Two hours later, Matt uses the radar one more time, this time he gets data on the telemetry, it's the mining vessel S.S. Extractor, he shouts with optimism of being saved.

He gets on the radio, "Mayday, mayday, mayday, S.S. Extractor, please reply, over."

"This is the Ex-T, please state your emergency, over"

"Copy, Ex-T, we are in an emergency escape pod, low on fuel and air, are we glad to see you, over."

"Copy, pod, we have you on radar, we will send a recovery vessel, stand by, over."

"Copy that, Ex-T, standing by, over."

On the camera, Matt watches the recovery vessel coming their way. As it gets closer, he can see it's a mining tug for harvesting frozen bodies of water out in the cold expanses beyond the solar system.

"Pod, this is griper one, you will feel a bump. Over."

"Copy, griper one, over."

Matt had no more said over when he and Connie felt the bump of the griper taking hold of the rabbit.

One hour later, they hear a knock on the canopy and it begins to open.

They are in a landing bay, there are five people around them, two with guns and only one in uniform. Matt can see two more in uniform up in the control room watching.

"Welcome aboard, do you have any weapons on you, if so, please surrender them."

Matt shakes his head no, then begins to remove his helmet. Connie follows his lead.

"I am Lt. Commander Banner, Second Officer of the Ex-T, can you give me your names?"

"I'm Matthew Dollar and this is Connie Burch."

"Looking at your craft, I would say you came from Biterin, would that be a correct assumption?" the Commander asks.

"Yes, sir, we escaped Biterin two days ago," Matt answers.

"Are you criminals?" the Commander inquires.

"No," Connie said with a bit of indignation, "we had to leave, the Royal Guard was trying to kill us."

"We need to contact the Steward's office," Matt tells the Commander, "it's urgent."

"All in good time," the Commander replies, "but in the meantime, you will be our guest in lockup as a safety precaution for us, as well as yourself."

"That is better than the fate we were going to have, so thank you, Commander, we accept your invitation," Matt said, "lead the way."

The two were led to the ships brig and placed in separate cells next to each other, so they could talk, given a change of clothes, access to a shower, then feed.

Sitting on the floor back to back, so they could talk.

"I am so glad to be out of that spacesuit," Connie said, "I don't know how they do it, Matt, the waste collector was leaking and now I have a rash on the inside of my thigh."

Matt laughs, "Welcome to the world of special operations."

"Do you think we can trust these people, Matt?"

"Yes, I do, Connie, did you see the Captain up in the control room as we were being escorted out? He's a Traayins and they have no love for the monarchy at Wolf Creek."

"I would have thought the same thing about the Parkins at T.S., Matt, but they were doing the Duke's dirty work, it was Mall people that was responsible for Kimmy's death, not the Guard."

"I have not forgotten that, Connie. Mall will pay for that, even if I have to do it myself," Matt feeling both anger and loss at the same time.

"I'm with you on that, Matt, Mall will pay."

"Let's get some sleep, Connie, that bed looks mighty inviting," Matt standing and stretching, "it's been seven days since I last had one."

"Sounds like a good plan to me," Connie said, standing herself and yawning. "I'm so exhausted, I'll sleep like a rock, good night, General."

“Good night, Bubbles,” Matt lays down and was out in seconds.

“What do you think, Simon?” Henry asks his first Officer, watching from the hanger bay control room.

“Don’t know, Captain, but what I do know is that pod they came in is a Rabbit, a GDF special operations insertion craft. Either there is a command ship in the area or they did come from Biterin, the thermal shielding would make me believe the later, and it would be an act of desperation to try something as foolish as going in to space in a craft that only has a two day range.”

“The man fits the profile of an operative, but the woman, that’s a different story,” Henry observes, “leave them till tomorrow. I’ll invite them for lunch at the Captain’s table and see if they will be more talkative after a good night sleep and a hot meal. Have Sidney download their log in the Rabbit; that will tell us where they came from and when they departed and, Simon, could you contact operations in Elbee one more time? Jasmine is worried sick about her brother James.”

“Will do, Captain.” Simon leave’s the hanger control room to carry out his orders.

Henry’s looking down in to the landing bay lost in thought over the events of the last two days, the destruction of Freedom Station and attack on Bentley, the senseless loss of life.

Elbee was attacked from one of the marauders, it missed, the shot was wide, impacting on the plain above the city. There was no reason for it, Elbee has no military value, it was built by the Drivers to help the Traayan’s transition from hunter gatherers to a technical culture.

“Bridge to Captain,” the intercom breaks his train of thought.

He hits the button, “Go, Bridge.”

“Captain, there is a problem with the heat ex-changer in number three engine, sir.”

"Contact engineering, I'll be on the bridge shortly, Captain out."

Damn it, he thinks to himself, we did not have these problems on the Ice Queen, the ship he was First Officer on; she was twenty-years-old, he reminds himself, not brand new like the Ex-T.

The image of the Ice Queen tumbling in to the atmosphere, burning up after the attack on Bentley is one, he will never forget.

53

It's totally dark now. Billy tried to follow James and the people that took them, but they were moving too fast and he did not wish to run head long into one of the captors unexpected.

Billy had misjudged his path on his return trip to James and the others, arriving too far up the gully while trying to decide on which way to go. Billy heard them coming from down the gully, he hid in the grass as they passed not more than two meters from him. The five adults were tied, Mae and the children were not, and they did not appear to be in any danger at this moment, so he followed.

The trail they were leaving was plain, even to a novice like Billy; after it got too dark to follow, he decided to rest and take it up in the morning. He could not afford to lose them leaving the gully and him getting lost.

The captors pushed on for over an hour after sundown, lighting torches to guide their way.

The gully they had been traveling in opened in to a wide canyon.

James could see a village down below, campfire burning in front of more than sixty huts and electric lights shinning in many of the windows.

They were not savages as some would contend, only behind the rest of the world in technology.

The trail continued to the bottom, it was well used and smooth from heavy use.

The captives were led to a large hut with lights shinning from the door and windows. They were told to sit off to one side by a fire, their hands were untied and they were brought food and drinks.

The leader enters the hut without a word being spoke to James or any of the captives.

An hour later, a runner came into the village and quickly entered the hut with only a momentary glance at James and the others.

10 minutes later, he comes out the door and ran off at a sprint.

This same scene repeated itself over and over with different people.

Every time any of the group would try to talk among themselves, a guard silenced them.

At around midnight, two warriors came and motioned James to follow them to the hut.

As James enters, he sees seven men sitting around a fire pit.

He is directed to sit opposite the man he thinks is the Chief.

He stands, "Tell us your name, stranger," then sits back down.

James understands the protocol, he stands.

"I am James Wildwind, son of Grand Chief Wildwind," sitting back down.

The man next to the Chief stands, "You said the son, not was the son of Grand Chief Wildwind, you lie, he would be over a hundred now," then sitting down.

James stands, "Yes, the Grand Chief lives to this day, yes, he is 103 years of life," sitting back down.

The man on the other side of the Chief stands, "How is this possible? Only the will of the Great Father could make that happen," sitting down.

James understands he must deliver a moving speech to convince them.

He stands, "There are few here that could remember the Metal Father and the day he changed the lives of the Traay people; he gave us gifts that made it possible to travel the stars, gifts that made it possible to talk to distant villages, electricity pointing to the light, and the most valued gift of all, no more sickness that take away the father from the son too soon. Two life times has my father been with me, he will pass one day, but the gift of two lives is one I shall not forget? Never in my life have I ever been hungry, it is the Great Father that makes this possible, using the Metal Father as his guide for any that will hear his words," sitting back down.

This time the Chief stands, "Your words ring true to my ears; why are you here and why do other men chase you in our land that your father gave us?" sitting down.

James stands, "The men that chase us are servants of an evil man, the woman and man child are the family of the outsider King who the evil man killed and wish to do the same to them. I have pledged to keep them safe. I travel to black rock where my friend and teacher, Charley White, showed me the ways of the Traay people, there I will teach the man child," sitting down.

The Chief stands, "I see honor in you and name you friend, you may travel on our land," sitting down.

James stands, "There is one that I call friend, he was separated from me yesterday, he knows not the ways of Traay, and it would sadden my heart to have harm come to him; if you find him, send him to me. I would be ever grateful, he is short and round with no hair," he sits down.

The Chief stands, "The friend of the friend will be safe, the evil men will not, go and take your rest, you may leave in the morning," he sits down.

James understood that the meeting was over; the fewer words that are spoken, the less chance of offending, that is the way of Traay.

The group are all asleep but Sandra and Ted.

"What's going on, James?" Sandra asks.

"We will leave in the morning, they have given their permission for us to travel in their land," James explains.

Any news about the Skipper?" Ted asks.

"They will find and bring him to us, Ted, don't worry," James said, "now let's all get some sleep."

As the sun came up, a group of maidens served the party breakfast, a flat bread with meat and cold water.

The party was preparing to depart when there is a commotion, four men came carrying Billy, tied to a pole like a hunting kill with two men leading the party. He had blacked eyes, busted lips, one man had his arm in a sling, all the hunting party had some kind of injury.

"Here is the friend of the friend," the man in the lead said, "this one looks tame, but he fights like a wild bear," as the four drop Billy still tied to the pole.

Billy was asleep in the tall grass when he felt his foot kicked, opining his eyes, he sees four men standing around him. Not thinking he jumps to his feet, punching the man in front of him in the chest, knocking the air from his lungs, and backwards. Two men grab him on both sides, the one on the left has his arm, the one on his right missed his arm and has him by the shoulder. Billy drops to his right knee, hooking his arm behind the man's legs, at the same time pulling the man on his left right, the man on the right falls on his back. Billy hunches his back with his head down, pulling the man on the left over him on top of the man on his back. Billy stands and pivots to his left, there is a man standing in front of him, he lowers his head and charges, striking the man in the abdomen, driving with his legs, the man goes down backwards and Billy runs over the top of him. He is struck from behind and sees stars, going down on his knees, with the world around him black from the blow. Billy feels himself pulled on to his back, both arms are grabbed and someone has his feet, still in blackness. Billy draws his knees in, pulling the man who has them forward at the same time pulling both arms in, then kicking his legs out, driving the one on his feet backwards. The two who have his arms collide over him. Billy falls to the ground on his back, rolling to his left getting on all fours, he pushes up hard, the pile of men scatter, standing up his vision begins to clear, standing in front of him is another man. Billy strikes him with his fist, knocking him backwards. Someone wraps their arms around Bill's waist; with his left elbow, he strikes the man's shoulder and the grip is lost, another blow strikes Billy on the back of the head. Billy is out cold.

"Everyone alright?" Billy asks as Ted untied him from the pole.

"We're good, Skipper, Ted explained what happened and the news that they would be going to Black Rock this morning unhampered.

The Chief walks up with three young men with him and greets James.

"They will be your guides," introducing the young men, Pandar, Gates, and River. The Chief keeps looking at Billy, "Tell me friend," addressing James, "my warriors call the friend of the friend Wild Bear. I do not see it, but the man who named him is truthful."

"I owe the man my life time's two, as do all of us."

"Wild Bear, I name you friend, you will be welcome here any time," the Chief nods his head to Billy, then turns back to James. "The evil men will be no more problem," the Chief waving one of his men forward with a bag.

The bag was opened and out came twelve radios, "Please take two," the Chief offers. "Now go and may your resting place be secret," the Chief said.

"Thank you, we will go now, may your resting place be safe," James replies.

The journey started with all in the village saying things like travel in peace and may your feet find a level path, waving good bye to the strangers as they departed.

They did not go west like they assumed but headed north up the canyon.

The canyon they traveled in was only about 500 meters wide at the bottom with thick woods and abundant wild life, a stream flowed through it, making a small pond with reeds growing on the banks.

The canyon has been getting narrower as they climb in elevation, passing dozens of ravines and gully emptying in to the canyon, some with water flowing out of them, others dry.

They made good time traveling about twelve kilometers by noon; coming to a small village, the inhabitants greeted them as they arrived, offering them food and drink.

They came to see the son of Grand Chief Wildwind and the little Wild Bear; runners had been sent ahead to prepare for the honored guests.

Billy was not happy about the newfound fame; the children would come up to him and touch his arms and the single women would smile and flirt.

The guides would only call him Wild Bear no matter how many times he would tell them to call him Billy. He finally gave up and started answering to it.

Shortly after they left the village, they turned west, climbing up to a ravine that was twenty meters across at the bottom, sandy floor, sheer walls, 100 meters to the rim, there was little lite making it to the floor, so vegetation was sparse, traveling was quick with the easy path.

They traveled another ten kilometers; the light was starting to fade.

Pandar announced, “We will rest here, we must climb to the top in the morning.”

River and Gates did not stop, they took off in a fast run on up the ravine. Pandar sees James's question on his face, "They will meet us on top," pointing to the north rim.

Everyone's very tired, and sleep takes them quickly.

James posted watches like he did in the first night, children and Mae in the middle, adults on both ends.

Pandar stayed by Mae, he said the old mother must be looked after.

At around three in the morning, James hears his relief coming to take over watch.

"I told Billy to rest a little more, James," as Sandra sits down next to him.

"This is a surprise, my lady," James greets her.

"How much further do you think, James? Mae is struggling to keep up."

"Another ten kilometers as the crow flies," he said, "it depends on how many times we have to go down, then back up, it could be two or ten. I have never been this far from Black Rock." Sandra shivers from the cool breeze coming down the ravine. "It may be summer, but at night, it gets cold," James said. Not thinking he reaches out and puts his arms around Sandra to keep her warm, pulling her in tight. He is struck by her scent, the softness of her hair, and the smoothness of her skin. "Forgive me, my queen, I did not think," releasing her and sitting up straight.

Sandra reaches over and takes James's hand, moving in close, pulling his arm back around her, "It's Sandra," she softly said.

For the next two hours, not a word was spoken between them, but volumes were communicated.

It was getting light when a rope came down the wall of the ravine. James stands and looks up and there is River and Gates at the top.

Pandar walks over to James, "We must eat quickly and be on our way," he said.

They all ate a hurried breakfast of energy bars and started the climb.

Pandar insisted Wild Bear go first, so he could provide weight at the end of the rope.

It took over an hour to get everyone up, James was the last.

On the rim of the ravine, the top of Black Rock could be seen northwest of them in the distance, it is only about five kilometers.

They go two kilometers, then come to another gully with an easy climb down, it goes in the direction of their destination, then makes a hard turn west, it goes another kilometer, then it empties in to a small canyon, the rim to the floor is about 200 meters high, the floor is 200 meters across, and there is a thick forest with a small stream running at the bottom with small ponds doting the floor, but the rim is 400 meters across, the side they are standing on has eroded away. Landslides have left the bank a jumbled pile of rocks, it was a very slow descent to the bottom, several times the rope had to be used to lower the group down.

"I know this place," James said, "we are here."

James spots a rock with an image scratched into it; next to it, a circle with an X in the center, all the legs were in the circle, but one was slightly outside. He looks around, looks at the sun.

"Ted," he said, "go to the tree there," he points, "and see if there is a flat rock on the other side, and if there is, lift the rock and see if there is something under it."

Ted does as he is instructed, finding the rock, then lifting it up.

"Jackpot," he shouts, "there is a waterproof box," he flips the rock to one side, reaches down and retrieves the box, carrying it to James.

James opens it and inside is a list of supply cashes.

Pandar, Gates, and River come and stand in front of James, "Our task is complete, we will leave now, son of Grand Chief Wildwind," Pandar said, "we will go by way of Black Stone," then turning to Billy, "friend Wild Bear, may your resting place be safe."

Billy returned, "May your resting place be secret." With that the three turned and ran up the canyon. "I'm puzzled, James," Billy asks, "why did they show me so much respect, all I did was defend myself."

"It was your size and age, Skipper, most old men like you and I who put on weight have no fight in them, and when it took six to subdue you, you earned their respect," James smiling at him, "Wild Bear. The last time I was here was thirty years ago," James tells Sandra, "but I re member it like it was yesterday." The camp site is up and to the right, just above the little pond, "Let's go make camp," James suggested, "we will have a fire tonight and a restful sleep."

The camp site is not visible from the outside, the tall trees and the shrubs hide it completely, James pushes his way in to revel a ring of trees sixty meters across, there is new growth all inside. He can make out the skeletons of the three shelters to one side, there is a fire pit in the middle all over grown.

James stops next to it, sitting his back pack down, the rest follow suit.

"I would need to set the camp rules," James announces, "number one, no going out of camp alone, no exception, number two, everyone works, and last, pay attention to the surroundings, there are wild things here that can take your life. We still have four hours of light left and there is much work to do, so I will assign jobs," James said. "We need the shelters cleaned out. Sandra, Mae, and Berrana, watch for spider, snakes, and rats. Fire wood collected, Bradly, Tyler, Tina, and Tamara, do it around the sit, there is plenty around, there is no need to go more than ten meters out. Skipper, Ted and myself will begin clearing the brush in camp, tomorrow we will start collecting the supply cashes and set some game traps."

Sandra stands, "Let's go, ladies," and heads for the shelters; they are in poor condition, the floors are covered in litter from the thatch that covered the roof, the shelter in the middle is four meters deep by six meters wide, sloping from the front to the back. Two meters on the open front to one meter on the closed back, closed on the sides.

The two shelters on both sides are smaller but the same design. Three meters deep by four meters wide.

Sandra, Mae, and Berrana had been working for about five minutes in the large shelter when all three screamed. James jumps up from the shrub he was trying to pull up, picking up a stick on the way as a weapon, charging in to the shelter ready to do battle. All three woman are cowering to one side, there in the middle of the shelter is a mouse, standing on its back legs threatening them. Billy and Ted enter right behind James with their own clubs; the three men look at the mouse, then look back to the woman, then back at the mouse, all three-start laughing a hard laugh.

Sandra pleads, "He startled us," then watched the mouse scurry away and she, too, started laughing, then Mae and Berrana join in, the four out gathering fire wood came running in to camp to aid in the battle only to be confronted by six hysterically laughing companions, and before long, they, too, were joining in on the laughter.

By sundown the camp was in fair order, tools were found in the shelter under the litter that added in the removal of the over growth, shovel, ax, saw, and a few more things.

Bradly gathered the children, Tina, and Ted and showed them how to start a fire using the material collected around the camp sight and had a good fire burning in the pit.

All the companions gathered around the fire having a festive time, forgetting the war raging across Severus.

54

It has been seven days since the attack, there was a few tense moments in the first few days, a group of die-hard Guardsmen tried to commandeer a supply boat and make an escape, lethal force had to be applied and the remainder of those men were separated from the rest, sent to a prison on Miller Island.

The fight was out of most of the POW's, few were free of injuries; broken bones, bumps, bruises, and burns were the most common, they were treated in the B-ward as Doctor Fields called it, some were critical and the surgical staff was not equipped to handle it on Edgefield Island, so they had to be sent to Vision Island for surgery.

In front of the destroyed lab building is the command tent with the communications center, contact had been reestablished with GDF Command, Tom learned New Hope was abandoned, Command was moved to Four Rivers.

The GDF Rapid Deployment Division had survived the opening attack and stopped the Guard's advance on Four Rivers with the help of the Navel air support.

A 1,000-man militia joined the fight from Elbee, complements of the Treey.

Cranstan Point is in the Guard's hands, but they do not have control, remnants of the GDF are harassing the Guard with hit and run tactics, keeping them from consolidating their hold.

Tom talked to Steward Smit, briefing him on the battle and subsequent victory.

"You were up against Colonel Brine Alvarado," the Steward told him, "as I understand it, he is a very competent and effective Commander; what you did impressed the GDF Chief of Staff, he recommended I give you an accommodation and a promotion for the victory."

"It was dumb luck, Steward Smit, and the fact that the Duke is a fool, ordering him on such a mission with no intelligence or support, all it did was throw away lives."

"Call it what you like, Tom, it was a win for our side," Peabody remind him.

"I think we can turn Colonel Alvarado," Tom tells the Steward, "he still had us out numbered with better trained troops, but he saw the suffering of his men and wished to end it with no more bloodshed, his heart was not in the fight, and I think deep down he knows he was on the wrong side."

"If you can pull that off, Tom, that would be a second victory for you, the philological value would be worth more than a division in the field, making every Guardsman rethink their commitment to the Duke, saving countless lives," the Steward told Tom.

Tom's new mission was clear in his mind, show Colonel Alvarado the truth; he contacted General Kroger and had him send over copies of the most convincing evidences against the Duke.

The Island of Edgefield looks like a tent city, where the hanger was is now rows of tents for the Guard POW's.

Out behind the tents is a massive mountain of debris, in the pile are two heavy transports, Adam's transport, and the debris of the hanger.

Only one of the heavy's was salvageable, it was flown to a GDF airfield.

Tom, armed with the evidence of truth, went to visit Colonel Alvarado and check on his condition; he was in the first heavy to land like Tom predicted when the transport runs off the runway in to the trees. He was thrown in to a bulkhead, breaking several ribs, then a branch pierced the fuselage, nearly impaling him, he is lucky to be alive. Ten centimeters higher, it would have pierced his heart.

"How are you today, Colonel Alvarado, are you being treated well?" Tom asks.

"Yes, Colonel Dearman, they are," he replied, "have you picked up any more survivors from the heavy that ditched?" Alvarado asks.

"There is good news there, we recovered five rafts with over 100 survivors, including Major Tibits," Tom told him, "they should be here within the hour. I will have Major Tibits escorted to you."

"Thank you for that, Colonel Dearman," he said with evident relief in his posture. "Tell me the truth, Colonel, how did you know we were coming? I only found out about the mission ten hours before I landed," Alvarado asks.

"We didn't, we played to the Duke's egotistical nature, we denied him something he wanted, then made it available for the taking; he played right in to our hands, it's too bad your men had to be the ones that payed the price for his delusions of grandeur."

"Colonel Dearman, it was the Drivers that started the war with the help of the Steward, killing the Queen and the Prince," Alvarado accused.

"No, Colonel, it was the Duke using drones piloting transports, controlled by his men that attacked the Queen; you're a veteran of the Trotter revolt, are you not? if the Drivers wanted a war, why would they not use their war drones, you know their destructive capability," Tom asks.

Tom could see Alvarado's mind processioning the information. "Think, Colonel, why is it there has been no more attacks by drones, and was it not your mission to secure the drivers and the drones here, transferring them to Wolf Creek, for what, to sit in a warehouse to collect dust? No, the Duke started this war to make himself King and he cares nothing for the blood he has spilled in his attempt, and furthermore, Tom tells him, "the Queen and the Prince are not dead, they are in Traay, Sub-Drive Clarence warned them right before the attack."

"Can you prove the Queen is alive, Colonel Dearman?" he asks.

"No, we lost contact with her shortly after the war started, but what I can prove is the Duke's use of drones, that was the reason I was on this island. I and a team of investigators were sent here to shut down his lab; we were attacked, and they escaped, but we have all the evidence, his people failed to destroy it and to keep that information secret. He started a war, not only did you have hundreds of casualties, there are hundreds of thousands of dead across Severus."

"Stop there, Colonel Dearman, you expect me to believe you're an investigator, not a special operations battalion commander?"

With that Tom smiled, "I have not been in the GDF for seven years, Colonel. I am a Senator for the Newland Islands; my rank is with the reserves. I originally came here with fifteen men to arrest a Doctor Pierce, the force you engaged was the Stink Water GDF security detachment, 400 men tops. Most are military police and support units with lawyers and engineers."

"I'm a fool," Colonel Alvarado sighs, "to be bested by a politicians, police, and mechanics."

"No, Colonel, you were beaten by the element of surprise, unfamiliar terrain, and men with a just cause, your leader had no regard for the safety and well-being of his. Why did you commit your men to something so unknown with no exit plan or any reserves, did that not sound warning bell in your head?" Tom asks.

After pondering the question, Colonel Alvarado conceded, “Yes, it did, but I’m a soldier and do what is asked of me, even at the price of my life.”

“And the lives of your men,” Tom added. “I have come prepared, Colonel Alvarado,” Tom waves a Lieutenant over with a file box; for the next two hours, he and Colonel Alvarado go through the evidence.

The most damming piece was Doctor Pierce’s own journal, his meeting with the Duke, and their discussion on riding the plaint of Drivers with their own drones, Doctor Pierce outlining how the subject dies after three day in a irrelevant fashion with no more remorse than killing a cockroach with the Duke’s support and encouragement.

At the end, Alvarado’s eyes close and his head dropped in shame, thinking about all his men that will never see home again, the children now missing a parent or a parent who will never see their child grow into an adult, all for the Duke’s ambition to have power.

Colonel Alvarado feels a hand on his shoulder; opening his eyes, he sees Tom looking at him with compassion, not hate or judgment.

“We all make mistakes,” Tom told him, “the trick is to learn from it and not repeat it. I would like you to share what is in the file with Major Tibits. I’m going to go now, but I will return tomorrow, rest well, Brine tell then, good bye.”

Leaving the hospital, Tom calls the Lieutenant over, “Go find Major Potter and have him meet me in operations ASAP.”

Tom had a plan, and he was going to put it in motion, he saw the reaction in Alvarado and Tom knows a good man when he sees one. With his help, this war will come to an end and the Duke will stand justice.

Tom and Adam are in the communication tent, in front of them is a video screen with the Steward and five of his war Ministers.

"Outline what you told me, Tom, to the Generals," the Steward said.

Tom begins his presentation.

"First I would like to alleviate any concerns you may have about Colonel Alvarado. I saw with my own eyes his reaction to the evidence about the Duke; he is a professional soldier, he respects and cares for the men under his command, he could have continued to fight losing more men, but he knew he was the aggressor deep down and what he was asked to do was wrong, and I can guarantee his cooperation on the grounds of his moral commitment to his men. If you could find the Queen and have her give her approval, that would seal the deal."

"I will work on that, Tom," the Steward replied.

"We have the Guard's heavy transport, fly it in to Wolf Creek with a team of special operations and Alvarado's hand-picked men and raid the Duke's command center, taking him prisoner."

"That simple," the General from GDF command said in a condescending way.

"Nothing is simple in war, General," Tom replies.

"How do you get there without being shot down, Tom?" the Steward questioned.

"We use deception," Tom answers, "we fly in under the radar to New Hope from the east, popping up halfway between Wolf Creek and New Hope, use a pair of GDF fighters to simulate an attack on the heavy. We send out a distress call claiming to have wounded on the way to Wolf Creek. Guard fighters show up escorting us to the airfield, a smoke grenade popped in an engine and we have an emergency, we will be cleared for landing with no questions."

"Your plan for the trip from the airfield to the operations center GDF fleet?" Admiral asks.

"The Duke's command center is right next to the hospital, the Duke knows we will not bomb a hospital, that is the reason it's there, to protect it, but we will use it to our advantage.

Only a few of the wounded will be wounded, they go first clogging the processes, the walking wounded will be asked to wait. We assemble outside in two teams, one to raid the command center, the other to secure transportation for the extraction, then make our move, we should be in and out in ten minutes."

"The wounded in the hospital, Tom, will they be left behind?" the Steward ask.

"Unfortunately, yes, each one will have to volunteer and know the risk of doing so," Tom answered.

"Very well, Tom, you have a go, but I still have the right to scrub the mission," the Steward said.

"Yes, sir, I understand, we will have a better chance with the Queen's support, Steward Smit," Tom reminds him.

"I will have someone on that by the end of the hour, Tom, start making the preparations," the Steward told him, signing out.

55

The brig guard and Matt have been playing chess all morning having a good time.

"A good night sleep will do wonders, Connie," he told her, "and I have been in brigs that make this place seem like a resort.

Connie has been sitting on the bed squirming all morning, the rash from the leaky recycle unit has her in a miserable state.

Right before noon, Commander Banner came by to get the pair for lunch with the Captain.

"I like your ship, Commander Banner," Matt tells him, "she is sleek and well-designed."

"Thank you, call me Tim or Timothy if you would; we do not fallow military protocol on the Ex-T, we are a family-oriented ship."

"In that case, call me Matt."

"I'm Connie," she adds.

They walk in to the dining hall and it's spacious with a high ceiling to dampen the noise from the chatter, making it feel like a nice restaurant, not a mess hall, there are pictures on the wall and fresh flowers on the tables.

In the corner is the Captain's table with low partitions around it to keep the conversation private.

Sitting around the table are six people.

The Captain stands on their arrival; and welcomes them to the table and begins the introductions.

"I am Captain Henry Carver, this is my wife, Doctor Jasmine Carver, my first Officer Simon Banks, Chief Engineer Sidney Cane, my Operations Officer, Chris Hascals, and Consultant Ben Driver. Our guest Matthew Dollar and Connie Burch, please sit," the Captain invited.

The servers started bringing the meal as soon as they were all seated.

Sidney started the conversation, "I downloaded your Rabbit's log, so you came from Biterin four days ago, was that not a bit risky?" looking at her watch, "if we had not intercepted you, you would have been dead ten hours ago."

Connie squirmed but said nothing.

"Yes," Matt answered, "our fate would have been the same if we stayed on Biterin, the Guard and the local authority were looking for us, and if they had found us, we would be dead for certain, no maybe."

"What was your crime?" Simon asks.

"Connie and I work for the Steward; we had arranged equipment to be delivered to Biterin to stop a work slowdown, awaiting the first shipment we took a tour of some of the caverns. We discovered Drivers and Drones that the Guard was dissembling. To protect their secret, they attempted to kill us, we fought back; in doing so, three were killed and two more three days later after they killed one of our companions."

Connie squirmed but said nothing.

"When you first came aboard, you asked to contact the Steward, can you enlighten us on the subject?" asks Chris.

"I know our supervisor is worried and that would be the best way to contact him," Matt said.

Connie squirmed but said nothing.

"Dear, are you alright?" Jasmine addressing Connie.

Connie turns a bright red with embarrassment, "I have a rash," she sheepishly replied in a timid voice.

Matt comes to her rescue, "The waste recycle tube was leaking, the generic spacesuits, they never fit."

"Poor dear," Jasmine reaches across the table, patting Connie's hand, "after lunch you and I will go to the infirmary and I will take care of that for you."

Lunch was over and Captain Carver turns to Simon, "Can you see to our guest and find them rooms? I see no need to keep them in the brig any longer, I'll be on the bridge," Henry excuses himself and heads off.

Jasmine stands, "Come, dear," talking to Connie, taking her by the arm, "we'll go to the infirmary and make you more comfortable."

"Simon, there are two rooms next to mine that are empty, they can have them if you have no objection," Ben said.

"Sounds good to me. Ben, can you show them the way?"

"Certainly, would you follow me, Matt? I have additional questions I would like to ask you."

"The Captain called you a consultant, what is your expertise, Ben?" Matt inquired.

"Engineering and space travel, my sisters and I have signed on in that capacity," Ben explained, "and I'm interested in hearing more about the Drivers you observed on Trinity Station, and I can answer any question you may have about this ship?" The two enter the corridor, "It's a long walk to the rooms or we can take the shuttle tube if you prefer," Ben indicating a door across from the mess hall.

"How long of a walk?" Matt asks.

"Seven hundred meters, my room is near the stern of the Ex-T, right above the landing bay," Ben said.

"How big is this ship?" Matt asks.

Ben brightened with obvious pride, "1,087 meters from bow to stern, 210 meters diameter." The door opens to the Shuttle tube and the two get in. Ben speaks, "Section fourteen," the shuttle starts moving.

"Wow, that's bigger than the early carriers," Matt showing more interest.

"Yes," Ben continued his description, "400 single cabins and 200 family units, the mining operations are outside of the inner hull, the double hull design is to keep the human population safe from radiation, all ship operations, living and recreation areas are in the inner hall, we grow all our own food. We are here," the shuttle stops, the door opens, and they get out.

"What's the ships complement?" was Matt's next question.

"The Ex-T was designed for 1,000 crew members, but with families, we lowered that to 500 working crew and 400 dependents, giving us a 100-person margin."

They walk down the corridor a few meters, then enter a side hallway going in thirty meters in to another hallway, then turn right four doors down is Ben's room, he points to the number on the door, it is 1425.

"You have 1426 and Connie has 1427," Ben tells him, "would you like to come in for a drink, Matt?"

"It's been a hell of a week, yes," Matt said with a big smile.

Ben opens the door and invites Matt in.

Entering the room, Matt can see it's small but comfortable, sitting at a desk is a woman with jet black hair, average build, very pretty.

"Oh, great, Ben, another one," the girl complains.

"Matt, I would like to introduce you to my cranky sister, Beth, she is the ship's Botanist."

"Hello, cranky sister Beth," Matt smiles and winks. Beth gets up, makes a grrr sound shaking her head, and goes to the back room, but before she closes the door, Matt sees her take a quick peek at him with a hint of a smile. "I like your sister, Ben, she's forward and not a bit shy," Matt said loud, so Beth could hear him.

"Bell will be here in a few minutes with Connie, should we wait for her or would you like that drink now?" asks Ben.

"I'll take mine on the rocks, barkeep," Matt getting his jubilant self-back.

"On the rock it is," Ben returning with two glasses.

Matt lifts his glass in the air, "To the Ex-T and her fine crew."

Ben follows Matt, "To the Ex-T."

They click their glasses and down the drink in one gulp.

The door opens and in walks Connie and a red head woman.

Matt stands.

"Matt, this is my other sister Bell; she is the ship's school teacher," Ben introducing her, "she loves children."

"Nice to meet you," Matt extends his hand.

"Likewise," Bell returns taking his hand.

"Another drink, Matt?" Ben offers. "How about you, Connie?"

"Yes," Matt answers.

"Yes please," Connie said.

Ben goes to the counter and retrieves two more glasses and a bottle of whiskey.

"To new friends," they all lift their glasses clicking them together, "to new friends."

Ben turns to business, "You both saw the driver the guard was disassembling, can you describe it?"

"Yes," Connie said, "I got the best look, it was two meters square, the back had a panel removed, there were five rows of components, two rows were missing, the three renaming rows were different, two rows had fifty centimeters square components, the other had smaller ones, same width but shallower, none were missing on that row, why the interest?"

"Occupational curiosity," Bell answers, "our father is a physicist."

The party continued for several hours; two bottles of whiskey was consumed. Matt told funny stories about his time in the GDF, sang a couple of songs. Matt was back to his fun and happy self. He was trashed by the end of the night.

"I think it time to put this one to bed," Connie tells her host, helping Matt to his feet, staggering to the door and out, "good night," she tells them.

Beth had been watching through the cracked open door, wishing she would have joined in the fun.

56

The encampment is starting to come together nicely; there are two new shelters, and the main shelter has been repaired and functioning as their kitchen. James located the supply cashes and the camp is well stocked now, there is a wild deer carcass hanging from a tree curing for their meat, two privies were dug, so each sex could have privacy.

Pandar came in to camp early in the morning, telling them two more evil groups of men entered their land and had to be dealt with; he brought a medical pack with the Guard insignia on it, in case they needed it.

James started thinking, I need to give a gift also, what do I have? The pendent around his neck, he removes it, handing it to Pandar.

James sees Tamara looking at him, they lock eyes. She has a question on her face, she reaching in her shirt and brings out a pendent like the one he just gave Pandar. I will need to talk to her later, he tells himself.

"A gift for Wild Bear," Pandar said, "a twenty-five-centimeter knife with belt and sheath, also with the Guard insignia."

James looks at Billy, then taps his collar where his Captain's bars are.

Billy understands, reaching up he unfastens the bars and hands them to Pandar.

"To the friend of Wild Bear," he tells him.

Pandar's face lights with pride as he accepts Wild Bear's gift.

Pandar did not walk on his way out of camp but ran, no doubt to show his friends the gift Wild Bear had given him.

After Pandar had left camp, James invites Tamara to go on a walk with him to get the story about the pendent in privet.

Sitting on a fallen tree by the stream, 100 meters from camp so they would not be interrupted, James begins, "That pendent was given to me right after the King was killed from Sub-Drive Clarence," he tells her, "I was only to use it in cases of dire need; in the fifteen years I have carried it, only twice have I done so, once to warn the Sub-Drive of the potential assassination of the Prince and once for the Queen."

James stops to give Tamara a chance to give her story.

"Master-Driver Michael gave me mine four weeks ago."

"Master-Driver Michael," James said, "to my knowledge, no one has ever talked to him."

"I was to keep it secret, he is my friend, he was my grandfather's friend as well as my great-grandmother's friend," she admits, "up until six days ago, I talked to him every day, now there is nothing, I have tried and tried but nothing."

"I, too, have tried to contact Sub-Drive Clarence, and like you, there is no response. I think we are alone now. That is not a bad thing, it only means we must take care of ourselves from now on," James consoles her, "that is what the Sub-Drive and Master-Driver hope for us, to stand on our own."

"It hurts," she said with tears starting to run down her face, "I am alone."

"You will never be alone, sweet girl. The Queen thinks of you as the daughter she never had and will love and protect you with her very life if need be, and I do, too," James reaching out giving her a hug, "you are part of this family now, let's get back to camp, daughter," he called her with a smile.

James and Sandra went on a scouting trip, at least that was the story.

James is sitting with his back against a tree, Sandra is laying down with her head in his lap, he is absently stoking her hair, looking out at a pond, not thinking about anything. The grass is high, providing a soft bed, there is a sweet aroma in the air from the wild flowers and a dove is cooing in the distance.

"Have you seen Ted and Tina?" she smiles looking up at James.

"I've seen it, those two think they're being sneaky, but I was out of camp yesterday and watched them coming back to camp holding hands," he laughs.

"You know they probably say the same thing about us," Sandra reaching up and pulling James's beard, "you need a shave."

"When we get back to civilization, this is my mountain man look," bending over and kissing her on the forehead.

"I think I could spend the rest of my life here; I can see why you loved it so much, James, it's tranquil."

"Yes, it is," he agrees, "we need to get back, the kids will be wondering about us if we stay out too long."

"You're right," she tells him, reaching up pulling his lips to hers, moments go by, she lets go.

On the way back, they hear splashing water and laughter, parting the undergrowth, peering out, it's Tina and Ted skinny dipping.

"Let's go around, I don't want them to see us, it would embarrass them," Sandra whispered, "they make a sweet couple."

Back at camp, Bradly has the kids continuing their education giving a civics lesson, Billy is cutting strips of the meat with his new knife to make jerky, Mae is cooking lunch.

"I love our new family," Sandra tells James, "is this the way a tribe works? If it is, count me in," giving James a little bump with her hip.

"Yes, it is, my love, a tribe is all about family," taking her hand and giving it a tender kiss.

Sandra starts in giving Mae a hand with lunch, and James starts placing the meat Billy had cut on a make shift rack to dry.

Tina and Ted come in about thirty minutes later, all giggles and smiles; they, too, go right to work.

Lunch was served and eaten, everyone was resting, letting their food settle, the children were running about just being children.

James hears a distant hum, "Quiet," he calls. Everyone stops, he is trying to determine the direction, "It's coming our direction, get ready to bug out," he shouts. The scenario has been planned from day one, four packs were ready by the bug out direction, the fire was put out, Sandra, Billy, Tina, Mae, Bradly, and the children are going up canyon one kilometer, depending on the intruders direction, they will go east or west, the path has been predetermined and the rally point.

James and Ted will be the decoy, leading the intruders away.

The plain comes in to view.

"That's a bush plane," James tells Ted.

The bush plain is a converted seaplane with a high wing and on the bottom instead of pontoons; there are wide skis for landing in the high grass, James intended on using one like that to get himself and Tyler to Black Rock.

The airplane circled the camp above the rim, dipping its wing three times, then landing above on the grass.

"Go tell them to hold for twenty minutes, then come back," James tells Ted.

He takes off in a run.

Ted was back in ten minutes all out of breath, their holding Ted manages to get out.

James hears his name called from the rim, "You down there, James?"

"Go give the all clear, Ted, that my brother's son, Fredrick."

Fredrick is eight years younger than James, the two of them spent two years together with Charley in James's final years here at Black Rock.

Twenty minutes later, James and Fred are hugging a welcome.

There are two men with Fred in uniform.

"How did you know I was here, Fred?" James asks.

"The Steward told us."

"How did he know," James started to ask, but he realized it could have only come from Clarence.

A Captain steps forward, "I'm Captain Brunswick from GDF Headquarters, Ambassador, the Queen is needed and I'm here to escort her back."

"What?" is heard from the side of the camp as Sandra steps out, "the Steward is asking for me, why is that?"

"Your majesty," the Captain bows, "yes, he replies, "it is a matter of great importance, it may end the war." The Captain explained the plan on taking the Duke captive but stressed it would only work if the captured Royal Guard participated, and the only way to do that would be for the Queen to give her consent. "They believe you to be dead, killed by the Drivers and the Steward."

"It was the Duke that tried to kill me and the Prince," Sandra said, "not the Drivers, Clarence saved our lives."

"I know that and you do, your majesty, but the rest of the world does not," the Captain replied.

"Please give us a moment, Captain, I will confer with my advisers," Sandra said, calling James, Billy. and Ted to her side. "What do you think?" she asks, "could this be a trap by the Duke?"

James speaks up, "No, only Clarence was aware I would be bringing you here, and Fred would not be a part of anything like that."

"If we could take the Duke out, it would save countless lives," Sandra told them, "and I think it is my moral responsibility to save all I can.

Billy, you and Ted are members of the Royal Guard, would my word carry any weight over the Duke's?" Sandra asks.

"More than you realize, my queen," Billy bows.

"We will get everyone together and leave immediately," she tells them.

"No, Sandra," James said, "that bush plane only carries four people, the rest will have to stay behind."

Sandra stands there for several moments, "I have made my decision. James, Billy and myself will go; if things go badly, Tyler and the others will be safer here. Ted, you will be in charge, Bradly and Mae will help you, and I know Pandar will return soon ask him for assistants, tell him Wild Bear said so," smiling at Billy. Sandra orders a meeting, all are in attendance, children included. "We have found a way to end this war, I will be going with the Captain to Edgefield Island, James and Billy will accompany me. Fred, you and the Sargent must stay behind, there will be no room in the bush plane. Ted will be in charge. Mae, Tina, and Bradly give him all the assistance he needs. Tyler, Berrana, and Tamara, you will be safer here if things go badly, I love you three, so it must be that way, mind the adults."

With all the orders given, Sandra said that will be all.

Captain, we will be ready in ten minutes."

Sandra gives each a good bye hug and an I love you.

James approaches Fred, "Sorry to leave you stranded here, but the Queen is right, if we can end this war, we must take every opportunity to do so."

"No worry, Uncle James, I have wanted to come back to Black Rock for twenty years, now I'm here and Dad will be fine with it."

"Give Ted some lessons in trapping and other things, he is a good kid but a bit green when it comes to surviving the wild," James asks.

"Will do, Uncle."

"Did you know a marauder fired a kinetic weapon at Elbee? It missed, but a 500 meters part of the canyon wall collapsed killing hundreds. Dad was so pissed, he sent 1,000 volunteers to Kranstan Point to assist the GDF," Fred told James.

"How's my father?" James asks.

"The Grand Chief is frail but still hanging in there, Prince Robert is in charge. Do you believe that, Dad makes me call him Prince Robert now," Fred said?

"Protocol is all," James answers.

The flight from Black Rock to Elbee only took one hour, a GDF fast transport was waiting and they left immediately for Edgefield Island.

57

The GDF fast transport is long and sleek, three meters wide and fifteen meters long with cantilevered wings, it only seats twelve passengers, six seats on each side with a narrow walk way down the center, it can out run all, but the interceptor class and the Guard have none in their inventory.

Captain Brunswick escorted the three to the transport.

"She's a beauty," Billy tells Captain Brunswick, "I bet she will do over 2,000 KPH.

"Try 3,000 KPH, Captain Zercoff," he told him, "and operate at a ceiling of forty kilometers, are you impressed more?"

On board Captain Brunswick make the introductions, this is General Roberts from the GDF Intelligence Division and his aide Major Butterflied, gentlemen, I give you Queen Sandra."

Both men bowed.

"Welcome aboard, your majesty," the General welcomes her, "please have a seat, we will be departing soon, and I must warn you the acceleration is very intense, I will have the pilot try to be gentle."

"Do what it takes, General, every minute we delay is more death of our people, so just get me there," Sandra sits down.

The takeoff was incredible, for five minutes all the passengers were held in their seats, pressed back in to the thick foam padding of the seats. Sandra could not even lift her head.

The fast transport could not land at Edifier Island, the runway was not long enough, they had to go to Miller Island first, then take a small transport to Edgefield.

By the time they reached the final destination, it was dark; without fan fair, Sandra, James, and Billy were whisked to the command center along with General Roberts and Major Butterflied.

There was a conference tent prepared for the arrival of the Queen, waiting was Tom and Adam.

"Welcome, my Queen," Tom greets her, bowing. Adam does the same, "would you please have a seat and we will start the conference."

With all seven participants seated, Tom begins, "As you have been told, this Island is where the Duke developed the technology for controlling the drones he used in the opening assault; nine days ago, a team and I raided it and captured the evidence of the Duke's crimes, he sent a force here to take it back but was defeated. we captured over 600 men, their officer, and an intact heavy transport. In my interrogations, I learned that the force sent beveled you to be dead, killed by the Drivers and the Steward. I had all the evidence needed here, so I shared it with the captured command staff, they have been convinced of the Duke's crime's and will assist if you give them your approval."

"I give my approval then, Colonel Dearman," the Queen said.

"You will have to tell them yourself, they will not take my word for it," Tom answered, "Major Potter, would you please bring in Colonel Alvarado."

Adam leaves the conference for several minutes, returning with Colonel Alvarado in a wheelchair being pushed by Major Tibits.

When Colonel Alvarado sees the Queen, the room can see he is emotionally struck.

"My god, what have I done?" he utters. "All my men dead for a lie," his head drops to his chest, he begins to weep.

Sandra stands and walks over to the Colonel, kneeling in front of him, lifting his chin, she softly calls Colonel Alvarado, he opens his eyes, looking at her.

"I forgive you, Colonel, now let's avenge your men and make this right."

Looking up she sees Major Tibits is crying also, her heart is moved for these men that sacrificed their men in the name of honor, only to find out they were deceived for someone's hunger for power.

Alvarado, still shaken by the reality that he was a part of the Duke's plan, he declared "We will make him pay, my queen, this I pledge with my life if necessary."

Sandra stands up and places her hand on Major Tibits' shoulder, "Go and rest now, we will discuss what needs to be done, and in the morning, I will visit you then," she said. Major Tibits pushes the wheelchair for the Colonel and they returned to the hospital. Sandra returns to the table and sits down and said, "Let's go over the plan."

General Roberts said, "We will take it from here, my Queen."

James is smiling, he knew what is coming.

"General, did I say you would discuss the plan or did I say we?" Sandra looking straight at him, "you involved me and these are Royal Guardsmen, am I not the Queen?"

"But "is all the General was able to get out when Sandra held her hand up.

"This is not up for discussion; I will be part of this. Did the Duke try to kill you three times in three days? He did my son and I, along with the ambassador and the Capitan, so please, Colonel, proceed," Sandra looking at Tom.

Tom outlined the plan, "Stage an attack on the heavy returning to Wolf Creek with wounded, fake a fire on board to preempt any questions and delays, ambulances show up taking the wounded right to the hospital next to the command center. Ten are real wounded with the rest walking wounded, we form up outside of the hospital, group one secures transportation for the trip back to the airfield, group two assaults the command center; if all goes well, we should be in and out in twenty minutes before they can respond. By the time they know what has happened, we will be back in the air."

"The real wounded?" Sandra asks.

"They will be heavily sedated, they will be unaware of the plan, but we will leave them," Tom answers.

"I do not like that part, Colonial, they may be executed for there part of the raid," Sandra said.

"It's war, your majesty, none of us like it, but it is the only way to gain access, any other way and the casualties would be in the hundreds on both sides and a direct assault would only harden the Guards resolve," Tom explains.

"I will accompany the raid," the Queen announces.

"No, Sandra," James jumps up and shouts, "I will not allow it."

Everyone around the table is looking at James.

Sandra looks at James, "I know it's dangerous, the men that we will be sacrificing know it, the others on the assault team know it. I will not ask them to do what I will not. John would do it and you of all people, James, knows this."

James know there is no persuading her, "Then I, too, will go," he sits down.

"How soon are we talking about, Colonial?" Sandra looking to Tom for an answer.

"We can be ready in three days, my lady."

"I would like to address all who are going in the morning, Colonial, the wounded and the assault team. Can you make that happen?"

"Yes, my lady, would 10:00 be acceptable?" Tom asks. "We will use the mess tent."

"I'm tired, Colonial, do you have a place I can lay my head down for a few hours?" Sandra asks.

"Yes, my lady, we have a tent for you all ready. I'm sorry it's a bit primitive," Tom said.

The laugh was jubilant, "My dear Colonial, for the last week I have not seen a bed, we," indicating James, Billy, and herself, "we have been sleeping on the ground, a tent will be welcomed," smiling at Tom, "thank you."

Major Potter escorted them to their tents, they were next to each other, a cot and blanket is all there was, no pillow.

"I will have a meal brought to you in a few minutes."

"Before you go, Major, there are two thing I need, a fresh change of clothing and a shower, we all have been in these for a week," Sandra told him.

"That can be taken care of, there is a portable shower across and down fifty meters to the left, the water is cold and I will send the quartermaster to you," Adam said.

"Thank you, Major," Sandra bowing her head.

Adam bowed and went to see to the food and get the quartermaster.

Ten minutes later, there is a voice outside the tent flap, "Hello," James hears.

Another voice, "This could not be were the Queen is, you lunkhead."

A third voice, "Yes, it is, the Major said the fourth tent."

James gets up and opens the flap and there are three enlisted men around eighteen-years-old standing there with trays of food.

"You're in the right place," James tells them, "the Queen is right there," pointing to Sandra.

All three looked shocked.

James had to prompt them to enter the tent, "Please serve the Queen first," he said.

The one in the front could barely hold the tray, he was shaking as he offered it to Sandra.

James takes the other two tray and hands one to Billy.

Sandra stands as she takes the young man's tray and bowed her head to the young man, telling him thank you for the food and your service to the empire.

All three bowed and nearly ran out of the tent, not speaking a word to them.

James hears one telling his comrades, "Wait till I tell my mom, she will never believe me."

All three look at each other and smile, "Good kids, I would say," Billy remarked, then devoured the food, they were all hungry, but with all the commotion, they had forgotten.

The quartermaster came by with the clothing, they were all uniforms from the GDF, also soap and towels for the shower.

The three walks to the showers, there are two, one for the men and one for the woman, and the Major was right, the water was cold. Billy screamed when the water hit him, but he washed vigorously and enjoyed it.

Billy understanding that Sandra and James needed a little time alone, he excused himself and went to bed, saying good night.

James tried one more time to talk Sandra out of going on the raid; as soon as he started, she placed her finger on his lips, then put her arms around his chest and snuggled in to his embrace.

There was no talk, only the sharing the night in each other's arms in the small cot, letting the warmth of their bodies mingle, sleep came quickly.

The sun had not breached the horizon when Billy exited his tent; it's going to be a beautiful day, he thinks to himself, looking at the wispy clouds high in the sky over the sea.

This week has been the wildest week of Billy's life, an assassination attempt, shot down and crashed, a mad trek through the wilderness, captured my primitives, appointed to be the Queen's adviser, and now a raid on his own Guard post, all in seven days, what next, he muses, a trip in to orbit, that would top it off, laughing to himself.

Billy looks at his watch, it's 05:00, the mess might be open and it's been over a week with no coffee, so he decides to go see.

Walking in there is only a few people there. Getting his coffee, he starts to sit down by himself, then he sees a familiar face.

She is deep in thought looking through papers and did not see him approach.

"Like some company?" he said to Carole.

She turns around and sees Billy.

Jumping up she throws her arms around Billy's neck with a little squeal of joy, "I'm so happy to see you, Billy, I have been worried about you ever since this crap started." Releasing him she steps back, "You're in a GDF uniform?" she inquires.

"Long story, Carole. he replies.

The two friends sit down to catch up on the events of the last three weeks.

"You know, Billy, I was so relieved when I saw the new transports dropping the Guard troops on the island, I knew I would not be shooting at you."

"I was over Traay being shot down by Guard fighters on that day," smiling at Carole, "I'm glad I was not part of this rebellion and being shot at by you, too."

"Where is Ted?" she asks.

"He's out in the wilderness of Traay looking after the Prince, a lot has changed since this coupe started."

"I would say, you in a GDF uniform and Ted with the Prince, I cannot guess what's next."

"I see you have met our man of the hour, Captain," Adam talking to Carole. The two look up to see Major Potter standing there. "May I sit?" he asks.

"Yes, sir," Carole said, "please join us."

Adam sits down, "You two old friends?" he asks.

"Not old but friends, Billy replies, "we met about a month ago."

"I was on a mission for the Senator and Billy, I mean, Captain Zercoff was my pilot," Carole explained, "and did you know our man of the hour is also friends with give'em hell Gab?"

"You are a man of mystery, Captain Zercoff. The Queen, Ambassador Wildwind, and General Boot, who's next, the Steward or a master-driver?" Adam smiling at Billy.

"Not a Master-Driver but a life like Sub-Drive," Billy responded, "nothing I planned for," blushing a little from the attention.

Someone calls "Attention!"

The dining room is now at full capacity and everyone stands as the Queen, Ambassador Wildwind, and Colonel Dearman enters the room.

Sandra spots Billy and heads for his table.

"Good morning, Skipper," she greets him sitting down.

Carole gives Billy a side ward smile and a wink, "I will need to be going, I have work to do," bowing to the Queen, then exiting the mess hall.

"The Captain was just telling me about meeting a life like Sub-Drive Colonel, can you explain it in a little more detail?" looking at Billy, Adam asks.

Billy explained the encounter with Bell and the night they spent out drinking and dancing with Ted and himself and the way she was naive to simple things.

"Skipper you said life like, how life like?" James questioned.

"If I had not met her with Sub-Drive Ben at the depot in Cranstan Point and the tour of their ship, I would have never known she was not human," Billy answered.

"You have been inside one of their ships also, Captain? Tom asks. "I have been dealing with the Sub-Drives for over twenty years, I have seen inside large transports, the ship they use as an embassy and manufacturing ships, you are the first person that I know who has ever been inside a Sub-Drive's ship."

"Luck of the draw I guess," Billy shrugs.

"I fear the Duke has deprived us from learning from the Drivers and them learning from us," Tom said.

James and Billy look to Tom with a question on their faces.

Tom understands and elaborates, "All the Drivers are gone, any that were not taken were destroyed; the Drivers will not return to the ground until we grow as a culture, however, they will assist in deep space exploration only, in the form of technical support and guidance."

Tom looks at James, "We need to do something about that uniform, Ambassador."

The uniform is too small for James, the buttons around the chest are pulled so tight, making it look like five smiling faces sideways, the sleeves are one third up above the wrist to the elbow and the cuffs are at the shin, not the ankles.

"The quartermaster is taking care of that, I should have my Guard uniform in an hour or so," James told Tom, "one for the Queen and the Skipper also, the Queen will be in a nurse's uniform and I will be an orderly. The Skipper will be in a pilot's uniform, he knows too many people at Wolf Creek to put him in anything else. The Skipper should be our pilot for that reason."

"Good planning, Ambassador," Tom said.

“I prefer James, Colonial, less formal.”

“We still have three hours before the meeting, perhaps you would like to rest until then,” Tom suggested.

“Yes,” Sandra said, “I am still tired.” On the way to their tent, Sandra sees the hospital tent the other direction. “I need to go see Colonial Alvarado James, the nap can wait, will you accompany?”

“I go where you go, my lady.”

The hospital was crowded, there are no private rooms, everyone is in long tents with a nurse’s station at one end; there are three tents like this, one for the wards and two for the operating room and examination rooms.

The sign over the entrance reads Officer’s ward.

As soon as Sandra enters, the tent become quiet. She sees broken bodies, suffering like she has never experienced before; it moved Sandra’s heart, going from bed to bed trying to comfort them, giving them words of hope, finally she came to Colonial Alvarado’s bed.

“How are you today, Colonial?” she asks.

I am better, my Queen, and thank you for spending time with my men, I know they are only words, but they come from someone who cares and it gives them hope.”

“I do what I can, Colonial, and thank you for caring for them, the Duke only cares for himself and what can help him only, you are a good man; you will be rewarded.”

“I have already, my queen, you are here,” with that Colonial Alvarado stands shakily and bows.

Those in the tent that could followed suit, standing and bowing.

Sandra tried to hold back the tears, but they would not stop, they streamed down her cheek.

James reached out and put his arms around her as she cried, standing in the middle with many eyes watching.

Sandra did not get that nap, she visited every ward, touching the hearts of the wounded with kind words and a genuine smile.

"It's time to go," James tells her, "it's 09:50, the meeting will be starting soon."

On the way back to the mess tent, Colonial Alvarado, Major Tibits, and five Captains are heading that way. Sandra and James join them for the walk, not speaking but contemplating the future.

The mess hall was packed, all the tables had been removed to make room for more people, there are nine chairs facing the audience, General Roberts, Colonial Dearman, Major Potter, Major Butterfield, and Capitan Zercoff are all waiting for Sandra, James, Colonial Alvarado, and Major Tibits to arrive.

As soon as the four entered the room, Captain Tucker standing by the door called, "ATTENTION, all rise for Queen Sandra."

The room fell dead quiet as they all stood to attention.

The four went to the front where the chairs had been reserved for them, Major Tibits pushing Colonial Alvarado in his wheelchair, James stood in front of his chair, and Sandra helped Colonial Alvarado to his, Major Tibits stood in front of his chair as Sandra took her seat.

Captain Tucked announced, "Be seated," all did in an orderly fashion.

Tom was first to speak, "First I would like to say is there any one that objects to being hear, if so you are welcome to leave without penalty," all remained seated. Tom continued, "Thank you for participating in this meeting it will save lives. I would like to introduce our honored guest, Queen Sandra."

When Sandra stood, the room remained quiet.

"Thank you, Colonial Dearman, I would like to say the rumor of my death is false as you can see, but there was three attempts on three consecutive days, first was the sabotage of the transport I was traveling in, the Captain's attention to details prevented that attempt. The second attempt was the bombing of the palace at Crown's View, Sub-Drive Clarence warned me of it in time to escape, the third time we were shot down by Royal Guard Fighters over Traay, the true King still lives. Prince Tyler is in hiding until the Duke is dealt with. I would like Colonial Alvarado to speak to you now," Sandra walked over and helped him stand and remand there, holding his arm.

All the Royal Guards stood for him.

"Be seated," Colonial Alvarado told his men; all did so. "We all lost brothers on this Island. We all suffered, we all bleed. We all cried for what? Our orders were to secure the Drivers and Drones on this island and return them to Wolf Creek, not to destroy them but bring them back intact, at all cost, no matter the losses. My command staff has seen the evidence. Are there any of you who dispute it? Speak up if you do. You know I never hold my officers back for their opinions. Speak up if you have something to say. Their silence is conformation of what I'm telling you. The Duke sacrificed your brothers for his goal to be King with no more concern than a rancher has for his cattle going to market. I will support the Queen in her mission if I have to do it alone. Never disrespect the Queen in my presence again; if you do, you have no respect for me. Colonial Alvarado releases Sandra's arm and turns to her. "My queen, I am at your service," bowing to her.

Like a cascade, one stood up and bowed, then another, then ten, then fifty, then the entire audience was standing, bowing to Sandra.

Colonial Alvarado straightens and takes Sandra's arm once more, "I need fifty volunteers, we are going after the Duke to avenge our brothers."

58

"Captain, our shadows back," Simon tells the Captain over the intercom.

The shadow has shone up three time in the last twenty-four hours, painting them with radar, then moving off out of range.

"This is the closest it has come yet, Captain, it's paralleling our cores and speed at a distance of 225K/KM. Change cores, ninety degrees to them, let's see what they do, I'll be there shortly."

The Ex-T is in the middle of her night watch.

Another interrupted night's sleep, Henry tells himself, welcome to the world of command.

Last time the shadow made an appearance, Henry tried to close the distances to get a better radar image, but the shadow moved off at a high speed.

This time he is going to try to get it to follow them, the second planet Crescent is not that far away, he will orbit its moon and see if he can surprise it as he comes around.

"Report," Henry said as he enters the bridge.

"They are 245K, KM out now, the Captain of that ship must have been sleeping when we changed course, it took him ten minutes before he did the same," Simon said.

"What's our distance to Crescent helm?" Henry asks.

"3.5M, KM," Captain, Roger replied.

“Twelve hours to Crescent at this speed, Simon, let’s give this young lady a work out,”

Engineering Henry calls on the intercom.

“Go, Captain.”

“Sidney, give me full power to the engines.”

With the artificial gravity, the change in velocity was hardly noticed, a slight pull was felt as their speed doubled.

“What do you think it is, Captain?” Simon asks.

“It could be a Guard marauder or a pirate, with the GDF fleet occupied, they may be getting braver and coming in closer,” Henry poses.

“Betty, put the Crescent system on the screen.”

The main viewer comes to life with the planet Crescent and its tiny moon.

Crescent is the largest rocky body in the solar system, second from the sun, with twice the gravity of Tarkaneay with a thick atmosphere and temperatures in the hundreds. making it unusable as a base.

Its moon is very small, no more than 200 kilometers in diameter with a weak gravity field.

“Here’s the plan, Simon, Crescents moon is between us and Crescent, we are going to make a tight orbit around it, then head for Crescent. Our shadow will be up orbit of us, as we orbit the planet. We will shoot past him as we break orbit of Crescent and there is nothing he can do; he will be too long to try the same thing. Then we will get a good look at him.”

“I like it, Henry,” Simon tells him.

“Radar,” Henry calls, “update on the ship.”

“He has closed 2K, KM, Captain,” radar reported, “he’s faster than us, but we have too big of a head start.”

“We have five hours to Crescent, Simon, I’m going to get something to eat, care to join me?” Henry asks.

“Sounds good,” Captain Simon answered.

"Shelly, you have the bridge."

On the walk to the dining hall, Simon comments, "You know if it's a Guard marauder, we may be in trouble, Captain, they have a rail gun and can spray us as we go by."

"Yes, I have thought of that, Simon, the Guard uses strength and the pirates uses stealth and speed, I would bet it's the later," Henry answered.

Entering the dining hall, Henry sees siting at a table Matt, Connie, Ben, Bell, and Beth.

"Our guest seems to be fitting in quite well," Henry nodding in the direction of the table.

"Yes, they are," Simon answered, "they have even got Beth to come out of her shell," hearing her laugh at something Matt said.

It's been four days since they were rescued.

Two days ago, they received a message form Elbee, relaying a message from the Steward for them, telling them to stay on the Ex-T for now.

"We need a security officer, that slot was never filed," Simon told Henry, "Matt has an in with the Steward and I think it would be a good match for the Ex-T."

They hear Beth's laughter.

"Matt seems to have a good rapport with the Sub-Drives," Henry said, "I think I'll make the offer."

"Do you think he has any idea those three are Sub-Drives are not humans?" Simon asks Henry.

"How could he; if I did not know it, I would be fooled myself," Henry answered. "Can you go ask them to my table and I'll make the offer right now before we make contact with our shadow?"

Simon gets up and goes to the table and makes the request, he returns with the five.

They all sit down, Beth sits next to Matt.

"Mister Dollar," Henry starts, "I looked up your service record and I liked what I seen, the only flaw was your discharge, can you enlighten me on that?"

"It's public record, Captain," Matt said, "I refused an order I felt was immoral and my commanding officer court-martialed me for it."

"If I gave you an order and you felt it was immoral, you would refuse it?" Henry asks.

"I must live by my conscious, Captain," Matt replied.

Henry looks over at Simon and he gives a nod.

"Mister Dollar, I would like to offer you a position here on the Ex-T, Security Officer, it's a command grade slot, so you will carry the grade of Lieutenant Commander."

"That would be wonderful," Beth said, putting her hand on Matt's forearm.

Henry looks over at Ben to see his reaction, he only smiles.

"Miss Burch, it's a joint offer; we could use your help in Operations."

"I don't know, Matt, Dale may feel betrayed," Connie told him.

"Let's do it this way," Henry said, "do the job temporarily until you talk to Dale, and if he cannot let you go, we will find someone else. I hate to do this to you, Matt, but you are going to be initiated under fire, can you report to the bride now? There is a matter that we will be taking up in two hours."

"Yes, sir, Captain, the only problem is, I don't know where it is," Matt said.

"I'll show you," Beth volunteered, standing up offering Matt her arm; the two head for the Bridge arm in arm.

"Bell, ask Connie if she would come with her to the quartermaster's room to get Matt a uniform, we can't have our newest bridge officer out of uniform," knowing Henry wished to speak to Ben privately. With all gone, Henry, Simon, and Ben have their private conversation.

"You aware of the mystery ship, Ben?" Henry asks.

"I have been monitoring radar, yes, I'm aware, your plan is a good one. You will be back at Tarkaneay before they can overtake you, and I agree it's not a Royal Guard ship, it has all the trademarks of a Parkins ship," Ben explained.

"I am glad to see Beth finally coming out of her shell, Ben, she is like a different person," Henry commented.

"It was Matt that did that, he would call her the grumpy sister. Before long she could not get enough of his hummer, it's a very good thing to see it," Ben said, "she will be a much better crew member this way."

"You know things may change when I tell him she is a Sub-Drive," Henry told him.

"Somehow, I do not think so, Captain. Matt seems to be a good man, not one to judge one on superficial maters, at least I hope so," Ben concluded.

On the walk to the bridge, Matt complimented Beth on her knowledge of the Ex-T.

"Thank you, Matt," she tells him with a bit of a giggle, "but I should know the Ex-T. I helped design her, I assisted my father in the construction of her life support and communications."

"I thought you are a Botanist," Matt stated.

"I have many talents; Matt botany is my passion. I love to see things grow, the smell of flowers, it makes me feel alive," looking at him. "Do you know what else?" Beth said, looking in to Matt's eyes. "For so many years, I secluded myself from human contact, throwing myself in to my work, thinking contact unnecessary and irrelevant, you have changed that and I know not why." He reaches down, takes her hand, placing his other hand over it, noticing the smoothness of it and the incredible softness,

"We all need contact to make us aware of our needs and the needs of others."

"Matt, is there something wrong?" I am sensing your blood pressure elevating and your respiration has increased, are you not well?" Beth asks.

"You are so beautiful, has no one ever told you that?" Matt said smiling at her.

"Never," she replied, "nor have I ever been kissed."

Matt releases her hand, gently taking her face in both hands, pressing his lips to her lips, he fills her body starting to tremble, "Now you have," he said.

"I don't understand, my mind feels weak. I wish to flee, but I cannot, I fill fear of this but a desire to re-experience it, help me, Matt," she pleads.

He can see she is in distress, so he reaches out and pulls her in to his embrace, the trimmers slow then stop and he can fill her body relax.

"Are you alright?" he asks her in a soft and gentle voice. "I would never harm you," he said, "I was only trying to give you a taste of life, forgive me."

"I could stay this way forever, Matt," she said. She suddenly releases Matt and takes a half step back, still holding his hands, looking him in the eyes. "Is this love?" she asks.

"Only you can answer that," Matt tells her, "as for me, I will say like with a capital L, only time will tell for love."

"We must hurry to the bridge, there are things I must go over with you before the encounter with the mystery ship." Beth grabs Matt's hand and starts leading him to the bridge.

The bridge is a busy place, the command crew is all there with the exception of the Captain and first officer, every station has the primary and secondary crew.

Beth escorts Matt to the tactical station, more than three quarters of it is blank. "We only have defensive counter measures, no offensive capabilities," Beth explained. "We have projectile counter measures here, it's a canon that shoots an expendable mass of sticky foam, this is radar jamming and this is decoy projection, that's all we have, Matt," Beth told him. "Sit down and familiarize yourself with the targeting and limitations of the system," Beth prompted Matt.

Henry, Simon, and Ben enter the bridge.

"Report," Henry orders.

"Vessel is 125K/KM, sir, 25K/KM, up orbit from us."

"Distance to Crescent," the Captain orders.

"65K/KM," radar calls.

"Helm, status the Captain call."

"We will be at the moon of Crescent in ten minutes, sir."

"Keep us as tight as you can, Helm," Henry tells Shelly.

Henry calls, "Decoy projection, as soon as we are behind the moon, project it out 10K/KM, above the moon."

"Tactical copy," Matt replies.

"Helm, status," the Captain calls.

"Five minutes," Helm replies.

"Radar, any change?" the Captain calls.

"No, sir, still on intercept," radar answers.

"Shelly, as soon as we are behind the moon, put us nose down to the moon, keep the power to the engines, use the gravitational pull to keep us low. Now, Shelly," the Captain orders.

The Ex-T pivots, the view screen is filled with the image of the moon rushing by. "Decoy projection now," the Captain orders.

Matt pushes the control and the image is projected out 10,000 kilometers above them.

Helm calls, "Sixty seconds to break orbit." Everyone is holding their breath. Helm calls, "Ten seconds to break orbit."

"Radar, any change?" the Captain calls.

"He changed heading, sir, he went after the decoy."

"Helm, right us, head for Crescent," Henry said, "and put us on a heading for Tarkaneay."

The mystery ship changed its heading, making it unable to use Crescent's gravitation to swing around and head back out in the opposite direction.

Radar painted the ship and now has a high-resolution image of it.

"As I suspected, Captain, Ben said, "it's a Parkin ship from Trinity Station. We have suspected them of piracy for some time now."

"What class is it, Ben? I have never seen one like that," Simon asks.

"It's really two ships made in to one, do you recall the sweeper program twenty years ago?" Ben asks.

"Vaguely," Henry said, "it was to clean up the debris in orbit, was it not?"

"Yes, after the last big war, there was so much trash in orbit, no one could achieve orbit safely, a program was started to remove the space junk, that was a relic of that program."

"How did the Parkins get it?" Henry ask Ben.

"They were decommissioned and sent to Trinity Station to be dissembled, apparently someone there has found another use for them," Ben said.

"That would be Floyd Mall," Matt spoke up, "he is the man running things at T.S. and he is the one that was going to kill Connie and I; he did have one of my friends killed, so piracy is right down his ally."

"So, it's this Mall and the Guard on T.S.?" Ben asks Matt.

"Yes, they are of the same mold, no regard for life."

"Radar status on the ship?" Henry asks.

"It's out of range, Captain, but last return he was heading toward the sun."

"I would say that confirms your suspicion Ben, about it coming from T.S.," Henry said.

"Communications, contact GDF fleet and let them know we will be in their vicinity in two days and tell them to be on the lookout for that ship," Henry ordered.

In a quiet voice, Beth asks Matt, "This Mall, he killed your friend?"

"Yes, two of his men knifed her, she bled out in minutes, trying to save me and Bubbles."

"Bubbles, who is that?" Beth asks.

"That would be Connie," Matt answered.

Beth looks at Matt, "Connie makes Bubbles."

Matt could not help it, he busted out in a booming laugh.

Reaching over and giving Beth a kiss on the forehead, "I love you." That is when he noticed the entire bridge is looking at them. "Sorry," Matt said, "my fault, it will not happen again.

"You may want to have that talk with Matt a little sooner than you think, Ben."

"You may be right, Henry."

59

"My lord, Cranstan Point radar reported a small aircraft landing, then taking off in Traay, it's in a very remote part, twenty-five kilometers from the crash site," the General tells the Duke.

"That's it, send in a Battalion this time, I want her dead," the Duke screams.

"My lord, if we do that, we lose the war," the General said, "Four Rivers will consolidate with Cranstan Point."

"Am I surrounded by fools?" the Duke screams, striking the General with the scepter on the side of the face, knocking him down. The Duke tells the General not to move, "Stay on the floor where you belong." The other Generals are watching this. The Duke begins his pacing back and forth mumbling to himself, "The bitch and the brat must die. If I lose this war and they're alive, I'm dead, but if they are dead, there is no one to take the throne but me," reinforcing his delusions of self-worth. "Get me Steve Carter now," he screams again. "It's all Alvarado's fault," the Duke tells himself, "if he would have brought me the Driver like I told him, I would not be in this position. His Commanding Officer pleaded with me for his life, but I had to make an example to the others."

His body hung out front for three days until the stink of the rot forced the Duke to have it removed.

"My lord, how may I serve you?" Steve Carter said as he bows to the Duke.

"I have a new lead on the bitch and the brat, take five men and go kill them," the Duke stops, "no, that's the problem, too many men. Take two, ones that you do not need, and leave them there, do you understand my meaning, only you return."

"Yes, my lord, I understand," Steve said.

"Good. General, you can get up now, take care of Carter and get him to the sight and never question me again, do you understand?" the Duke orders.

"Yes, my lord," the General bows.

"That's by your command, my lord," the Duke sneers, "now repeat it."

"By your command, my lord," the General bows one more time.

"Now get out," the Duke shouts.

The Royal Guard space fleet is doing no better, they are low on fuel and supplies. The only place they have for that is Trinity Station, the Admiral failed to secure Z Point Station, he is floating in space without a spacesuit, another example.

60

The bush plane circled the canyon once before it departed, leaving the rest of the party behind.

"So, your James's nephew?" Ted asks Fred.

"James is my father's little brother, the baby boy of the family," Fred laughs, "not so little is he, he dwarfs my father and every one of his brothers."

"I think he is the biggest man I have ever met," Ted comments, "I would not wish to be in front of one of his punches, he would knock someone's head off." Ted turns to the Sargent, "We were never introduced. I'm Lieutenant Ted Linch, call me Ted," offering his hand to the Sargent.

Sargent Peter Roads taking Ted's hand, "What do we do now, sir?" asking him.

Peter is a fair size man, the same height as Ted but broader at the shoulders and from the insignia patch, he's from the infantry.

"We wait," Ted answered, "it's a beautiful place to sit out the war. I will say a bit primitive, but I like it."

"Me, too," chimed in Fred, "as a boy, I would spend two weeks four times a year here. They are my best memories of childhood, the first two of those years James was here with me.

Let's get you two settled in, you'll be bunking with me," Ted points to the last shelter. "We have yet to find the weapons stash, do you have any idea, Fred?" Ted inquired.

"I bet old Charley moved them to the cave, it's about a kilometer up canyon, we can go have a look if you like?" Fred asks.

"I think that would be smart," Ted picking up the knife Pandar brought, "this is our only weapon."

"Let's go take a look, we can be back in two hours," Fred said.

"Peter, I would like you to stay with the camp, two men are better than one if something happens," Ted told him. "Shall we go, Fred?"

"I'm coming, too," Tina informs him, "let me get a few things."

Tina gos in to the shelter and comes out with a rope and flashlight, Ted's flashlight, he gave it to her so she would not trip over anything at night on the way to the privy.

On the way, Fred is pointing out game trails for Ted, places they can place snares for rabbits and the likes.

Fred calls Ted's attention to a berry bush, "This is poison," he said, "and that one over there is eatable."

"They look alike," Ted said, "How do you tell them apart?"

"This one has a death shroud," Fred picking one, "see here, around the stem, that one does not." Fred continued pointing things out to Ted on the walk to the cave, like James asked him to do. "I'll make a Traayen out of this boy, thinking to himself and make James proud."

"I think this is the place," Fred told his companions, "it's been twenty years, things have changed." Fred walks over to a bush and peers behind it, "Ha-ha," he shouts.

Behind the bush is a mark on a rock, like the one James found on their first day in the canyon, a circle with an X in the center, one longer than the other three. Like James did, he looks to the sky to get his bearings. "It's that way," Fred announced, pointing across the canyon.

"There is a small ravine up the rim, we climb for that," Fred said, "it's on the left halfway up."

The wall is not sheer but a difficult climb; they come to a small ledge leading to the left, they follow that for forty meters. In a washout on the wall, there is a crack no more than a meter wide. "This is it," Fred said, "I'll go in first, can I have the light?" he asks Tina.

Tina passes it to him; he turns sideways and squeezes in.

Five meters in, it opens in to a small cavern ten meters wide and over fifty deep with a ceiling twenty meters high.

"Come on in," Fred shouts.

The three are now standing in the middle of the cavern, Fred shines the light to one side, there is what looks like blankets rolled up and several boxes.

Fred unrolled the blankets and out comes two old hunting rifles, single shoot breach loaders covered in oil.

"It will take hours of cleaning to get them usable," Ted remarked.

Tina opened one of the boxes to find ammunition, five knives, three hatchets, and a string saw.

Ted opened the next box and in it were three revolvers; they, too, are covered in oil, with holsters, belts, and ammunition.

The third box had string, arrow heads, and shafts, all the needed materiel for making a bow for the arrows.

"We will only take half," Fred said, "the rest must stay in case someone after us needs them, that's the Traay way, think about the next person, not only about one's self."

They repackaged what they were not taking to keep them preserved and headed back to camp. The sun was below the rim of the canyon when they got back to camp.

Ted sits down and started the job of cleaning the weapons. Peter volunteered to help him.

Fred gathered the children and started the search for the right trees to make the bows, Bradly accompanied them.

Tina and Mae started diner.

After diner they all sit around the fire and talked.

Fred was working on the bow, shaping it with one of the knives they brought back.

"You're very good with the children," Bradly tells Fred, "do you have any?"

Fred's face brightened with pride, "I have five," he said, "three boys and two girls."

"I understand you're the son of Prince Robert, an heir apparent?" Tina ask him.

"Yes," Fred answered, "my father has been running thing for over ten years now, the Grand Chief has been too frail to govern, the elders do not dispute his leadership."

It was a joyful night; the war was forgotten and peace was in their heart as they slumbered.

Up on the canyon rim, the three men watched as the fire started to burn low.

"The tall blond, that's the Queen," Carter tells his companions, "get some sleep, it's too dark to try to descend the canyon. First light we will go down canyon two or more kilometers, so we will not be seen and take them the day after tomorrow morning. I'm planning on having myself a little fun with the Queen," Steve laughs. "You two can have the other two girls, that will be your bonus."

Everyone slept in late, last night's conversation went in to the early morning hours, there was laughter, stories of Traay from Fred, Ted's account of meeting a Sub-Drive, and Berrana's story of the trip to Tarkaneay from T.S..

This had Ted's full attention, anything about space, he would be all ears.

The camp was coming alive around eight in the morning.

Mae was the only one up at sunrise; by the time the others had started waking up, Mae had breakfast ready.

After breakfast Tyler, Tamara, and Berrana ask Fred if he could show them how to track.

"James said he would, but he never had the time," Tyler explained, "then he left with Mom, so I was hoping you could."

"I think that would be an excellent idea," Fred complimented Tyler, "I have just the task.

I would like you three to retrace mine, Tina's, and Ted's path to the cave yesterday, no one has been back that way, so the track has not been disturbed. We will make a short practice run the other direction and I will give some pointers," Fred told them. "Rule one, never leave camp unprepared, water, one meal, knife, and something to start a fire. Rule two, communication, tell someone where you are going and when you are expected to return, this is very important," Fred said, "it may save your life."

They spent all morning and part of the afternoon perfecting their skills.

How a track can tell you if a person is carrying something, a line of dirt on a disturbed rock, broken branches and leafs knocked off of shrubs, all the signs.

Tamara was a natural at it.

Fred would try to confuse her by jumping to a rock in the opposite direction, but she remembered the dirt line on the disturbed rock.

On the way back to camp, Fred told them they're ready, "First light tomorrow, the test will be make your way to the cave and bring back one arrow head, pack tonight, we will make three torches from available materiel before the day is spent."

Before dinner Bradly had the children come with him to fill the water flasks from the stream.

When Mae found out Fred was going to let the children go off on their own, she objected.

"They're only children," she said.

"The Prince is going to have to grow up," Fred explained, "he is going to be King one day, you need to stop pampering him; his father by this age was doing thing like this with James."

"He's not John," Mae argued.

"And he never will be if you don't let him grow up," Fred countered.

"Let's do this," Ted interceded, "Tina and I will leave before the children, we will walk on the opposite side of the canyon staying out of sight, letting them believe they are on their own, will that satisfy you, Mae?"

"I still think it's a bad idea," Mae objected but relented.

After dinner they all called it an early night and went to bed.

By ten that night the fire had died down and the camp was quiet.

The three intruders were only fifty meters down canyon from the camp waiting for first light.

Ted and Tina spent the night next to the fire, so they would not give away their plan to watch the kids on their adventure.

At four in the morning, Ted heard the children starting to stir; he bent over and kissed Tina on the forehead.

"It's time to go," he whispered.

"This was your plan all along," stroking his face, pulling him closer, giving him her own kiss, "this was an excuse to get me alone," smiling at him.

"Can you blame me?" he teased.

The two picked up the packs they had ready, Ted buckled on the pistol, and Tina had the bow and arrow.

In high school, Tina took two years of archery and she was a fair shot, she has been practicing with it, and if she gets the chance, she will try to score some meat for the camp.

The moon was waning, so there was a little light. Ted and Tina crossed the stream, then climbed up the side of the canyon a little way, so they could watch the children as they exited the camp.

Carter walked up one the sentry he posted, "Hear anything?" he whispered.

"There was some activity ten minutes ago," he said "but it's quiet now, someone must have been using the head."

"I'll be back in thirty minutes, be ready," Carter told him.

Tina and Ted watched the children leave camp and make their way to the trail going up canyon; they would stay on this side, so they could see them from a distance.

The three children stopped about 200 meters from camp and waited for the sun to start giving more light. They know Fred, Ted, and Tina came this way; they would start doing the circles pattern like Fred showed them to pick up the trail.

As soon as the kids started moving again, Ted sees Tamara wave the other two over and point to the ground, the hunt was on.

The three intruders are now on the outside of the camp, peering through the trees, they see Mae putting wood on the fire to start breakfast.

Three men emerge and sit by the fire talking.

"The bitch must be sleeping in," Carter tells his men, "circle around on the left and right, if any try to run, stop them. Wait for my signal," Carter reminds them, "if any get away, the Duke will have your head," he smiles inward, knowing these two will not be going home.

Carter takes aim at the big guy, he's the only one that would be any problem, the other two are smaller and look like he could take them both at the same time, feeding his own self-worth.

Fred is looking right at Peter when he hears the gun shoot, he sees a red dot right below the left shoulder, it begins to spread. He knew what had happened.

He shouts at Bradly, "Run!"

Fred did not run away from the shot; he ran toward it.

Bradly stood there for s second, then did what he was told, he sprinted for the trees.

Mae stood there in shock, with her hand to her mouth, stopping a scream.

As Fred neared the tree line, a man steps out with a rifle, the barrel was hung up in the low hanging tree branches.

Fred tackles him mid chest, knocking him off his feet.

Bradly comes around a tree and is face to face with a man with a gun, he stops dead in his tracks.

"Hit me hard," the man tells Bradly, "then run." The man drops the gun and offers the side of his face to Badly, "I can't explain now, just do it."

Bradly strikes him hard, then runs in the direction of Ted and Tina.

Fred has the man down, striking him repeatedly, then everything goes black.

As Carter gets to his feet, he points at Fred, "Secure him," he tells his accomplices, kicking him twice in the ribs.

Mae is kneeling over Peter, trying to stop the bleeding when Carter butted her with the rifle, knocking her out.

With a smile, Carter approaches the shelter, "Come out, come out, your royal bitch-ness," he sneers. Looking in there is no one there, he runs to the next, same. He checks all the shelters; the Queen and the Prince are gone. "The Duke will kill me if I fail," Carter's starting to panic.

The other man came stumbling into camp with his mouth and nose bleeding. "Where is the other one?" Carter yelled at him.

"He hit me and got away," is all he said.

"Great," Carter screamed, "now we have two men, the Queen, and three kids to go find."

Ted hears the gun shot and turns facing the camp.

He looks to the children and Ted can see they also heard the shot.

"What do we do, Ted?" Tina asks.

"Go get the kids and head for the cave, I'm going back, be safe my love," Ted tells Tina, then takes off in a run back to camp.

On his way, Ted hears rustling in the bushes, he stops and hides behind a tree.

Out comes Bradly.

Ted tries to stop him, but Bradly is in a panic and runs over him, knocking them both to the ground.

Bradly finally recognized Ted. Out of breath, he blurted out, "Someone shot Peter." Ted gave Bradly time to calm himself to find out what happened. He heard the story about the gun shot and the red-haired man letting him go. "What do we do?" Bradly asks.

Head up the canyon, keep looking on the left wall, you should see Tina and the kids making their way to the cave, go with them and stay there," Ted instructed. "I'm going to camp."

He started to walk back to camp more slowly, stopping every few meters and observing the surroundings.

We have at least one friend in the group, Ted thinks, he checks his pistol for rounds in the chamber.

He has been making his way to the camp stealthily, making as little noise as possible.

Ted hears movement behind him, spinning around, pointing the pistol at whoever is coming.

Out comes Tina with her bow notched with an arrow.

Lowering the gun Ted reprimands Tina for coming but is glad to see her.

"Bradly is taking the kids to the cave, I came to help," she said.

They sneak up on the camp from the west side, there are no paths coming out that way.

They hear Mae scream in pain.

On their bellies, they crawl to the clearing to get a better view.

They see three men standing over Fred and Mae.

Fred is beaten bloody, his head is leaning forward, he is unconscious.

The black-haired man is putting Mae's hand to the fire, she screams again.

"Where is the Queen," he shouts.

"She is gone," Mae cries, "she left two days ago with the Ambassador and the Captain to Cranstan Point."

"Who was the blond that was here last night?" Carter asks a little calmer.

"That was Tina, the Queen's servant," Mae answered.

"Then where is the Prince?" Carter shouts, his anger back, "I saw him yesterday."

"Pandar came last night and took him to their village, all the children and Tina," Mae whimpered.

"Why didn't you go?" Carter said, looking at Mae.

"I would have slowed them down," she answered.

"This is a waste of time, wake that one up," Carter told his companion. "I want him to be awake when I kill him."

The man retrieved a water skin and poured it on Fred; he lifted his head and looked at the leader.

"You're never going to leave this canyon alive," Fred told him in an act of defiance.

Carter told his companion, "Shoot him in the gut, so he dies slowly."

The man pointed his gun at Fred, smiling, "I'm going to enjoy this," he said.

A shot rang out, the man pointing his gun at Fred fell over.

The other man turned his gun toward Carter, but it was too late, he had drawn his pistol and fired three shots at him, striking him twice.

Walking over to him, Carter pointed his pistol at his head, you were never going to leave alive anyway, nor was he," pointing at the man dead next to Fred.

A twang was heard as Tina let an arrow fly, striking Carter in the side, he turned and fired in the direction of the arrow, then fled, leaving a blood trail.

"You go untie them," Ted told Tina, "I'm going after him." The trail was plain to see, he was bleeding profusely. Ted found him not fifty meters from camp; as he approached, Carter tried to raise his gun, but it fell to the ground. Reaching down Ted picks up the pistol, then kneels down next to him. "You will be dead in two minutes, anything you would like to say before you do?" Ted asks.

"I would be dead anyway if I failed the Duke, he's crazy you know," Carter said, spitting up blood. "Tell me the truth, is the Queen really not here?" Carter asks.

"No, she left two days ago, the GDF is taking the war to the Duke, his own men are going to help," Ted explained.

"I'm not surprised, he has killed his own Generals for nothing," Carter coughing blood and fighting to breathe. "There is a satellite radio in my pack," Carter tells Ted, "the Duke is expecting my call with an update, it will send the Duke in to a rage," he smiles. "If I can't win, I want him to lose."

"Why would you work for such a man?" Ted asks.

He only looked at Ted and died.

Ted pulls the man's billfold from his back pocket to see who he was.

Ted can see this is where the three intruders spent the night, there are three back packs next to fallen tree.

He can see the radio on the side, pulling it out, starting his walk back to camp.

Back at camp, Ted sees the body of Peter covered with a blanket.

The man that saved Fred's life is still talking, but the blood flowing from his side tells Ted that he will not survive much longer.

"Tell Ambassador Wildwind the undercover agent said we are even for the punch, he will know," then he died also.

"You doing alright, Fred?" Ted asks. "He really gave you a beating."

"I can deal with the face, it's the broken ribs that is giving me the most pain," Fred said.

"The man's name was Steve Carter," handing Fred the billfold, "we talked some before he died, he asked me to call the Duke for him," Ted told him.

"Why would he do that?" questioned Fred.

"To torment the Duke, they are of the same mold, vindictive and egotistical," Ted answered, "but I think we should do it, that will keep him from thinking about other things and feeding his anger, bad decisions are made in anger."

"You're right," Fred said smiling, "he may send another hit squad our way," he reminded Ted.

Tossing the radio to Fred, "I'm going to get the kids, we will handle anything the Duke throws our way." Ted takes off for the cave.

Tina was listening to their conversation as she was rapping Mae's hand.

"He is right, Fred, the more we distract the Duke, the better the odds we have of defeating him," Tina said.

Ted returned with the children and Bradly before nine in the morning.

As the children enters the camp, they see three dead bodies, Peter among them.

"Kids," Ted calls, "you will have to go with me, you, too, Bradly. There is equipment and a body to retrieve."

They go to where Carter is and the backpacks.

Each child grabs a pack, Ted and Bradly carry Carter back to camp to bury him.

It took the rest of the morning and part of the afternoon to complete the task of burying the dead.

The contents of the pack are laid out to see what was there; besides the food and blankets, there were three assault rifles, three automatic pistols, three flashlights, ammunition, and three hand held radios.

"What do you think, Fred?" Ted asks. "Should we call the Duke or not?"

"I thought it was a bad idea in the beginning, but you and Tina have a point, we are not out of this war, only a side note. Let's do it but not today, we will give him more time to stew, his imagination will keep him from sleeping, day after tomorrow morning I think."

"Then it's settled," Ted said, "we make the call and let Tyler talk to his uncle."

61

Camp Edgefield, as they are calling it now, is a busy place.

There are several new tents added to the camp, one is for the mission, inside there is a modal of Wolf Creek, laying out the airfield, hospital, and command center.

On the tarmac sits the heavy Guard transport that will be used for flying the mission.

Billy met his crew this morning, his copilot he knew from his squadron, Captain Greg Carpenter.

The first thing Carpenter noticed is Billy is no longer a Captain, he is wearing a Major insignia.

"I see you have your Majors rank back," he tells him, shaking Billy's hand.

"Last night the Queen promoted me," Billy explains, "she said I deserved it and it would look better with the change to the heavy. "I have never flown a heavy," Billy told him, "so I will be depending on you to keep me from making a mistake."

"You'll do fine, Billy, everyone knows you are really the best pilot in the squadron," Greg said.

Greg went over the flight caricaturists of the heavy with Billy. "Let's go have a drink afterwards," Greg asks Billy, "the Colonial set up a recreation tent with a bar."

"I'll go, but I have not touched alcohol in over a month. I think I will stay the cores and have coffee."

"You have changed," Greg said, "there was a time you would be the first one there and the last one to leave."

"My priorities have changed," Billy told him, "and look, I have lost five kilograms of fat and put on more muscle," flexing his biceps, smiling at Greg with obverse pride in himself.

The fifty man combat team has been going over the plan, brainstorming different scenarios trying to anticipate any unforeseen problems.

One of the most critical problems is keeping the ambulances from leaving, stranding the team with no way to get back to the airfield.

"Why use ambulances?" one of Alvarado's Sargent suggests. "They only hold eight people, we would need at least seven to have enough to hold everyone, one bus would do the job. I have a friend at the motor poll, it's on the way to the hospital, drop me and an officer off, I'll get us that bus."

Tom looked to Major Tibits.

"Sargent, do you think you could get two?" Tibits asks.

If you send a hard ass officer with me, yes."

"He's right, sir," the Major said, "we could send Captain Warren with him and two drivers. Warren will not take no for an answer."

That would do it, sir," the Sargent replied, "Captain Warren can be a real ass sometimes, no offense, Captain."

"None taken, Sargent," Captain Warren returned, "I'll take it as a compliment."

Tom goes over the plan one more time.

"Once the explosives are placed in the park across the street, that is when we signal the fast movers to make their run. It will take them ten minutes to arrive, simulating an air raid.

As soon as they go over, we detonate the charges in the park, that is the signal to move, it will be chaos for ten minutes. A team secures the front entrance, then starts moving toward the command center. B team moves on the door facing the hospitals, then starts moving toward the command center. C team takes up position to guard our exit. D team breaches the west wall with a shaped charge, gaining entry to the command center. We will come at them from three directions. Remember the Duke is the target, use deadly force only as the last resort, these are your brothers, they are not the enemy," Tom reminds them.

For the next two hours, they go over the plan honing their rolls, making adjustments in timing and execution.

"I think we are ready," Tom tells Sam, "release them early, so they can write letters and get some sleep this evening, we will assembly at 01:00, takeoff at 02:00."

"Will do," Colonial Sam replied.

"I need to go see Colonial Alvarado; he is insisting on going with his men and adding authenticity to the plan," Tom said.

"Yes," Sam replied, "the infection is spreading, this will kill him. I'm afraid, but he will not say behind, he is a good man and a there is no better commander to serve under. He feels this will make up for the death of so many men under his command."

"He was following orders, Major, there is no blame from the Queen, the Steward, or from me," Tom said, "it is a soldier's duty to do so, the Duke is the one that is responsible for their deaths, not Brian."

"Thank you, Colonial, it means a lot to me that you have respect for Colonial Alvarado, and I see a lot of him in you, the two of you could be great friends if this works out in our advantage."

"It will, Sam, we are on the right side," Tom putting out his hand to him, "you are a good man also. I will be honored to serve with you." Sam took Tom's handshake, and Tom could see he was moved as a tear streamed down Sam's cheek. "I will see you later, Sam, go get some rest with the men, tomorrow will be a day for the history books."

Tom looks over to Adam and motions him to accompany him on the way to the hospital.

"Major Tibits is a fine officer," Adam tells Tom.

"Yes," Tom agrees, "it takes more than giving orders to your subordinates to make a good officer, you must feel their pain as well as their joy, to put it simply have a heart, the Colonial and the Major have one."

Entering the officer ward of the hospital, Tom sees the Queen sitting next to Colonial Alvarado's bed and James standing beside her.

"Good afternoon," Tom greets them. "Your Majesty," Tom bows to Sandra.

Adam does the same. "How are you today, Brian?" Tom asks.

"Better today, Tom," he responded, "I am ready to go, the Duke will be in our custody by this time tomorrow."

"You are not better," Sandra said. "The Doctor told me not more than an hour ago if you go, you will probably be dead in two days. I'm going to order you to stay."

"Your Majesty, do you trust me?" Tom asks.

"Yes," Sandra answered.

"Then you cannot order the Colonial to stay behind, that will kill him just as well as going; he may live for years, but the guilt would be a life sentence for him, give him a chance at redemption," Tom explained.

"But" is all Sandra got out when James placed his hand on her shoulder, looking into her eyes, shaking his head no.

"I thank you for your concern, Your Majesty," Brian said, "but this is something I must do, my men will look after me like I do them."

"I still do not like it," Sandra protested.

"I do not like you going either, Sandra," James said, "but this is something you must do, so I support your desire to participate, even at the thought of the danger you are putting yourself in."

"It just sems unnecessary to use injured men, it's like we are using them twice, then throwing them away," Sandra told them. "Is there no other way?"

"No," Tom replied, "if we us healthy people, they will know something is up; we need to swamp the emergency room with real wounded, giving us the chance to position the assault team, otherwise we are wasting our time and the lives of all involved."

"We are all volunteers, my Queen," Colonial Alvarado said, "let us do our part," placing his hand on hers.

Sandra sighs deeply, "All service men are the same; how many wounded are we sending?"

"Ten in total," Tom answered, "all critical, that should keep the walking wounded out of the emergency room. We should all eat and get some rest, tomorrow will be hectic," Tom said.

"I don't see me getting any rest until this is over," Sandra replied, "but food will help. You get some rest, Colonial Alvarado. I will see you tonight," Sandra reaches over and gives him a kiss on the forehead, "I wish you would stay, but I understand."

"If you were the one controlling the Guard, we would not be in this position, my queen, you are a good person," Brian said, "someone I could follow knowing your commands were moral and just."

"Thank you, Colonial, that means a lot to me and I believe you to be the same, rest well."

Sandra and James, arm in arm, head for the mess tent.

As soon as Sandra was out of the hospital tent, Tom turned to Brian, "They will execute you and all that we leave as soon as we grab the Duke and make out escape."

"Yes, I know Tom, but this will make up for the men I sacrificed for the Duke's plan to be King. I should have refused his orders right from the beginning."

"No, Brian, that would have served no purpose, he would have killed you and sent someone else, you were meant to be here," Tom reminded him. "The loses could have been greater if your replacement was of the Duke's mind set, you saved countless lives, your men and many others."

"Do you really think we can pull this off, Tom?" Brian asks. "If it goes badly, we will be delivering the Queen right in to the Duke's hands."

"Yes, I do," Tom said, "I have not given you all the news from Wolf Creek, the Duke has been executing his Generals, your Commanding Officer was the last one; he blamed you for losing the Drivers, so he took it out on him."

"Why would he do that?" Brian asks. "Robert Davidson was a good Commander; it makes no sense."

"I cannot say for sure," Tom responded, "I believe he has gone mad with power; the Guard Space Fleet has started surrendering also after he executed the Admiral for failing to secure Z point Station."

"How could we not see this from the beginning, Tom, there must have been warning signs, no one gets that bad this quick, did we all just ignore it?"

"No, I think there was clues, but the hope was the Prince would take charge before he did anything like this."

"I am afraid the Duke has killed the Guard forever; it will never be trusted again and it was fine origination with history and honor, Tom, all for one man's greed," Brian looking at him with apparent shame and loss in his eyes.

"Maybe not," Tom giving him a smile, "as long as it has men like you who are ready to take charge, there is hope, now get some rest. I will see you at 01:00."

62

The gardens on the Ex-T are large, more than 300 meters long and fifty meters wide with every kind of vegetable growing in a hydroponic solution, miniature fruit and nut trees growing down the center, with more than twenty different flowering plants for the dining room tables all under grow lights to scrub the carbon dioxide out of the air.

Matt has been off duty for the last two hours sitting next to the fish pond used for growing fresh sea food, listening to the trickle of water, watching Beth work her magic with the growing things.

She is so delicate, taking each tender sprout and lovingly placing it in the growing bed; he was amazed to see her encourage a bee to pollinate a flower.

She scolded him for swatting one away that buzzed his head, telling him to be gentle with them, they will not give up their life unless the hive is threatened and a sting is the end of their life.

In Matt's entire, life he has never met anyone so gentle and loving of other thing, even the rabbits and chickens that the crew uses for food; she talks to them and treats each one delicately as she feeds them, tending to their needs.

Normally Matt is drawn to a woman of the rough and tumble kind, one that will stand and fight, then ask questions later, but Beth is different, soft and sweet, a bit naive about life, a thinker, not a fighter.

Lost in thought, Matt looks up and sees Beth looking at him with a smile on her face. She, too, is lost in thought, she is unaware of the leaf that has become entangled in her hair.

Matt gets up and starts the twenty-meter walk to where she has been working, passing by the flowers, he reaches down and picks a small crocus flower.

Now standing in front of her, he reaches and removes the leaf from her hair, stroking the out of place hair behind her ear, then places the flower there, the orange and yellow contrast to her jet-black hair moves Matt's deep emotions.

Reaching for her hand, Matt lifts it to his lips and gently kisses it.

Still holding Matt's hand, her other hand goes to her mouth, her lips begin to tremble, she is on the verge of tears.

Matt can see she is in distress, so he releases her hand and gently puts his arms around her and pulls her in to his embrace.

"I have never felt like this, Matt," she tells him, "I feel joy, and at the same time, I feel fear."

"There is nothing to fear, my sweet," he tells her.

"But there is," she replies, "if you know my secret, you would hate me I fear."

"That's not possible," he said, "there is nothing you could have done that would change my feelings toward you."

"It is not what I have done but what I am that you will hate I fear."

Matt takes a step back and touches her chest, "It's your heart," then moves his hand to her head, touching the side of her face, "and your mind that has my attention, everything else is irrelevant."

Beth steps in close and puts her arms around Matt's chest, "I hope you are right; I never wish for this to end." They remain that way for several minutes, locked in a mutual embrace.

Suddenly Beth steps back, "You must get to the bridge, Matt, we are in danger."

"What do you mean?" he asks.

"No time to explain, I will be there soon, now go please and be fast."

Beth turned and ran to the aft of the ship.

The elevator to the interior of the ship is only a few meters from where they were standing. Matt runs for the exit like Beth asked him to do.

As Matt hits the call button for the elevator, the alarm starts sounding, all crew members to their duty stations, this is not a drill.

Matt enters the bridge, and the first thing he sees is the view screen has seven ships on it, a Guard Carrier, four Marauders, and two heavy Frigates, the Carrier in the center with the Marauders surrounding it with the Frigates in line behind the Carrier, he goes straight to the tactical station.

Moments later Henry enters the bridge, "Report," he orders.

Timothy responds, "They came from nowhere, Captain, one-minute radar is clear, the next, they're only 2,000 kilometers out."

"They must have used radar scattering technology," Henry told him.

"Captain, we are being hailed," communication reported.

"Send it to my chair, Rodney," Henry tells him.

The view screen at his chair comes to life with an image.

"To whom am I speaking?" the image asks.

"I am Captain Carver of the S.S. Extractor, and to whom am I speaking to?" Henry asks.

"Admiral Rimes," he answered, "commanding the 7th Royal Guard task force, I would like to present my fleet to you for surrender."

Henry turns and looks at Simon with a question on his face, "Do I understand correctly, you wish to surrender?"

"Yes, Captain, surrender; the Duke lied to us and cost me five ships and the men that crewed them. I or my men will no longer participate in this coupe, this must be done quickly, not all of my Captains agree with me, and if we give them too much time, they may mutiny."

"Admiral, we are a commercial vessel, how can I help?" Henry asks.

"You can start by reporting our location to GDF fleet and letting them know our intention; hopefully they will send ships to handle this."

"Com, send a message to GDF fleet and inform them of the situation," Henry tells Rodney. "Anything else, Admiral?" Henry asks.

"No, Captain, that will do, but if you can get a bit more speed out of your ship, I would. I think at least three of my Captains are not going to surrender, there may be a fight and I would like you as far away as you can be, God's speed," the Admiral said. "Rimes out."

"Sidney," Henry called engineering, "give me everything she has. Helm, fastest course to the nearest GDF ship you can find. Radar, keep a close eye on that fleet. Tactical, ready the canons."

"Captain Radar called, the Frigates are firing on the Carrier and one Marauder is in pursuit of us, they have fired three missals."

"Tactical, jam their radar and project a decoy," Henry ordered.

The three missals arc for the decoy and fly by the EX-T harmlessly.

Radar called out one more time, "Three more missals, Captain, they appear to be visually targeting us this time."

Of the five screens on the bridge, one has the Guard fleet on it; the bridge crew watches as a Frigate explodes, the other is severely damaged, one of the Marauders is spinning and the Carrier is venting badly.

Matt starts firing the canons hoping to at least stop one or two of the missiles. He watches on his radar screen as two streaks shoot from the aft of the EX-T, one intercepted the missiles, the other struck the Marauder.

"What was that?" Henry asks.

"That was me, Henry," Ben said from the com on his chair, "I could not stand by and see this ship destroyed, the battle is over. May I suggest we go back and see if we can save a few lives. Helm, turn us around and go back to the Guard fleet, there may be some we can help."

On the way back to the fleet, the EX-T went by the Marauder that fired on them, there is a hole through the center of it all the way through, from bow to stern, ten meters wide, there will be no survivors there.

As the EX-T arrives, the Marauder is still spinning out of control, the Carrier is badly damaged on the port side, the venting has stopped, but the landing bay on that side is a mangled mess, no fighters will be landing on that side.

One Frigate is completely destroyed and the other is missing the top quarter where the bridge was.

The two remaining Marauders have damage but are under their own power.

"Com, see if you can raise the Admiral."

Moments later the image of Admiral Rimes is on the screen.

"Thank you for returning, Captain, we can use the help, that Marauder, if the spin is not stopped soon, all on board will be lost."

"We can help with that, Admiral, we have lots of experience stopping spinning things in space," Henry told him, "stand by, we will dispatch some of our harvesters, we also have a well-staffed and supplied sick bay. If you would send over your wounded, we will help there as well.

It only took a little over an hour for the harvesters to stabilize the Marauder and five shuttles has ferried over wounded from the Carrier and the damaged Frigate."

In the mist of all this activity, Henry gets a message from GDF fleet asking to clarify their last message, "What do you mean Admiral Rimes wishes to surrender to you?"

"Send a reply, com, not wishing to surrender but has surrendered, send medical ship and a recovery ship for the disabled vessels, a Carrier, a Frigate, and four Marauders, add a video with the message, Rodney, so you do not have to repeat it, put my name on it," Henry said.

Twenty minutes later, Henry gets a reply, fleet at your location in six hours, “Arrest Admiral Rimes and the Captains.”

“Rodney, get me the Admiral. I need to tell him he is under arrest; do you think that would do it, Simon?” Henry asks his first officer.

“Yes, sir, they did not say put him in the brig only to arrest him,” Simon laughed.

As soon as Henry had Admiral Rimes on the com, he told him he was under arrest and not to flee the area, “So if you are ask Admiral, tell them I arrested you and your Captains.”

“Thank you, Captain Carver, for all the help and may I ask you something? What did you fire at the Marauder that was attacking you, the shuttle we sent said there was a hole all the way through her?”

“That was not us, Admiral, that was the Sub-Drive that was escorting us,” Henry replied, “so you see if the Drivers were here to dominate us like the Duke said, we would be a defeated race in a matter of hours.”

“I never believed his story, but I had to follow orders, you do understand, don’t you?” Captain Admiral Rimes said. “As soon as the Duke started executing command staff for failures, I knew we were in trouble, more than half of the fleet has surrendered, there is only a small minority that is planning on fighting to the death. Three got their wish here today and took their crews with them.”

“Let’s hope we can avoid any more like today, Admiral, there has been far too much death already,” Henry told him.

“Yes, Captain, you are right, thanks one more time. I will sigh off now, there is much work to do before the fleet gets here to arrest me, safe travels to you and your crew.”

Simon give the stand down call, “There is no need to keep the crew at all stations now, you have the bridge number one. I’m going to see Jasmine and see if she needs anything.”

“I have the watch, Captain.”

63

"The heavy transport has been in the air for three hours now heading north, the sun can be seen starting to light the horizon, soon the transport will be turning west to position itself northeast of Wolf Creek, when we do," Billy told Greg, "we will descend to 1,000 meters to stay below the radar, we will not pop up until we are in line between Wolf Creek and New Hope, make our final turn southwest, ascend to 5,000 meters, and make the distress call."

Tom enters the bridge and asks Billy if there is anything to report.

"No, sir, radar has had no returns and there has been no radio traffic, we are two hours out, we should be at Wolf Creek just as the night crew are getting off and the day shift is starting. It's always a bit hectic at that time of the morning."

In the back, the assault team is resting. Tom looks them over, they are dirty with dried blood on the uniforms, most have bandages on arms, legs, and heads; they look the part of wounded soldiers just in from the front line, no one will question why they have their weapons, a soldier only gives it up in death.

The real wounded are all in the back, so they will be the first off the transport. Doctor Fields and three nurses are there to tend to the wounded during the trip but will stay with the transport. Sandra and James will accompany them to the hospital; they, too, are in soiled uniforms. The doctors briefed Sandra and James on what to tell the attending doctors upon arrival at the emergency room, each patient has a chart pinned to their hospital gown.

Tom feels the transport make its turn west and the start of the descent, the next turn will be southwest. At that time, he will start getting the team ready, they will only be thirty minutes out at that time.

Tom takes a seat next to Sam and Adam, "We are only forty-five minutes out, anything you two can think of?" he asks.

Both shook their heads no.

"I do have a question though," Adam asks, "why is the Duke in charge of the monarchy when the Queen could be doing it? She is apparently qualified and has leadership qualities, she is forceful, compassionate, direct, knowledgeable, and thoughtful. I can see people following her and being loyal at any cost. Now the Duke on the other hand is rude, selfish, condescending, and downright stupid, people only follow him out of fear. I don't understand how he ended up in charge."

"It was a man's world," Sam answered, "few if any would follow a woman in the past; it has only been a few years that a woman can hold a leadership position. Before the Drivers, a woman was considered property of the man, not even considered intelligent, now they are excelling and thriving. Take your Captain West for example, in the GDF, she has a chance at becoming a General, in the Royal Guard, she is as high as she could ever get; it will change after this I think, the Guard is dead as it should be."

Tom fills the transport bank left and starts its climb, "Get them up, we are thirty minutes out, but before you go, I would like to say it has been an honor serving with the two of you; seven days ago, you were on opposite sides and today you are making history."

On the bridge, Billy starts his deception, "Mayday, mayday, mayday, this is Heavy 499 in route from New Hope to Wolf Creek, do you copy, Wolf Creek?"

"Copy, heavy 499, this is Wolf Creek, declare your emergency."

"In route to Wolf Creek with wounded, some critical, was strafed by GDF fast mover, have fire in number two, having trouble maintaining altitude."

"We have you on radar heavy 499, you will be cleared for emergency landing, use runway 175."

"Copy, Wolf Creek tower, runway 175, feathering number two, have fire and ambulances standing by, we have fifty plus wounded."

"Copy, heavy 499, fifty plus wounded, fire and ambulances dispatched."

"Wolf Creek in sight, Greg, hit the smoke."

The original plan was to use a smoke grenade, but one of the engineers came up with the idea to use motor oil and a small pump, injecting the oil right in to the intake, keeping someone from discovering the smoke grenade as the fire department puts out the nonexistent fire, nor can we risk them damaging the engine making it impossible to takeoff, the fire will be out as we taxi to the end of the taxi way, an engineer will be out on the wing with a hand held extinguisher finishing the ruse.

Tom is looking out the window at the number two engine, smoke is billowing out of the exhaust.

"Two minutes," he calls to the team, "remember you're wounded, put on a show."

The wheels touch down and the smoke stops on cue.

Tom can see the fire trucks coming and the ambulances all lining up ready to do their jobs.

Looking forward he can see the engineer out on the wing using the extinguisher, making a show of his courage in the line of duty; the transport stops and he spring into action, opening the inspection cover, giving one more blast of fire retardant, standing up he signals all clear.

The fire trucks are all around the transport, giving back up just in case the fire starts up again.

The back ramp comes down, medics rush in and start taking the wounded to the ambulances, first in is Colonial Alvarado and a Sargent in a coma with brain damage. Sandra and James are with them, the first ten are away in five ambulances, there are three buses for the walking wounded. Tom, Adam, and Sam are mixed in to the three buses, it's only ten minutes to the hospital.

64

Ted, Tina, Fred, Tyler, and Bradly are up before the sun today; they are aware that the Duke is expecting a call from Steve Carter this morning and they are planning on giving him one.

The five of them around the fire pit eating an early breakfast and having a festive time, only Ted, Fred, and Tyler will be climbing to the top of the canyon to make the call.

"What should I say?" Tyler asks Fred.

"Just let him know you are still alive and you will bring him to justice," Fred told him, "other than that, say what you would like to, remind him you will be King and he will be in prison or hung for his crimes."

"That should set him off," Ted remarked with a laugh.

"He may send more people to kill us," Tyler said.

"Make him understand you are not afraid of him any longer, Tyler," Bradly suggested, "that's the best way to confront a bully, and if he sends more people, we will deal with them like we have the others."

Tina reaches out and places her hand on Tyler's shoulder, "You are growing in to a man, my prince, let him understand that."

Everyone around the fire can see Tyler is getting more confident with the encouragement from his friends, and friends they are, no longer does he consider them servants. The last two weeks, he has grown to love every one of them and trust their advice.

Fred stand up, "Let's get this over with, the climb will take about an hour to make, that puts us on top around 6:30, just in time to disturb his sleep."

They started the climb on the same side that Sandra, James, and Billy did four days earlier.

Like Fred predicted, they arrived right at 6:30.

Ted removed the satellite radio from his pack, switching it on, "I will be Carter and get the Duke on the radio, then pass it to you, Tyler. This is Steve Carter. I have an urgent message for the Duke."

"One moment, mister Carter. I will let the Duke know you are calling."

It was ten minutes before there was a new voice on the radio

"Carter, is it done?" they hear. Ted gives the radio to Tyler. "Carter, answer me," the Duke commands.

"Well, Uncle, Carter cannot speak right now. Do you know why, Uncle? I killed him and the two men you sent, you are pathetic in everything you do; my mother is coming for you, she will have your head and I will be King, not you. Your war is failing, your men have deserted, my father will have his revenge in the end, send more men, so I can kill them also. I have 2,000 warriors at my command, the Traayans call me the grand chef, so take your best shot, Uncle. I'm waiting." Tyler turns off the radio, then turns to Fred, "I hope I did not insult your grandfather or you with that."

"Not at all, Tyler, I loved it, and the grand chef would be proud that you put the Duke in his place."

The Duke just stood there, he could not move, fear was running through him, how could that boy beat him, how did he git 2,000 warriors. I need to send a division to stop him, but if I do, I lose the war and the GDF comes for me; if I don't, he gets stronger and comes for me later, is the bitch really coming?

His mind is racing, not staying on any one thing, his rage builds coupled with fear.

"Your majesty, is everything all right?" the General in charge of the Duke's Intelligence Division asks.

"No," he screamed and hit him with the scepter, knocking him down, "it's all your fault I am going to lose this war, yours and Hartwell. Hartwell," he screams, "he is the one that failed me first, if he would have done his job, we would be celebrating the victory already, he needs to be hung as an example for not doing his job. Have Hartwell hung out front, so I can see him swing in the breeze," he screams, "do it now!

Pick him up and take him to the hospital," the Duke orders, and as soon as he recovers, have him hung like Hartwell. I do not hang unconscious people; I need them to suffer some first."

A Colonial waves two security men over and they grab the General under the arms and drag him out, heading for the hospital next door, with the Colonial following and a Captain next to him.

As soon as the pair are out of ear shot of the Duke, the Colonial turns to the Captain, "We are all going to hang one at a time if we do not stop the Duke."

"But how?" the Captain asks.

"I do not know yet, but we have to do something soon," the Colonial said. "I'm going to take the General in to the emergency room, get him checked out, then get him to a safe place, you go find Hartwell and let him know his life is in danger, tell him to run."

"You know, sir, if the Duke finds out you did this, he will hang you too."

"I'm aware, Captain, but we have to start somewhere and this is a good place to start, so get going."

65

Sandra and James are getting Brian on to a hospital gurney when they see two security men dragging a General in to the emergency room, they push the gurney with Alvarado on it right behind them.

The orderlies grab the General and place him in a wheelchair and start taking him back.

A doctor comes up and looks at Alvarado, retrieving the chart pinned to his gown.

Flipping through it, he said, "Don't worry, Colonial Alvarado, we will take good care of you here."

"Brian," Sandra hears from behind her, turning she sees a Colonial standing right there.

A look of relief was on the Colonial's face, then it was replaced by dread.

Coming up to the gurney, the Colonial reaches out and places his hand on Brian's shoulder, leaning down he whispers, "It's good to see you, my friend, but if the Duke finds you here, he will have you hung."

"Bill, we need to find someplace to talk," Brian told the Colonial.

The Colonial turns to the doctor, "Can you bring him to a private examining room, we need to have a private conversation."

"That will not be a problem," the doctor replied, waving over an orderly, "bring him to room seven, I will be there shortly."

The orderly grabs the hand rail and starts moving the gurney, followed by Sandra and James, who only look at each other and shrug.

The orderly pushes the gurney through the large emergency room to the back where there is a row of rooms at the back, making for room seven, it's clearly marked over the door.

The orderly parked the gurney, then set the brake, turning to the Colonial, "Is there anything else I can do for you?"

"No, that's it, shut the door on your way out if you would," he then turns to Sandra and James, "if you would please wait outside? he asks.

Brian reaches up and places his hand on the Colonial's forearm, "They need to stay, Bill."

With the door closed, the Colonial turns to Brian, "What are you doing here? I thought you were captured by the GDF."

"I was, we are here for the Duke, he is a criminal and a psychopath, everything he told us was a lie," Brian told Bill.

"Then who killed the Queen?" Bill asks.

"I'm not dead," Sandra speaks up from behind him.

"Bill, this is our Queen," Brian told him, "please show her respect."

"But how," Bill stammers, "I saw the photos of Crown's View, it was completely destroyed."

"I was warned about the assassination in time to escape, along with the prince and Ambassador Wildwind," she nods to James. "Time is short," she said, cutting off any more questions, "we are here to arrest the Duke, are you with us or against us? I need to know now."

Brian speaks up, "It is our only chance to end this war and save lives."

"Bill looks at Brian, "If he thinks it's the thing to do, I'm in."

"We only have about twenty minutes before the team is in place," Brian said, "it's my men that will arrest him," seeing the question on Bill's face, "so please help our Queen do this."

Bill turns around and gets down on one knee, "I am at your service, my queen."

"We need to go now," James reminds them.

Sandra turned to Brian, reaching out touching his hand, "Please don't die, we need men like you," giving him a friendly smile.

Turning for the door, not waiting for his response, Sandra leads the party out the door, heading for the rally point out front.

Exiting the emergency room, Sandra sees the buss unloading the fake wounded at the end of the parking lot.

A doctor is there telling them it will be a little wait and there is no room in the emergency room for them, so if they would wait on the bus, they will come out and get them in batches; phase one is working.

Sandra sees Tom, Adam, and Sam standing next to the bus and makes her way there with James and the newly recruited Colonial.

The look on Tom's face was one of concern about the Colonial.

As he arrived, Sam puts his hand out and greets the Colonial, "Bill," he said.

All the Colonial said is, "I'm with you, Sam."

Tom has already directed C team into position in the park and placed the explosives in the trash cans like they planned as the diversion.

"Colonial, I can get your team in to the building without any bloodshed," Bill told Tom, "I'm head of security at the command center. I don't know your plan, but ten of us can enter the front door unopposed and go straight to the operations center, that is where the Duke is right now."

Tom looks to Adam and Sam for their input.

"I trust him," Sam spoke up.

Tom stood there for a few seconds, pondering his options.

"OK, Colonial, we will follow your lead, but if you show any sign of betraying us, I will personally put a bullet in your head, do I make myself clear?" Tom looking him in the eyes.

"Understood, Colonial," Bill returned, "let's stop this mad man before he kills more people. Sam, get your men, Adam, stand by out front with teams D and B."

Sam hurried over to team A and selected seven men, then sent the rest to Adam.

"We have four minutes before the fast mover arrives," Tom told team A, standing right out front of the main door of the Command Center.

Looking over at James, Tom tells him, "No matter what, keep her safe," referring to Sandra.

"He will, Tom," Sandra said, "he is my rock and I will never doubt him," smiling at James.

"One minute," Tom said, "let's go inside, it will be chaos as soon as the charge goes off."

They had entered the main lobby and the four guards ask the Colonial if he needed anything, eyeing the group that followed him in.

"No, Sargent," Bill tells him.

Then the scream of the fast mover can be heard coming their way, as soon as it went over the pitch shifts to a lower frequency as it moves off, then the blinding flash of light from the explosion; moments later the report from the detonation rocks the lobby.

"Air raid," the Colonial shouts, "everyone down to the bomb shelter," looking at the Sargent. "Move now," he orders. The lobby empties and Tom and his team are the only ones there now.

"This way," Bill directs them down a long hallway, and as they go, he is ordering people down to the shelter.

Without question they go, clearing the way for the team to the Operation Center.

As soon as Bill enters the O.C., the Duke is shouting. "What's going on?" he demanded.

Sandra and James steps around the Colonial, so the Duke can see them, "You are going to stand trial for your crimes."

All the color drains from his face as he realizes who is speaking to him; he begins to tremble, then his knees buckle and he falls to the floor.

Two team members reach down, picking him off the ground, handcuffing his hands behind his back, then places a hood over his head.

Now Tom is speaking directly to him, "You are under arrest for the coupe and all the deaths that you caused by order of the Steward."

One of the Generals started to object, but Sandra cut him off, "I am Queen Sandra," she tells the room, "this man tried to kill me and the Prince; if you do not wish to share his fate, I would stand down and let things take their course."

No one made any attempt to stop them as they escorted the hooded Duke back the way they came.

The buss was ready out front, Adam standing at the door.

"Have your men load this bus and the one over there," Tom told Sam.

"Sorry, Colonial, my men and I are remaining with Colonial Alvarado, team A will escort you to the airport, but that is as far as we will go."

Tom did not argue, he understood Sam's loyalty to his Commanding Officer, this too only strengthened Tom respect for the Major and his ability to lead. There is still hope for the future of the Royal Guard with people like him in their ranks.

There were only thirteen people on the bus, not including the driver.

The Duke was put in the middle on the floor with a guard sitting next to him with one in front and one behind.

The trip to the airport was slower than the drive to the hospital, there are emergency vehicles converging on the park adding to the confusion.

"Adam," Tom called, "contact the heavy and let them know we are on our way with the package with an ETA of fifteen minutes."

Tom had no more than told Adam that when a military police vehicle stops them with it parked in the middle of the intersection.

A Sargent is holding his hand up, stopping all traffic.

"I'll handle this," Sam announces, standing up and exits the bus, making his way to the Sargent in the middle of the road.

Tom can see the Sargent snap to attention as Sam addresses him, then points to the bus. Moments later Sam is back on board and the Sargent is waving them through the intersection.

As Sam takes his seat in front of Tom, he volunteers the conversation to him.

"I told him if one of my men die on that transport because he delayed our trip, I will have him court marshaled, he was not eager for that to happen."

The GDF has not targeted non-military targets in the Guards controlled sectors, the population in Wolf Creek has not experienced the terror of war first hand, so with the simulated air raid, the population is in near panic.

The roads are filled with people fleeing to anywhere and nowhere, it is pure chaos like expected.

It took over twenty minutes for the ten-minute drive from the Command Center to the airfield with the extra traffic.

By the time the bus reached the airfield, they were the only vehicle near the base.

The guard at the gate did not stop the bus, he waved it through.

As the they passed the gate, Adam radioed Billy at the transport, telling him to start getting ready to leave, they are only three minutes out.

Billy gives the engineer the signal to close up the engine cowling and take his seat, then he radioed the second flight of fast movers to strike the airfield with fire bombs on both sides of the runway, filling it with smoke, then pull any defenders away from the transport for their escape.

The co-pilot is standing by at the loading ramp awaiting the package.

As soon as the bus stops, the team is on the move with the Duke.

Sam waves a good bye to Tom as the bus pulls away.

Tom stopped for a moment before he enters the transport, looking around watching the bus leave, thankful he did not need to fire a shoot and take any lives on this mission.

On the way forward, Tom hears the ramp door lock into place behind him and the engines winding up.

He takes a quick head count as he makes his way to the bridge.

Susan and her team.

Check.

Sandra, James, and Adam.

Check.

And the reason for the mission, the Duke.

Check.

At this point, the mission cannot fail, even if the Guard stopped the transport, the Duke would not make it out alive, ending the war.

As Tom enters the bridge, he hears Billy telling the tower he is moving the transport to the maintenance hangar on the other side of the airfield.

"Copy, heavy 499, you are cleared to preceded," Tom hears the tower reply.

The transport starts its trip down the taxiway. It's about 1,500 meters to the end of the runway where they must cross the runway to make the trip to the maintenance hangar.

Tom hears the radio crackle, then a voice comes over it, "Fire in the hole," is the only words spoken.

Out the front window, Tom sees the four fast movers shoot by, two on each side of the runway.

Then a row of flashes as the fire bomb explodes along the sides of the runway with flames shooting high in to the sky and black smoke billowing.

Still 400 meters from the cross over, the tower advises all traffic to stop in place to let a dozen fighter take off to challenge the GDF fast movers.

Barely viable through the smoke, Billy can see the fighters taking flight.

Billy never stopped like instructed and the tower never noticed.

He is at the end of the runway now, making his turn. Billy advances the throttle to full power and the transport follows the fighters.

The transport was in the air before the tower noticed them.

"Heavy 499, this is tower, why are you air born?"

"Tower, this is heavy 499, the ground is no place for an aircraft in an air raid," Billy replied.

"Copy, heavy 499, continue on course to ten kilometers, then orbit the airfield until safe to land," the tower told him.

"Copy, tower," Billy said, but he never gained more than 500 meters altitude to stay under the radar, setting a heading of west for Four Rivers and the GDF stronghold.

Billy can hear the radio traffic, the fighters are chasing the GDF fast movers east, but they will never catch them, giving the transport time to make its escape.

Tom pats Billy on the shoulder, "Well done, Skipper," he said, "send the message, we have an hour and a half before we get to Four Rivers," sighing his relief.

"Will do, Colonial," Billy adding his own sigh of relief.

Billy turns the radio to the predesignated channel, then sent the message.

"Bird cage, this is raven, package airborne, will be your location, ninety minutes."

"Copy, raven, escort will be your location in ten minutes."

"Copy, bird cage, awaiting escort, raven out."

"I'm going aft, Skipper," Tom told him.

As soon as Tom enters the cargo bay, he sees James has the Duke's hood off and is glaring at him.

The Duke is whimpering and pleading to be set free.

"It's too late for that," Sandra tells him, "you will be tried for your crimes."

"But I am the King, you cannot do this to your king," he tells her.

"No, my King was John, you killed him for your lust for power," James shouted, "he was a good man, you killed your own brother, then tried to kill his widow and his son."

"No, that was the Drivers that did that," Kin objected.

"No, that was you and we have all the evidence to prove it," Tom said. "If you are lucky, they will not hang you, but you will spend the rest of your life in prison."

All Kin does is cry, he knows his fate and there is nothing he can do to stop it.

The intercom crackles, "Fast movers on our wings."

Tom looks out the window and sees two on each wing.

The rest of the flight was smooth and excitement free.

Four Rivers came in to view and they all knew it was over.

Right before landing a broadcast was heard from Wolf Creek telling all units to stand down, the war was over.

After landing the ramp was lowered, and standing there was Steward Smit and the legal team to arrest him and formally charge the Duke for subversion and treason.

He was led off in chains still crying.

"Your majesty," the Steward greeted the Queen, bowing low.

"It's good to finally meet you, Steward Smit. I hope we can work out an end to all of this madness, so we can rebuild the trust that was lost between the Empire and the Federal Government," Sandra said.

"I look forward to it," Peabody replied. "I think you will be taking my place at the end of my term," Peabody told Tom, "there is no one I would rather see take it than you. You deserve it for your actions over the last two weeks, you, the Queen, and Ambassador Wildwind are all heroes and I will see to it that everyone knows who was responsible for the victory."

"Steward Smit, can you arrange transportation for me back to Traay? I would like to reunite with the prince as soon as possible," Sandra asks.

"Yes, my queen, I can, but if you would, we have arranged for you to address the country by way of video transition, that way everyone can see you are alive, putting to rest the assumption of your death and placing the blame where it belongs, on the Duke."

"I think that would stop the dissent in the ranks of the Royal Guard, so yes, that would be a good idea," Sandra agreed.

"It is already prepared for you in the hanger, we can do it now, the way you are dressed just coming back from the mission," Peabody said smiling.

Tom turns to Adam, "I should have known he would be ready for this; he never misses a thing."

They both laugh.

Steward Smit looks at Tom and Adam with a question on his face, Tom only smiles and winks at him.

Ten minutes later, Sandra is in front of a camera ready to make her address to the Nation.

The video crew tried to straighten Sandra's appearances by brushing her hair and cleaning any blood off of her, she waved them off, saying she will be herself as she is.

Standing next to Sandra are James, Tom, and Billy.

The light on the camera comes on.

"My fellow citizens," Sandra starts, "I would like to put to rest any rumors of my death. I am alive as you can see. This morning with the assistance of the Steward, the GDF, and elements of the Royal Guard, I and a team of loyalist arrested the Duke at his Command Center in Wolf Creek, he will be tried for crimes against humanity and the attempted assassination of myself and the Prince. I hereby order all Royal Guard forces to disengage in all hostilities and return to your bases. I am also issuing a proclamation granting pardons to all involved, this is a time of forgiveness, not revenge. I would also like to make it clear, my priorities are mother first, nation second, and queen after that, not that any are less than the first, but all are important to me.

To be a good mother, we must have a stable and just government, one where the law is followed by all, even those in power. To have a prosperous Empire, it must be compassionate to its subjects, ensuring their needs to live a healthy and happy life. For the reasons I have stated, I will assume control of the Monarch until the Prince becomes of age, and I pledge my life to see it is run justly for all. I will be gone for the next week retrieving the Prince in the wild lands of Traay; until then I am appointing Major Sam Tibits as my Chief of staff, follow his orders. I am also appointing Colonial Tom Dearman as my representative to the Federal Government," nodding to Tom. "Next I am appointing Major Billy Zercoff as my liaison to the Royal Guard," indicating Billy standing next to her. "I do not think I have to introduce Ambassador James Wildwind," he is standing behind her towering over. Sandra turns and looks up to him, nodding to him, "He will be my adviser to the Royal houses. They have earned my trust and respect. I will end now and leave you with this thought, may any pain inflicted on you be healed. Good day."

As soon as the light gos out on the camera, the Steward stands and starts clapping, all in attendances follow suit.

"Well done, my queen," Peabody tells Sandra, "I did not expect the pardon yet, but it will help in bringing the Guard home."

"The Guard's heart was not in this fight, they were only following orders, so there is no condemnation for them on my part," Sandra said, "let's get them home."

Billy is looking at Sandra with a question on his face, and Sandra sees it.

"I know, Skipper, you never expected this. I need people I trust in key positions and there are none I trust more than you," Sandra tells him.

"Thank you, but what do I do?" Billy asks.

"Go back to Wolf Creek and see Sam; between the two of you, you will have things working in no time," Sandra smiles at him. "I will be heading to Traay soon to get our family," Sandra tells Billy, and a family they have become.

66

The EX-T has spent the last three days escorting the limping Royal Guard fleet back to Tarkaneay, assisting the GDF using the harvesters to power the crippled Frigate and Marauder back. The Carrier and two of the Marauders are under their own power, the other Frigate and Marauder are total losses.

They are still more than a week out traveling at 25k/kph, any faster and they run the risk of losing control of the Frigate.

Henry is on the bridge when Rodney in Communication turns to him, "Captain, there is an emergency broadcast from GDF headquarters."

"Put it on the screen, Rodney, let's see what's up."

The screen comes to life and on it is James standing behind the Queen, "Record this, Henry," instructs Rodney, "Jasmine will want to see this."

They all listen as the Queen orders the Guard to stand down ending the war, the bridge erupts in cheers, and for the first time in days, the atmosphere is jubilant.

Henry calls Jasmine on the comm, "I'm sending you a message, love," he tells her.

"What is it?" she asks.

"It's a surprise," he teases, "it will make you happy, I promise, watch the link," he tells her.

Moments go by, then he hears Jasmine shriek with joy, "I love you, you old space dog," she tells him.

"I love you, too, my sweet. I will see you later, bye." Henry hits the comm on his chair, "Attention all personnel, this is the Captain, the war is over, there is a message on the log channel from GDF headquarters, give it a look, Captain out."

Matt is with Beth in his room when suddenly Beth begins to cry.

"What's the matter?" he asks her.

"You will be leaving soon," she sobs, "the war is over."

He reaches out and takes her in his arms and pulls her in to his embrace, trying to soothe and reassure her.

About that time, the Captain comes on the comm and announces the war is over.

Matt is puzzled. "How did you know?" he asks Beth.

"If I tell you, you will hate me. I know it," she continues her sob.

"No, I will not," he said, "I could never hate someone as pure as you."

There is a knock at the door.

Matt releases Beth to answer it to find Ben and Bell standing there.

"Can we come in, Matt?" Ben asks.

"Yes, please do," Matt answer them, moving out of the way, motioning them in.

"We need to talk to you, Matt," Ben explains. Bell goes straight to Beth and puts her arms around her, consoling her like any sister would. "Let's sit down," Ben said to Matt, "there is much to explain." They all have a seat, Matt in a chair and Ben, Beth, and Bell sitting on the couch facing him, all holding hands. "So, you know, Matt, this is new to us, only last month did these emotions become real to any of us. We had some, but the level was subdued; with these new avatars, it has become intensified, sight, smell, and touch, we never expected this, not at this level anyway."

"I'm confused," Matt tells Ben, "avatars what do you mean?"

"We are not human, Matt, at least our bodies aren't, our minds are as human as yours, but our bodies are artificial. I am, or should I say we, are a Sub-Drive."

Matt is torn, parts of him are appalled at the thought of it, but his heart hurts for this woman sitting in front of him.

How could he reject her, she is the most tender person he has ever meet! The loving way she treats things, animals, plants, and even insects, her gentleness is like a light shining in the dark.

Beth begins sobbing with her face in her hands, tears at his heart.

Getting down on his knees in front of her, Matt pulls her hand away from her face, holding them in his.

"No, I could never hate you," he tells her, "not for anything. I love you for what you are."

Beth falls to her knees with Matt throwing her arms around his neck, still sobbing, but this time it's with joy. "I will tell the Captain I'll stay on permanently; will that make you happy?" he asks Beth.

All she could do is say yes between the sobs, still holding Matt in her embrace.

67

Fred, Tina, and Ted are out hunting for wild game down canyon from camp when they hear a bush plain coming their way.

It makes two passes dipping its wing, telling those on the ground they know they're there and are friendly.

"I bet that's James," Fred said, "but to be on the safe side, let's get back to camp to be certain."

It took them ten minutes of hard running to get to camp; upon arrival Mae and Bradly had the kids ready to bug out with packs on at the first rally point.

As soon as the three arrived, everyone knew what to do. Mae, Bradly, Tina, and the children started for rally point two.

Fred and Ted would evaluate, then send word to either come back or a shot in the air to run.

Fred hears his name called from the rim, "It's James," he tells Ted, "go get them."

Ted takes off in a run.

Thirty minutes later, there is a reunion in camp.

Sandra hugs each one with a loving embrace, including Fred, who was supersized.

"Where's the Skipper?" Ted asks James.

"He's back at Wolf Creek supervising the surrender."

"The war's over and the Duke is in jail awaiting trial," Sandra told them.

"We are going to spend four days here relaxing before we head back," James said.

"I would like to make an announcement," Sandra told the group, "James and I are going to wed, if there is no objection," looking to Tyler.

All Tyler did was offer his hand to James like a man would, "Welcome to the family," he said.

THE END.